Also by Sandy Kendall:

The Boy from the O: A Novel

The Youngest Son

A Novel

Sandy Kendall

authorHOUSE®

AuthorHouse™
1663 Liberty Drive
Bloomington, IN 47403
www.authorhouse.com
Phone: 1-800-839-8640

Published by AuthorHouse 10/17/2013

ISBN: 978-1-4918-2437-5 (sc)
ISBN: 978-1-4918-2436-8 (hc)
ISBN: 978-1-4918-2435-1 (e)

Library of Congress Control Number: 2013918009

To Ted and Sarah—How did I get so lucky?

"EVERY SAINT HAS A PAST AND EVERY
SINNER HAS A FUTURE."

Oscar Wilde

Dear Reader

To my dear Catholic friends. I have tried to be as respectful as possible in telling my story of a priest who leaves the priesthood. I stressed that he left in good standing, without any conflict, and with a continued love for the Catholic Church. I have great respect for priests and the Roman Catholic Church and sincerely hope that the story reflects my admiration. In every other way, it is a work of fiction and was never intended to reflect exact facts concerning the Jesuits.

Thank You

To my editor, proof-reader, advisor, confidant, best friend, and husband, Dan.

To my ever-supportive family: Stephanie, Ed, Sarah and Ted, each so beautifully talented in their own way, thank you.

To my faithful friends who encouraged me to write and then to write a second book. You bought books; told your friends; hosted book clubs and discussions. You know who you are. I am grateful.

Prologue

My mother is an attorney; not just an attorney, but she is a well-known advocate for abused women. She's amazing. She went back to school after my parents were married. She was pregnant with me and my sister most of the time she was getting her law degree, and never missed a day of school.

My father is a physician and a PhD medical researcher of some renown. He's brilliant. Well, people say he is. I know he is smart. What's more, people also say he is that rare combination of incredibly good-looking and nice guy. It is hard to judge your own father. I see the reaction of women, however, when they are around him. He is crazy for my mom though and would never look at another woman.

We are a *his*, *hers*, and *theirs* family. My sister and I are theirs. I have two half sisters; one is CEO of a big recording company in New York, the other a pediatrician in Boston. They are my mother's contribution. My dad has two sons from a first marriage. One is a judge in California and the other is a college professor here in Philadelphia. My little sister is Director of Nursing in a large teaching hospital here. Is it any wonder then, that I have had trouble making a name for myself in this family of achievers? Or, that I have just left the only job I have ever had with no inkling of what I am going to do with my life. I turned thirty-four last month, and today I left the priesthood.

I say I left today but the process of leaving the priesthood is a long one. I have been leaving for some time. I just went out the door today. My family doesn't know. I have kept it from them all this time; months and months of counseling. My mother can handle it; she is a converted Catholic. But, my dad—he is the real McCoy. My dad should be the picture in the dictionary for Catholic. He was raised by nuns, literally. He was in a Catholic orphanage until he was sixteen. His identity is Catholic more than anything else; more than doctor, researcher, husband, father. He is CATHOLIC. He would have become a priest himself if he hadn't found out that his biological father was a doctor. Once he knew that, all he could think about was becoming a doctor.

My father was so happy when I told him I wanted to be a priest. I know in a way it broke my mother's heart. She thought about how little she would see me; how I wouldn't get married and have children. But my dad, he was thrilled. I know he loves me and will accept me now, but I worry that he might be disappointed in me. That would kill me. He is the greatest man alive. In all the counseling sessions, it became apparent that I probably did try to fulfill his dream instead of my own. That isn't what he wanted. He wanted it to be my dream; but I had this overwhelming sense of wanting to make him happy.

Where do I go from here? I have had some counseling in that regard and some references for organizations that help ex-priests. But, I am heading for my parents' house and I don't have a clue how to tell them what I have done or what I am going to do in the future.

Chapter One

As the taxi pulled up in front of the house, Nick began fumbling through a wad of bills to pay the driver. Vow of poverty notwithstanding, this is a big amount for a ride from the airport, Nick thought. He tried to calculate how much to tip but then just rounded it off to the nearest twenty and hoped for the best. He wasn't sure of the going rate for tipping cab drivers. He felt very out of touch with many things right now. His only bag, a small beat-up Nike gym bag he had had since college, was beside him on the seat. He picked it up, thanked the driver, and opened the door.

Nick stood at the bottom of the steps leading to the front door of his parents' home. What a magnificent house, he thought. It was a large English Tudor that his parents moved into before Nick was born: six bedrooms, five full baths, a kitchen as large as most family rooms, and a magnificent library with full shelves and a moveable ladder on a rail that he loved as a child. This house has character, he thought. Nick remembered going to Biltmore House in Asheville one time and thinking he liked his house better. So, it wasn't the Biltmore mansion, it was everything a person could want in a home. It was located in the Philadelphia suburb of St. John's Village, and every house around it was also magnificent.

Calpurnia, the family black Lab, was sleeping on the lawn in front of the house. Nick knew that meant someone was close by. She was old now, the last of several sweet Labs the family had lavished love upon, even though his dad, Kris, claimed to dislike dogs. Cal looked up at Nick drowsily and cocked her head, until she somehow recognized him, or thought she did. Her tail began to thrash against the boxwood. "Hi, girl," Nick said, as he sat down on the ground and scratched her behind one ear. She lay over on her side in pleasure.

"Some guard dog you are," Kris said as he came around the side of the house. "You'll let anyone in here, won't you old girl?" Kris beamed at his son. The father and son looked very much alike. Both were tall and lean with incredible deep-blue eyes. The two men embraced, stood back to look at each other and embraced again. Nick felt his eyes begin to well but he blinked to control it. Kris patted Nick on the back. "Your mom's going to freak. Did you tell anyone you were coming? How long can you stay?" his father asked quickly.

"As long as you will have me," Nick answered softly. Kris looked at his son to see if he heard him correctly. By that time, Nick's mother, Emily, came around the house. Emily was small compared to the men. She was trim and attractive and exuded energy. She practically ran to him. Kris stood back to let Emily get to her son. Kris pondered Nick's comment as he came around to the other side of him, picked up his bag and the three of them went in the front door with Calpurnia close behind.

"Oh, if we had known you were coming, honey, we could have had everyone come for the weekend. Well, the girls, anyway. Mike needs a little more notice to get here from San Francisco." Emily was rambling and trying to remember if they had made plans for the weekend or if they had enough groceries to entertain Nicky. What must he miss, she thought? What would he like? They got to see Nick so rarely, she wanted everything to be special. "Can you stay a while?" she asked. Nick nodded but didn't explain. Kris looked at his son and contemplated the situation. Why was Nick here unannounced? Was he ill? He did look thin, and pale, Kris thought. Or, was one of the other children having some kind of problem Nick had been asked to help with? "Get us a drink, darling," Emily said as she looked at Kris. She turned back to Nick, "How shall we celebrate? Would you like a glass of wine, or a beer? It should be champagne but we don't keep any on hand. We should do that, Kris. Why don't we keep champagne on hand in case of special occasions?" she asked. Just for a second, Nick pictured an emergency magnum of champagne behind a glass enclosure with instructions, "Break glass in case of celebration." He smiled warmly at his mother. It was wonderful to be home.

Kris got up to get the drinks and Nick watched his dad walk out of the room. He thought his dad had aged a little since he saw him last. It had been quite a while since he had been home. His dad moved more slowly and maybe had a bit more white hair now. He still looked great though. Emily pressed against her son on the sofa. "I am so glad you are here. We miss you terribly, you know."

"I know."

"We'll have a cookout tomorrow night. Tonight it will be just be the three of us," Emily rambled on. "Is that okay? I'll have Dad call Beau and he and some of the family can come then. I just want to look at you. You aren't wearing a collar. Is that what is done now? You don't have to wear a collar when you travel?" It was a family joke that Nick wore his clerical shirt to get a better seat on the airplane. "This is a vacation, isn't it? You aren't going to one of the universities or anything on church business are you?" Nick came home one time to go to a seminar at nearby Villanova University.

"No. I am not on church business...or anything."

Kris came into the room with a tray, three glasses, and a cold bottle of Stag's Leap. Well, they are prepared for some emergencies, Nick thought.

Kris poured the wine. When he raised his glass to Nick, he noticed the pink blush on his neck and a tan line where his Roman collar had been. "To Nicky. Welcome home."

Emily repeated, "To Nicky. Welcome home."

The three of them settled comfortably into the family room. Emily had pictures to show Nick. She had recent ones of Michael's family and some of Alison's family at her birthday party last month. They ordered pizza for delivery; it was what Nick said he wanted. He didn't want his mother to go to any trouble. His parents spent the evening filling Nick in with family details. Tomorrow night, his half brother, Beau, who lived nearby and as many of his family as possible would be there for a cookout. They left his sister Laurie, who also lived in the Philadelphia area, a message and invited her and her family too. Next week they would try to get Alison and Mandy and their families to come from New York and Boston. Emily called it a progressive family reunion. Most of the evening was just spent in comfortable, pleasant conversation. Though Nick gave out little information about why he was there or for how long. He would shrug his shoulders when asked. Emily didn't seem to care. She was just glad he was home.

After dinner, they went out to the patio and sat. It was a beautiful starry night. The back yard was as inviting as Nick remembered. Clematis was climbing gracefully up a narrow trellis. Day lilies were blooming along with other flowers he couldn't name, in what Emily called the Yellow Bed. Another bed had blue and purple flowers, aptly named the Blue Bed. In the back, at the edge of the property, was a large English garden. Emily had it designed as a birthday gift for Kris one year. He had described for her the garden he worked in as a child at the orphanage where he grew up in London. Interesting flowers and plants of various colors were growing at different heights, giving a very beautiful random appearance that had been carefully planned. Despite the fire in the pit, mosquitoes began to bother Emily and she decided to go in to bed. "Don't stay out too long, boys," she pleaded. "You will be eaten alive." She kissed Nick on his forehead and then Kris. "Love you both," she said. They both smiled at her in response.

The two men sat in silence for several minutes. It was a lovely evening, perfect temperature to enjoy the fire. Nick thought about sitting there with his friends when he was a teenager and other times when he was young and would spy on Alison and Mandy and their friends from an upstairs window. He was brought back to the present when Kris spoke. "What is going on, Nick?" Kris asked. His mood was somber, the question serious.

"What do you mean?" Nick answered cautiously.

"You know what I mean," Kris stated flatly. When Nick didn't answer, he tried again. "Why are you here, Nick? Unannounced, without a schedule," he said softly. Then he added, "Without your clerical shirt." He sat, his hands folded between his knees, biting his lip slightly. "Tell me what's wrong."

Nick was looking down also biting his lower lip. He was seated directly across the fire pit from Kris and when he looked up at his father, he felt a tear begin to slowly make its way down his cheek. He made no effort to wipe it. He closed his eyes and sighed. "I left," he said simply. A few seconds went slowly by and he added, "I had nowhere else to go. I came home."

Kris now took a big breath. He exhaled loudly and smiled. "Then this is where you belong!" He started to say something else but thought better of it. He smiled tentatively again at his son.

"Dad," Nick began. "I know you have a lot of questions. I don't really know where to begin. It might take me a while to tell you everything. Let me just start by saying that I am not in love. I am not in any trouble. I am not gay. Most priests leave because they are upset with the Catholic Church. They are angry because the church requires celibacy of priests and they have fallen in love with someone or want to. I haven't," he explained. "I am not upset with the Church," he said emphatically. He paused and closed his eyes for a few seconds, then opened them and looked at his father. "And I haven't fondled little girls or abused little boys. I don't lust over other priests. It is just that I…I," he began again, "I," but the words didn't come. Finally he said, "I just didn't want to be a priest anymore. It just didn't seem right… I mean, it didn't feel like it did in the beginning. I mean…."

Kris put his hand out to tell Nick he needed to say no more. "It's okay, Nick. This is your home. I would want you here even if you were in love, or in trouble, or if you were gay. There is no need to go into it further tonight. You can tell me, tell us, whatever you want, whenever you want. I was proud of you when you went into the priesthood, but I am proud that you had the courage to leave if it was not right to be there." He looked at Nick and thought he looked exhausted. "It must have been really difficult, Nick." He went on, "I am sorry we weren't there for you when you were going through this. But, we are here now." With finality, Kris stood and indicated for Nick to stand too. He put his arm around his son and said, "Let's go in and get some sleep. Everything gets better with rest. Your mother and I love you, unconditionally. It is okay. Maybe, you have no longer been called to be a priest, then you have been called to do something else. Let's get some sleep and talk about it tomorrow."

Nick went into the house with his dad and Kris pointed him in the direction of a "guest" room. It had been his younger half sister's room when he was growing up. He was so glad he wasn't being put in the bedroom of his childhood. The house had been redecorated several times. None of the kids' rooms were shrines. They had all been made into functioning guest rooms for when family in various configurations come to stay. Some of the rooms had bunk beds for kids, or cribs for little ones, others queen-sized beds for couples, or in his case…disenfranchised priest, he thought. It was good to be home. He was so fortunate. His parents were wonderful. His dad took it much better than he expected and his mother would be no problem. Not that she isn't a strong, opinionated woman, he thought. But she is my mother! The lamp was barely out when he fell asleep. Finally, sleep without waking until morning light. A first.

Chapter Two

When Nick came downstairs for breakfast, his sister, Laurie, was at the table waiting for him. Nick and Laurie were only fourteen months apart in age and were exceptionally close. His sister was a perfect combination of his parents; lean like the Millar men and taller than her mother but with Emily's outgoing personality and wit. Laurie ran to Nick who came in the room sheepishly. "It is about time! I have been waiting hours for you to get up," Laurie said trying to sound put out. They rocked back and forth as they hugged each other.

"Hours?" Nick questioned. "It is only eight-thirty now." He looked around for any evidence of his parents being home, but finding none asked, "Where are Mom and Dad?"

"Went out for coffee. I think they wanted us to have some time alone."

Nick put his hand on his forehead and pushed his hair away from his face and then patted it back in place again. "Laurie," he began. He looked directly at her now. "I," he began again.

"Mom told me," Laurie said flatly. She gave him a sympathetic smile.

"Things do get around quickly, don't they? I told Dad just as we were going to bed. He told Mom, and she told you. Who did you tell?" he asked smiling at her.

"Jack and Pippa. It seems right that I told my husband and daughter, doesn't it?"

"Sure."

Nick was barefoot, in jeans and a white tee shirt. His hair was still damp from the shower. He slowly put his arms around Laurie and hugged her again; a long, warm hug.

"My God, you look like Dad! You are incredibly good-looking, you know, just like he is. Why do guys always get the good looks? It's not fair." Nick smiled at his little sister, who was trying to pout. "And you are much too good-looking to be a priest. They are all supposed to look like Charles Durning. And besides," Laurie was babbling now and Nick loved watching her do it. "Besides, seeing you in a collar always made me nervous."

"In all fairness," Nick quipped, "it was supposed to make you nervous. The appearance of a priest is intended to be a sobering influence on people."

"It worked. I never wanted to do drugs around you when you were a priest," she said jokingly.

"You've never done drugs in your life."

"How do you know?"

"We know these things."

Nick sat at the table and Laurie poured him a cup of coffee. "Well, I am glad you aren't a priest any more. I've missed you."

"I've missed you too. And now you can do drugs."

Laurie laughed. "So what happens now? I mean do you have to report in at all, or what? Do you just start looking for a job? Will it be church-related? What do you want to do? Will you date? I know lots of single girls." Laurie's eyes lit up.

"Stop!" Nick nearly shouted. Then his tone relented a little. "I don't know what happens now. No, I don't report in—I left the priesthood, I am not on parole. And I have no idea what I want to do. And no," he said emphatically. "Don't even think of fixing me up with a date. I may date in time, but I can find my own dates, thank you very much. Remember, I am good looking like Dad, not homely like you," he teased. Then he smiled. "What are you doing today?" he asked.

"I'm working, bro. We do that when we are married with children, not married to the Church." Then Laurie quickly put her hand over her mouth. "Nick, I'm sorry. I was trying to be cute. I didn't mean to insult you or the Church. I'm sorry," she repeated softly.

"I forgive you," Nick said with a twinkle in his eye, as he made the sign of the cross in the air. "Look, Laurie," he began. "This is all new for me too. I am still sorting it all out. I just can't jump into anything—make plans, or decisions at this point. I just need to take things a day at a time for a while. Can we just pretend I am on some sort of vacation? I am just here to enjoy being with my family and get some rest. I have had some pretty sleepless nights lately."

"I'm sorry. I really am. I will try to be better. I have to go now. I think we are coming to dinner tonight. See you then." She began to walk backwards to the door. "I do love you, you know. And I have missed you. And I can't hide the fact that I am glad you are back. I have really missed you," she said slowly.

"I have missed you too," Nick responded sweetly. "I need clothes," he said rather randomly. "I have nothing to wear. I was hoping you could go with me today."

"Go with Mom. No, go with Dad. No, Mom." Laurie couldn't decide who would be best. On second thought," Laurie began to ponder. "Why don't you call a dresser? Remember Mom said when she met Dad she thought he had such great taste and she found out that he had a personal shopper from Nordstrom or somewhere help him choose clothes. They always called her 'his dresser'. She would go around the store with him and show him what was 'in' and find things to fill out his wardrobe. Dad still has a good-looking wardrobe, but I think Mom has taken over. But, wouldn't it be great to have someone help you choose a wardrobe? I mean, you can find some of your own knock-around stuff at Target or wherever, but to have someone work on your entire wardrobe; wouldn't that be great?" Laurie smiled as she backed out the door, "I just decided what Jack can get me for Christmas this year!" She waved as she closed the door and headed for her car. "By the way," she shouted back to him, "you need a haircut!"

Nick shook his head. Man, I have missed her too, he thought.

Nick was reading a magazine at the table, eating a piece of toast, when his parents came home. Emily came in and put her arms around him from the back. "Did you get to see Laurie?" she asked as she kissed him on the head. Nick nodded.

"How did that go?" Emily asked, not knowing how to phrase the question.

"She's insane, you know," Nick stated frankly. Kris was standing across the room and laughed.

"So," Emily began feeling her way. "What did you two talk about? I mean," she paused not knowing what to say.

"Mom, I know you know! I told Dad, he told you, you told Laurie, she told Jack and Pippa. I am no longer a priest! We all know. It's okay. I'm okay." He paused, "Are you okay?" he asked softly.

"I am better than okay. I have my son home," Emily beamed.

"And are you okay, Dad?" Nick asked looking across the room at Kris.

"I am definitely okay. I am happy. And you?" Kris asked.

"Well, I am going to need some money, I guess. Are you still okay?" Nick asked with a smile. "And clothes, and maybe a car eventually," he added as an afterthought. He immediately was overwhelmed with guilt. I have nothing, he thought to himself. And now I am asking my parents to provide for me as if I am a dependent child. He put his hand over his mouth.

Kris was beaming. "No problem."

"Starting over at my age isn't easy. I might need a little grubstake. I don't need much, just a little to get started," Nick admitted apologetically trying to soften his earlier list of needs. "I just need a few clothes. Just basics. I don't really even need a car; there is good public transportation here. If I could just borrow a little money to get started," he murmured.

Kris looked directly at his son. "Your trust fund is still intact," he said factually. "I never did anything with it. It has just been accumulating. Well, some years accumulating better than others." He smiled, "It is your money, Nick. You can do anything you want with it."

It took a minute for it to sink in but now Nick smiled, "Of all the things I contemplated about coming home, having a trust fund waiting for me wasn't one of them." He was genuinely touched. "I don't think I will need very much."

"I didn't keep it because I thought you would come home some day." Kris wanted Nick to know he never considered that possibility. "I just couldn't decide what to do with it," he admitted. "It is your money, Nick," he repeated.

Nick was unsure that he ever knew he had a trust fund. He hadn't thought about money for years. "One man shouldn't be this lucky," he responded. "Love and money, it just doesn't seem right."

"It's not *that* much money," Kris responded.

"Next to a vow of poverty, any is a lot."

"Enough said." Kris smiled at his son.

Emily drove Nick to Target and he picked out a few things. Emily choked up a bit when she realized he had obviously brought very little with him. She found the coat, tie, and shirt Nick had worn home in the trash in his room. They had obviously been given to him; the neck was too big, the sleeves too short. He put into the cart all of the basics: razor, shave cream, shampoo, nail file, comb, brush, toothbrush, toothpaste, deodorant; everything that everyone else takes for granted. Then he went on to underwear, socks, handkerchiefs, tee shirts, and a belt. A belt, she thought. Who doesn't even own a belt! Why did I get rid of all of his things? She remembered the day when she and Laurie packed up all the clothing Nick had left at home, with tears streaming down their faces, and took the boxes to a church donation center. Not their church! She couldn't bear to see someone wearing Nick's clothes. It would be like he died. They took the boxes to a church across the bridge into New Jersey.

After Nick had selected a minimum of clothing items he asked, "Could we go look at a few groceries?" Emily nodded. They cruised the aisles with Nick asking occasionally about a product, or if they had peanut butter at home, or about whatever looked particularly good to him at that moment. Emily loved shopping with him and seeing him select cereal he loved as a child and cookies she knew he must not have had for a long time. He seemed stunned by the vast selection of ice cream. But then Nick seemed to tire quickly. "I'm finished," he said rather abruptly. But then as they started to enter the check-out line, he slowed his pace and looked at every candy bar, pack of mints, and gum. He threw gum in the cart first and then took a long time selecting a candy bar. When they did check out, he put the bags back in the cart as soon as the checker had filled them. He bit his lip as he heard the total and watched as Emily slid her card to pay. He seemed overwhelmed with the entire process.

Back at the car, Emily asked Nick if he would like to drive but he declined. He couldn't remember the last time he drove. He slumped in the seat and didn't talk at all for several minutes. Emily wondered if spending money after the vow of poverty and working with the extremely poor was bothering him now. For several years he had worked in impoverished areas in different cities, each one sounding more dangerous to her than the last. Both Kris and Nick had tried to convince her that priests were safer than others who roamed the streets.

Emily wondered if Nick thought their life totally decadent. Well it is, she thought. We have "stuff", lots of "stuff". But, she continued in her thoughts; we have worked hard, educated six children between us, and given to lots of charities. Not to mention, she thought now that she was trying to justify their lifestyle, we built a women's shelter and run it! One year early in their marriage, Emily, and Kris's sons had a shelter for abused women built on the grounds of a previous shelter, where Kris's youngest son had been killed while volunteering. An irate ex-husband was determined to take his wife and children out of the shelter with him and the teenager tried to protect them and was shot. They named it Millar House and dedicated it on Kris's birthday as a gift to him. Kris has been on the board since the day it opened. It has been a tremendous success and two other shelters have been built by the city using Millar House as a prototype. Still, she reasoned as she came back to the present, maybe we should curb our spending for a bit around Nicky.

Later Nick and Kris were sitting across from one another at the kitchen table. Nick had a half-eaten peanut butter and jelly sandwich in front of him and a glass of water. Kris had obviously finished lunch and his empty plate remained in front of him. Both men were engrossed in books they were reading. Emily entered and exclaimed, "Nicky, is that all you are eating? I would have fixed you something. I can warm up something. Anything sound good?" she asked.

Nick looked up to the ceiling and said to his father, "Do you hear that? There must be a helicopter around here. I can hear hovering. Do you hear hovering?" Kris laughed loudly.

Emily tried not to laugh. "Nicholas Millar, I have this uncontrollable urge to kick you as hard as I can in the shins. I do not hover! Well, maybe I do a little. But, I'll stop. You can take care of yourself from here on out! So there!" Nick smiled at his mother.

"So who am I, Mr. Nobody? You didn't offer to fix my lunch," Kris complained.

"It is in our pre-nup, I don't have to fix your lunch."

"How about a cup of tea then?" Kris asked.

"Get your own damn tea. I am sick of men," Emily answered trying to sound angry.

"Okay then," Kris said as he got up and put his plate in the dishwasher. "I'll make it. Who wants tea?" Both Emily and Nick raised their hand. Kris smiled and shook his head.

After the tea was finished and the table cleared, Kris asked Nick if he might like to go to the bank. "We can set up a checking account for you, get some checks ordered and a debit card," he reasoned. "Then eventually we can have funds transferred into the account. As you need them," he added.

"Dad, I can't handle any large sums of money right now. I really just need some pocket money," Nick explained.

"Nick, you are going to need some things like a computer and a cell phone. And, I am a little concerned that you don't have any credit record. We have got to get some things going eventually so you can have a VISA or Master Card, to buy airline tickets when you want to and things like that," he explained. "I am not trying to rush you, son. I know this is all coming at you at once. Let's just get an account open and get a debit card to start. Then you have pocket money. You can have your mother's car for now. We were thinking of getting her another one anyway. Emily and I can share mine for a while. We go most places together anyway. I'll put you on my VISA for now. Is that a good plan?" Kris asked. Nick nodded. Kris went on, "Go with one of the girls when you buy a computer if you want help. I can barely turn mine on. If they come next weekend, I know they would love to go with you."

"Great Dad," Nick answered. He smiled at his father. He had forgotten his dad's accent. He sounds so British, he thought. I guess he always has and always will sound British. I had just forgotten. Isn't it funny, he thought, that Dad came to the U.S. as a teenager and he still has an English accent. I guess your first six years are the most important as some say. His thoughts drifted off to his young childhood and how wonderful it had been. The house was always full of action. Laurie chasing after him and he annoying his older half sisters, Mandy and Alison, who lived in the house with them. His dad's sons, Mike and Beau, came in periodically. Mike stayed in California after he graduated from Stanford but came home occasionally. Nick was crazy about Mike as a young boy. Beau had an apartment in Philadelphia near their house. He first lived there alone and then married Khiem Li and eventually they bought a house nearby. When his parents traveled, Nick and Laurie would sometimes stay with Beau and Khiem Li. Beau and Khiem Li have six children, the older ones just a few years younger than Nick and Laurie. Nick came back to the present. "Give me ten minutes and I'll be ready."

Saturday night Beau and Khiem Li and four of their children and two of their grandchildren came for dinner. Laurie and Jack, her husband, and three year-old daughter, Pippa, arrived a few minutes before them. Nick saw them getting out of the car, Laurie leading the way. Just as she opened the door he jumped out and scared her. "Grow up!" she shouted at him as she patted her heart. Jack was still getting Pippa out of the car. When they got to the porch, Nick went to meet them. He shook hands with Jack. They had only met once before, for a very brief time at Nick's grandfather's funeral. Pippa was just a baby and didn't remember Nick. Jack was carrying her and she refused to get down, burying her head in his shoulder. She turned to look at Nick and as she did, he put his hands out to take her if she would come to him. She looked him up and down, and began to wail. Laurie tried to come to Jack's aid but Pippa would not let go. She screamed.

"I often have that effect on women," Nick quipped.

By now Emily was at the door. "What's wrong?" she asked.

Now Pippa was looking at Emily and continued to cry. Finally she shouted, "Gran Kris!" Emily called for Kris to come. When Pippa saw Kris, she had a look of relief and held her arms out for him to take her. Then she pointed to Nick and shouted, "No Gran Kris!"

"I told you, you look just like him," Laurie said. "You confused her. She thought Dad would answer the door and you did instead. We told her you were here but it didn't compute."

The rest of the evening was almost as wild. Beau always called Nick, 'Saint Nick'." It sort of irritated Nick now. He was never that crazy about his half brother calling him that as a child, but it seemed particularly annoying at this time. Still, Beau was a jokester. He meant well. Why should he change just because Nick was super sensitive. Kids were shouting, crying, laughing, eating. The grandchildren were chasing after each other, running around the room. Everyone was talking at once. Nick was quiet. After dinner everyone was in the family room and Emily went into the kitchen to get something. Nick was sitting at the kitchen table alone. He had pulled up one of the chairs and had his feet propped up and was drinking a beer from the bottle. Calpurnia was lying near him.

"Too much?" Emily asked.

"Well, it is loud," Nick answered softly.

"I'm sorry. It's like that here. Always is, always has been."

"I know," he answered but didn't move.

A tear ran down Emily's cheek. Nick sat up and put his feet on the floor. "Mom, what's wrong?"

"I'm afraid you'll leave again." She sat down at the table. "This is all too much for you. I'm sorry. We shouldn't have invited them. I don't want you to go back." She began to sob.

"Mom," Nick went over to his mother, crouched down and put an arm around her. "I am not going to leave, not for a while anyway. And I am certainly not going back. I couldn't really if I wanted to. I have been laicized; reduced back to the lay state. I am not a priest and will never be one again. I'm sorry if I can't fit back into the family…" he struggled for words, "'dynamic' instantly. Give me time. I will. I promise, I will." Nick continued to try to comfort his mother. "I am sort of disoriented right now. I was successful living a modest life and I will be successful living a secular life. But, I can't change overnight. I'm sorry. I never wanted to upset you. The last thing I wanted to do was upset you by coming here."

By now Nick's father had entered the room to see what was keeping Emily. "Everything okay?" Kris asked.

Nick went on seamlessly, talking to the two of them now. "I would like to live here for a while, with the two of you, if that's all right. I'm very tired. I need sleep and rest. I need to decompress. I want to see the family. I am glad they are here. I want to see Alison and Mandy and their families, and Mike. But I have to take an occasional break. I know it might seem rude, but once in a while I need a break. I'm sorry. I'm really sorry. I thought…maybe I didn't think, about what living here would be like for you. I'm sorry. I'll try to be better." He paused and looked at Emily, "Now what did you come in here to get?"

"Dessert. Cobbler and ice cream. The plates and forks are right there," she pointed.

Kris spoke up, "I'll get the ice cream."

"And I'll bring the plates. Mom can bring the cobbler. But I have to warn you, I can't eat any right now. I am stuffed and if I eat one more bite, I will be ill. It won't be pretty. But, if you hear someone in the kitchen at midnight, it might be me." He smiled at his mother and then his dad, and added, "I'm going to be a porker if I am not careful."

The rest of the evening went well. Pippa eventually made up with Nick and sat on his lap and finally fell asleep on his shoulder. He was teased that his quiet demeanor would put any woman to sleep. He didn't comment. No one asked him what he was going to do or how long he was going to live with his parents. He was grateful for that. One of Beau's sons did ask him if he planned to go back to school. Nick said he had had quite enough of school. He thought to himself about all of the years of theology, Greek, and philosophy classes, and silently wondered what courses he had taken that would be helpful in gaining employment. The phone rang and Kris answered it. "For you, Nick. John."

When the entire room seemed to look at Nicky for an explanation, he answered simply, "My sponsor." For an instant he resented their interest. Then he added to put the topic to rest, "I am assigned to him so he can help me through the rough spots. He's an ex-priest." Then thinking he needed to clarify, he added, "He's married. Three little kids. Not all priests are gay! I'm not gay!" he mumbled. He went upstairs to talk on the phone. The room got silent, temporarily, and Nick thought to himself, I am becoming totally paranoid. What in the world is wrong with me?

Chapter Three

"Hi, Mom," Nick said into his cell. Dad and I will be home in about twenty minutes. We stopped and got a cell phone for me after we played a few rounds. I would have texted you, but I kept screwing it up." Nick scrunched down in the front seat of his dad's car and continued his conversation with his mother. "After golf, we got haircuts. That should make you and Laurie happy."

"Did Phyllis cut your hair too?" Emily asked.

"No, another woman cut mine. She had pink stripes in her hair."

"So what does your hair look like?" she asked.

"Dad says I have a purposely disheveled look. It is sort of rumpled, sticking up here and there. He says I look like I just got out of bed."

"I can't wait to see this!"

Laurie was there when the guys got home and squealed when she saw Nick. "Oh, my God! Nick, you are hot!"

He laughed her off, "When you're hot, you're hot. When you're not, you're not. So, I've heard."

"I'm not kidding, Nick. You look hot. Get out in the sun and get a little color and you will be on the cover of Spotlight Magazine as Bachelor of the Year." Nick rolled his eyes at her.

"I'm going up and shower."

As soon as he was out of earshot, Laurie and Emily began to giggle like school girls. "He looks adorable," Emily said.

Kris looked at them totally disgusted. "You two better shape up. If you ridicule everything he does, he is going to rebel," he said sternly.

"We are not ridiculing him. Complimenting!" Laurie protested.

"Nevertheless, read my lips—leave him alone, or you will regret it."

"Okay, you're right. But, he is the most handsome man I have ever seen!" Emily said laughing.

"Thanks!" Kris responded and left the room to go shower. The women continued to titter.

Nick had been on a long run and had just turned back onto their street, when he slowed and finally decided to cool down by walking the rest of the way home. A car slowly pulled to the curb next to him. He thought he had seen the car go by before. The window went down so he walked over to see if someone needed directions or something. A young woman leaned across the passenger side to talk to him through the window. "Hi. Are you new in the neighborhood?" she asked.

"Hi. I'm just visiting my parents down the street," he answered.

"Oh? Who are your parents? I know most of the people on this street. I live in the next block." The woman was an attractive blonde, well dressed in crops and v-neck top.

"Kris and Emily Millar are my parents. I'm Nick."

"Hi, I'm Kat. Short for Katherine. I know Laurie a little bit. She was a few years ahead of me in school. I'm living with my mother, Jane Evans, down the street. I just got divorced and my little girl and I moved in with my mother to get things straightened out," she summarized. Then suddenly it seemed to dawn on her. "Oh," she gasped. "You are Nicholas, the priest. I'm sorry, Father. I didn't realize. Don't let me keep you." With that she pushed the button and the window went up before Nick could even straighten up. The car took off.

Well, that was weird, Nick thought.

When he went into the house he asked Emily. "Do you know the Evans, Kat and her mother? I guess they live down the street a block or so. I don't remember them."

"I know her mother a little bit. She and her husband moved here not long after we did, I guess. He died a few years later and she stayed in the house. Her daughter and granddaughter moved in recently. Did you meet Kat when you were out? I have heard she is a bit on the wild side. She just got divorced. I would stay away from her if I were you."

"No problem."

"Nicky, I invited someone to dinner next week. It is someone I worked with in the law department at Manner and Gross. She is more your age than mine but we really got on well and I see her now and then. I just wanted you to know that she is here as my friend. I am not trying to set you up with her. She may be going with someone anyway. She has political aspirations. She works for the governor now and is going to be in Philly for a few days, so I invited her. Is that okay?"

"Of course, Mom. This is your house. You can invite anyone you want."

"I know, but I want you to meet her. She is just so neat. I really like her and would like you to know her. But, again I don't want you to think I am setting you up. If Laurie were living here, she would be included. So, will you have dinner with us?"

"Sure. By the way," Nick began slowly, "I am going to have dinner tonight with John and his wife."

"Oh, that's nice. Where are you going?" Emily asked.

"Their house. I have the address. I am not sure how to get there. I should look at a map," he said mostly to himself. "Do you have a street map?"

"My car has a GPS, have Dad put their address in it. Or I can."

Nick paused and looked very somber. "Cars still take gas, don't they? And the rules of the road haven't changed, have they?" he asked sarcastically but with a sad tone. "We still drive on the right?"

Emily looked at Nicky and her heart broke, not knowing what to say. She said nothing.

Nick grimaced and said, "I'm sorry. Yes, please put the address in the GPS. Maybe you could teach me to use it."

"Sure, it's simple."

"Thanks."

John met Nick at the door and let him in and introduced him to his wife, Janey. Their three kids were in front of the television. "You two talk in the den, while I finish dinner," Janey said. John led the way to the den and offered Nick a seat on the sofa. He sat across from him in a chair. It was a comfortable room. There were a few toys scattered about but the room looked to be used mostly by adults. There were bookshelves on one wall and a desk with a computer against another. One entire wall was covered with family photos.

John was older than Nick, in his forties. He was nice looking. Not as tall as Nick and certainly heavier but not overweight. He was fair and his hair was cut short making his face look round and pleasant. John was dressed in chinos and a sport shirt. Nick was in the same thing he had worn since arriving in Philadelphia; jeans and a short-sleeved tee shirt. He had bought several colors when on his shopping trip, none black. He apologized for his appearance. "I haven't been able to sort out the clothing thing," he told John.

John laughed, "If that is your biggest problem, you've got it made. How is it going?"

"Okay. It may be a little harder than I thought. My parents have been great, but I seem to keep saying mean things to them. Especially my mom, I guess. I don't know why."

John listened and asked, "Tell me, how do they treat you? Like an adult? Like a child?"

"Sometimes like an adult. Mostly like a child I guess but maybe I am acting like a child. I don't know what to do, so I don't do anything."

"Does your mother treat you differently than your dad?" John asked.

"Yes, my mother is terrified I will leave and go back. She cried. I felt terrible. I tried to tell her I won't go back but I am the one who told them I would be a priest forever! My dad is pretty quiet. We did go play nine holes the other day. That was good. It's when I am confronted with something new, that I don't know anything about, that I get defensive— like the GPS," he explained. "I can't seem to make all of the decisions that a normal teenager could make about cell phones, computers, cars and stuff and I'm in my thirties! I get easily overwhelmed. I feel like I am either in a state of panic or completely stoic. My family just looks at me to see what I am going to do next." He added, "My sister isn't too bad. She still treats me the way she always has. But even she has a life. I mean," he stammered, "she has a job, a husband, and a daughter. And she is my little sister. All my older siblings are established. Even their kids are established. Some of my siblings have grandchildren; though they are lots older than me," he explained. "I'm just frustrated that I have no idea what I am doing. I'm living with my parents! I guess I thought I would leave and come home and suddenly something would come to me about what to do and how to go about doing it. It hasn't. Sometimes I feel like I am the stereotypical youngest son; the underachiever; overindulged and unambitious."

John began, "I told myself the one thing I wouldn't say to guys going through this is 'this is normal', and yet I have to say it. The other thing I said I would never say is 'it takes time', but here goes. It takes time. Maybe if I tell you what it was like for me, it might help."

"I went to my mother's house. My dad had passed away about three years before. I had felt really bad about not being there to help my mom at that time, but when I got there I gave her nothing but grief; ironically," he said smiling. "For the first week, I don't think I got out of my pajamas or went out of my room. I am not kidding. I was there several days before I took a shower. No matter what I did or didn't do, my mother wouldn't criticize me. She tried to act like nothing was wrong. She brought food up to my room. Finally, my brother came and told me to get up, or get out. He gave me one week to get myself in shape (clothes, haircut, etc.), one month to get some plans down, and six months to get a job. I bawled like a baby! Had a complete meltdown. Called him names, said he didn't understand. I ridiculed my mother and made her cry. They left the room. I am sure they thought I should be institutionalized. But, after I calmed down, I took a shower, got dressed, went downstairs and offered to fix dinner. I had cooked a lot at the rectory. After that, I cooked dinner nearly every day and started to feel better. It still took a long time to get out and meet people. I didn't have a job in six months, but I had applied for some. It took me four months to go to mass. But once I got over that hurdle, I went several times a week for a while. I tried a shrink but he truly did not understand. Finally, a friend of a friend, knew another guy who had been a priest and he talked to me—listened to me. It was so helpful, just to know someone knew what I was going through. That's why I volunteered to be a sponsor."

Nick sat with his hand resting on his neck.

John asked, "What did you like to do before you went into the priesthood? You were in college, right? What did you like to do?"

Nick thought before answering, and finally said, "Just college stuff. I dated some, and I went out in groups. I went out a lot to drink and dance. My friends and I did a lot of dancing. We listened to music; went to movies; played poker. Just normal stuff single young guys do, I guess."

John smiled, "Well, here is a bulletin for you…you are still a single, young guy. I am not saying you are ready to date. I think that might take a while. I didn't date for close to a year. I met Janey two years after I was out and we married a year after that. She had no idea when we met that I had been a priest. I sort of needed to be anonymous for a while. I went out by myself a lot and didn't talk to many people, just observed. If a girl came up to me, at first I told her I was married. Later, I could talk about my job, music, whatever. I traveled a little by myself. When I traveled, I could be anyone I wanted. No one knew me in Atlanta or Chicago so I felt comfortable. At home it wasn't that way. I felt like everyone was trying to catch me being un-priest like, or priest-like, I am not sure which."

"I just had a crazy thought. How would you like to go out with Janey and me tonight. We sometimes go to a club near here. There is a live band. We can listen to music, and dance. You can dance with Janey, or anyone else," he added. "You are free to dance with anyone you damn please. Make up a name. Make up a life. All I ask is that you don't take down any phone numbers or give yours out. Be totally anonymous. How does this sound to you?" John started to think maybe this was a bit premature for Nick. "You don't have to dance. You can just listen to music if you want. I'm not trying to push you to do anything you don't want to do. You know, there aren't any rules to this." John smiled and looked directly at Nick, "Some people 're-enter' one way, some another. If you say 'no way', we'll stay here and play Scrabble. It is totally up to you."

"Let's go listen to music!"

After dinner, Nick, John, and Janey dropped the children off with grandparents and went to the Circus Club. Nick liked the music. The band played music he had known in college. For the first time since he arrived home, something felt familiar. After two beers, he danced with Janey. After that, girls came from everywhere. He danced nearly every song but didn't really talk. When they would ask him anything personal, even his name, he acted like the music was so loud he couldn't hear and would wave them off and go to someone else. Janey drove him home in his mom's car and John followed to take her back home.

It was eleven-thirty when he got home. Even though Emily and Kris would usually go to bed by ten, they were up as if they always watched the late television programs. "Nice dinner?" Emily asked.

"Great. Swiss steak, baked potato."

Kris didn't want Emily to interrogate Nick so he tried to conclude the conversation and go to bed. "Good. Glad you had a good time. We should get to bed."

"Then, we went out drinking and dancing!" Nick blurted out and then waited for their reaction.

"You did?" Emily asked sincerely.

Nick smiled, "But I didn't drive home. Janey, John's wife, drove as my designated driver. The car is safely in the garage."

Kris and Emily looked at each other. Finally, Kris said, "Really, Nick, you went dancing? That's great, son."

"It was great, Dad. I'm sorry I have been so grouchy. I promise to try to be better. I still have a long way to go to normal, but this is a start. By the way, John would like to talk to you one day. Would that be okay?"

"Sure. Goodnight. Love you, son."

"You must."

John met with Kris at a Starbucks. When Kris stood as John approached, John said, "I would have known you anywhere. Nick looks just like you. Same eyes."

Both men sat down and John began, "I want you to know first of all, I am not a professional therapist or psychologist. I have no professional credentials to counsel Nick. But, I have experienced many of the same things Nick has experienced, and will experience, because I was once a priest also. I left for some of the same reasons that Nick left. Like him, I just didn't feel called to be a priest any more. I wasn't angry with the Church and I left in good standing, if you will. I later met my wife and we married and now have three kids. So, I thought maybe you might have some questions for me that you might feel awkward asking Nick, or that he may not be ready to answer. Obviously, I can only tell you what it was like for me. I can't speak for Nick. But I feel sure some of the things he is feeling, I felt also. So are you comfortable speaking to me? I know you are a doctor and maybe you don't feel I am qualified."

Kris listened intently and then answered John, "I am sure you are more than qualified to counsel Nick. His mother and I, the entire family, want to do anything we can to help Nick transition back into a secular life. I am so glad he has you to talk to. None of us know what to say to help."

John smiled, "You have an English accent. I wasn't prepared for that. Is your wife British also?"

Kris answered factually, "No, Emily is American. I came here as a teenager."

John asked, "How do you think it is going for Nick?"

Kris was somber. "I don't know. He's moody. Sometimes he seems like Nicky, other times he seems out of place, sort of from a different world. I can't believe he went dancing. When the family storms into the house, he retreats. Why can he take groups of strangers and not his family?"

John laughed, "Nick wasn't exactly social at the club. He didn't really talk. He just danced. The music, and I suppose the beer, helped him relax. Nick is going to have a special problem that most of us didn't have," John said smiling. "He is incredibly good-looking! Women are going to pounce on him. They did at the club. He won't be ready for a relationship for a little while. So, he ignored them for the most part. He just danced, sort of in a parallel universe, if you know what I mean. He has made it very clear that family means everything to him. That is the relationship he wants to work on."

"How do you think or feel you treat Nick now, compared to when you last saw him when he was a priest?" John asked.

"I am very tenuous. I feel so guilty. I feel like it is my fault that he became a priest and was in that situation for so long. And now I feel guilty that I don't know what to do or say to make his homecoming easier." Kris was obviously emotional.

"Nick is scared, or at least I was when in his situation. Look, people revere priests for the most part. They are treated pretty well by the public generally. But for ex-priests, it is a whole different story. Most people assume ex-priests have been asked to leave the priesthood. It is a big fall. Even if someone doesn't think that, they are usually uncomfortable being with an ex-priest. The celibacy thing scares people to death. What woman wants to date an ex-priest? As soon as you say you were a priest, women treat you like a thirty year-old virgin. My wife said when she told her friend she was dating me, her friend called me John Two Shoes, as in Goody Goody Two Shoes. I looked up the story to understand what it meant. The expression means, as you might know, sort of smugly virtuous. I hated that. I finally told the girl off. I felt better for a while. Then, of course, I felt guilty. I am getting off track. The point is, Nick will be confronted by some pretty negative behaviors."

Kris asked, "How can we help with that?"

"I don't know that you can. It has to play out. Just be there when he gets slapped down. The job thing is a case in point. Nick thinks he is only qualified to be a missionary and a scholar. He feels all those years of education have bitten him in the butt. He has to come up with something he feels passionate about that he will be accepted doing. He is qualified to teach some things, but schools will stay away from him like the plague. They are afraid of scandal. Besides, he signed an agreement that he will not teach in the Catholic schools or teach religion in other schools. It is pretty normal to ask a priest to agree not to influence others about religion after he leaves. The assumption is that an ex-priest harbors some animosity toward the Catholic Church. Nick doesn't, any more than I do, but it is a standard part of laicization. Nick doesn't want to be a missionary any longer. Who can blame him? We called those who did what Nick did 'street priests'. He worked in city filth for years, ministering to drunks, druggies, prostitutes, and runaways. He says he can still smell the vomit and urine when he tries to sleep. He needs to be in a clean environment. He loves being home for that reason. He needs a lot of rest."

"So how are we to treat him?" Kris asked. "Do we treat him like a guest, or our son home on vacation? Emily wants to do everything for him. She worries about him every time he goes out the door. I guess the time to worry was when he was with drunks and dealers," Kris said with a smile.

"First of all, you didn't know what he was doing so you didn't worry. Secondly, it wasn't as dangerous as it sounds because he was a priest in appearance. Rarely is a priest hurt on assignment. But, as for now, give him a little room." John paused and slowed his pace in speaking to Kris. He leaned in a little to explain. "Nick has been leading a very modest life. He lived in very simple surroundings, with simple food. So everything will take a while. It will even take a while for his stomach to adjust. On mission assignments, they ate very small meals. They didn't have cooks when they worked in the inner city, like priests do in residence. They were confronted with so much worldliness on a daily basis, they tried to keep their own environment extremely simple. Did you know he is sick after nearly every meal?" Kris shook his head. "He needs to make small changes in his diet, not dramatic. He doesn't want to upset his mother, so he eats. We fed him broth, bread, and rice. He told me he told you otherwise. He's embarrassed."

Kris shook his head in disbelief, "I'm a doctor. I can surely help with that."

"Sure, tell him I told you about it. I don't want him to stop trusting me—or you. Maybe you can give him something and have some simpler food around. Let him fix his own meals, what he feels like eating. Have him go get his own groceries. He isn't helpless. Find some things for him to do."

"He didn't go to mass, Sunday," Kris announced out of context.

"Well, he doesn't know what to expect. Sometimes even priests are rude to ex-priests. Do you have a good relationship with your home-church priest?" Kris nodded. "He needs to talk to Nick. Nick wants to be a good Catholic. He wants to stay in the Church."

"I looked up *laicization*," Kris said. "From what I understand, Nick can't really do anything in the Catholic Church again. He can't celebrate any of the sacraments or give homilies. I think it said the only thing he could do was give deathbed or emergency Last Rites."

"That's right," John said. "There are a lot of restrictions. But, I don't think any of that bothers Nick. I think he is looking to do something completely different. I was. He just doesn't know what it is yet. I think Nick is going to be okay. I really do. I think in a few years he is going to be riding in car pools and playing with his kids when he gets home from work. It just takes time. Nick will adjust. I really believe he will."

Kris was glad to have talked to John and told Emily everything he learned. They vowed together to do everything they could to help Nicky even if it meant leaving him alone sometimes.

The next weekend Emily's two daughters from her first marriage came for the weekend. They did not bring their families. Emily thought it might be too much for Nick. Alison and Mandy were twelve and fourteen when Nick was born. They treated Nick like a pet. When they had time, he was fun to play with. When they were busy, he was a nuisance. The more they tried to get away from him, the more he tried to be with them. Because of the age difference, they had little in common when they lived at home. But, still they had genuine affection for one another.

Mandy moved to Boston and became a pediatrician. Alison graduated from Harvard and moved to New York to work for a recording company. So, they didn't see much of Nick as he grew up except on holidays. None of Kris and Emily's children had any ill feelings for the others. They actually all got along amazingly well. And the older four, were happy that their parents met and fell in love and had a family together. At holidays, they all got together. But, Nick of course, had been out of the family loop for several years when in the priesthood. He didn't know either girl's spouse or their children.

Alison brought Nick a gift and handed it to him right away. It was an iPod and she had every family member e-mail her suggestions of songs to download on it. It was loaded with three hundred and eighty-four tunes from Rod Stewart to Black Balzac. It would be an instant music appreciation course. He was thrilled and appreciative. Nick had a cell phone in the field but it belonged to the church and he had to turn it in. The cell was very basic and did not have a keyboard and he never learned to text. He had access to a computer, so he could e-mail home when he had a chance but they didn't really use it for much else. But, he did not have an iPod or any way to play music. He did not have a television. In the field, the men took inexpensive, furnished rooms, usually sharing a room in a down-market apartment building in the neighborhood where they were ministering. It was probably music, secular music, that Nick missed the most. He loved the iPod.

Alison, looked like an Emily clone. She was petite with dark hair and bright brown eyes. She was very animated. She loved music as much a Nick, which is why she went to work for a recording company. "Nicky, come to New York. You'll love it. You can live at my house for a while. Notice, I said for a while. I still remember how annoying you can be," she laughed. "Seriously, there is everything in New York: music, art, theatre, and women!" she added quickly.

"Thanks. I'll think about it," Nick said with a smile.

Mandy was also small but more serious than Alison. She adored her stepfather, Kris, and it was because of his influence that she became a doctor. The only person she admired as much as Kris, was Kris's father Nick, for whom Nicky was named. Nick, the elder, had been a noted pediatric orthopedic-specialist in Boston and Mandy went there to follow in his footsteps. They were in practice a few years together before he retired. Both girls kept the name Millar after they married. Kris adopted them soon after he and Emily were married and they both claimed they were so happy being in the Millar family they would never give up the name. Alison named one of her two sons

Kristopher. Mandy and her husband have four girls. Her husband is an OB/GYN. Now Mandy and her husband have practices in the same building. "Boston has more class than New York," Mandy joked saying it with a Boston accent, "Come to Boston."

Kris and Emily went to bed early, but the girls and Nick stayed up until 2 a.m. sharing stories of childhood, college and after. "Nicky," Mandy said, "do you remember Halloween when you were little? Alison and I would dress you up and take you out to get candy. We taught you to say, 'one for my sisters, please?' Everyone thought you were so cute that we got tons of candy."

"Remember, Mandy, one year we lost him," Alison said. "We were talking to some guys our age and we looked around and you were gone. We knew Mom and Dad would kill us if we let something happen to you. They liked you for some reason. You were really little. Laurie was just a baby, too little to go with us. We were scared to death. We looked everywhere and couldn't find you. We had all our friends looking too. Finally, one of our friends found you in a window well of a house. I guess you just fell in. He heard you crying. Thank God you were unhurt. We didn't tell Mom and Dad. You tried to tell them you fell down a hole and we told them it was just a hole in the street." The girls were laughing.

"Mom!" Nick yelled, kidding them.

Before they left to go home the next day, the three siblings went to Buy Rite and got a computer tablet for Nick. Alison made sure it had everything loaded on it that he needed, in her estimation. A few days later Beau looked at it and thought it was lacking games. Nick was content with Solitaire and Hearts. Beau thought it should have Bee Mangle and Nuke Duke. Beau installed them, Nick never played them. One day, Beau stopped in and went to see Nick in his room and he was playing Solitaire. "That is so eighties," he said adding, "and I mean the age not the decade."

"Mom," Nick shouted, "Beau is picking on me."

Emily was coming up the steps, and sounding like a mother of small children said, "Nick, learn to stand up for yourself."

"See, she doesn't like you best," Beau sneered.

Chapter Four

Nick walked to the train station. It was a beautiful day, clear and sunny. There were only a few people on the platform since rush hour had been over for some time. He was going in to meet his mother for lunch and then they were going to shop for a sport coat and some other clothing. Not much! He had agreed to a sport coat so he would have one when needed and a few knit shirts with collars; he had borrowed one from his dad to wear today. And maybe a pair of pants. He was in jeans today as he had been since arriving except for occasionally wearing some old athletic shorts he wore to run.

A young woman approached him after a few minutes. "You've been staring at my legs," she said smiling as she spoke.

"I'm sorry," Nick gasped. "I didn't mean to. I didn't realize I was doing it. I am sorry." He thought for a minute and said very seriously, "I know this sounds stupid but I guess I was thinking about skirts. I mean, my mother wears her skirts long, well not long, but past her knee. My sister wears hers just above the knee I guess, like yours. My young nieces wear them really short, barely covering their underwear. So, I was thinking, how do women buy skirts? Guys buy pants by inseam length. Are skirts all one length and you have them altered or are all skirts available in every length? I am going to meet my mother to buy some clothes and so I guess that is why I was thinking about it. I mean…I am going to buy clothes for me, not skirts." Nick flushed and touched his neck. Realizing he had done that, he then put his hand in his pocket and felt his rosary there. He moved his hand to his back pocket.

"Wow, and I thought it was because you thought I had good-looking legs," the girl said smiling. "Do you live around here?" she asked.

"I am visiting my parents a couple of streets over. Do you live nearby?" he managed to say.

"No way. I am working as an au pair this summer for a family on Harper Drive. Today is my day off and I am taking a class at the University of Pennsylvania. It is my first law school class. I am a teacher's aide, third grade, but I want to be a lawyer and I'm going to take classes part time."

"My mother is an attorney," Nick said supportively. She went back to school and got her law degree when I was little. Actually, she had me while she was in law school. Congratulations for making that decision," he said beginning to relax a bit.

"Is she in practice?" the girl asked.

"She used to work for Manner and Gross but she is semi-retired now. She does a few projects for them once in a while and she volunteers at Millar House helping battered women."

"I know Millar House. We have some homeless kids at the school where I work and the ones who come from Millar House are right up to grade level. It is amazing. Usually the homeless kids are so far behind, they eventually drop out. I'm Paige by the way."

"Hi, I'm Nick Millar. My parents will be happy to know what you said about Millar House."

"Oh, boy. So you are part of the Millar family that Millar House is named for?" she asked.

"Guilty."

"I am the first in my family to go to college. This neighborhood freaks me out. The privileged few," she said somewhat sarcastically. "I mean I know your family has done good things but," she trailed off.

Nick bristled a little, "My parents have worked very hard, their entire lives. I don't think my dad ever worked less than a ten hour day. I guess we are privileged. I don't know about the neighbors. I never thought about it." The train was approaching and Nick wouldn't be heard, so he stopped talking. The door opened and Paige got in,

Nick let another woman on and then he got in. He saw that Paige had taken a seat at the front, so he went to the back and sat by himself.

Nick met up with Emily. Two of her friends from Manner and Gross were with her when she met him and she introduced him but they didn't stay to talk. They ate in the department store restaurant. Nick had a half sandwich and a cup of soup. Emily didn't say anything about what he chose. Nick began rather out of context, "Mom, when you met Dad, did you think he was of privileged background?"

"Well, yes. He was. He was already a doctor when I met him. He went to Boston College and Harvard. It wasn't until later that I learned he grew up in an orphanage and met up with his father as a teenager."

"Did you compare it to how you grew up?"

"I guess so. I lived in a working-class neighborhood with working-class parents. My parents didn't go to college and didn't think girls needed a college education. Finally they said my sister and I could go to university but they wanted us to be teachers. I started out in business education but then finally switched to the business school. By that time, my parents didn't seem to care that much. I went to law school because I had always dreamed of it; your dad encouraged me and paid for it after we were married. Kris didn't flaunt money. Although he had a sports car when I met him," she reminisced.

"You're kidding! I never knew Dad had a sports car. He drives boring cars now."

"I don't think the sports car ever meant that much to him. I think his friend David talked him into it. Kris never really cared about status."

"Do you think our neighborhood is 'privileged'?" Nick asked.

"Don't you? Every home in the neighborhood is expensive. But I think the people are nice. Most have worked for their money. They give back. Why?"

"I just wondered. It's funny, I have worked with a lot of dirt-poor people but I never thought about us being rich. I just accepted our lifestyle because it is all I had ever known. That's sort of insensitive, isn't it?"

"I don't know. It is probably pretty normal to accept your lifestyle as normal. I love our house but I have always worked. Your dad always worked. We have always been generous in our help to others. I know we have a lot but I don't feel guilty about it. Ask Laurie how she feels."

"I just think it is funny how I just kind of separated off my past life when I became a priest. I love our house too. If you had moved and I couldn't have come back to that house, it would have been harder I think. A girl, today, told me I am privileged and I was sort of shocked to be judged by my address."

"What girl?" Emily asked.

"At the train station."

Emily was afraid to ask more.

Emily's friend was coming to dinner and Emily asked Nick to pick her up at the hotel and bring her to the house. Nick parked in the hotel lot and walked into the lobby. Only one woman was standing in the lobby. She smiled as Nick walked in. "Hi, I'm Abbe Metzger. It was nice of you to pick me up."

"Hi, Abbe. I'm Nick."

"Your mom said I would know you. She's right, you know, you look just like your dad. You both have those amazing blue eyes. Your mom calls them azure blue. I'm not so sure now that I look at them. Maybe they are more…cornflower or French blue."

Nick frowned and bit the inside of his mouth. Finally he said, "Thanks, I think," but then he smiled. "What are you doing in Philadelphia? Mom said you work for the governor," Nick said as they headed for the parking lot.

"I do, but his term is about up and I will be out a job. I have been meeting with the Democratic Party here. We are trying to strategize about what I should do."

"Have you come up with anything?" he asked.

"Well, I don't know. They are talking about me eventually running for mayor. I could start out as City Prosecutor or something and keep going. I am not sure I ever want to be mayor. I don't know if I could take the pressure of keeping the snow cleared and trash picked up in Philadelphia," she said. "I am not kidding, people get more upset about those two things than crime, jobs, education or anything else."

Nick listened. Abbe was indeed closer to his age than his mother's. She was just a year older than Nick. She was very attractive, five feet nine, slim, a thick mass of jet black hair and dark eyes. She was comfortable talking and Nick was glad to listen and not talk. But finally she said, "How is your re-entry going?"

Nick was somewhat surprised by the frankness of the question. Most people avoided any reference to his past life. He answered vaguely, "Better some days than others." He smiled and looked at her, "Today's good."

The rest of the way to the house, Abbe talked about Emily and how they met and how helpful Emily was when she interned at Manner and Gross. Nick felt very comfortable with Abbe. She was like meeting up with an old friend. It helped that she knew his family. She had been coming to their house for years, first when she worked with Emily and later when she moved to Harrisburg. Emily sort of took her under her wing when she was interning and loved her like a daughter.

Nick helped clear after dinner and while in the kitchen got a cell phone call. He was still unused to getting calls and it startled him. "Nick," he answered.

"Nick, when I tell you who this is, don't react, okay? For God's sake, don't say my name."

Nick answered back hesitantly, "Okay."

"It's Jack, but I don't want your parents to know I am talking to you. Will you meet me somewhere tonight?"

"We have a dinner guest. I have to take her back to her hotel later. I can meet you after that. She is staying downtown."

"Can you meet me by ten?" Jack asked.

"I think so, she says she is tired so won't want to stay late."

"Meet me at the bar in the Sheraton. I'll be there from nine-thirty on." Jack hung up.

How strange, Nick said to himself. Why would my sister's husband want to meet with me?

Nick walked Abbe into the hotel even though she said he could just drop her off. They exchanged pleasantries and then she hugged Nick goodbye thanking him for the ride.

Nick contemplated what to do. Do I call my mother, like a teenager and report in, telling her I will be late? Or, be inconsiderate and not phone and she wouldn't know why I didn't come home after taking Abbe to the hotel? Not wanting to upset his mother, he phoned home and said he was stopping for a drink. "Do not wait up!" he commanded. Then he felt like a jerk.

Jack was seated at a small table when Nick arrived. There were no other patrons in the bar. Jack was dressed in jeans and a sweatshirt. He looked tired, Nick thought, though he did not know Jack well. Laurie had wanted Nick to officiate at the ceremony when they were married but Nick was in Rome and couldn't even get back for the wedding. Jack seemed very nervous. The two men shook hands and Nick sat down. Someone came to the table right away and Jack ordered a light beer and looked to Nick. Nick held up two fingers to indicate he would have the same.

"Who came to dinner?" Jack asked but didn't seem interested in the answer. Finally he looked directly at Nick and said, "I'm in a mess. I messed up. I don't know what to do." Nick continued to look at him but said nothing.

"I have been seeing someone at work. Today she told me she is pregnant. She says she will keep the baby no matter what I do."

"Does Laurie know?" Nick asked.

"No! And you can't tell her. Not yet."

"What is it you are going to do? How do you feel about this woman?" Nick asked.

"I am in love with her." Jack looked down at the floor and covered his eyes with his hands. Then he looked up at Nick. "Do you have any idea how hard it is to compete with your family? I have never felt good enough for Laurie. She always talks about her siblings as if they are perfect. My God, your parents are icons in the city. She wants to know why I don't have Mike's drive and ambition, or Beau's love of children. I love Pippa but I don't want six kids. I didn't want any more children. That's ironic!" he said in a sarcastic voice.

Jack paused so Nick took over. "What do you intend to do about this? You have to tell Laurie."

"No."

"Jack, is this woman going to go quietly into the night?"

"No. She wants to get married."

"And you want to marry her?"

"Yes. But I don't want a big ugly scene with your family. I just want to divorce Laurie and marry Lydia. And I want joint custody of Pippa."

"Well I don't know about a scene with the family, but Laurie isn't going to be happy about this situation. Are you sure you don't want to go to counseling with Laurie and see if you can't save your marriage?" Nick felt some kind of obligation to at least suggest reconciliation, but it sounded ridiculous even to him as he said it.

"I know Laurie," Jack answered. "One strike and you are out. Besides, I don't want to hear the rest of my life how I let her down. I hear that enough now. I want a divorce."

"Why did you call me here if you already knew what you wanted?" Nick asked sincerely.

"I needed to say it out loud. I had to tell someone and since you are a priest, well…," he trailed off.

"I am not a priest! Don't make me your confessor," Nick was angry. "If you don't tell Laurie, I will. She needs to know and the sooner the better. No matter what your decision is about divorce and remarriage, you have to tell Laurie. Do you think this woman is lying to you? Are you thinking she may not really be pregnant?"

"No. I know she is pregnant. I just can't face Laurie. She is going to have me for lunch."

Nick answered, "So be it. Tell her. Right away, Jack. Tell her!" Jack threw some money on the table and started to get up, so Nick did also. They walked to the parking lot together. Finally, Nick asked, "How long have you been having this affair?"

Jack answered, "About a year."

Nick opened the car door and sat down. "Tell her." He slammed the door and took off.

Two days after Nick met with Jack, Laurie came into the house, as usual, through the back door. Kris was in the kitchen and she handed Pippa over to him asking him to take her outside to play. Kris did. Then Laurie flew into the living room where Nick was sitting on the arm of the sofa, taking to his mother across the room. As Laurie got to Nick she put both hands on his shoulders and she shoved him as hard as she could onto the sofa. "What is wrong with you?" Nick asked, as he righted himself.

"You knew! You bastard! You knew about this and didn't tell me!" Laurie was furious. Emily was completely baffled. Nick and Laurie always got along. Even as children, they hardly ever fought.

Laurie looked at her mother. "Ask Nicky who he had a drink with last week," she demanded. Emily looked at Nick blankly. Nick chewed on his lip. Laurie turned to Nick. "Tell her! Tell her, damn it. Tell her you met with my husband behind my back!" With that Laurie started to cry.

Nick sighed loudly, stood and walked to Laurie and put his arm around her. "I listened, and told him to tell you. I just listened. I wanted *him* to tell you so I gave it a couple of days. Obviously, he finally got around to telling you." Nick looked directly at his sister, his eyes deep with sympathy. "I'm sorry, Laurie. I am sorry this happened. I am glad Jack finally told you. He never should have let it get this far."

Finally Emily shouted, "Will someone tell me what is going on around here?"

Through her sobs, Laurie told of Jack's long infidelity and subsequent paternity and asked if she and Pippa could move in. Nick thought to himself, Jack is right about one thing, Laurie's reaction. But how else could she react, he thought? Nick had counseled for a short time and he learned that forgiving infidelity was one thing, but paternity something else. Yet, it had been his job to try to keep marriages together. He wasn't going to try in this case. Emily, however, saw the situation in a legal sense. She counseled Laurie to think about staying in the house. Not to let Jack stay there. She also said they would go see a good lawyer tomorrow and start to sort things out. Laurie agreed to going to the attorney, who was a friend of Emily's and was very well-known in divorce law. But, she would not stay in the house. She would tell Jack to get out and she would start to get it ready to sell. She was not going to live in the house they had been in together one more night.

That night after Pippa went to sleep, Laurie went in to Nick's room. He was propped up in bed reading when she tapped at the door. Calpurnia was curled up next to him. Nick looked at his sister sadly. "I'm sorry, sis," he said. "I really felt *he* needed to tell you, not me. I wouldn't have let it go on for long. Honest, I wouldn't have."

"I know. I'm sorry. When he told me he had talked to you, I went crazy. I am crazed. I don't know what to do next. I think I hate him. I have never hated anyone in my life and I hate my husband, the father of my child. I don't know what to do."

"When I would counsel people and they would say they didn't know what to do, I would always suggest they not do anything. At least for a while." Nick then broke the solemn atmosphere by smiling and saying, "Of all the kids our parents have raised, we two are the ones who lived in the totally functional home. We are the two who had both parents. Two loving parents! And here we are, adults, living at home. We are pathetic. You have to admit it is kind of funny, don't you? Dad raised boys by himself, before he and mom were married and they are successful and happy. Mom lived with an adulterous husband and raised two great daughters. What in the world happened to us?" And then they both laughed.

"What are you reading?" Laurie asked.

"Porn."

"You wouldn't know porn if you saw it."

"Yes I would, I went to high school. Anyway, it's a brochure about a class my sponsor says I might think about taking. It is a basic computer technology class. I don't really think I need it. I am okay with most technology. Not that much has changed since college. I haven't been living in a cave, like most people think. I used a cell phone and e-mail. I still can't use the camera on my phone though," he said with a chuckle. "Well, I can use the camera, I just can't do anything with the pictures. John said he took the computer class to get back up to speed. He said the class is mostly made up of the elderly, ex-cons, or others of us who have fallen off the face of the earth. Again, pathetic! Not you; just me. You actually have a career; a well-paying job."

"And an adulterous husband," Laurie added. "Pathetic."

Nick thought for a minute, "Laurie, maybe we should take off and go to Disney World," he said.

"Say what?"

"I am just saying, let's take advantage of our 'in limbo' situation and go to Disney. Pippa hasn't been has she? Of course, Mom and Dad should come too so they can watch Pippa, when you and I want to ride a coaster." Nick began to laugh. "This is great. A family vacation. Mom, Dad, and the loser adult kids go to Disney World." The next week the five of them went to Disney for four days.

Chapter Five

Nick heard a light tap on his bedroom door and turned to see his sister-in-law, Khiem Li standing there. Khiem Li had been married to Beau for as long as Nick could remember. Even though she was too young to be his mother, she was like a second mother to Nick. As a young child, Nick would have to beg other adults to play the games he liked, but Khiem Li would come into the room and ask Nick to play a simple matching game or Chutes and Ladders. She could get the whole family involved in a rollicking game of Old Maid or Spoons. He loved those evenings when the house would be full of people playing games that he liked and were his age level.

As a teen, Nick often talked to Khiem Li about dates; where to go, or what to buy a girl for her birthday that wouldn't make it look like he was going to ask her to go steady. Khiem Li was a full professor at the University of Pennsylvania in the School of Education. She and Beau met while they were both working on their doctorates; Beau's in Chemistry. Khiem Li seemed ageless. She bore six children and was still a size six. Her raven black hair did not have a sign of gray, and was worn most often in a pony tail straight down her back. She was attractive but Nick also always considered Khiem Li so wise.

Khiem Li's parents were immigrants. They came to the U.S. when reparation was slow in Viet Nam and Khiem Li's father, Hak, wanted to come to experience the American dream. He had been a librarian in Viet Nam and her mother, Lia, was a midwife. Neither profession transferred well. Hak ended up working in a warehouse at night and as an orderly in a hospital during the day. After Khiem Li was born, her mother worked in a kitchen of a Thai restaurant until a Vietnamese restaurant opened in the area.

Khiem Li's father passed away several years ago. Lia, her mother, spoke very little English, even after all the years she had been in the U.S. She lived with Beau and Khiem Li until her passing rather recently. She had been very much a part of the Millar family. She attended every celebration and was loved by all. She prepared medicines from herbs and concocted medicinal soups that became standard fare when someone in the family had a cold or flu. Nick was sorry she was no longer there with them. He missed her. He hadn't had any time to be with Khiem Li since he had been home except when the house was full and he was glad to see her standing there.

"I am sorry to disturb you, Nicky," Khiem Li said. I knocked at the front door but no one answered, so I used my key. I saw your car. I hope you don't mind me stopping in to see you."

Nick smiled and stood. He walked over to Khiem Li and put his arms around her. After they embraced, he kept one hand on her shoulder and guided her out into the hall. "I am glad you came, Khiem Li. I haven't had a chance to talk with you without twenty other people in the room. Let's go have a cup of tea or something. Mom has something tempting down there I bet. She seems to think I am malnourished," he said with a smile.

"I think maybe Emily thinks everyone is malnourished. Well, not Beau," she laughed. "But you and your dad are thin by design as I am. Emily is also trim and very attractive. But Emily works at it. She watches everything she puts in her mouth and cannot understand why we can eat without worry. The truth is you, your dad, and I are not as fond of food as most people are. Is that not true?" Nick shook his head in agreement. "My parents lived in Viet Nam when it was very poor. They had little to eat. Even as the country began to prosper, the people did not take food for granted. It was a necessity. My mother always prepared simple meals. Most Asians eat less than Americans. Well, some come to America and begin to eat like Americans. And then get fat, just like Americans." She laughed and Nick smiled at her.

"Tea?" Nick asked.

"Please."

"It looks like we have some kind of cookie here." He brought the plate over to the table.

"Those are Rachel Ray cookies I think. Emily told me about them."

"Who is Rachel Ray?" Nick asked.

"Oh, you have been away! She cooks on television. There are lots of cooking shows on television now. It is interesting because so few people cook. I guess they just like to see other people do it. I've missed you, Nicky. I wanted to tell you how glad I am that you are home."

"Thanks. You don't have any advice for me about what I should be doing?" Nick asked sarcastically.

"I didn't hear you ask for my advice. I do have an invitation. I will give you my card, and it has my class schedule and office hours and you can come to see me any of those times at school, if you would like. We could have lunch on campus one day. I want to spend some time with you. I have missed you," she repeated.

"Thanks Khiem Li. That would be nice. I have missed you too. I am sorry I couldn't come when your mother passed away. She was a wonderful lady. I had the flu one time when I was living in St. Louis and I would have given anything to have had her soup."

"She had a happy life. She loved seeing our children grow up. She was very fond of you, you know," Khiem Li said. Then changing the subject a bit she said, "In Viet Nam many religions have been co-existing for centuries. Beside Buddhism, Taoism, and Confucianism, there are a small number of Catholics and Protestants too. My mother, like many Vietnamese, considered herself non-religious even though her parents were Buddhist. But after you left to become a priest, I heard her tell her friend that she was Catholic. I was surprised because she never expressed any interest in religion. I asked her why she told her friend she was Catholic. She said because I want to support Nicky and his decision." A tear formed as she recalled her mother and her love for her.

Nick put his hand on Khiem Li's cheek. "She was a wonderful lady and she has raised a wonderful daughter." With that the tea kettle whistled and she got up to fix tea. Nick got up too and walked over to the kettle. "My job," he said. "You sit, I serve."

The next week Nick did go in to the university and met Khiem Li for lunch. They had lunch at Shady Gables, a college hangout near the building where she had classes. Nick had spent many years on college campuses. After he became a priest, he went to Holy Cross and received a doctorate in ancient languages. He took classes at other universities at various times in things ranging from theology to criminology. But, this was the first time since he was twenty-two that he had been on a campus without a collar and quite frankly he felt naked. Girls paid attention to Nick now. They smiled at him. He suddenly felt old among these twenty year olds. He tried to concentrate on Khiem Li. She noticed his discomfort. "Nicky, I'm sorry. I shouldn't have brought you here. I didn't think about how crowded it always is," she said. Someone walked by their table and spoke to Khiem Li but looked only at Nick.

Khiem Li smiled. "Because you are my brother-in-law, I sometimes forget how appealing you are to the opposite sex. College girls are very flirtatious. I'm sorry if that makes you uncomfortable. They are very young. I should have taken you somewhere off campus." Nick didn't react but took a long drink of his soda.

"I asked you to meet me for lunch one day because I enjoy being with you," Khiem Li explained. "I wasn't trying to get you into the university environment. It is only because I work here that I invited you here," she explained.

"And I am happy to be with you, Khiem Li. Everything is sort of a new experience for me now," he explained. "I just wasn't prepared for how insulated I had been in the cloth. I didn't realize how hard it would be to just be Nick again and not Father Nicholas. I have spent the greater part of ten or twelve years off and on campuses as a priest and was always comfortable. I was comfortable, as an undergraduate before I was a priest. So, why am I uncomfortable now?" he asked.

Khiem Li thought for a minute. "You know, Nicky, I bet the first time you stepped on the campus at Notre Dame when you were eighteen years old, you were not that comfortable. And I bet the first time you went on a campus as a priest, you were not comfortable either. They were both new situations and generally we all have to adjust a bit to new situations. Now this is a new situation. You will adjust to it as well. You are a very flexible young man."

"Thanks Khiem Li. I can always count on you to put things in perspective. May I walk you back to your classroom?"

"I would love that. Maybe I will get a new reputation by walking with a handsome stranger," Khiem Li said. "Would you like to stay for my class? I often have visitors. You are very welcome. It is an elementary education seminar class for seniors. They are doing presentations."

"I would like that, Khiem Li. Though I would rather see you teach. I remember coming here in high school a couple of times and sitting in on your classes. I think my mom worked it out. She thought maybe I might fall in love with education and give up on the priesthood."

Khiem Li laughed. "Don't be too hard on your mother. I would probably have done the same if one of my sons had said they wanted to be a priest. I would have exhausted every avenue to see if I could talk him out of it. That sounds terrible, I know, but sometimes a mother's love is very selfish. When it became apparent that you were determined to be a priest, your mother supported you all the way. You do believe that don't you, Nick?"

"I do. Mom is great. I have no complaints. She really wanted what she thought was best for me. It just wasn't what I thought was best for me. But maybe now, we know she was right. If I had listened to her, I wouldn't be in this mess."

"In Viet Nam there is a saying, 'Everyone has to find a way to get across the water.' It means that some swim, some use a bridge, some go around. But each has to find his way or he will get stuck on one side and never get over. Maybe you chose to swim and your mother would have rather you had taken the bridge. But what if while you were swimming, you saw beautiful fish and enjoyed the water while you were making your way. Then swimming would have been the best way for you. And you are on the other side now, so does it make a difference? Besides," she added, "I don't think you really regret your decision. I think you know it was the right thing to do at the time."

Nick smiled at his sister-in-law. "I love you, Khiem Li. Does Beau know how lucky he is?"

She laughed, "He doesn't have a clue. But speaking of Beau, you really should see him teach. He is a wonderful teacher. You might think that chemistry is a boring subject but he can get quite excited teaching it, and then the students do as well. Do you know that he is the most popular chemistry professor on campus? There are waiting lists for his classes. He truly is very good. When you can find humor in chemistry, you have a gift, I think."

Khiem Li pointed out the chemistry building and Nick walked over. He passed mostly young men on the path. He concluded that there were still more men than women in the sciences. When he entered the building, however, there were more students milling about, both male and female. Most looked at him and acknowledged him in some way. He responded with a nod. He found room 321 and opened the door. The room was a lecture hall with the rows stepping down to an almost stage-like platform with a podium for the instructor. It made him smile when he saw Beau with a large cluster of students surrounding him. Nick walked down to the front row and took a seat at one end. A bell rang and more students poured in from the back and the ones with Beau began to take their seats. Beau was looking through notes after all the students were seated and looked up and announced, "Ten point quiz!" There was a slight collective groan from the students. A young man walked up to the first row at the opposite side from Nick and handed the quizzes to the first person to be passed down the row. Nick assumed he was Beau's teaching assistant. Nick was impressed with Beau's professional demeanor. He rarely saw him in a serious mood. He was suddenly struck with how he misjudged Beau. Beau was still looking at notes and someone handed Nick a copy of the quiz. Nick took the paper, wadded it up and threw it at Beau. It arced and came down on the podium in front of Beau like a perfectly executed basketball through a hoop. Beau looked up and saw Nick laughing. He walked to him and Nick stood. "Hey, everyone, this is my little brother." He gave Nick a bear hug. "In honor of my brother, Nick, I will forget about the quiz." A cheer went up. "But I suggest you look at the questions and learn the answers because they will probably be on the mid-term." He then addressed Nick personally, "What in the hell are you doing here?"

"I had lunch with a beautiful woman on campus and she suggested I come here and see you perform," Nick answered. And Beau did perform. Nick thought he was amazing. He explained things so well there were few questions but even those were handled well. The hour went quickly. Nick was entertained and impressed. "You were amazing," Nick told Beau. "I took Chemistry. We all did, or Dad would have disowned us, but I never had a prof like you."

"Wow, I impressed St. Nick. I didn't think that was possible. Now if my kids were only that generous." Beau had to go to his office after class so Nick walked to the parking lot alone. He was feeling better. He still didn't want to take any classes or teach, but he had a good day and that was enough.

Chapter Six

"**D**ad," Nick said softly.

"Yes," Kris replied looking up at his son who was across the room.

"I think I would like to drive in and talk to Father Pat. Would you like to come with me and talk to one of the others?" He knew Kris often stopped in and chatted with the priests.

"Sure, son, I'll be ready in five." This was what Kris was hoping for. He didn't want to suggest a meeting but was happy Nick finally wanted to talk to one of the priests. Father Pat was perfect. He was getting old, but wasn't judgmental or rigid. He had known Nicky since he was a child. He surely would make Nick feel comfortable.

Nick was driving Emily's car and had been ever since he arrived. He usually asked her first and she was more than happy to let him use it. Kris said to Nick, "Why don't you keep Mom's car and I will get her a new one? Unless you would rather have a new one?"

"I couldn't care less. I will drive anything. It's a nice car, though. Would you rather I just get a used clunker? Maybe Mom really likes this car."

"She doesn't care. She'll like getting a new one."

"Dad," Nick began, "I didn't know you once had a sports car. How did that happen? You just don't seem the sports car type—not that you aren't cool Dad."

Kris laughed. "I am not the sports car type. I don't know why I got it. I think my friend talked me into it. The boys were getting older and maybe it was a mid-life crisis. I hated it in the winter. It was totaled in a simple fender bender. I like sturdier cars now I guess."

When they got to the church, Kris started to point out where to park, but Nick obviously remembered from all the times he went there when he first made his decision to be a priest. The two of them walked into the rectory and were greeted by Father Pat and Father Marcus. Father Marcus embraced Kris. He also was born in England and they liked to talk about their early lives there over a cup of well-made tea. Father Pat first patted Nick on the back and then he hugged him. Kris was encouraged that it would go well for Nick.

Father Marcus and Kris first sat in the kitchen of the rectory and had tea, and then moved outside to sit in the garden. Father Marcus loved to work in the garden and it was a beautiful, peaceful refuge. The two men talked for a while and then they sat and contemplated the beautiful surroundings. At the back edge of the property, there were bird feeders and song birds were flitting from one feeder to another, occasionally jousting for dominance. A hummingbird feeder was much closer to them on the edge of the patio and both men watched the dance of the tiny birds diving and feeding. Sometimes the two men sat in the tranquil setting without talking for several minutes, just enjoying the secluded area and quiet.

Nick was with Father Pat for well over an hour. Kris hoped that was a good sign. He tried to look for any signs of upset on Nicky's face when he came out into the garden but he seemed fine. Father Pat's expression didn't betray anything either. Finally, in the car, Kris was anxious to know what Nick was feeling and asked how it went.

"Good." Then Nick paused and said, "Father Pat says I am trying to hide who I am, or I guess he is afraid I might try to hide who I am. He doesn't think I should have remained, he just thinks I should be doing something Jesuit—you know, being a soldier for Christ. In other words, he thinks I should be doing paid mission work, like working for a not-for-profit, or social work, social justice or something. I don't know, maybe he's right." Nick looked unhappy; he was frowning and biting the inside of his mouth.

"Nick, you don't have to decide today."

"Dad, is this an embarrassment to you? Have I failed you? I really want to know if you think I have done the wrong thing. Just because

I can't change it, doesn't mean you can't give your opinion. I feel so guilty that I may have let you down."

"Oh, Nicky. I am the one that feels guilty. I feel like I forced you into something, when you were young and impressionable, that you never really wanted to do."

"We are a sorry lot, Dad. Believe me you never forced me to do anything, except be polite and use good grammar!" Nick smiled at his dad. "Seriously, I wanted to be a priest so bad I could taste it. I truly felt called. I did. I loved it in the beginning. I just fell out of love, not with the Church or God, just with being a priest. I guess in a way, I can't decide what to do because I'm afraid I'll make another mistake; not a mistake, another… I don't know, I guess in a way I thought I could come home and just start in where I left off when I finished up at Notre Dame. But the truth is, I'm a different person now; a lot older anyway. Sometimes, I don't feel like I even know who I am. I was Father Nicholas for quite a while. I am having trouble knowing who Nick is. That's really stupid, isn't it?"

Kris swallowed trying to get rid of the lump forming in his throat and hoping he didn't tear up. Finally, he was composed enough to say, "It isn't stupid at all, Nick. This must have been," he changed the tense and said, "this must *be* really difficult, Nick. I don't think any of us can imagine what you have been going through and are now experiencing. Cut yourself some slack, Nicky. It hasn't been very long. You need some time to rest and recuperate. Come to think of it, it is sort of like leaving the military. You need some time to get back into the life you had before. And it won't be the same life. Things have changed since you have been away and you have changed too but some things have stayed constant. You have your family, Nick. We all love you and want you to be fulfilled and happy. And we don't expect it to happen overnight. I am so glad you talked to Father Pat. That must have been a big hurdle and you got over it. I am so proud of you. Even John said it took him a long time to go back to church. You are making great strides, Nick. Give it time, son."

That night Nick went to a club by himself. This week he had conquered some of his fears. He had spent some time on campus around people and he had talked to Father Pat. Surely I can go to a bar alone and have a drink without freaking out, he thought. He sat at the bar and slowly drank a beer and watched the dancing. He definitely was not going to dance. He just wanted to watch; observe the customers. He knew he couldn't make himself get on the dance floor without John or his wife there.

It was a small club. He had been there once when in college. He tried to remember, he thought maybe he went with a friend he had brought home with him from Notre Dame. The bar had ten barstools and three small booths. The rest of the space was dance floor with small tables around the edge. A young woman sat down on the bar stool next to him. She had been with two other friends, but she walked away from them to sit by Nick. "Hi," she said.

Nick answered, "Hi."

"I haven't seen you here before," she stated.

"I haven't been here before," he said, feeling his face flush and wishing he had not come into the club at all.

"I'm Lisa."

"I'm Nick." Nick realized he had put his hand on his throat. He was feeling exposed without his collar; the feeling of being naked. He moved his hand and put it around his beer. The cold felt good and he wanted to bring the bottle to his flushed face, but didn't.

Lisa was clearly looking to get to know Nick but he wasn't buying into her attention. He sat, nervously handling his beer bottle; now peeling the label from it in tiny strips. Lisa was thirty, blonde, cute, and curvy. Her friends were watching from a table across the room. She tugged on her v neck shirt which allowed a little more cleavage to appear. Then she smoothed down the front of her jeans. Nick tried not to look at her wardrobe adjustment.

"What do you do, Nick?" she asked.

Oh no, the dreaded question. Nick wasn't prepared. He chewed his lip and then said, "I'm sort of between things right now." He didn't want this conversation to go on. He was ready to get out of there. He couldn't think of something to make up and he didn't want to tell the truth. He turned away from Lisa and looked at his beer, his back to her.

Lisa was not to be spurned. "What did you do?" she then asked.

Several things quickly ran through his brain but with each contrived answer he was frightened there would be a follow up question he couldn't answer. He was in a state of panic. I'm a terrible liar, he thought. What was it that John said that he told people, he asked himself? He was paralyzed in thought. Lisa thought the long pause was the cold shoulder. She was clearly insulted that he turned from her and wouldn't talk to her, or even look at her.

"Sorry to have bothered you, asshole," she said. "Just because you are good-looking doesn't mean you have the right to be obnoxious," she said as she was getting up.

Nick turned and looked at her. "I'm sorry," he said as earnestly as he knew how. "I was trying to think how to answer your question." He looked directly at her. "You asked what I used to do. I used to be a priest," he stated affirmatively. He waited patiently for her response.

"Yeah, right, asshole," she said as she got up and walked back to her friends. Nick left without finishing his beer.

By the time Nick got to his car, he was even more upset. He was kicking himself for being unable to answer a simple question, and not too happy about being called an asshole for finally answering it. He did not want to go home. He began to chastise himself. What is wrong with me? Why can't I just make conversation with someone? I just wanted to be around people without freaking out and look what happened? I just wanted to listen to a little music and maybe talk to someone. He further reflected, who am I kidding? I came out tonight with the specific goal of meeting a woman and perhaps having a sexual relationship. Hell, I just wanted to get laid. Is that criminal, he asked himself? I am single, over twenty-one, and no longer have the damn celibacy thing over my head. The car ahead of him stopped for a four-way stop and Nick had to slam on his brakes to avoid hitting it. That calmed him down for the moment and he tried to focus on driving. He had no idea where he was going. He made a right turn and continued on Rahl Street then at Martindale turned left. He proceeded for a while along Martindale. He did not know this neighborhood. He didn't think he had ever been here before. But he wasn't going home. He would just drive for a while. He made another left-hand turn. Now things were beginning to look a little seedy. Some of the row houses were boarded up and others had windows broken. Trash was littering the street and sidewalk. People were standing around in front of the row houses, sitting on cars, and wandering into the street. Odd, he thought, I used to be very comfortable in similar surroundings; lived in neighborhoods just like this. A siren blared and Nick had to pull to the curb to let the police car go by. Once it passed, Nick continued on a few blocks and then turned back toward the hotel district. As he entered the fringe, he saw the girls walking in front of the cheap hotels. Bingo, he said to himself.

Nick slowed the car and went on cautiously down the street. One woman waved to him. He continued driving. Two women were walking together arm in arm. They were both in skin-tight pants and glitzy tops that dipped into their cleavage. They gave him a wave and indicated with gestures that they were open to a ménage a trois, but he drove on. A man, it seems, dressed as a woman, approached his slowing car but Nick continued down the small street. Nick had an overwhelming feeling he was looking for something but this certainly wasn't it. Finally, a few blocks later Nick thought he saw what he was looking for. He pulled to the curb and a young, attractive, petite woman came over to the car. She was wearing black shorts that fit tight and were as short as physically possible and still have two separate leg openings. With them she wore a thin, white peasant-style blouse that was loose around the neck and showed most of her small breasts that were pushed up by a black bra. She had on black stilettos that strapped around her ankles. "What do you want?" she asked without expression.

"Want a ride?" Nick asked.

"Are you a cop?" the girl asked in a naïve way.

"No!" he said affirmatively. "I just wondered if you needed a ride somewhere," he then said softly. He added, "If you want to go somewhere with me." Nick felt like he was making this up as he was speaking. He had no idea what he wanted or how to express it. He repeated politely, "Would you like to go someplace with me?"

"Yeah. The Almont Arms. You want to take me there?" She seemed extremely nervous. She was small and pale. Her mousey brown hair had blonde roots showing and she had on black eyeliner and red lipstick, both too dark for her complexion.

"Sure."

"I can't be gone long. Can we be out in an hour?" she asked in a panicky tone.

"Of course we can."

She got in. "It is just around the corner." Nick turned where she indicated. "Cops watch the place," she said. "Drop me here. Then you park down the street and come up to room 223," she instructed.

"Okay."

"Want to know terms?" she asked awkwardly.

"Sure."

"One hundred and fifty. You look like you can afford that. And nothing rough or kinky. Okay?" Then she nervously asked, "Is that too much? Maybe one hundred and twenty," she said breathlessly.

"Okay." Nick was puzzled by her "unprofessional" demeanor. But he knew nothing of the going price of a car or house, let alone this. She got out of the car and turned to look at him through the window. He could see fear in her face.

"You are coming up, aren't you?" she asked. He nodded.

Nick parked down the street and walked back to the crummy little Almont Arms. It was a pathetic-looking building, as gray as the night. The only illumination was the 'vacancy' sign. The 'l' was missing from the name of the hotel. People were milling about in front. He had to step over a couple sitting on the stoop. When he went inside, only one person was working at the desk and he didn't look up from his newspaper. Nick saw the elevator in the hall but took the stairs instead. The stair runner had at one time been a green pseudo-oriental print, but was so threadbare it had little color. He tapped on the door of 223. His heart pounded and he chewed the inside of his mouth. Quickly the door opened.

"Come in," the girl's little voice said in a whisper.

The room was small and dark. In it there was only a rickety, stained, upholstered chair and a bed with a satin sheet over it. The heavy brocade drapes were pulled and the only light was a small lamp on a stand on one side of the bed. Nick sat balanced on the narrow arm of the chair. When the girl turned around to look at him, he saw how young she looked. "How old are you?" he asked.

"Old enough," she answered.

Nick continued to stare at her. She was awkward; nervous, he surmised. She tried not to look at him; avoided eye contact. She was standing straight in front of him but not looking at him. She was fingering the string on her shirt. She was carrying a small silver bag which she put on the floor in front of her. When she dropped it down to the floor, it popped open and a plastic photo case fell out. Nick picked it up for her. In it was a picture of a child. "Who is this?" he asked as he handed it to her. He moved from the arm, to the edge of the seat of the chair.

"None of your business!" she bellowed. She snatched the photo. "Do you want to get on with this or what?" she asked.

Nick didn't answer but sat with his elbow on the chair arm and his hand covering his mouth. He slouched in the chair. The girl began to undress. Nick didn't move. She unbuttoned her shorts and stepped out of them revealing a black thong. He noted her small frame. Her hip bones were prominent but she had a tiny protrusion of belly. She has given birth, he told himself.

"I can't stay long," she said. She looked at him in the chair confused by his inaction. He continued to watch her.

"How long have you been doing this?" he asked.

"Why does it matter to you?"

"It matters. How long have you been doing it?" he asked again awkwardly.

She refused to answer the question. Her chin began to quiver and she bit her lip. "I thought you wanted to have sex. You want to have sex with me don't you?" She was puzzled.

"Of course I do. Do you want to have sex with me?" he asked.

"Do I want to? I'm paid to, remember. You pay me, I do it," she said clearly aggravated.

"But," Nick asked again, "do you want to do this? You don't really want to, do you? You don't really want to have sex with me."

55

"It doesn't matter what I want. Sometimes we have to do things whether we want to or not," she answered impatiently. She turned away from him.

"Why do you have to?"

"Look, I thought you came up here to have sex with me. I have to get going. I have to make some money and get out of here." The girl took off her blouse and unhooked her bra. She took it off and put it on the blouse on top of the bedside table.

Nick continued to sit. His eyes moved from her small breasts to her face. "Is that your child in the photo?" he asked.

The girl was about to cry but quickly stopped herself. She straightened and seemed to regain her compose. "Yes. I have got to get going. I can't leave her long."

Nick asked, "You didn't leave her alone did you?"

"No, she is with my friend!" She was outraged by the question. Then she pulled herself together a bit and said, "Why do you care?"

"I don't like to think of children left alone."

"She's not. I would never do that!" she said, clearly insulted that he would suggest it. "But I can't be away long. My friend has to leave soon."

"I won't keep you long. Just tell me," he asked in a sincere voice, "why you are here?"

I should be asking you that question, she said to herself. "Because I like to eat," she said to him angrily. "Have you ever been hungry?"

"No."

"Well, at least you are honest."

"My name is Nick. What's yours?"

She paused and finally said, "Della."

"Della, how old is your little girl?"

"So you want to talk or have sex?" Della asked. Then she added, "It's the same price."

"I'm not sure at this point. What do you want?"

"Why are you doing this to me?" Della asked, clearly perplexed.

Nick, seeming equally confused by the entire situation and clearly bothered by it, said, "Do you have no other way to get food?"

Della picked up her blouse and covered herself with it. Finally she decided to let him have it right between the eyes. "I do it because my boyfriend makes me. I have to take the money to him. If I don't give him some money, he'll beat me. So what do you think of my sad little tale?" She looked at him trying to judge his reaction. "Don't tell me you don't want to have sex with me anymore. You have already wasted my time. I could have had a paying customer in here. Are you going to stiff me?"

"No!" Nick peeled off a roll of twenties and handed them to her. "Why don't you leave him if he beats you?"

"He would find me."

"Do you really want to get away from him?"

"Of course, I've tried but I have no place to go," she mumbled.

"What about a shelter for women?"

"They wouldn't take me."

"Why not?"

"Because I am a hooker and I have a little girl. No place would take me," she said stating what she thought was the obvious.

"Would you go if they would?"

"Of course, I'm tired of this crap. I'm just tired. I have tried to get away before but he found me. So if you really want to help me, let's get on with this. I'm not going to take your money and not have sex with you. You could call the cops and tell them anything. They would believe you. You look like Mr. Perfect and I look like...." She shrugged her shoulders, "Hell," she finally said. "I look like hell," she repeated softly as if to herself.

Nick took out his cell. Della flinched at first thinking it was a gun or knife.

"I won't hurt you, Della." Then into the phone he said, "Dad, do you think Millar House has any rooms available?" He listened to his father's answer and said, "I'm going to take someone there. Will you call them and tell them I am coming? She has a little girl." Kris said he would make the call without asking any questions of Nick.

"Della, get dressed. Where is your little girl? We'll pick her up and I'll take you both to a shelter where no one will ever bother you again."

Della was clearly frightened. "Are you crazy? He'll find us. He will. He will find us and beat the hell out of me. I can't go. You must be crazy. Get out of here."

"He won't find you, Della. We won't let him. This place is as secure as they get. There is a guard and electronic monitoring. No one can get in without going through security. He won't be able to get to you or your little girl. They will help you. Whatever you need. They can help you find a job, a place to live, go to school; anything you need, Della. Do you trust me?" Nick asked.

Della stepped into her shorts, put on her bra and pulled on her shirt, wiping her nose on it as she did. She nodded that she would do as Nick said. She was physically tired; too tired to argue. She wanted to get away but she was frightened. "I guess I trust you. I don't know why. I have trusted other guys and they turned out to be creeps. But for some reason, I trust you." Oh God, she said to herself. I should know better than this. Creeps don't always look like creeps. That Jeffery Dahmer guy, looked like anyone else, I think. Still, this guy called someplace. I know I shouldn't trust him, but I think I do, she thought to herself. But could anything be any worse than this?

Nick took Della's elbow and guided her quickly down the stairs and out the door. They practically ran to the car. The child was just two blocks away. Nick sat in the car while Della went in to get her. She brought her out wrapped in a blanket. Nick said they should sit in the back, so Della could buckle the toddler in as best she could. She sat low, hoping not to be seen from the street, with her arm around the child. Nick looked at her in the mirror. The little girl was frightened also. He thought she was about Pippa's age, but he wasn't sure. She had just been awakened so was cuddling up to her mother, her hair in damp ringlets around her face. Della never took her eyes off Nick. Each time he looked in the rear-view mirror, she flinched. "What's her name?" Nick asked.

Della considered before she spoke, "Angel. Her name is Angel." Nick smiled.

They drove the short distance in silence. Della was still unsure what was happening; what was going to happen. She was afraid to trust him. Nick parked the car and opened the door for Della and put his hands out for the child. He carried the little girl up the walk to Millar House with Della beside him. They were greeted at the door by a middle-aged woman who smiled at them. "Welcome," she said softly. "Dr. Millar said you were on your way." She looked at Della and the fear in her face. "It is okay now. You are home, dear. Safe at home. Come in and get something to eat and get ready for bed. We have things you can use. We'll take care of you." She handed the little girl a plush rabbit. The child grabbed it and hugged it with both arms.

"Are you okay, Della?" Nick asked, as he passed the child back to her. "Will you stay and get things straightened out?" He touched her for the first time, putting his hands on her shoulders, facing her as he spoke.

His touch was electrifying. "Yes," she answered with tears streaming down her face. "Why are you doing this for me?"

"I don't know," he said honestly. "I just know you deserve better." He watched the door to Millar House close and then he turned and walked to the car.

Chapter Seven

"Uncle Nicky, will you play with us?" Pippa asked. Her friend Olivia was spending the afternoon. Laurie was working but Emily had agreed that Olivia could come over a play a few hours. The girls went to pre-school together and often played together at one house or the other. Laurie didn't want there to be too many changes in Pippa's life since she was already confused about them moving in with her grandparents and her dad not living with them. "Gran Kris was playing with us but he had to go to a meeting," Pippa complained. The girls had on large straw hats, lacey gloves and pink boas were wrapped around their necks. Emily had lightly touched their lips with lipstick. "Please, Uncle Nick."

"Sure. What are we playing?"

"Tea party," both little girls shouted out.

Nick looked apprehensive. "Okay. Where are we having tea?"

"In the living room. The table is set but first you have to get dressed up," Pippa announced.

"I don't think so, Pippa. I don't dress up for tea."

"Gran Kris does!" she said pouting.

Emily was standing in the doorway and shrugged her shoulders.

"What do I have to wear?" Nick asked, standing there in his usual jeans and tee shirt and bare feet.

"Dress up clothes," she demanded.

Nick looked at Emily again but she wouldn't save him, so he gave in and said he would be right back. The girls squealed with delight.

In a few minutes, Nick came bounding back down the stairs wearing white tennis shorts he snagged from Kris's closet, white tee shirt, white athletic socks but still no shoes, and a navy tie knotted and loose around his neck. The girls cheered and Emily laughed out loud. It has been years since I have seen Nick act silly. This is wonderful, she thought. Then she patted him on the back. He gave her an icy look.

The girls took turns serving lukewarm, orange Kool-Aid from a small plastic tea pot into equally small mismatched cups and saucers. A plate of Mini Chips Ahoy cookies were on a plastic plate and were handed out with little fingers. Nick sat sideways at the small oak table so that his knees wouldn't knock it over. Emily got the camera and he mugged it up for her to get some shots. He kept his pinky finger extended at all times while drinking, much to the delight of the girls. They would beg him to finish his "tea" and then quickly fill his cup and beg some more. "Are you going to take us to see *Muffin Top?*" Pippa pleaded.

"What's that?" Nick asked.

"A movie! Gran Kris was going to take us. Please Uncle Nick," Pippa begged.

Then Olivia chimed in, "Please Uncle Nick."

"Where is it playing?" he asked Emily.

"Just over at the Walnut. Your dad was going to take them but someone from the hospital called and asked if he could go talk to someone about something," she said with disproval.

"What time?"

"You'll have to leave in about half an hour."

"Okay. I'll take them. It surely doesn't last very long, does it?" he asked optimistically.

"No, kids' movies are pretty short. Thanks sweetie. They have been talking about it all day."

Nick addressed the little girls, "Okay guys, now I have to change into my movie clothes. I'll be right back." But, before he got up from the table, the door bell rang and Emily went to the door. She came back in with Olivia's mother. Her mother explained that she had forgotten to give Olivia her allergy medicine and wanted to have her take it now.

"Ellie, this is my son, Nick. Nick, Olivia's mom, Ellie."

Nick stood and said, "Hi, Ellie. We have been having tea. I am going up to change for the theatre," he stated in an uppity voice to entertain the girls. "Please excuse me," he said and ran up the stairs.

Ellie was suddenly flustered. "Ah, Olivia, I think maybe we had better go home. You didn't take your allergy medicine and I think you had better come home and rest."

"But, they were going to the movies. We talked about it on the phone just a few minutes ago," Emily said.

"I know but…" she stammered.

"But?" Emily pressed.

"I thought you or your husband was taking them. I don't feel right having your son do that. He doesn't have to take them. They can go another day."

"He said he would. The girls are excited about him taking them," Emily went on.

"Mrs. Millar," Ellie began seriously. "I'm sorry, I just don't feel right having your son take the girls. It just doesn't, ah, look right."

"Why?"

Olivia's mother was starting to get very worked up. "Let's go Olivia. Now!"

"Mommy, I want to go to the movie with Pippa and Uncle Nick. Please."

Nick came down the stairs back in his jeans and felt the tension in the room. "Problem?" he asked.

Pippa said, "Olivia's mommy won't let us go to the movies with you."

"Well, how about you two going out to the front porch for now," Emily suggested. "We'll get everything straightened out while you swing your dolls in the porch swing." The two little girls scampered out to the porch.

"Okay," Emily began. "What is going on?"

"I'm sorry but I can't let my daughter go with him," Ellie said very pointedly.

Nick didn't say anything. Emily, however, was livid. "Why?" she demanded.

"I am not letting my little daughter go with a man I don't know."

"But you know Laurie. You know me. Kris was going to take them. Why was it okay for Kris but not for Nick?"

"Because," Ellie said in an exasperated voice, "he was a priest. But now he isn't." She struggled trying to think how to express her thoughts.

"What are you suggesting? My son was a priest and decided he no longer wanted to be one." Again, she asked, "What are you suggesting?"

"It is just that there are a lot of rumors about priests these days. Maybe he left because he fondled little girls. How would we know? The church covers all that stuff up. I can't take that chance."

Emily was outraged. "How dare you insult my son and my family." Before she could go further, Nick came up behind her and grabbed her shirt in the back and pulled her back to him out of Ellie's face. "Stop," she shouted at Nick. Nick put his arm around her and kept her from going closer to Ellie.

"Let's keep this out of the range of the kids, Mom," he lowered his voice as if to show her. "Tell the girls the movie has been cancelled for some reason," Nick said. "It's okay, Mom. People will think what they want to think. There is nothing we can do about that. It's okay," he said in a calm voice. "The girls have a good time together. Let's not ruin that."

"He's right," Ellie said. "Pippa is welcome to come to our house any time."

Emily sputtered and finally said softly, "And how do we know that your husband isn't a pervert?"

Nick put his hand over his eyes. "Mom, let it go."

Ellie walked to the porch and said to Olivia, "Darling, the movie has been canceled today. The machine is broken. They will show it again another day. Say goodbye to Pippa." She grabbed Olivia's hand and headed to the car.

"This isn't right," Emily said facing Nick. She said it again and tears began to fall.

"I'm so sorry, Mom. Now you are upset and Laurie is going to be upset. Pippa is going to be upset. I'm sorry. I shouldn't have gotten you all into this."

"Nick, this isn't your doing."

At that point, Pippa came in the house crying. "Why did Olivia have to go home? Why can't we go to the movie?"

Nick answered. "You can see it another day. Olivia's mother wanted her to go home so she could rest up and go another day. You can play a game on my DS. Get it from my desk and take it into your room."

"Yeah!" she shouted and ran upstairs. Nick walked Emily into the library but neither wanted to talk about it now. Nick went into the kitchen and brought Emily a wet wash cloth and a Diet Coke for each of them. By the time Kris came home, they were more relaxed about it and Emily told him what had happened.

"Show Dad the pictures you took of the tea party," Nick demanded. She handed Kris the camera and he and Nick looked at the photos of Nick hamming it up in his tea party outfit. "And you wonder why she didn't want me near her daughter?" Nick said.

"I'm not sure that even I want you near children after seeing that, son," Kris said laughing.

Emily stopped in Nick's room. Nick was propped up on the bed reading a book his dad had just finished and passed on to him. "Want to go Christmas shopping with me, Nicky?"

"No thanks."

"Are you going to be doing some Christmas shopping soon?" she asked picking her way in the conversation and hoping he would agree.

"No."

"Nicky, we celebrate Christmas here," she said tentatively. "We have a tree, hang stockings, give each other gifts, and have a big family dinner. This year it is at Beau and Khiem Li's house." She waited for him to respond.

"What time do you have dinner?" Nick asked barely looking up from the book.

"Late afternoon, about four or five o'clock usually."

"Okay, I'll go there for dinner."

"Nick," Emily was getting irritated now, "we celebrate Christmas as a family. We buy gifts."

"I know, hang stockings and have a tree. I celebrate Christmas. But I don't want any gifts and I don't want to buy any gifts," Nick said.

"Nick," Emily said pleadingly. "Are you just going to mope around in your room on Christmas Day?"

"No, Mother. I told them at the shelter I would serve meals. That is what I would like to do for Christmas. If someone wants to buy me a gift, they can give a donation to Barrington Mission. I will give a donation in my family's name. Then I will go to dinner at Beau's. Is that acceptable?"

Emily pondered the situation. How can I argue with that, she asked herself. "Nicky," she said. Nick looked up. "Is is okay with you that we buy each other gifts?"

"Of course," he said emphatically. "You should celebrate however you want to celebrate. You should celebrate as you have been celebrating. Maybe next year I will want to celebrate like that too. For now, I would like to just go to church on Christmas and serve at the shelter. I can't handle much more than that. Is that okay with you? I really mean it, Mom. I am not trying to be difficult. Is that okay?"

"Of course," Emily answered. Emily thought, all the time your children are growing up you are trying to develop them into good, caring citizens. Then they are, and you are stymied. "Nicky, I love you. I won't bother you about shopping any more. I am happy that you want to work at the shelter and we will all love having you come to dinner." After all, she thought, all of these past Christmases, we haven't bought him gifts and he hasn't bought them for us. And now he is with us. That is the best gift; more than I ever imagined.

Emily loved Christmas and everything about it. Laurie and Pippa helped her decorate and put up the tree. Ornaments were on the tree that had been used ever since Emily's girls were born. Some were made by the children. This year it seemed particularly festive.

Emily wanted everything perfect for Pippa. She had garland on the stairway banister and some of Pippa's little stuffed animals were peeking out from the rails of the stairs as if they were looking for Santa to arrive. The fireplace mantel was festooned with greenery and crystal candlesticks were artistically placed. The dining room was decorated in a Williamsburg manner with fruit in a three-tiered pedestal dish. Candles graced the table and a setting of Spode Christmas china was at each place along with silver cutlery that had been Kris's stepmother's. She had left it in her will to Emily. Kris hired someone to decorate the outside as he had been doing for some time. The homeowners' association put lights on all of the trees in the strip of lawn near the street. A single candle was in every window in the house and there was a huge wreath on the front door with a big red ribbon. The entire house smelled of peppermint, cinnamon, and evergreen. Pippa decorated a gingerbread house that Emily had made and assembled. Emily had baked cookies for days.

"It's beautiful, Mom. I love it," Nick said enthusiastically when he came into the house the day they had completed the work. He put his arm around his mother and asked if she would come with him into the living room. He sat at the beautiful grand piano that only Kris and Nick could play. Laurie had been forced to take lessons as a child, but Emily could only tolerate the tearful scenes about practicing for one year. They were both glad to put lessons for Laurie behind them. Nick, however, enjoyed playing. Kris had always played the piano and played even now occasionally. Nick sat and motioned for his mother to sit with him. He first played, *It's Beginning to Look a Lot like Christmas* and then went on to *We Three Kings* and finally, *What Child Is This?* Emily had tears in her eyes when he finished. Nick played beautifully. It had been a very long time since she had heard him play. Laurie and Pippa came in when they heard the music and finally Kris came downstairs and joined them.

Pippa demanded Nick play *Jingle Bells* and he did. He played some more carols and then he played *Ave Maria*. Nick played music boldly, dramatically. Kris watched. Though Kris had many years of piano lessons, he marveled at how beautifully Nick played with much less instruction. Nick felt the music. He performed it. Kris was awestruck.

When he finished they all went into the kitchen for dinner. "Nick," Kris said. "The Millar House Christmas party is Friday. Would you like to be Santa? You could help pass out gifts and then play the piano for a while?" he asked.

"Sure," Nick replied.

Nick was a big hit as Santa, though he was a much younger and more active Santa than most. He played with the kids and their toys after they opened them. At one point, he saw Della out of the corner of his eye while he was looking at the instructions for a board game. He touched the tangle of beard that was part of his costume and kept his head down. Angel had an ear infection, he heard his dad say, and Kris gave Della a gift for her. She promptly went back to their room. Kris came up to Nick and asked if he wanted to change clothes before he played the piano. "No, I'm okay like this," he said, and he moved to the piano and started with *Jingle Bells*.

Chapter Eight

Abbe called the house and Nick answered. "Hi, Nick. I was hoping I could get you. I am going to be in town tonight and I wondered if you could meet me for dinner."

"Sure. Where and when?" Abbe told him she would meet him at Blakely's Steak House at seven and asked if he could take her back to the hotel after. "Sure," he replied again.

Emily and Kris were both working at Millar House. Kris had a board meeting and Emily went in to counsel some women on legal issues. Nick sent a text to his mom that he was going out and added in caps, DWU. He hoped that was correct for "don't wait up". He didn't bother to tell them he was going to dinner with Abbe. He could fill them in later, besides he still wasn't as quick at texting as the rest of the family.

Nick stood only a few minutes at the door, inside the restaurant, until Abbe arrived. She was dressed casually when she came to the house but today she had obviously come from a meeting. She had on a short skirt and silky blouse and had a jacket over her arm. Nick did a double-take, he was so struck with how great she looked. She ran up to him and hugged him warmly. She smelled great too. She reached down for his hand and held it as they followed the waiter. They sat across from one another at a small table. Abbe took over the conversation. "I've been in meetings all day with old men. Sorry if I came on too strong. I am no shrinking violet and I have never been accused of being one. You are sight for sore eyes, after the day I have had."

Nick smiled.

She went on, "Tell me what you have done since I saw you last?"

"Started a rock band," Nick said with a smile. Not getting a reaction, he then said cautiously, "I am not sure you are ready for this; it's almost as weird. We went to Disney World, the whole ' *fam damily*': Mom, Dad, Laurie, Pippa and I went to Disney! There has got to be some kind of label for our kind of family." He waited for her reaction.

"Cool!" That wasn't what he expected. He thought because she is so driven, she would think he should be working by now and certainly not going off to Disney with his parents, for goodness sake. Abbe laughed. "That's great. I should take my mom and sis sometime. I never think of that."

"Have you decided what you are going to do when the Governor leaves office?" Nick inquired.

"No. They are still working on it. Maybe attorney general or something. None of it sounds very thrilling," she lamented.

"How did you get started in politics," Nick asked.

"My father was Governor for several terms. He left office and promptly had a massive heart attack and died. That should have put me off but it didn't. I was always crazy about him. He was a judge when I was a kid. I would go to the courthouse as a little girl and watch him in action. Then he became a state representative. I followed him around then too. Then he ran for Governor. I thought the election was the most exciting thing in the world. It was more fun than living in the Governor's mansion, which wasn't that nice, by the way. So I sort of inherited his passion for politics. I am not crazy for the back room stuff but I love the challenge of taking on a cause and seeing it to fruition; making a difference."

Nick said, "I am sorry I didn't know about your dad. I should have recognized the name. I have been isolated for so long, I don't even try to make connections, I guess."

"Have you thought more about what you want to do?" Abbe asked. "How do you feel about politics? It is good for people who have no direction." Then she considered her wording, "I hope that didn't sound like a slam. I didn't mean it as one. I was just talking about me."

"You sound as if you do have direction. I can't see you taking instructions from anyone else. I, however, am very good at following orders. I could join the Army except for that combat thing. I am a pacifist."

"Yeah, can't see you doing that," Abbe said.

The evening flew by. Abbe and Nick got along very well, telling each other things they had not confided in other people. Abbe confessed she doesn't drive; never did, doesn't want to. Nick said he never wants to be a boss, in charge of lots of people. Abbe told Nick she was superstitious. Nick told Abbe he was afraid of heights. Abbe told Nick he had the most beautiful blue eyes she had ever seen. Nick told Abbe he had never known a girl to be so open; so easy to talk to. She said she would like to see him again. He said anytime would be good for him. They left the restaurant at ten o'clock though the waiter had cleared the table by nine and the check had been paid shortly after.

Nick and Abbe walked hand in hand into the hotel. Abbe opened her purse and handed Nick the key card to the room. He pointed to the elevator and they walked to it and got in. When the door closed, Abbe turned and wrapped her arms around Nick and they kissed until they reached her floor. For a nanosecond, Nick wondered what his parents would think if they knew he was with Abbe at her hotel. But only for a nanosecond.

Nick woke around one a.m. He dressed and quietly left the room. On the way to the parking lot, Nick's phone vibrated. He was sure it was his mother or Laurie. It was Abbe. "Hey, you're pretty good, all things considering…"

"Like riding a bicycle," Nick said interrupting her so she couldn't finish her sentence.

"Want to get together the next time I am in Philly?" she asked.

"Sure."

The next morning Emily was in the kitchen when Nick came downstairs. "Have a good evening, honey?" she asked.

"Great. I had dinner with Abbe," he said rather sheepishly. "She was in town for a meeting yesterday and we had dinner at Blakely's. She called yesterday while you were out. She went back home this morning."

"I'm sorry I missed her. Well, it was good you got to spend some time with her. She said she would help you with your resume. Did you take it?" his mother asked.

"No. I'll e-mail it to her," he replied.

"But she was helpful?"

"She was really helpful, Mom," he said and he thought, you have no idea how helpful.

Chapter Nine

Nick was listening to his iPod in the library of his parents home, staring off into space when his mom, sister, and his little niece, Pippa came in. "Mail call!" Pippa shouted, clearly having been rehearsed. She handed Nick an envelope and climbed up onto his lap. Her grandfather, Kris, and now Nick, were her two favorite people. Emily and Laurie stayed to see Nick's reaction to the letter.

"It's from the high school," he said factually.

"It's about a reunion," Laurie informed him.

"You'll go won't you, Nicky," Emily pleaded. "You have never been able to go before and besides, you'll see some people you know."

"People I used to know," Nick corrected. Nick tore open the envelope and looked at the form.

"When is it?" Emily asked.

"A week from Saturday."

"That's crazy," Laurie suggested. "They send those things out weeks, months ahead of time. Someone must have heard you were home. Go Nick," Laurie pleaded. "You can check up on people and tell me if anyone else is as screwed up as we are."

"Laurie!" Emily hated it when Nick and Laurie acted like their lives were in shambles. She had every confidence that both of her children would bounce back from these *challenges* in their lives, as she had told them many times.

"I went to one of the class reunions a few years ago and it was fun. Do go, Nick. I dare you!" she finally shouted.

Nick took a pen from the desk and checked the box "Will attend". He had promised his sponsor that he would make an attempt to meet up with someone from his past. This should take care of it, Nick thought.

Laurie shouted, "Hooray," which made Pippa shout it too. Emily was gleeful but tried not to react for fear Nick might change his mind if they made too big a deal of it.

"What do I have to wear?" Nick asked in a sad voice. "Please don't tell me I have to go shopping again."

"It's usually pretty casual," Laurie answered. Nick sat with his hand over his mouth trying to think how he could get out of this but came up with nothing. So, he stood up with Pippa in his arms and put her on his shoulders, ducked through the doorway and went into the kitchen to get them each an ice cream bar. He took her outside and sat on the lawn with her while they ate their ice cream.

A few days later the phone rang. "Nick," he answered.

"Hi Nick, this is Amber Nelson Bryant. I don't know if you remember me. We were in the same class in high school."

Nick did remember her. It wasn't that hard. She was a cheerleader, prom queen, and class president the year before he was. Besides, he dated her a few times. "Sure," he answered.

"I am so glad you are coming to the reunion. I don't think you have made it to any before," she paused but Nick didn't say anything so she went on. "We were thinking, since you were president of the class our senior year, that maybe you could start the evening off and introduce faculty who are attending and make any announcements we have. We can give you the information that night if you get there a couple of minutes early. Would that be okay?" she asked.

"Sure, that's fine," he answered without further comment.

As sort of an afterthought, she then added, "And then you could say the invocation."

Nick felt his face flush. "Ah," he started. "I'll do the introductions but why don't you get someone else to do the invocation. Sort of spread it around. Okay?"

Amber thought it was a little strange that he didn't want to say the invocation but she could get someone to do it. "Sure, Nick. I'm sorry, should I be calling you something else?"

"No, Nick is fine."

"Well, see you Saturday night," she said pertly.

"Bye."

The evening of the reunion, Nick came downstairs wearing chinos, striped shirt, sport coat and topsiders. He had his hair cut again and was wearing aftershave he got from his dad, for he had none. Both Emily and Laurie squealed when they saw him. Both were worried now about him not being prepared for women chasing after him. He looked fantastic. "You're beautiful," Pippa said.

Nick actually smiled at that.

"What will you do at the party?" she asked.

"Sit around and drink beer," Nick answered.

"And dance," Laurie added. "They usually have great bands."

"Okay. I would tell you not to wait up but I don't plan to stay that long, and besides you will wait up anyway," Nick said clearly irritated.

Emily took Nick's arm and said, "Nicky, try to have a good time."

"I will, Mother," he said through gritted teeth. "I am not the total social misfit you obviously think I am."

Emily started to say something and Kris grabbed the back of her tee shirt and pulled her away. He smiled at his son. "I will try to keep them under control," Kris told him. "Though it won't be easy," he added disgusted with both women. Emily turned to Kris and took his hand and squeezed it.

There were only a few people in the ballroom of the country club when Nick got there. He was about fifteen minutes early. He didn't want to get there too far ahead of time. He was actually a little more nervous than he thought he would be. He had spoken before groups many times. Maybe he did use the clerical collar as a crutch, he said to himself. He was thinking how he would like to leave. This was not how he wanted to make his reentry back into society. What was I thinking! He said a quick prayer and fingered his rosary in his pocket. Old habits die hard, he thought. Not that he had given up on prayer. He was devout. He had morning prayers and evening prayers, though it was usually in the privacy of his room. Once or twice his dad came to his room, however, and asked if they could pray together. He went to mass faithfully Sunday mornings now. Again, sometimes he and his dad would go to mass together, just the two of them, during the week. Why was he thinking about this he wondered? Get a grip!

A woman approached him and he immediately recognized her as Amber Nelson. She looked good; had not changed that much. She smiled and said he hadn't changed a bit. He paid her the same compliment. Two other women then came up to them that he didn't really recognize. One stuck out her hand, "I'm Lizzie Myers. Do you remember me Nick?"

"Sure," Nick flashed a smile. He tried valiantly to try to remember something about her.

"We were in Biology together. Your friend Curt, was my lab partner and you two were always cutting up. Curt and I got C's and you got an A," she said.

"Oops, sorry," Nick said with a grin.

The other woman looked familiar. She was pregnant. "I'm Stacie. Please don't tell me you have forgotten me, Nicky!"

"Stacie!" Nick exclaimed. "I'm sorry, I didn't recognize you. You look great." Nick and Stacie had been friends since kindergarten. They never dated but it was a strong friendship. She was the first person he told that he was going to be a priest. She cried. Stacie had highlighted her hair and it was nearly blonde now. Even though she was pregnant, her face had lost the round baby face, he remembered, and she was very pretty in an older more sophisticated way.

"Are you in Philadelphia for long?" she asked. "I saw your mother a few years ago at Strawbridge's, well back when there was a Strawbridge's. I guess it was more than a few years ago. She said you were in New York then, I think. You had just moved there from St. Louis, I believe."

"I am here for a while. I don't really know how long. What is up with you?"

Stacie filled him in on her life and told him this will be her third child. She said her husband came with her and she pointed to him sitting across the room. She would introduce them later. The room began to fill up and Amber brought Nick some notes so he could make the announcements. Then he would pass things along to Sarah Taylor and she would give the invocation. Everyone was given a name tag with their senior picture on it. Nick put his on his jacket and walked up the steps of the stage and stood in front of the microphone.

"Good evening," he said in an announcement voice. Some voices quieted but there was still chatter in the room. He began again a little louder, "Good evening." People began to end their conversations and turned to face the stage. One more time he said again, "Good evening," his pitch lowering this time. By now every eye was on him. "Now I know how Mr. Daggert used to feel when he couldn't get our attention to start government class." The audience laughed. Mr. Daggert had no control of the classroom.

"I'm Nick Millar," he stated with authority. The class applauded.

"Wow, I didn't see that coming. I have never been applauded for saying my name. Anyway, I have been asked to welcome you tonight. This is my first reunion so most of you probably know more about what is going on than I do, but I am to tell you that we will eat dinner after the invocation, socialize after in the Terrace Room while they take down the tables, and then we will have dancing back in here."

"My little niece asked me what we were going to do tonight," he told the audience. "I told her sit around and drink beer." The group laughed. "I was thinking that sitting around and drinking beer would have been an ideal evening when we were in high school. We talked about it a lot; a lot more than we did it," he added. "I do seem to remember actually having a can of beer at school one time. Someone, who shall remain anonymous, put a can in my locker. I was sent to the Dean of Boys, my parents were called, and they grounded me for two weeks. They said they believed me that I did not put the beer in my locker. But they thought I showed bad judgment, walking around the hall showing it to anyone who would look and trying to act drunk. They also suggested that I consider making some new friends." The crowd roared and several people turned and looked at Curt Norris who looked incredible guilty. Nick flashed a smile that lit up the room and made the women swoon. Everyone was whispering about Nick.

"Anyway," Nick said to get back on track, "we are privileged to have several faculty members with us tonight." He went on to make introductions and then turned the microphone over to Sarah for the invocation. He remembered Sarah, a really pretty, petite girl; was in every play and musical, he said to himself. Amber told him Sarah is now a Lutheran pastor.

After the prayer, Nick needed to find a place to sit to eat dinner. He saw an empty chair at Curt Norris's table and walked over. "May I sit here?" he asked. He had not seen Curt since he left for Notre Dame. Actually, Curt had stopped coming by after graduation. Even though Nick took a rather general course at Notre Dame, Curt knew Nick was set on going into the priesthood and after he was told, never really spent any time with Nick. Several of his friends behaved similarly. A couple of girls even tried to talk him out of going.

"Sure," Curt said. Curt had not aged well. He had gained at least thirty pounds since high school and football training. After graduation, he went to Drexel University and lived at home. He now ran the real estate agency his grandfather had started in Drexel Hill. He was married for the second time but his wife was not with him tonight. Curt didn't stand up when Nick came to the table; no warm embrace, no handshake, and he didn't talk to him at all. Nick sat next to Pete Garrison and his wife, Anne, who turned out to be very friendly. Pete was in the debate club with Nick one year and they traveled to tournaments together. He is now an attorney. "Do you have a family?" Anne asked Nick. Everyone at the table turned to see how he would answer. Amber and her husband were also at this table. Amber tried to make the situation less embarrassing but only managed to make it more so.

"Nick is a priest," Amber announced.

Nick waited until the shock registered with Pete's wife and then shocked the rest of the table by saying, "Not any more, actually." The table was quiet for several minutes. No one reacted; perhaps didn't know how to react. Nick panicked. He tried to think of something witty to say. It didn't come. Finally, side conversations started and Nick quietly ate his meal. Nick and Curt's eyes never met. At last, they were dismissed to the other room. Nick was thinking of making his way to the door. Maybe he could get out. He would have to drive somewhere for a while. He couldn't go home this early without a major scene with his mother and sister.

A man Nick didn't recognize came up to him. "Nick, I'm Jonathan Wright. We had a few classes together. You actually tutored me in Latin our first year. I heard you went into the priesthood. Is that right?"

Nick liked straight conversation better than circumvented, so he answered directly. "I was a priest until recently. I am not now. I am in the process of finding out just exactly what I am." He smiled. Several others had joined the conversation.

"Wow," one of the other women said. "What a difficult decision that must have been. I think it is hard to just change churches." She laughed. Nick laughed too. She put out her hand. "Alice Van Kiel."

Nick remembered Alice. She was a nice girl. He tried to remember if they had ever been out. He didn't think so, but tried to think why not. Then she said, "Maybe you don't remember me. Jason Ruby was my boyfriend at the time and he didn't like for me to socialize very much. I transferred here late in my sophomore year and went with him for most of my junior and senior years. Come to find out, he was schizophrenic, poor thing. They would probably call him bipolar today. Anyway, he committed suicide the next summer. I wasn't going with him then, thank heavens. But anyway, I didn't get to know many people in the class."

"What do you do Alice?" Nick asked.

"I'm a nurse. I work at University Hospital. I know your dad. Well, I know who he is. Everyone does. He doesn't know me. Before he retired, I was working in pediatrics and he would sometimes come in to check on studies. The kids loved him."

"And do you have a family?" Nick asked, though he hated the question when posed to him. He instantly felt guilty for asking.

"No, I've never married. I blame it on nursing. It's our curse. We only meet sick people and arrogant doctors. Don't tell your dad I said that. He was always friendly and sweet." Alice smiled.

"Well," Nick said, "my profession kept me from having a family too," he joked. "But, we aren't old. We still have time. Although my sister's little girl wears me out. I don't know if I could handle raising children. Odd, since I am from a big family."

"I do know Laurie. Of course, she works at University too. We have lunch sometimes. She's great. She told me she is living with your parents, but she didn't tell me anything about you. If you ever come in to see Laurie, drop by to see me. I'm in oncology now."

"Thanks, I will." An announcement was made that the room was now set up for dancing. Nick gestured for Alice to go ahead of him. When the music started, he pointed to the dance floor and she went with him. He danced quite a while with Alice, including one slow dance. But then women started to cut in when he was slow dancing and just joined in the fast dances. Most of the time several people were all dancing at the same time. After a while, Alice was dancing with other people and so was Nick. He did think he might go into the hospital sometime and meet her for lunch. She seemed very nice and not hung up on his past.

The evening went better than he had hoped really. He met up with some old friends and made some new ones and exchanged a few phone numbers. Most people treated him in a civil way. Only a few seemed to shy away. Curt never came around. When he went home, he was in a good mood. He filled Laurie and his mom in on those he spoke with, and they were delighted to hear about it.

Chapter Ten

Nick was still bothered by Curt's brush-off at the reunion and decided to confront Curt head on and see if they could talk things out. Nick didn't expect to become best friends again, but it would be nice to at least exchange pleasantries. He drove to Drexel Hill and looked for Curt's real estate office. After only going up and down two streets, he saw Norris Realty. He walked in and Curt was the only one in the office, looking at his computer, his back to the door. In a loud voice, Nick said, "You got any property for sale around here?"

Curt spun around in his chair and was obviously surprised to see Nick there. Nick was wearing jeans and a light blue tee shirt and sneakers. Curt was dressed for work in a broadcloth shirt and a tie, loosely tied. He started to get up but didn't. Curt looked Nick up and down.

Nick smiled. "Got a minute?"

Curt shrugged his shoulders.

"How long have you been doing this?" Nick asked sincerely as he looked around the room.

Curt didn't answer.

"Is the housing market picking up? I heard it is getting better every day. Is that right?"

Curt continued to stare at Nick.

"Look, Curt, we haven't seen each other since we were eighteen years old. Surely we have something to say to one another. Can I take you to lunch?"

"I can't leave until Lillian comes back." He did not say who Lillian was.

"Can I wait?"

Curt seemed to be thinking about it and softly said, "Sure."

"Can I sit down while I wait?" Nick then asked.

Curt nodded his head affirmatively.

Nick sat across from him and began, "Curt, I know I hurt you some way. I'm sorry. I know my wanting to be a priest upset you. I...," he struggled to find the words. "It was just something I felt I had to do."

"How long have you been out?" Curt asked.

Nick smiled. He thought it was interesting phraseology. "Not long. I was pretty happy until the last year or two and then I felt like I needed to leave." He waited for Curt's reaction. Getting none he went on, "I never understood why it bothered you. Can you explain it to me?"

"Is it really so hard to understand?" Curt asked, his voice a little louder. "We were friends. We did stuff together. All kinds of stuff. Got into trouble together; not serious stuff but, you know. And then, you decided to be a priest. You were going to be the saint and me the sinner. It felt crappy."

"I'm sorry, man. But it surely wasn't a shock. I always talked about being a priest. My dad wouldn't let me go right after high school. He wanted me to be sure, so he talked me into waiting until after college. By eighth grade I was talking about being a priest!"

"I don't know...maybe it wasn't even you being a priest. When high school ended you were going away to school anyway. I was staying here. I felt stupid and abandoned. It was like," he pointed across the room, "All you smart kids line up to go away. You stupid kids, line up over here to stay home."

Nick sat with his hand on his mouth listening. He waited for Curt to go on. "I guess I never wanted high school to end," he said sadly. "I went to college here and lived at home. Commuting students are never a part of anything. I wasn't a very good student anyway. You were smart. You were good looking. Your parents had money. I knew everything would go your way."

"Yeah, but I had to live in South Bend, Indiana. Do you know how cold and windy it gets in South Bend?" Nick said to lighten the conversation. Curt attempted a small smile. "You are married, Curt. You have kids. You've accomplished something I haven't," Nick said in an attempt to flatter Curt.

"I screwed up my first marriage. I married a girl I hardly knew my junior year, and then went out with other girls. She dumped me and she was right to do it."

"But now?" Nick asked.

"Lillian is great. She helps me with the business. She is better at it than I am. We have two kids, girls. They are the best thing I have ever done." Curt was feeling more comfortable now, beginning to loosen up.

"Is that them?" Nick asked looking at a photograph on the desk. Curt nodded and smiled.

"I have fifteen nieces and nephews," Nick stated. "I really don't know how people do it—raise kids. My brothers and sisters are all great parents. It seems so natural for them. Is it natural for you?"

Curt's confidence was building. "It seems pretty natural. I like being with them. My little one is a riot. She will do anything. She'll try anything. She's fearless."

"Wonder who she gets that from?"

Just then a woman came in the door. "Lillian, come over, I have someone I want you to meet."

Nick stood as Curt introduced them. "Lillian, this is Nick Millar."

"Nick Millar, the priest?" she said. "Curt has told me so much about you. He is so proud of you."

Nick looked to Curt who now looked him in the eye for the first time. "I guess I was proud of you. I just wasn't proud of me and took it out on you."

Nick walked over and put his arms around Curt and hugged him. "I missed you Curt and I'm proud of you!" He hesitated and then said, "Can you give me a job?" Then he laughed and Curt laughed with him. Curt suggested they go to the sandwich shop next door for lunch so he wouldn't be gone too long. He would have to be back in time for Lillian to pick up the girls.

"I'll buy," Curt said, "since you are unemployed." He smiled sheepishly.

"Yeah, but I have degrees in things like Greek and Philosophy!" Nick said.

"And that will get you what?" Curt asked flippantly.

"A free lunch from my old high school buddy."

Nick loved being at home but everyone had something to do but him. His mom and dad were always busy volunteering or going somewhere with other retired friends. His parents invited him to come along but he didn't want to be a fifth wheel. Laurie worked full time and even Pippa went to day care. Nick realized he had never done "nothing". He had always been busy. All through school he was busy with activities. When he was working in the field, he worked until exhaustion. Even as a priest in residence, he had a schedule. That was the problem, he had nothing to schedule. He called Mike and tried to find a time when he could go out to San Francisco to visit his half brother and his family. Mike was the oldest in the family and was grown when his dad married Emily. Nick didn't get to see Mike much when he was growing up but he always liked Mike. He didn't really know his wife or daughters. Nick tried to be casual. He didn't ask to visit, he just asked how they were keeping busy and Mike told him the litany of activities in which he and Alice were currently involved. Mike's girls were both out on their own now. One was married and was a teacher. She lived in Walnut Creek and Mike and Alice saw them as often as possible. Their other daughter lived in San Francisco and was an attorney. But, as new "empty nesters" they were anxious to do some traveling, just the two of them. Mike apologized for not coming to Philadelphia to see Nick but they had travel plans for the next two months and just couldn't work it in. He promised they would try to come as soon as they could.

Mike must have sensed Nick's disappointment for he talked with him for a while. "I was thinking about you the other day," Mike said.

"I have always felt so guilty about your accident when you were a kid. I sort of felt like I caused it," he said with a chuckle.

"You tampered with the zip line?" Nick questioned flippantly.

"No, but I always felt like I put some kind of curse on you that caused it to happen. I was home for a visit then. Do you remember?" Mike asked.

"Not really."

"Well, you were nearly sixteen and Dad told me he was getting you a car for your birthday. I was sort of pissed because Beau, Geoff and I all had to start out driving this ugly old Subaru that Dad had. It was old when I drove it, so come to think of it, poor Geoff was driving it when it was really old. Geoff was like you though, and didn't really care. He didn't even really like to drive and got out of it whenever he could. The car Dad was thinking about getting you, was not that wonderful, but it was nicer than the Subaru that we had. And it was new. Emily and Dad both liked their cars and didn't want to pass them down to you, so that's why he was getting you a new one. Theoretically, I think you and Laurie were supposed to share it since she is only a year younger. But, I didn't think that would happen."

"Anyway, if you were almost sixteen, I was in my thirties. I had just left the big law firm and was trying to get out on my own and it was going very slowly. My girls were probably about eight and ten and Alice was running them around all the time and was working only part time so things were getting tight. I love living in California and Alice is from here and would never move, but it is as expensive as hell so things weren't going well. I came to Philly for a few days just to get away. Alice and I were starting to get on each other's nerves. You, Nick, had the ideal life. I frankly was just jealous. I wanted to be a teenager again and be carefree, like you."

"When Dad told me about the car, I was really irritated. I told him how spoiled you were, how they babied you and how you would never be able to take care of yourself because they did everything for you. I even flared up at you one evening at dinner and told you to grow up. Early the next morning you left for junior year outdoor camp. That night Mom and Dad got the call no parent wants to get. You had been in an accident zip lining. You broke your hip, didn't you?"

"Well, that big thigh bone up by the hip and another bone in the other leg," Nick answered.

"Emily and Dad were frantic. Dad drove down to be with you and Emily stayed because of Laurie and me. I was flying out the next day and Laurie had something big going on. Anyway, I always felt terrible because I was so mean to you."

Nick laughed. "Wow, you did me in with a curse!"

"I know," Mike said. "And you were laid up a long time."

"Tell me about it. I smashed into a big ole' tree like a cartoon character when the zip line broke, and then fell. From the camp they took me to a rinky-dinky hospital in the boonies. They wouldn't even set the bones. They let me lay there in pain. Finally, when Dad got there he wanted me transferred to a different hospital. They were talking about taking me to the hospital for children in Boston because Granddad had worked there and orthopedics was his specialty. But since he was retired, Dad decided to bring me back to Philadelphia. Then they had to decide and make arrangements to take me either in a helicopter or an ambulance. I thought a helicopter would be cool but in the end for some reason, I think the helicopter wasn't available, I went in an ambulance. The ambulance hit every bump for four hundred miles."

"It wasn't four hundred miles," Mike interrupted laughing. "It was about fifty or sixty."

Nick laughed, "Well it seemed like four hundred. Anyway, finally, Dad put me out or I passed out, but I woke up in University. I was there for a couple weeks and then at home in a hospital bed, then a wheel chair for several more. I really don't remember how long. It seemed like a long time. Don't break bones in both legs. One, you can walk on crutches, but two you end up flat. I spent my sixteenth birthday in the hospital and Laurie actually got her license before I did. It was miserable. I can't believe you caused that, Mike. I don't like you anymore," Nick teased.

"Well, you did get to have all the girls feel sorry for you and those good-looking nurses," Mike laughed.

"Yeah, some of the girls in my class would bring my homework and I would be prostrate with a catheter inserted and a bedpan nearby. It wasn't my greatest moment. Made me humble, I guess. Maybe that is when I decided I may as well take vows," Nick laughed.

"Well, I just wanted you to know that all this time I have felt guilty," Mike said.

"Good," Nick retorted.

"Does your leg ever bother you now?" Mike asked.

"Actually, I have no residual problems with either leg. I just ended up with a fear of heights," Nick said laughing.

"Hey, I gotta go. Alice has dinner ready. I really do want to see you, Nick. I will try to work something out so I can go to Philly or you can come here. I don't even know the last time I saw you. At a wedding or a funeral, I guess. I love you, bro. Sorry about the zip line."

"I give you absolution," Nick said. He added, "Not as a priest, as your brother. Just turn around three times and send me ten thousand dollars."

"Indulgences. That's disgusting. But I will buy you dinner when we get together."

Nick tried to remember friends from college and recall where they were living but had not kept in contact with any of them. Laurie mentioned the social network but Nick didn't want to track down people or troll for friends, he told her. He was feeling pretty lost and alone. He called John and asked if they could meet for a drink or something. John suggested lunch on Saturday. Nick didn't want to take John away from his family but John's wife and kids were going to be away that weekend with her parents.

Over lunch Nick explained his frustration in having nothing to do and no one to do it with. He explained that his family was great. His parents invited him to everything. He did play golf twice with his dad, but Kris had regular golf games with his buddies and Nick didn't want to mess that up. He also invited Nick to go to Millar House with him one time but Nick didn't feel comfortable doing that. His mom asked him to go with her every time she went out of the house. "Come with me to the grocery, Nick. Let's go to the mall, Nick. I'm going to

Target. Want to come?" Sometimes he went with her but he felt like he slowed her down from what she would be accomplishing and he wasn't into shopping. She would want to point out things she would like to buy him.

John listened. "It's hard, man," John said. "It takes time to meet people and get things going. I wish I could tell you it doesn't but it does. It's like being out of the country for a long time. Everything has been going on without you. Things don't stand still, just because you weren't around. Old friends find new friends. You have to find new friends too. It is particularly hard if you aren't working. Maybe you might like to do some part-time volunteer work or even a part-time job. Do something easy though, not anything taxing or emotional. Give it time. It has only been a few weeks. I know it seems like forever but it hasn't been very long. Hang in there."

Nick decided he would call Alice Van Kiel. She was nice to him at the reunion. He called the hospital and asked for Oncology. But, when someone answered he apologized and said he had the wrong number. Maybe another day he thought.

Chapter Eleven

Nick was starting to feel antsy at home. He drove by a couple of apartments in the area but couldn't face renting one when he had no job. Everyone had a suggestion for him. Emily wanted him to go back to school and study something completely different, like law or medicine. Nick couldn't even imagine going back to school. He had spent most of his life in school. Mike suggested he go into business for himself; insurance or something. Nick didn't think anything could be more boring. Laurie wanted Nick to do something at the hospital; work in the lab like Kris started out, maybe. Nick would never want to follow in his dad's footsteps. Kris was the only one without suggestions. He would just tell Nick to take his time, not to rush into anything. In the meantime, he enjoyed having Nick home to talk with him, or play golf. He tried to think up things for them to do together. They bowled one morning. Neither of them had bowled in years and they were pretty bad. In the lane next to them were two elderly women who were fantastic bowlers. They laughed about it over a beer at lunch.

Beau walked into Nick's room one day without knocking. The door was open and Nick was at his computer, his back to the door. Beau never seemed to age. Though he was considerably older than Nick, in fact he had children only a few years younger, he seemed close to Nick in age. Everyone in the family agreed that Beau is a child at heart. Khiem Li is the grownup in Beau's house.

"How's it goin', bro?" Beau asked as he walked up behind Nick. Nick was playing Hearts, which Beau had no time for. He liked action games, like his kids and now young grandkids.

"Okay," Nick murmured.

"Man, you got to get out of here. Don't you run anymore?" he asked. "Or do you just stay cooped up in here playing old lady card games?"

"I run."

"Are you filling out applications, or having job interviews?" Beau asked.

Nick ignored him.

"You've got to get yourself together man. You've got your whole life ahead of you. You know what you should do?" Beau said brightly. Kris walked up to the doorway just then and stood watching his two sons.

Nick rolled his chair back so quickly he nearly backed over Beau. Nick jumped up and faced Beau poking his finger into Beau's chest as he said, "I'm pretty freakin' tired of people starting sentences with 'do you know what you should do?'" He took a breath. "Do you know what you should do, Beau? Get the fuck out of my face." With that he picked up his car keys, walked past Kris without a word and went downstairs and out the door.

Beau was astounded. He looked at Kris who was grinning ear to ear.

"What in the hell was that all about?" Beau asked.

Kris continued to smile and said, "I think it's about him wanting you to get the fuck out of his face." Then he walked over to Beau and put his arm around his shoulders. "I think this a good sign. He is beginning to feel. He was numb for a while but maybe he is starting to feel now. Give him some latitude. He probably feels like hell now for yelling at you, but the pressure valve opened just a bit. He's got a lot going on inside. You were just in the way and were caught in the turmoil. Nick's a gentle soul. He doesn't know how to let things out like the rest of us."

Beau laughed. "How long do you think it has been since he said the word 'fuck'?" Then he laughed harder, "How long…."

Kris stopped him. "Don't go there. It's unfair." Beau nodded.

Nick showed his ID at the guard's station and asked them to call Della. Even though nearly everyone at Millar House knew Nick, they always followed procedures. She said he could enter and she met him in one of the meeting rooms. "Hi," he said sheepishly.

"Hi," she answered. "I wondered if you would ever come back."

"How is Angel?"

"She's good. She has a little friend, Shaundra. They are playing together outside and Shaundra's mom, Tamika, is watching them. I wouldn't leave her alone, even here."

"I know you wouldn't. How are you doing?"

"Pretty good." It was awkward. Neither knew what to say to the other.

"So your family owns this place?" Della finally asked.

"They don't own it. My dad is on the board." He considered how to explain it. "He helps run it, helps find ways to … keep it going."

"It's nice here."

"Good. I'm glad you like it. Would you like to go out? I could take you to Wal-Mart or something. Do you need anything? You want to go some place for lunch?"

"Where?"

"Where would you like to go?"

"You mean, a real restaurant? Not a fast food place?"

"Sure. There is a restaurant on the water not far away. Would you like to go there?"

"What should I wear? They gave me some clothes."

"You look fine as you are." Della had on navy pants and a nautical striped top. Her hair was in a pony tail and had a red scrunchie around it. She looked even younger than the last time he saw her. "I'm wearing jeans and a tee shirt," Nick said. "You are more dressed up than I am. Will you be ashamed to be seen with me?" he teased.

She blushed and shook her head. Nick wondered if Della would want Angel to come along but she said, "I'll go tell Tamika that I'm going out for a while. She won't care. She likes for the girls to play together and she don't have no place to go anyway." Nick didn't react to her grammar. She was back quickly and they both signed out. Nick opened the car door for Della and she blushed again. Nick thought about how she didn't blush when she had her top off. What a strange world, he surmised.

At the restaurant they were asked if they wanted to be seated inside or out. Nick looked to Della but she shrugged. "Inside today then," he said. "It is a little cool today in the shade."

Once seated, Della studied the menu for several minutes. "This is an expensive place," she stated. It wasn't really but Nick didn't react.

"Anything look good?" he asked.

"What's a panini?" she asked.

"A grilled sandwich," he answered. "Like a toasted cheese sandwich but it can have meat and things in it," he added to clarify. "What is your favorite type of food?" he asked.

"Anything someone else cooks," she laughed.

"That sounds like my mother," he said.

"Does she live in Philadelphia?" she asked.

"She does. I actually live with her and my dad right now. I just moved here from…somewhere else," Nick said.

"So you aren't married and have kids?" she asked as if she thought he did.

"No wife, no kids. Not now anyway. Maybe someday," he said wistfully. Then he added as an afterthought, "My mother volunteers at Millar House. She was there yesterday. Maybe you saw her. She is small with dark hair. She helps people with legal problems."

"Is she a lawyer?"

"Yes."

"Wow, your mother is a lawyer. My mother didn't finish high school. Is your dad a lawyer too?"

"Doctor," he answered.

"Wow, and what are you?" she asked sincerely.

"I'm nothing. Unemployed right now. That's why I am living with my parents. See, we all need help sometimes," he said to make her feel more comfortable.

The waiter took their drink order for lemonade. Della asked that Nick order for her. "I'll eat anything." Then she said, "I saw a movie one time and a guy ordered for this woman and told the waiter 'the lady will have'. I thought that sounded so cool; so rich."

Nick smiled and when the waiter came back he said, "I'll have the tuna melt and the lady will have a turkey and bacon panini." Della grinned.

"Can I ask you a question?" Della asked.

"Sure."

"Why did you pick me up the other night? Were you really going to have sex with me?" she asked pointedly.

"I guess you deserve an answer to that question." He took a deep breath. "I had had a bad night and yes I came to that street to pick up someone for sex. But when I saw the picture of your little girl, I felt horrible; really guilty. I just wanted you to be able to have a good life with Angel. Does that make sense?" he asked.

"I guess. But most men don't care about what kind of life I have, or Angel."

"Well, maybe most men in that neighborhood. Do you like Millar House?"

"It is wonderful. Who is that person whose name is at the front of the building, Gee-offery?" she pronounced with a question.

"The name is Geoffrey. It is pronounced the same as Jeffrey with a 'J'", he explained. "He was my brother, half brother really; my dad's son. I didn't know him. He was killed before I was born. He was volunteering at a shelter where Millar House is now and he was killed." He started to explain that the gunman came in to get his wife and children and Geoff tried to protect them and was shot, but he didn't want to scare Della. To change the subject Nick asked, "What have you been doing since I dropped you off?"

"I've had lots of meetings with different people. They are scheduling some things for me. A dentist is coming and going to fix my teeth. I have a couple that are chipped, and some are crooked. But, I take good care of them. I brush them and don't have cavities. You have nice teeth, really even," she said looking at him.

"I had braces as a kid," he said factually but then realized what a privileged thing it was to her, to have had braces.

"They might let me have braces," she replied. "There are people who do that for women in shelters. Free," she added. Then she went on, "They are going to help me get my GED. I didn't finish high school either, just like my mom. But, Angel will. I will make sure she finishes." Then she tried to remember the other meetings she had. "A group of us get together each day and talk about how we are going to get our act together. A lady helps us talk about how we shouldn't let anyone hit us. She says the first word we have to learn is 'stop'. She has us practice with each other. One person plays the bad guy and grabs our arm and we are suppose to say 'stop'. They talk a lot about how we have to feel good about ourselves and that no one person is more important than another and that if we want our kids to feel good about themselves we have to be role models. It is a little hard for me to think that I am as good as say, your mother. She has all that college and all, but I am going to work hard on 'self esteem issues'," she said with her fingers making quote marks.

"I can assure you that my mother does not think she is a better person than you are. She had just had some breaks that you haven't—yet," he said with a smile. "I bet you would be a great lawyer," he added.

"I made pretty good grades when I went to school. I just got mixed up with a bad bunch of kids and stayed out and didn't go to school much. I won't let that happen to Angel. What would your mother think of you paying me to have sex?" she asked suddenly.

For a second Nick was speechless. "I think," he said slowly, "she would be very disappointed in me. She wouldn't blame *you*, if you thought you had no other way to support Angel. But, I don't really have an excuse."

"I won't tell her then," Della said with a smile. "I won't tell no one. It will be our secret, okay?"

"Okay."

"You seem sort of sad. Not just today but that night too. Like someone you had loved had died or something. Or, like you lost everything you cared about and you don't know what to do or where to go."

"You are a very bright girl, Della. I do feel like I have lost something, or something has died. I guess I am grieving in a way. But you have helped me feel better. I think maybe I should start to feel good about myself too. I am a very fortunate person in reality. I, too, will work on 'self esteem issues'," he said with his fingers making quote marks. They both smiled warmly at each other.

"When you were a little boy," Della asked, "did your parents take you to museums and stuff? I heard there is a museum here where kids can actually play with things and learn stuff."

"The Please Touch Museum in Fairmount Park," Nick answered. "I loved that place. You want to go? I could bring my little niece and pick you and Angel up and we could all go one day."

"You would do that? You really aren't ashamed to be seen with me?"

"Of course not," he replied. "You are a better dresser than I am anyway," he teased.

"You are a really good-looking guy. Why don't you have a girlfriend? Don't you have anyone special?" she asked. "I mean, I know you and I are just friends. At least I hope we are friends. But a guy like you has to have lots of girls after him."

Nick thought it over. "There is a girl I sort of like, but she lives out of town. I am just getting to know her but…" he drifted off.

"Well, I hope it works out for you. Is she brilliant?"

Nick laughed. "I think maybe she is. But, I think she might like me anyway," he said with a grin.

"I don't want a boyfriend for a long time. I just want to be with Angel and make a home for the two of us. Then maybe someday I might think about having a nice-guy boyfriend. I didn't think there were nice guys until I met you. I am really glad you are my friend."

"I am too," Nick said.

When he dropped Della off, he gave her his cell number and told her she could call if she needed anything and that he would set up a day when they could all go to the museum. The women had all been given cell phones. She started to walk away after thanking him for lunch but she ran back and hugged him and kissed him on each cheek. "I saw a woman do that in a movie, too!" she said. Nick laughed.

"You look good happy," she said.

"So do you," he replied.

Nick drove over to Beau's and pulled up and parked in front of the house. Beau was playing basketball in the back of the house with his youngest son, Josh, who could easily outplay his father. Beau was bent over catching his breath when Nick walked into the yard. Several years ago, Beau had a half court put in the back and it was in use nearly every day for years. Now, only Josh was living at home and he would go out and shoot free throws and shots from the three-point mark, but he would occasionally beg Beau to play one-on-one or horse with him. It was far from challenging. Nick went onto the court and started playing with Josh. Slam, he took the ball from Josh and sent a hook shot through the net. Josh picked up the ball and tried to get around Nick but Nick slapped the ball again and ran to the basket and made the lay-up. Beau pulled up a lawn chair and sat at the side of the court. Josh threw the ball to Nick, wanting him to go for the basket so he could take it away. Nick took off for the basket, stopped and bumped Josh with his hip, faked, moved around him and nailed it. "Damn, bro," Beau said, "where did you learn to play basketball like that?" Before he answered, Nick grabbed another one from Josh and dunked the ball.

Nick stopped and turned to Beau, "In the hood. Not our hood, mind you. On the street in St. Louis, Detroit, and New York City. Some of those guys would be a challenge on any NBA team but they had bad habits they couldn't break. I'm six-one, and I was always the shortest guy playing."

Beau was amazed. "You just walked out and started playing with these guys?"

"Yeah."

"Why did they let you play?" Beau asked. But without waiting for the answer he continued, "What kept them from icing you?"

"The collar. No one wants to ice a man wearing a collar. They let me play because I brought the ball," Nick said with a sly smile. With that he took the ball away from Josh two more times and sank the ball each time.

"You are good, Uncle Nick," Josh said with astonishment. "I have to have a drink of water. Want me to bring you one?"

"No thanks," Nick said as he sat on the ground next to Beau's chair. He looked down at the grass for a while and finally said, "Beau, I'm sorry. I shouldn't have yelled at you." He then brought his head up and looked straight at Beau. "I'm sorry. I apologize." Then he put his hands behind his head, lacing his fingers together.

Beau was sincerely touched. "Nicky, I say lots of stupid things. I'm sorry," he said. "Usually no one listens to me," he added with a smile. "I'm not Mr. Sensitivity, you know," he said.

"And you're old and fat," Nick said grinning.

"Now that hurt," Beau said and picked up the basketball at his feet and thrust it at Nick hitting him in the chest.

"Love you, man," Nick said as he walked toward the car.

"Yeah, I know," Beau answered.

Kris, Emily, and Laurie were in the kitchen when Nick came home. "Hi," Kris said, cautiously.

"Hi Dad. Hi Mom. Hi Laurie." Nick was upbeat and cheerful. Before Kris could say anything, Nick said, "I stopped by Beau's and apologized."

"That's nice. But I don't necessarily think you needed to do so," Kris said. "Beau was out of line. He doesn't need to lecture you. He hasn't always had his ducks in a row."

"Well, it was necessary for me. I know I have been difficult and I will try to be better."

"Wow, where have you been?" Laurie asked. "I'll have what he had," she said laughing. "Was it legal?" she asked in jest.

"Just barely," he answered and left the room. Emily and Kris looked at each other.

Abbe called and invited Nick to Harrisburg for the weekend. Perfect, he thought. He needed to get away and he liked being with Abbe. He eagerly accepted her invitation. She asked him to meet her at a bar near her office when he arrived on Friday night. She and some friends from the office had drinks at a different place every Friday. He nearly asked her what he should wear. Thinking everyone would be coming from work, he decided to wear chinos and a sport coat. As it happened, it was casual Friday and they all had on jeans. He quickly shed his jacket.

Saturday, they stayed in the apartment nearly all day. They read the paper, listened to music, read books, and made love. That night they went to an early movie and then dinner at an Italian place. Nick hadn't been to a movie since college. Sunday, they slept in and then went to lunch at an old coach inn. Nick loved being with Abbe. He liked that she didn't try to fill every moment of their time with activity. She had work to do and would work at her computer while he read or listened to music. She didn't have suggestions of things he should be doing either. They had a great time.

Nick missed Abbe when he came back home. He liked being with her. He even contemplated moving to Harrisburg and trying to find a job there but Abbe wasn't likely to stay in Harrisburg. Besides, that would be a bit rash at this point.

Abbe was always upbeat. She was funny and intelligent. He loved talking to her. She never looked at him like a loser; he felt like others did. Not his family, really. They were supportive. But maybe, even they thought he had had enough time to get his act together, he pondered. He, however, didn't think he was any closer to a decision than when he arrived.

Emily was thrilled that Abbe and Nick got along so well. Nick did not have much to say about the weekend. He told her that Abbe had looked at his resume. The truth was, they laughed together about how anyone could have taken so many classes that had no practical application. Abbe said the worst part was that he had such a fantastic

GPA and both master's and doctorate degrees. At least she didn't say it was a waste. He couldn't tolerate that. It was not a waste.

Once back home Nick was bored again. On a whim, he stopped in at the local bookstore. It was a small chain store that had recently moved into the suburbs from Ohio. He walked around a bit and then went up to the information desk. "Excuse me," he said politely as a young woman looked up at him. "May I have an application?"

"A what?" she asked, a bit curt for Nick's comfort.

"An application," he repeated. "I thought maybe I would apply for some part-time work," he said with embarrassment.

"It's on-line," she answered.

"I'm sorry?" he asked not understanding.

"You apply on-line!" she said rather loudly as if he were elderly and hard of hearing.

"Sorry," he said sheepishly, and walked away and out the door, placing the two paperbacks he had selected on a table before he left.

Nick was in his room looking at his computer when Laurie went down the hall. "Hey Laurie, did you know that nearly every major company has their application for employment on-line?" he shouted out to her.

"Yes," she answered as if everyone should know that. Then she came back into his room.

"Colleges and universities, too," Nick exclaimed. "The application is right on the computer. What happened to all of the crap we had to go through to apply?" he asked. "Remember those ridiculous compositions we had to write?"

"Don't know about the compositions. Maybe they still have those. It has been a while, you know," Laurie said. "So you are sitting there looking up companies and reading their applications?" she asked.

"It's fascinating," he said.

"So are you going to apply for something?" she asked confused.

"No."

"You're lame!" Laurie replied.

Chapter Twelve

bbe came to Philadelphia on a Friday, was in meetings all day and Nick met her at a restaurant that evening. This time Abbe suggested that they have dinner at a well-known pizza place, Jock's in Center City. After pizza and beer they walked to the hotel. As they walked down Ninth Street, they passed City Mission. It was a stately old building that had seen better days. Dirty gray paint was chipping off and showing a pea green underneath. There was a notice board attached to the door with rules for when the men would be served a meal and when they could come in to sleep. The notice ended with a declaration that in the event that the beds were full, the door would be locked until the next morning. Several men were standing out front. Nick stopped to talk to them. He asked them how they were doing, where they were going to spend the night, and if they had had anything to eat.

Abbe was struck with the ease with which Nick was able to talk to them. Some were staggering, most were glassy eyed, none were very well groomed, or even clean. Abbe was, in fact, repulsed by the odor. Nick was in a blazer, conversing with them as if they were old friends. She didn't hear anyone ask him for money but he opened his wallet and took out five ones and two fives and divided them among the three men. He clasped his hand on their shoulder as he gave the money to each and Abbe heard him say a sort of blessing softly to them. When they walked away, Abbe said, "Some people say you shouldn't give them money. They might buy alcohol with it."

"But, they might not," Nick responded. "Besides, two hours ago I was buying alcohol with it. Actually," Nick said, "that is really a quote from C.S. Lewis. He and a friend supposedly were walking together and his friend didn't want him to give someone money for fear he would buy booze with it and Lewis made that statement."

Abbe ignored him and said, "There are services available to the homeless. When you give them money, you make it easier for them to ignore the services they could have," she lectured.

"However," Nick said, "the shelter was full. They came to the shelter to get food and a bed and it was closed." He had clearly heard this argument before. "Besides," he went on, "I did encourage them to come back the next day or go to St. Mark's. I heard they were opening up some new rooms."

Abbe took his hand and they continued on their walk to the hotel. Neither said anything for several blocks.

Saturday, Nick took Abbe on a drive through the Amish country. There was a fair going on and Abbe bought a quilt. She was thrilled with the geometric shapes and bright colors. She held it in her lap on the drive back. Nick thought she looked almost vulnerable sitting there, holding tight to her treasure. It was far different than when she was coming from work, so in charge. They stopped back at Nick's parents' house so she could show Emily the quilt. Emily was glad to see Abbe. She put her hands on her hips and chastised Nick, "You've stolen my friend! I hardly ever get to see her anymore," she complained. Nick grinned, "She likes me more than you, Mom. Deal with it." With that he went upstairs to shower and change. He came down in jeans and tee shirt, just a different color than the one he was wearing. He asked, "What are you guys doing for dinner?"

Emily said, "I was thinking about chicken and rice. Why?"

Nick said, "I was thinking we could mooch off of you?"

"Oh, I would love for you guys to stay for dinner. Are you going out later?"

"Dancing at the Circus," Nick answered. "John and his wife are going to be there. We won't go until about eight or after."

Abbe looked at Nick sheepishly and said, "Is that what you are wearing?"

"It is what I have on. Is that what you mean?"

"No, I mean is that what you plan to wear to the club?" Abbe said.

"I was, but obviously, I shouldn't have. What do you think I should be wearing?" Nick asked.

"Maybe something that isn't a tee shirt, like a shirt of some kind; with a—pardon the expression—collar!"

Emily and Kris cracked up. Nick tried not to laugh. "I will go up and try again," he said trying to act insulted. Emily and Abbe gave each other a high five.

"Emily," Abbe said slowly, "what was Nick like as a child?"

Emily smiled and said, "I have been asked that a lot. Sometimes people think that Nick must have been this angelic child and that we knew when he was born he was to be a priest. It wasn't like that. He was an ordinary little boy. Well," she said faking overblown pride, "not ordinary. But, he was just a good little kid. He drove his sisters crazy, me too sometimes. He got into things that little boys get into when they are growing up. As a teenager, he did all the things that teenagers do. He dated, went out with friends, played sports, got into minor trouble at school, and so forth. He was always kind," she said evaluating her son. "He was somewhat sensitive, not that he was easily hurt or upset easily, it wasn't that. He just looked out for the 'little guy', you know the kid that the other kids made fun of. He didn't want anyone to be hurt. So I guess he was very moral." She stopped to think back. "Kris made all the kids volunteer in the community. Nick was a camp counselor in the summers at a CYO camp when in high school. He loved it. I think maybe that is when the idea was formed. He was always very 'religious' for no better word. But, Kris is too. They are the two in the family who always loved going to mass. Anytime Kris wanted to go, Nick was there ready to go with him. They were tight. Still are. Anyway, he would come home from camp and would seem different. He had high standards. He was outraged by injustice. But, then school would start up and he would be involved in sports or student government and date the prom queen and it was life as normal."

"Then about Nick's junior year, he started hanging out at church and talking to the priests. He wanted to go into the priesthood right after high school but Kris wouldn't let him. Kris was terrified he had talked him into it and he wanted him to have a normal college experience. After a couple of years of college, it became apparent that Nick was determined to be a priest. I was in…not exactly shock, but he was my baby. Laurie and Nick were our…I don't even know what you call it. 'Our' children compared to his boys and my girls. I truly love all of the kids but Kris's boys were out of the house before we were married. They are the most wonderful young men I have ever known. He did a fantastic job with them. And I adore my girls. They are my firstborn. But Nicky and Laurie were our bonus babies. They are the kids from our love. We love them so much because they are the best part of me and Kris. I had never had a son and Nick was so like Kris. We were just this amazing family, and then Nick said he wanted to be a priest. I was in shock. I didn't think he meant it all those other times. But now he was making plans. I wanted him to get married and have my grandchildren. I couldn't think of him being a priest. The Jesuits vow poverty and chastity." Emily stopped and corrected herself. "Kris tells me celibacy and chastity aren't vows, they are solemn promises. Well anyway, poverty, I could handle, but I didn't think Nick, or anyone really, could take a pledge, or a vow, or promise, or whatever, of chastity. It is different than celibacy. Celibacy, as I understand it, just means no sex. Chastity is perfect self-containment; meaning purity in thought, word and deed. Who can do that? Kris said it was a challenge; one that few men would attempt. Kris tried to convince me that it wasn't about sex, it was about obedience. Nick was willing because it was a part of being a priest. He would do anything he was asked to do. I was a converted Catholic. Kris was a cradle Catholic, but even he didn't know if it was right for Nick. But, he had a faith though that I didn't."

"The day Nick was ordained was the worst day of my life. I saw him lying face down, prostrate, on the cathedral floor with his arms out, like Jesus on the cross and I was grief stricken and then guilt stricken. I think I reverted back to my Protestant bewilderment of all things Catholic. He was so happy and I was so miserable. The few times we got to be with him, in the next few years, he seemed so sure. I finally believed it was right. When he would come home, which was rare, he was content; quiet; tranquil. He studied for several years. It was almost like he was just back in college at first but didn't come home for vacations. He went to Holy Cross for at least two years and even though it isn't that far away, I don't think we saw him the entire time. He studied at other places too. After that, he was always moving around. He would work in missions in a city for a year or so and then he would be sent someplace else. We hardly ever saw him."

"The parish priests who are assigned to churches and who live in the rectory, have a semi-normal lifestyle. They see people; parish women cook for them, knit them scarves, and make over them. They get invited to dinner, to the symphony, to homes to celebrate birthdays and anniversaries. But after a while, Nick was put out into the worst parts of cities. He lived in minimum accommodations with several other priests, without any of the support systems of the parish priest. Old Father O'Reilly once told me he thought that maybe they had put Nick out in the field for fear he would cause a 'sensation' in the parish because he was so young and good looking. He was serious. He thought maybe they were afraid he would tempt young women or maybe young men, I don't know. But, they did keep him from the normal parish priest routine. Nick never complained. He liked the ministering aspect of the work, so maybe it was all his own doing. We will probably never know. And Jesuits are different than some other priests, I guess. Like I say, I am not the best person to ask about priests. But, for years Nick seemed happy, when we saw him. But we didn't see him very often. He phoned or e-mailed occasionally, but just enough to keep us from worrying. Weeks and weeks would go by and then we would get a phone call. When he walked in here that day a few weeks ago, I didn't have any idea he had left the priesthood. He never told us he was thinking about it. Evidently, it was a long process. We don't know what he went through. I don't mean to sound like anything happened to him that was wrong or unfair, I just think they wanted to be sure he wanted to leave and made sure he had time to decide. He doesn't talk about it. This is a long answer to a short question. Nick was a sweet, normal little boy; an active teenager; and a fun-loving college student. Then he was a devout priest."

"Do all priests take vows of chastity and poverty?" Abbe asked.

"I'm a bad person to ask. I think celibacy, not chastity. I always tried not to think about it. I'm not sure about poverty either. Kris used to say all priests were poor but only Jesuits were into poverty. But, I don't know much about it," Emily answered as a disclaimer.

Nick came back downstairs wearing a white knit shirt and black jeans. He got thumbs up from the women.

Pippa was with her father and Laurie was out with a friend, so the four of them had a leisurely dinner. After they left, Emily and Kris looked at each other. Emily said, "I think he likes her. Do you think he likes her? I mean, *really* likes her."

"He seems like he really likes her," Kris stated offhandedly.

"I know. But they barely know each other. I think he is trying to make up for lost time."

Kris frowned and said, "Nick isn't going to rush into anything. I think he likes her. I don't know how much. He is just getting back into the personal relationship thing. He is going to try some things out."

"I don't want him to get hurt. I love Abbe but I don't know if she is right for him. I mean, I just wish he hadn't fallen so soon," Emily lamented.

"A few weeks ago, you were afraid he would never fall, and besides," Kris said, "I fell in love with you the first time I laid eyes on you." He laughed and brought her to him. She put her arms around his waist and he hers and then he put his chin on the top of her head. A slow song was playing on the audio system and they began to dance, swaying to the beat in the embrace. "Who needs to go out?" he asked, meaning to the Circus to dance. Calpurnia, however, heard him and barked.

Kris, Emily, Laurie and Pippa were all at the kitchen table in the morning when Nick got home from taking Abbe to the airport. He sauntered in, said good morning, but no one seemed to take notice that he had not been home all night. They seem transfixed on the little television on the kitchen counter. Hey, I'm an adult. Finally, they get it. He smiled to himself, finally I get it. He went upstairs to shower and change clothes and was back down to find something to eat. "Did you hear that news bulletin?" Kris asked Nick, indicating the television.

"No."

"Senator Straub had a stroke; he died," Kris told him. Nick could only think about how upset Abbe would be. She talked about Senator Straub last night and how much she liked him. She was even thinking of trying to get on his staff. In the next several hours, Nick tried Abbe's cell many times but always got her voice mail. He left a message asking her to call sometime when she had a chance and he acknowledged knowing about Senator Straub and extended his sympathy. He didn't hear from her all day.

At four-thirty in the morning, Nick's phone rang. He jumped up to reach it. Calpurnia stood up on the bed, turned in a circle and lay back down where she was originally.

"Nick," he answered.

"It's Abbe. You won't believe what is going on. They want to appoint me to take Senator Straub's place."

"What? You're kidding! They can do that? Are you qualified? I mean what do you...? Are you old enough? You don't have to be elected?" Nick couldn't take it all in. He rubbed his face to try to wake up and then propped himself up with pillows.

"First of all, as you remember from high school social studies, you only have to be thirty. Though, I would be one of the youngest ever to serve. Secondly, the seventeenth amendment gives the responsibility to fill a vacant seat to the governor and state legislature. That, my friend, is a slam dunk. It will only be until the election. And I won't win the election. I won't even run. The Republicans will throw a heavyweight in and the Democrats will have to come up with someone equally well-known. They aren't ready to put someone in now who will run. They know who they want but they have to straighten some things out...in his life, I think. I think he is divorced but they think they can get his wife to remarry him before he runs. Until then, I will be holding the place. It sounds stupid I know, but it will give me experience. In reality, the rest of the senators will probably ignore me. I won't serve on any committees are anything. But, by God I will be in the Senate. Sorry about the 'by God' thing," she added.

"Abbe, that's fantastic. I am so happy for you." Nick was genuinely delighted that Abbe was going to be given this opportunity.

"Here's the best part," she said. "I want you to be my chief of staff." Nick was quiet.

"Did you hear me?" Abbe asked. I want *you* to be my chief of staff."

"Abbe, me?" Nick gasped. "I know nothing about politics. I just got out of the priesthood! It is sweet, but no one would want me. I mean surely the party wouldn't want an unknown ex-priest to go to Washington and be your chief of staff."

"Wrong! When I mentioned you, they went crazy. You being an ex-priest shuts up the so-called Christian Right. I don't mean to exploit you. I would want you no matter what. But, the press, the Senate, the staffers; they won't attack you. And Nick, you will be good at it. You are conscientious and smart. You have a social conscience, Nick, and no ego, and no political aspirations! And trust me, everyone will love you. You are so loveable, Nick. Please! I don't think I can do it without you."

"What exactly would I do?" Nick asked, somewhat more awake now.

"Well," Abbe began, "basically you would work with my direct reporting team. You would sort of be my own personal, human resource manager. You would deal with issues and mediate disputes within the staff before they get to be problems for me to handle. You would be great at that. You are so calm and cool. And you would act as a confidante and sounding board to me. I really need that and I respect you so much. I need you. I really do. Please say yes. Please, please, please."

"Yes."

In the morning, Nick came over to the breakfast table and sat next to Kris. He had talked to Abbe for more than an hour on the phone. He wondered if she had yet been to bed. He fell asleep for a short time but got up and showered and dressed when he heard the family up. Kris poured him some juice.

"Dad, I've been offered a job," Nick said.

Just then Emily came in and sat down at the table too. In an instant, Pippa was racing into the room. She ran around the table, tagged Kris and then jumped on Nick's lap. Laurie was following her. "Walk," she shouted. "No running in the house." Pippa covered her ears with her hands and almost lost her balance and started to slip off of Nick's lap but he caught her.

"A job?" said Emily.

"Yes," Nick answered. He had wanted to tell his dad first and get his input before telling the rest of the family but there were few moments of calm when he could tell him. Finally he blurted it out. "Abbe is going to be named to take Senator Straub's place to finish out his term. Then they will run someone else in the next election for the next term," he started to explain.

"Abbe?" Emily was overwhelmed with the news. "That's amazing. Abbe is going to be a senator? That's fantastic. I didn't know they could just appoint someone. Abbe must be going crazy. It is everything she has ever wanted."

Kris looked at Nick. "What is the rest of it?" he asked.

Nick answered looking directly at his dad. "She wants me to be her chief of staff."

Emily gasped, "Oh, my God, Nick. You don't have any experience in that sort of thing; politics I mean. Do you think you can do that? Abbe has been groomed for this sort of thing, but Nick, Washington..." What she didn't say but was thinking was that Washington would chew him up and spit him out. Nick, in politics? He's too nice, too sweet, too naïve, she thought.

"I have lots of experience counseling people, Mother. I have experience mediating. I have lots of experience listening to people," Nick said rather defensively. "Priests are trained to be masters of diplomacy."

"Sounds great, son," Kris quickly said trying to be optimistic. He gave Emily a look to assure her Nick would be fine.

"Where will you live?" Laurie asked.

The Straubs have an apartment in Georgetown. Abbe can live in their apartment. Mrs. Straub's mother lived in a small one across the hall. I can have that one. It will just be for a few months. Part of that time we will be in Harrisburg. We'll go back and forth. Abbe, of course, already has an apartment there. She will keep it."

Emily came around the table and put her arms around Nick. "I'm sorry. I didn't mean to sound negative. I think it is wonderful. I think you will be wonderful. Oh, Nicky. This is a good thing. I was hoping you would stay here in Philadelphia, but Washington is great."

"It is just a few months; less than a year, Mother. I have no idea what will happen after that. But at least I will be doing something that sounds somewhat interesting. I will actually be paid a salary," Nick said almost in a daze. It had been a very long time since he had earned anything. "Evidently, a rather substantial one at that," he added, somewhat amazed.

Chapter Thirteen

"**M**om, may I have a couple of car seats?" Nick asked Emily.

"Sure, there is one in my car, and one in your dad's trunk. Why do you need two?" Emily knew Nick was taking Pippa to the Please Touch Museum.

"I am taking a woman from Millar House and her little girl too," he answered but didn't explain.

She knew vaguely about Della. She knew Nick had brought her in but no one knew how he met her. Nick didn't volunteer and Emily didn't ask. "Oh," was her only comment.

"Elephant in the room, Mom!" Nick shouted out.

"What?" she asked.

"You want to know about Della. Why don't you ask me? Have you asked around at Millar House? Have you seen Della? Asked to have her pointed out?" he further asked her.

"No, I haven't asked around." She smiled, "So tell me about her. I am a little confused. I thought you liked Abbe. You are going to Washington with Abbe. How do you feel about this Della?"

Nick laughed loudly. "I do *like* Abbe. I might ask her to go steady in study hall tomorrow," he said sarcastically. "Now about *this* Della." He went on, "She is about twelve years old." Before he could add anything else, Emily protested.

"She is not. I have seen her. Someone just *happened* to mention who she was."

"Well, she is a lot younger than I am and I have no interest in her other than helping her out. She got herself in a mess and now she is getting herself out of it. She's bright, Mom, just uneducated. I think she is going to make it. You should meet her. She's funny. And as Dad would say, she is 'cheeky'—like you! You would like her. If she had been born in St. John's instead of God-knows-where, she would be like Abbe someday, or you, or Laurie. She just got all of the bad breaks. She isn't bitter though. If you are there this afternoon when we come back, I'll introduce you to her and you can fill Laurie in and you two can gossip or do whatever the two of you do." Nick flashed a smile and then came over and hugged his mother. "You are the only one I really love, Mommy," he teased.

"Good!" Emily said with triumph. "Liar!" she then said softly.

Nick shrugged his shoulders.

Nick was standing at the guard's desk filling out the form and holding Pippa in his one arm when Della came up with Angel. He put Pippa down and the two little girls began to check each other out. "You look great!" Nick said.

Della laughed, struck a model's pose and said, "I had a make-over. Like my hair?"

"I do." Her long hair had been blunt cut above her shoulders, longer on the sides; shorter in the back. And it had been highlighted and she was a blonde now and a very natural-looking one. Her hair was shiny and healthy looking. It moved as she talked and fell into place when the movement stopped. She didn't appear to have on any makeup, just a bit of lipstick. Her complexion was flawless and glowing. She looks like an adorable teenager, Nick thought. No traces of a hooker. She was dressed in jeans, tight, but no tighter than Laurie's or Abbe's, he said to himself. She wore a long-sleeved silver-blue tee that brought out the blue in her eyes. Adorable, he thought. No other word for her.

"I had a manicure and a foot one too," she volunteered. "Four of us went. We had facials and massages. It took nearly all day." Several companies and organizations volunteered services for the women and children at Millar House. Nick thought a make-over was such a perfect thing for Della.

Once they got the girls strapped in and they were on their way, Nick said, "You really look good, Della."

"I feel good," she said with a smile. "How old are you?" she asked out of context.

"Thirty-four," Nick answered and then thinking this was the perfect opening, asked back, "How old are you?"

"Twenty-three," she said with a smile. "How old is your girlfriend?"

"She's thirty-five," he said.

"Does everyone call you Nick," she asked, "or do your parents call you Nicholas?"

"No one calls me Nicholas, now." It slipped out. He meant now that he was not a priest. "Most of my family calls me Nicky," he went on to explain, "because my grandfather was Nick also. I was named after him. Most everyone outside of the family call me Nick."

"Does it bother you to be called Nicky?" she asked.

"Nope. Call me anything, just call me for dinner."

"That's funny," she said. "My real name isn't Della," she said softly. "I just used that name so people wouldn't be able to come after me. My real name is Ann Marie. That was what my mother called me. And my boyfriend—ex-boyfriend. I am never supposed to call him my boyfriend! If someone hits you, they don't love you!" she stated affirmatively. "They know my real name now at the house. They call me Ann. What do you want to call me?"

Nick thought for a minute. "I would like to call you Annie. How does that sound? You look like an Annie to me."

"Great. No one has ever called me Annie. It is the beginning of a new me," she said smiling.

"Annie," Nick began, "I have a job offer."

"Wow, that's good."

"It is good." he said. Then he said, "I have to move away."

"Oh."

"The job is in Washington, DC mostly. Sometimes I will be in Harrisburg."

"Will you be working for the President?" she asked.

Nick smiled, unsure if she was serious or not. "No, for a senator. My girlfriend; she is going to take a senator's place who passed away recently. It will only be for about a year, really less."

"Wow, and I have never even voted before."

"Della, I mean Annie," he corrected. "I want you to know I will always be your friend. I will always take your phone calls. And sometimes I will be back and I will come to see you wherever you are living then. And my parents," he added, "will be happy to help you if you need something too. They like to help people out; help them get on their feet and then off on their own. See, even I am about to leave the nest," he smiled.

"You seem very happy now. Maybe you found what you had lost," Annie said.

"Maybe I have," he said wistfully. "When I met you, I was really worried about you," Nick said. "I am not worried any more. I know you can do anything you want to do, be anything you want to be. You are one of the strongest people I know."

"And you are one of the nicest," she replied.

The rest of the way to the museum, they all four talked together. Pippa told them what she enjoyed the most at the museum and Angel listened wide-eyed, as did Annie. Not surprisingly, Annie enjoyed the museum as much as the girls and Nick had a wonderful time too. The girls loved beating the conga drums in the Rainforest exhibit and using the rain sticks. They enjoyed the Railway exhibit and took an imaginary trip to the 1876 World's Fair via the Pennsylvania Railroad. Angel particularly liked the train tables everywhere with classic wooden train sets to play with. Nick remembered how much he enjoyed trains as a little boy and how much both Angel and evidently Annie have missed compared to his privileged childhood. They all rode the beautiful carousel. Angel was apprehensive in the Alice in Wonderland area. She was frightened by the circular maze, but sat on Nick's lap to descend down the rabbit hole and laughed all the way. While the girls were in the restroom with Annie, Nick bought a four person membership and put it in her bag. Every child should see and do these things, he thought and Annie and Tamika could bring the girls anytime they wanted now. They stopped for sundaes at the

Cow Barn on the way back. Both Pippa and Angel fell asleep in the car on the ride home.

When they were signing back in at Millar House, both Kris and Emily were in the hall talking to someone. They came over when they saw Nick. "Annie," Nick said, "this is my mother, Emily, and my dad, Kris. Mom, Dad, this is Annie and her daughter Angel." They all shook hands and Kris knelt down and started talking to the girls. Emily didn't seem to notice the name change.

"This is a really nice place," Annie said. "I am really lucky that I met Nick and he brought me here."

Suddenly Nick said, "I just remembered who you remind me of… Anne in *Anne of Green Gables*!"

"Who is she?" Annie asked.

"She is a character in a book. I'll get it for you. You'll like it, I know."

"It is in the library here, I think," Emily said. "I'll go get it."

Two days later Annie called Nick. "I finished it," she said first thing. "I read *Anne of Green Gables*. I loved it. Did I remind you of her because she talked all the time?" she asked laughing.

"No, because she was precocious, and smart, and inquisitive," and then he added, "and she talked all the time."

"Well you remind me of Matthew Cuthbert; quiet and sweet," she said.

"He was also very old," Nick protested.

"Well, Anne was a child!" Annie volleyed back.

"How about lunch?" he asked. "I can be there in about an hour."

"I'll be ready."

Annie met Nick at the desk. "Where are we going?" she asked bright eyed.

Nick hadn't thought that far. "Let's see," he teased, "maybe the root beer stand?"

"No way!"

"Seriously now, there is a nice little local restaurant not far from where I live that I think you would like."

"I love it already. What is it called?" she asked.

"Yumsters. Silly name, great food. I worked there as a waiter in the summers when I was in college." Yumsters was a small restaurant, barely holding fifteen tables, and a few more outside on the street. "It's nice today. Want to eat out?" he asked.

"Sure."

"What have you been doing today?" Nick asked once they were seated.

"Working on a resume to apply for some part-time work. I also studied for my GED with a tutor from the university. I asked my tutor if she knew any of the Millars and she said she had a Millar for a teacher and that's who has the students come and help out. I think they get credit for spending time with us tutoring," Annie said. "And then I ran on the track," she said as an afterthought.

"She is talking about my sister-in-law. She is married to my brother, Beau. She is a professor in the School of Education." He changed the subject, "Are you a runner? I love to run. When I was a kid, I would go to Millar House with my dad and we would run with a group of moms and kids to get them started in running. My dad has been a runner all his life too. That's a great track. At least it used to be."

"I just started running but I'm pretty good. I mean, I'm not fast, but I can run a long time," she explained.

"Maybe you should do a marathon sometime," he said. Their food arrived and they began to talk about the meal. Nick got a salad with grilled shrimp. Annie had never tasted shrimp and tried one and liked it. She ordered for herself this time and chose vegetable quesadillas. She didn't know what they were and wouldn't let Nick tell her. She wanted to be surprised, she said. She said she worked as a waitress for a while but they only served plain food; meat and potatoes, she explained. They had flavored iced tea with their meal. She had raspberry and he apple. She was amazed that tea could taste so good.

"You don't eat very much. Is that how you stay so thin?" she asked.

"I guess I am just not really into food," he said. "I like to eat small meals. Sometimes I snack in between though. My dad isn't a big eater either and doesn't really care about food. It used to drive my mother crazy that we would never suggest anything but now she just makes what she wants and we eat it."

"Can you cook?" she asked.

"Not really, but I won't starve. I can warm up food and make peanut butter sandwiches, so I can take care of myself," he said.

"Can your girlfriend cook good?" she asked awkwardly.

"Well, she lives alone so she must cook sometimes. We usually go out when we are together. I haven't really known her very long. It is really a stretch for me to call her my girlfriend, but I don't know how else to explain her," he said seriously.

When they got back into the car, Annie asked, "How far is your parents' house from here?"

"A few blocks. Just north of Oak View over there," he explained.

"Could we drive by? I mean, not stop or anything. I would just like to see it. I have never seen a house where a doctor and lawyer live," she stated.

Nick smiled, "Sure. My sister is having her book group there now, so I really can't take you inside. I promised to stay away while it was going on. But I'll show you the house."

They drove up to the house and Annie was in awe. She was full of questions. "How many bedrooms and bathrooms do you have?" she asked. Before he answered she continued, "Did you have your own room as a little kid? Did you have servants?"

Nick smiled. He was unsure whether Annie was truly interested or just "pulling his leg". "It is a big house. We are a big family. It has six bedrooms and," he counted to himself, "four or five bath rooms and two half baths. I always had my own room but when I was small, my sister and I would like to sleep in the same room. We are close in age and got along pretty well. So my mom put twin beds in my room and my sister would sleep in there sometimes. As I got older, I didn't want her in there anymore and I got a queen size bed and made her stay out." He then remembered the other question. "We did not have servants. Or maybe we were the servants. My parents were fairly strict. We had to clean our rooms and bathrooms, and generally pick up after ourselves. We didn't have specific chores. We were expected to do things that needed to be done, like take out the trash, get the mail, clean up a spill, empty the dishwasher etc. We did have a cleaning lady who came in once a week, I think, and now my parents have a cleaning service. I mowed the lawn for a while as a teenager and my sister and I raked leaves and things. We didn't get paid for doing specific things but we did get spending money. Now my dad has a lawn service. The service is a lot more reliable and skilled than we were."

"It is the most beautiful house I have ever seen."

"It is a great house. You will have you come to dinner there sometime. I won't cook. My mom will." He smiled.

The Beatles song, *Yesterday,* was playing on the CD player and Nick was singing along. "You can sing!" Annie said.

Nick laughed and quickly said, "All priests can sing." Then he caught himself and looked at Annie, embarrassed.

Annie smiled at him. "I know you were a priest. Mrs. Walters called you Father the night you dropped me off. I asked someone else the next day and she said she heard you weren't a priest any more. It's okay. You don't have to talk about it."

"Thanks," Nick said. "I am not ashamed of it. I loved it most of the time. I am just going to do something else now," he explained. "I'm still a Catholic," he added, "just not a priest."

"I don't really go to church," she said. "I went a few times once when I was in foster care when my mom was in jail." She looked at Nick's reaction. "I am a believer though. At least I think I am. I was always afraid to go to church. I thought they would tell me to leave. I would like to take Angel to church now though. Do you think that would be all right? How do I know what church to go to?" she asked sincerely.

"Don't they have services in the chapel on Sundays?" he asked. "Just go to those for a while and see how you feel."

"They have different ministers come each week. Maybe I could see which one I liked best and visit his kind of church. They have a Bible study class on Wednesday nights too. I haven't been because I don't know anything about the Bible really," she lamented.

"The purpose of a class is to learn," he said.

"I might try it. Don't you want me to be a Catholic?" she asked. My boyfriend, ex-boyfriend, used to say the Catholics thought that only Catholics would go to heaven. He didn't like Catholics."

"I want you to make up your own mind. The truth is, most of us are whatever religion our parents presented to us. You get to chose. I know you will make the right choice for you and Angel. Annie," he began seriously, "no one should ever judge you. If they do, they are wrong, not you. Church is for everyone. It is like a hospital, where people go for recovery and strengthening. Each person is trying to be healed in their own way because each needs something different, usually. There are no perfect people, no perfect Christians, even Catholics. There is my high school," Nick said as they turned the corner, glad to get to another subject. He drove around for a few minutes pointing things out to her.

When they got back to Millar House, Nick said he could stay a few minutes and play with Angel and the kids. He obviously liked being there and remembered spending time there when younger. He climbed through the inflated tubing in the play gym and had to squeeze through the last section, because his body was so long. The children squealed with delight. Outside both he and Annie took turns going down the slide and pushing kids in the swings. They played tag for nearly half an hour. Finally, Nick said he had better get going but that he would like to come back and run with Annie on the track sometime.

When he was leaving, Annie kissed him on both cheeks as she had done before. Nick put one hand on her shoulder and made the sign of the cross on her forehead with his other hand. "You are a child of God. Go in peace," he said softly.

Annie looked up at Nick. "That made my stomach turn over," she said.

"I was just… I'm sorry. I shouldn't have…" He didn't go on. Finally he said, "I'll call you."

Chapter Fourteen

"**N**ick," he answered into his cell.

"Hi, Nick. It's Abbe."

"Hi."

"I have a shopping list for you. These are the things you need to get before you come to Harrisburg next week. Emily is a great shopper and has wonderful taste, so why don't you ask her to go with you."

"Shopping? What kind of shopping?"

"Clothes shopping."

"Abbe, you know how I feel about clothes. They are just meant to cover your body, not to identify you."

"Wrong, Nick. Clothes are important in politics. Do you have a pencil?" she asked.

"Yes," he said in a defeated voice.

"You need a tux. Actually, you should probably have one in Washington and another in Harrisburg just in case. Just get one and bring it to Harrisburg. When we get to Washington, you can get another."

"A tux!!! Really Abbe. Why can't I just rent one when I need it."

"Because rented tuxes looked rented. I want you to look good. Nick, you are a great-looking guy. You are tall, trim, very attractive. We don't want to spoil that. Anyway, get a tux, very modern. Get two, hear me, two shirts for your tux, so you will have one clean at all times. And shoes for your tux. Got that?"

"Got it, I guess. I think I have been tricked," he lamented.

"Keep writing," she said. "You are going to need two blazers: one black single-breasted and one navy double-breasted. Are you writing this?" she asked.

"Yes, damn it. I am writing it. I don't like it, but I am writing it." he said disgusted.

"Okay, you need at least three other sport coats, and they should be conservative, pardon the expression." She listed off other things: "At least two sweaters, v neck, dark colors. Five oxford-cloth shirts: three plain, two striped. Two suits: one black, one navy. Four white shirts, one blue shirt, one tan, and six ties. Some of this stuff we will duplicate for the other location. Six knit shirts: four plain colors, two stripe or whatever. Three pairs of dress slacks. Three pairs of chinos. Six sport shirts. You choose. Two pair of dress shoes, one pair of topsiders, and one other. You will need a raincoat of some kind, and eventually a winter coat but we won't worry about that. Are you with me?"

"Yes, I am not to worry about a winter coat."

"Get some pajamas and a robe. You never know when someone might drop in. You can have as many pairs of jeans as you want for around the apartment when no one is there; a sweatshirt or tee shirt or two."

"Oh, thank you."

"I am trying to help you Nick."

"Oh, I ...never mind."

"Get some running clothes."

"I have running clothes."

"No you don't really, Nick. You have old gym shorts and faded rock-concert tee shirts, and those were your dad's. Get some proper running outfits. Three," she shouted out. "And get two athletic sweats or track suits or whatever you call them."

Nick put his foot down. "Abbe, I surely can run in anything I damn well please. No track suit. I am not a Junior League blonde."

"Okay, okay. You can handle the really casual stuff. Anyway, bring it all with you for inspection when you get to Harrisburg next week. I'll get you some luggage. Just bring it in your car. Isn't this fun?" she asked, and Nick wondered if it was a sarcastic remark or she really thought it was fun.

"Mom," Nick said when his mother sat down for dinner.

"Yes?"

"Would you go shopping with me for some clothes for Washington?"

"Sure. What do you need?"

"I have a list," he replied. He handed his notes over to Emily who read through them.

"Oh, my! This is complete, isn't it? I knew Abbe was organized but I didn't know she was this… organized."

"I didn't either," Nick said. "I think this is insane," he said barely audible. Emily had a worried look on her face.

Kris held out his hand to see the list. He didn't say anything but passed it back afterward. Nick didn't have much to say during the meal. He was contemplating which things to eliminate from the shopping list and still stay on Abbe's good side. He hated clothes shopping. He hated dressing up.

Emily looked at Nick and said, "You aren't eating very much, honey." Nick didn't respond. "Honey?" she said again.

Finally, Kris said, "Nick, I think your mother is talking to you."

"Oh, sorry," he said absentmindedly. "I thought you were honey," Nick said, looking at his dad.

"No, I'm sweetheart. You're honey," Kris said.

Emily looked at the two of them. "I think you are both idiots!"

Nick was on his stomach on his bed with a pillow propping him up at his chest. The phone rang several times and then Kheim Li picked up. "Kheim Li, it's Nick. How are you?"

"Nicky, it is so good to hear from you. We are well, and you?"

"Good. I just have a question for you. That is, I need some advice."

"Oh, oh. When you were a teenager, that would mean a girl situation."

"I guess some things don't change. I consider you my go-to person when it comes to gifts. I need suggestions."

"Is it a gift for the woman who has everything? I have heard a lot about Abbe from your parents. It would be hard to find a gift for someone so accomplished."

Nick winced and sat up on the bed. "Actually, it is for the woman who has nothing. It is for a girl who lives at Millar House with her little girl. She just mentioned that it is her birthday tomorrow and she has no family or anyone really, and I just thought I would get her something. But, I don't want it to look like...ah," Nick paused trying to explain. "We don't have any kind of a relationship," he announced. "I just try to help her out sometimes. Would it be lame, if I got her a gift? Would it look like more than it is? I mean, she isn't into me either. She knows I go with Abbe. I just feel sort of responsible for her since I was the one who brought her there." Nick now thought it maybe wasn't such a good idea to have called Kheim Li or have even considered a gift.

"I understand, Nick. Some of my students have tutored her I believe, and they like her very much. I see nothing wrong with you getting her a little gift," Kheim Li said. "Did you have something in mind?"

"Well, I was thinking about a cross. You know, a necklace with a small gold cross. She expressed an interest in church. I'm not trying to convert her or anything. I just thought maybe she would like that. What do you think? Too lame? Maybe a cross coming from me, would be strange."

"Nick, I think it sounds very appropriate for a friend to give a friend a cross. It is very ecumenical really. I think it would be sweet. Women give other women crosses. A heart might be misleading but a cross would be very nice, in my opinion."

"Thanks Kheim Li. You are always a big help."

Kheim Li smiled wondering exactly what she did to help since he seemed to know what he wanted to give the young woman. She wondered why he didn't just ask his mother. Emily has wonderful taste and ideas for gifts. Maybe he didn't want it to get back to Abbe that he was buying something for another woman. She made a mental note to get out to Millar House and meet this girl. Every one of her students who worked with her thought she was very intelligent and an amazing learner. What a blessing that Nick brought her in, she thought.

"Oh, Nick it is beautiful. I have never had anything like it before. Thank you so much," Annie said beaming. "Will you put it on me?" she asked him.

"Did you see that in a movie?" he asked. She looked at him puzzled and pulled her hair up in back so he could attach the clasp.

Then she understood his remark. "Yes, women always have men put their necklaces on them don't they? It is so beautiful, Nick. I won't ever take it off. I will use it as a talisman for good luck. Talisman is a word in a vocabulary list I saw of words every college graduate should know."

Nick had to laugh. He didn't think the Catholic Church or any Christian church would think much of calling the cross a talisman. Still, if it made her happy. What a complicated and yet sweetly simple person she was. Then he thought, Kheim Li was right. What in the world would he have to come up with to give a meaningful gift to Abbe?

Chapter Fifteen

*E*mily, Kris, Laurie, Pippa and Calpurnia were all at the door to say goodbye to Nick. "We have your address, well, Abbe's address," Laurie said. "We will miss you."

"We have your cell, son," Kris said. "We will call you, you will call us. It isn't the moon, girls. Let him take off."

"I can't believe I ever functioned on my own before. How did I get to be this pathetic? I feel like a character in an Anne Tyler novel. I am an adult. I can drive one hundred miles or so by myself and live in Harrisburg for a few weeks without help. I think." He added cautiously.

"Of course, you can, sweetheart. We just love having you here and will miss you. Have a wonderful time." His mother added, "Nicky, take care of yourself. Abbe is one of my favorite people but she is ....a little controlling."

"You think?" Nick said.

Kris looked at his son and pulled Emily, grabbing her shirt in the center of her back and bringing her back to him, as he so often did when she was in his opinion, getting out of control. Bye Nick. Have a good life. Let him go girls. Goodbye."

"Thanks Dad for trying to leave me one shred of dignity. I love you guys." And then he kissed each of them.

Half way to Harrisburg Nick took out his cell and punched in #2. "Hey, it's Nick. What's up?"

"Not much. Where are you? Are you there yet?"

"No, about an hour away. What have you and Angel been up to?"

"I passed my GED. I passed it, Nick, first try! I am so excited. I sent for some college course catalogues and I can't wait to enroll. Are you proud of me?"

"I am. I am so proud of you. But, Annie you have to be proud of yourself. That is what really matters. What other people think isn't nearly as important as what you think of yourself."

"And, oh, I forgot. I am going to take some speech lessons. Elocution lessons. Actually, I guess in a way they are grammar lessons." She started over, "Someone from the university is going to teach me to speak correctly. They say speaking incorrectly hurts you when you apply for jobs. So I signed up. No one else in Millar House wants to take it. I think it sounds great. This one girl said I would be like Liza Doolittle," Annie said. "Do you know who Liza Doolittle is," she asked.

"I do. She is the main character in the movie *My Fair Lady*. It was taken from the play, *Pygmalion*."

"I saw the movie last night. It was funny. I hope I don't sound as bad as she did. I didn't know there was a play," Annie said seriously.

"What is Angel doing?" he asked.

"She's right here; on my lap. I think she hears your voice. She is trying to listen," Annie said.

"Put her on. Hey, Angel, it's Nick. *Sup?*" She replied by giggling. "Your mom is a very bright lady. Give her a hug from me to congratulate her for passing the GED, okay?"

"I just got a slobbery kiss. What was that all about?" Annie asked.

"I said a hug, but a kiss is good too. To congratulate you," he added a little embarrassed. "Traffic is getting a little heavy, so I had better go so I can concentrate on driving. Take care, Annie."

"Bye, Nick."

Nick could hear Angel say "Bye bye," when he ended the call.

As soon as Nick rang the bell, Abbe opened the door to her apartment and ushered him in. She was in jeans and a sweatshirt. Nick had not seen her this casual before. She looked cute; younger;

less professional. Throwing her arms around him she said, "Where are your things?"

"In the car," he answered. "You want me to go get everything now?"

"No, we'll wait until dark," Abbe said laughing. Nick was unsure if she meant it or not. Then she added, "No one here is going to make anything of you staying in the apartment with me. In Washington though, we will have to be more careful. You'll have to go over to your own apartment every night. In Washington, they are always snooping for something. We have to be pure as snow." Then as an afterthought she said, "We aren't going to have any displays of affection around the staff, even here. No one is to know that we sleep together on occasion. You are just a staff member, like everyone else." Nick thought the wording odd, to say the least.

"Okay."

"Tonight I have been invited to a district party fundraiser. It is a dinner dance. I told them my chief of staff was coming into town and you are invited too. As my date," she added. "Governor Parker and his wife will be there. Also the Lieutenant Governor and her husband. And other muckety-mucks," she added. "You get to break in your tux," she said excitedly.

Nick tried to smile. A tux was actually one of the things on the list he did buy.

Nick and Abbe had to be the best looking couple in the room, and certainly the youngest. Abbe had on a long, black, form-fitting gown that was stunning. Her sometimes unruly hair was wrapped tight and twisted and held with a clip, and zillions of unseen pins. Tiny tendrils fell from her temples to nearly her earlobes, softening the look to a gentle sophistication. She was wearing long diamond dangles, a gift from her father when she turned twenty-one and a diamond evening ring he had given her for graduation from law school. Her neck was unadorned making the low cut and cleavage even more sensuous. Nick's tux outfit was classic. His sun tan and modern haircut gave him the appearance of a GQ model.

"Abbe, introduce me to this young man," a voice said from behind them.

"Governor Parker, Mrs. Parker, I would like you to meet Nicholas Millar. Nick, this is Governor Parker and Mrs. Parker," Abbe beamed as she spoke.

"Nicholas, so glad you are here. Did you just arrive, son?"

"Yes, sir, about two hours ago. Please call me Nick," he said as he flashed a million dollar smile.

"You are from Philadelphia, is that right Nick?" Governor Parker asked.

"Yes sir."

"No yes sir, no sir, here young man. You will get to know us as Jake and Lindsey. 'Governor and Mrs.' is okay for formal occasions but we are going to get to know each other very well in the next few months. Do you have any political ambitions for yourself?" he asked.

"No, Governor Parker. I am just here to support Abbe," he said.

"Good answer. Abbe is going to need people around her who are watching out for her and just her. You sound perfect for the job. She has told me of your *church background*," he said in sort of a whisper. "I suggest you just tell people you worked for the diocese. Later if need be, it can be spelled out. Is that okay with you young man?"

"Yes sir, ah Governor Parker"

"Let's go meet a few people before we sit for dinner," the governor said. He took Abbe's arm and left Nick to walk with Mrs. Parker. Nick had a feeling he should get used to walking behind Abbe. "Gentlemen, I want you to meet the young lady who is going to be the new Senator from Pennsylvania, Abbe Metzger," Governor Parker announced as he went up to a group of men.

"I knew your father, Miss Metzger. He was a wonderful man. I would have voted for him for president," an elderly man with a cane said to Abbe. "How is your mother?" another asked. "I haven't seen her for ages. Where is she living now?"

"She is in Florida. She can't take the winters anymore she says. She lives in Palm Beach. I am hoping to get her to Washington for a while anyway. Thank you for asking, Mr. Towson. Mr. Towson," she said, "I would like for you to meet my chief of staff, Nick Millar, from Philadelphia."

"Philadelphia," he exclaimed, "I love Philadelphia. Where is your home?"

"In St. John's, sir," Nick answered.

"I know it well. Lovely area, lovely area. Do you know the Duggans?" he asked.

"Slightly, sir. Their youngest went to my school. He was a few years ahead of me, I believe." Nick thought to himself, the Duggans. We called them Duggans' Hooligans.

"What does your father do in Philadelphia," the old gentleman asked.

"He is a doctor. He worked in medical research at University Hospital."

Abbe elaborated for the group standing there. "Nick's father is a well-know researcher. He is also Chairman of the Board of Millar House, a shelter for battered women, that is named for the family. Nick's mother is an attorney for Millar House too. I met her at Manner and Gross when I was an intern there. It is a brilliant family." She smiled at Nick.

"Well, maybe we should consider Nick for an office," Mr. Towson said laughing.

Nick shook his head while smiling.

Abbe took over again for Nick, "Nick is more into community service and not-for-profits, like his parents," she said.

"Isn't that what elected office is all about; community service and not-for-profit?" the governor asked. Everyone laughed politely.

Nick and Abbe were seated at a table with business people who were high contributors to the party. They all knew of Abbe's father and most had met her parents at one time or another. Nick was wishing he had brushed up a bit on Mr. Metzger and knew more about him. He made a mental note to look into it. Abbe was radiant. She listened intently to each boring story and fired back compliments and anecdotes. Nick had his father's quiet charm and was the golden boy of the evening. Nick had traveled, lived in several places, could talk about art and music, so had no problem finding topics other than politics. He let Abbe take care of those conversations.

"Where did you go to school, Nick?" one dinner guest asked.

"Notre Dame and Holy Cross, Sir," he answered. Nick didn't want to give out too much information but he thought that was safe.

"My God, we've got ourselves a good Catholic, Kathleen," he said to his wife. "Tell me you are Irish!" he went on.

"Sorry sir. My father was born in England."

"Well, good schools," was his ending comment.

Another guest talked about recently going to Italy. "Have you been there, Nick?" she asked.

"Yes, ma'am, I was in Rome for about a year doing some studying," he answered. Abbe turned to look at him.

"I never knew that," she said to him quietly.

"Art or music?" the guest then asked.

"Theology and ancient languages," he answered as vaguely as he knew how.

The music started and Abbe said she would like to dance. Nick and Abbe danced very well together, so well most people did not want to interfere. The band played mostly slow dance tunes with some swing numbers thrown in. Governor Parker did come to the table once and ask Abbe to dance. Nick danced with Lindsey Parker who was very sweet and friendly on her own. "Tell me about your family," she asked openly. It was a comfortable subject and Nick explained his blended family members and what they are presently doing. He then asked about her family and she told him of her children and grandchildren and pledged him to looking at photographs later.

Late in the evening, the guests at Nick and Abbe's table were fairly incoherent. A great deal of wine was consumed with dinner, and that was preceded by numerous cocktails, and was followed by after-dinner drinks. Both Nick and Abbe had soda water before dinner and one glass of wine with the meal. They agreed that it was a good policy for this type of function. Their table mates talked mostly among themselves, not relating to the age group that Abbe and Nick represented but happy to be in the presence of the future senator.

Abbe greeted guests on their way out and they were the last to leave. They were invited to the Governor's mansion for dinner next week. There would be no other guests and it would be a strategy meeting. Abbe seemed born into this role and Nick carried his own very well. The Governor whispered in her ear that she chose well. "He will wow the women and he is intellectually superior to the men," he told her. "Let's keep Nick in our pocket, Abbe, in case we decide to run him for something," he said in a stage whisper. Nick gave an ingratiating smile and shook his head as if to say 'thanks, but no thanks'.

The next month in Harrisburg was filled with strategy meetings, meet and greets, and two community town meetings. Abbe was good, talking with the constituents. Nick wondered how she would appear to them. He knew she could be condescending but she had obviously been groomed for this and was at her best. He wondered if the experience of being the Governor's daughter was the contributing factor. Whatever it was; it worked. The constituents liked her and liked talking to her and telling her their worries and fears. Abbe took notes and listened attentively. One afternoon, they were quickly whisked off and Abbe took the oath of office to become the senator. The days had become so hectic, it was anticlimactic. Nick wanted to take Abbe to dinner somewhere or do something to celebrate but there really wasn't time. He had no experience buying gifts and he certainly couldn't afford to compete with the jewelry her father had given her, so he opted to have roses delivered.

Four people from Senator Straub's staff agreed to stay on and operate Abbe's office for her in Harrisburg. Senator Straub went back and forth to Harrisburg from Washington, frequently. Abbe said she would try to be back in Harrisburg at least once a month. The party agreed Abbe could use the same office as Senator Straub since it would be such a short time there was no need to make a move. Quickly, Nick and Abbe found themselves packing for Washington, DC.

Abbe wanted to get to Washington as quickly as possible so she left Nick to handle the last minute details with the Harrisburg staff and she flew to Washington two days before he drove. Though a short trip of less than three hours, Nick found the solitude refreshing after the hectic schedule they had been on. He relaxed and called his mother. "Nicky, how are you?"

"Fine Mom. It has just been a whirlwind. How are you and Dad?" he asked.

"We're good. Dad has had a little heart episode but he has an appointment with his cardiologist tomorrow. Laurie had a date with a doctor at University. She seemed to have a good time. Oh," she said, "I looked into Annie's situation and had an investigation done on her boyfriend. It seems he is living in Iowa now. He promptly got arrested and is on parole, so most likely he won't come back here. She seems relieved. I think she was still afraid he would show up. Did you know he is not the father of her little girl?"

"I never asked," Nick said. "Is Dad there?"

"No, he went to the drug store. He will be sorry he missed you. He will probably call you later."

"Okay, Mom. I better go. Tell Dad I said hello and I will try to call him in a day or two if he doesn't get back to me. You are sure he's okay?"

"Yes, the doctor said it was just a little blip. The cardiologist might prescribe something."

"Okay then, Mom. Love you both."

"Love you too, Nicky."

"Nick, where in the hell have you been? I have been waiting for you," Abbe said as she let him in her Georgetown apartment. Her hands were on her hips and her face flushed. "I thought you would be here an hour ago. I left you a message on your cell. Didn't you get it?"

"Oops. I turned it off and forgot to check. Roam was wearing down the battery." Nick was calm. "What's up?" he asked innocently.

"What's up, is that I wanted to have our first staff meeting but my chief of staff wasn't here," she said with irritation.

"I thought you knew what time I was leaving. I met with the Harrisburg staff until noon. Then they brought in lunch for me," he said. "Anyway, I am here now."

"Well I don't want to have it now. I'll meet with everyone tomorrow. I sent an e-mail to everyone a few minutes ago to meet here tomorrow. Three o'clock. I haven't met with the staff yet. I have been trying to get the apartment straightened out. Some of the furniture they left is butt ugly. I am having someone from building maintenance take it down to the storage room. I went to the interior design shop down the street and they are going to bring me a new sofa and two chairs tomorrow. They were expensive but have class. I don't want to look like an amateur. I should have had your mother come and help me decorate. She has impeccable taste. Oh well, I'll muddle through. The decorator is going to make some suggestions when they deliver the stuff."

Abbe was babbling on about the apartment and decorating for some time. Finally, Nick said, "So, can I see my place?"

"Oh, yeah. I have the key. It is directly across the hall. How convenient is that?" Abbe started to calm down. "It is rather drab, but suitable I think. I liked the china in yours better than mine so I switched with you. You don't care do you?" she asked but didn't wait for an answer. Nick smiled. "Also, you had a better floor lamp in the living area. Since you will be at my place most of the time, I didn't think you would care if I took it," she said in one breath. Nick smiled again. They walked across the hall and Abbe unlocked the door. "It is sort of plain," she said. "What do you think?"

"It is fine," Nick declared. "It doesn't matter to me. I just need a place to sleep and someplace to sit. I'll be fine." He reached over to Abbe and pulled her over to him. He put his hands on each side of her face tenderly and said, "Whatever you want Abbe, I want for you." Then he kissed her lightly, once, then again, then a third time. Then he led her to his bedroom.

The next morning Abbe was orchestrating furniture movers. "Get rid of these things," she instructed the maintenance people. "Put them in storage out of my sight." Within minutes, the new furniture arrived. The decorator did indeed have some suggestions to the tune of several thousand dollars. A Persian rug would be gracing the floor before noon and other small adornments would give the room "lift", "credibility" and "substance," the decorator said. Abbe was pleased. Nick was amused.

By two fifty-five, the eight member staff had all arrived. Abbe put their names and numbers in her iPad and Nick wrote them down on a legal pad, Leo Press Secretary; John, Martin and Lenny, Political Strategists; Amy, Appointment Secretary; Samantha, Party Coordinator; Stacie, General Secretary; and Nick, Chief of Staff. Senator Straub had had a staff of fourteen but only these staffers had stayed on to meet Abbe. Each person told what they had been doing for Senator Straub and how they would continue to do as much for Abbe. The men were mostly in their thirties, Samantha and Stacie were in their late twenties. It was one of the youngest teams in Washington. It was obvious from the beginning that they did not think the work they would do in the few months left would be very meaningful. They had already been told that Abbe would finish out the term but would not run in the next senatorial race. Therefore, they each had begun to vie for other positions that would be more lasting. Abbe was full of enthusiasm but was playing to a subdued audience. Most of her suggestions met with cold stares. Finally, Nick suggested that he meet with Abbe to sketch an outline of her goals for the remainder of the term and then get with the staff tomorrow and they could tell how each could work to help fulfill the objectives. Abbe was relieved to have a plan and grateful to Nick for thinking of it. He stood at the door and shook hands with each staff member and said he looked forward to working with them. They each took his cell number and were to meet with him in the senate office at three the next afternoon, Thursday. Amy had explained that Friday and Monday were off days for the Senate this week and most would be going home to wherever they lived if they had homes nearby, or off to somewhere else otherwise. Therefore, tomorrow was the last hope of getting anything started for several days.

Abbe was discouraged. She had dreams of working on social reform, bank legislation, or even tax reform. The next couple of weeks nothing was accomplished. There were no invitations to social events. Abbe was not asked to participate in any committee meetings or discussions of any kind. She pouted and was constantly complaining to the staff. The following week didn't go much better. Washington seemed to be on a holding pattern. Three staff members, knowing it would be slow, scheduled vacation. Abbe was ticked. Nick finally calmed her and they drove to Rehoboth Beach. Nick suggested they take the remaining four staffers with them but Abbe wouldn't hear of it. It was a beautiful day at the beach. They took books and note pads but did nothing but walk, read, and eat crabs at a local crab shack on the way home. Abbe was cheered a bit. But by Tuesday, Abbe was on the war path. It seemed that any question she had of the political strategists was met with shoulder shrugs. "When will things pick up?" Shrug. "What should we be doing?" Shrug. "What would have Senator Straub been doing?" Shrug. "Thanks so much for your frickin' help." Shrug. They didn't meet again until the next Thursday. Nick had Abbe try to list things she thought would be helpful to accomplish and to assign specific tasks to people. Abbe couldn't come up with much and it outraged her. Nick tried to convince Abbe to have a wine and cheese night with the staff at the apartment or to take everyone out to a working lunch, but she had no interest in his suggestions.

Kris called his son. "Nick, it's Dad. How are things going? Has Abbe arranged for world peace and a balanced budget?" he said sarcastically.

Nick laughed, "No, but not that she hasn't tried." He went on, "It has become pretty apparent that Abbe was put here as a place marker until the election. She isn't included in anything generally that the Senate does and this is sort of low season for them anyway. They have more recesses than most first graders. The ones up for re-election are all home campaigning most of the time. I guess the others know nothing will get through, so they vacation or just meet with the 'good old boys'. She met Senator Wilson for dinner and had hopes that as the other Pennsylvania senator he would treat her like a cohort, but it didn't happen. Like Senator Straub, he has been senator forever, and he doesn't have time for a substitute. He just met with her to be polite. He knew her father."

"The junior senators here are even worse," Nick said. "Some of them are still living in their offices and they know she is living in Senator Straub's place in Georgetown. And their staffers aren't all that friendly either. Basically, I would sum up Washington as everyone covering their own backside. Our staff is okay. They are nice guys, just bored with the scheme of things. They aren't crazy about Abbe or she them. I play basketball with a couple of them in the gym nearly every day and they come to my apartment sometimes and we play poker. Some guys from other staffs come too. Basically, there are lots of us in the same boat. There just isn't much to do right now. No senator is going to make waves before an election. Those up for re-election are at home wining and dining voters. It makes you proud to be an American," Nick said sarcastically. "You know they say you never want to see two things being made: laws and sausages."

"Sorry," Kris said.

"It doesn't really bother me. I have read several books, listened to my iPod all the way through a couple of times, and I am trying to learn my way around DC. There are wonderful museums and fantastic restaurants here. I am trying to take advantage of the situation but I can't convince Abbe that is the way to go."

"I saw Annie the other day and she asked about you. She said you have been sending her menus from restaurants," Kris said.

"Yeah, she likes to learn about food she hasn't tried before. Does she seem to be doing okay?" Nick asked.

"She's fine. Her little girl is a doll. She is talking more and more every day. She is bright as a penny, just shy at first. I took Pippa back one day to play with her."

"How is Laurie?" Nick asked. "I haven't talked to her for a while either."

"She's fine. I don't think Jack is going to protest anything in court. He may even give up the joint-custody fight and just have Pippa on some weekends and vacations. Laurie gets a bit vindictive, and says she won't let him have her at all, but I think she will see reason. She gets a little outraged about things like your mother," he laughed.

"I think I may come home in a few days," Nick said. "Because Abbe is getting the cold shoulder here, she wants to spend more time in Harrisburg. It makes sense, really, since she is looking for something after this and there are people in Harrisburg who can help her. I can probably take her to Harrisburg and then come home for a couple of days. The staff there is self-sufficient. How are you feeling, Dad?" he asked.

"Okay, son. The cardiologist put me on some medication. It seems to be working. I'm fine," he said reassuringly. "Hope to see you soon," Kris signed off.

"Love you, Dad."

Chapter Sixteen

Their trip to Harrisburg didn't happen right away. The Straub family, had a change of heart and decided that lending the furnishings for the two apartments was too generous, and asked that the furniture be returned to Harrisburg where Mrs. Straub was living. The party had agreed to lease the two apartments from Mrs. Straub because Abbe was going to be there such a short time and out of compassion for Mrs. Straub. The lease would be up at the end of the term anyway. However, now they decided two apartments excessive and asked that Nick find another and they would sell the lease. Nick was happy to take a room in Georgetown but Abbe was becoming very depressed at this point and began not to care what people thought, and had Nick move into her apartment. Abbe rented some furniture to fill in with the pieces she had bought. Nick insisted he only needed a bed and a desk. Abbe's apartment had a second bedroom and she announced to her staff that for the sake of the budget, she would have Nick as a roommate. The staff was beginning to dislike Abbe so much at this point, they couldn't and wouldn't believe that Nick would be interested in her sexually. He was beginning to feel similarly.

As soon as the furniture thing was worked out and Nick moved in, Abbe decided to go to Harrisburg without Nick. She wanted him in Washington to rub elbows with the other staffs and let her know what was going on while she worked on her career out of Washington. Nick could entertain himself. He liked cities and would play pickup games of basketball at recreation centers and would walk around in neighborhoods he probably shouldn't, looking for games.

One night, Lenny and John, two staffers Nick particularly liked, asked if he would like to go bar hopping with them. They ended up at a club in Georgetown. Most of the patrons there were much older than the young men and the average income level far exceeded theirs. They started to leave to go home but were invited to stay by a table of four young women who had just come in. Nick had told Lenny and John that they could stay in the apartment that night since they were all drinking quite a bit and therefore, they continued to drink knowing they could walk to the apartment. Lenny was a little short and chubby to physically attract these women but he was a comedian and everyone was amused by his take on Washington and imitation of Abbe. John was an average-looking young man, quite serious most of the time, but could enjoy himself when given the chance. But, all four women were after Nick. Two different women at the table were vying for his attention when he went to the restroom. When he came back, one was gone, the other sitting next to his empty seat. He looked to John and Lenny for an explanation but got none. This woman, Jeannie, began to fondle him, running her hands over his thigh. Nick took her hand and raised it in the air for all to see saying in a Shakespearian voice, "Look at this tiny hand, so delicate but so deadly." Not liking to be rebuked, she picked up her glass of beer and threw it in Nick's face. Nick didn't flinch. Everyone gasped. Finally, he took out his handkerchief and wiped his face. "I think I have had quite enough beer," he said. "I believe I will go home now."

"I am so sorry," the girl cried. Sobbing, she said, "I shouldn't have done that. I'm sorry. I'll make it up to you."

"It's okay," Nick said goodheartedly as he started to leave the table. The other two young men got up also.

The young woman grabbed a napkin and sprawled her phone number on it and stuffed it into the pocket of Nick's jeans. "Call me. I will make it up to you. I promise." Nick waved to the table as the three men walked out of the bar and headed to the apartment. Once inside, they each found a place to sleep, Lenny the sofa, John in Nick's room and Nick took Abbe's room. There was no way the other men would consider sleeping in Abbe's room. Lenny and John slept soundly but Nick was awakened at seven a.m. by Abbe shaking him.

"What are you doing?" she asked. She was furious that Nick had brought the guys back to her apartment.

"I *was* sleeping," he muttered. "Late night," Nick then answered. He added, "Too drunk to go home. You don't want your staffers arrested do you?" and tried to lie back down.

"Get them out," Abbe said through her clenched teeth. "It smells like a brewery in here."

Nick sat up a little and propped himself up with two pillows. He tried to smooth down his hair a bit. "Abbe," he said very seriously, "we need to talk." He yawned as he patted the mattress next to him to indicate she should sit. "Abbe," he said again, not quite knowing how to begin. He rubbed his face with his hands trying to wake himself up so he could be articulate. "I think I haven't been doing my job. I haven't been an advisor to you. I let you say what you want to say, but I don't contribute. You surely want me to be more than that, so I am going to say what I should have said a long time ago. When I am finished you can decide if you want me to go back to Philadelphia or stay on your staff until the end. Are you ready to listen?"

Abbe thought about it for a minute. "Shoot," she said with exasperation. "Say what you want to say and get on with it."

"The staff doesn't like you," Nick said bluntly. He paused to see if she wanted to listen.

"Thanks a hell of a lot."

"You say you want a team, but you want to *have* a team, you don't want to be part of a team." He let Abbe digest that thought before he went on. "These guys are really pretty good at what they do. They have some experience here in Washington that we don't have. They know people that we don't know. They could really help you." Abbe started to speak but Nick put his hand up to indicate that he wanted to finish before she responded. "We all know there isn't much to do here now. I know you are disappointed that you haven't been able to step in and do something, but it is not going to happen. The other senators are either ready to vacation or to campaign to keep their seat. Either way they don't want to involve a newbie, especially knowing you are temporary. So I think you should take advantage of the situation and learn what you can from your staff! You need to get on their good side. Stop complaining about Washington and singing the praises of Harrisburg. Let's do Washington! Let's take advantages of the wonderful cultural charms of this city. Let's learn what it was like to work for a senator who had been here for eons. Let's pick the brains of the staff and let them tell us how things work. Then some day, you can come back as an elected senator, and be ahead of the game."

Instead of being furious, as Nick thought might happen, Abbe was reasonable. "What should we do first?"

Nick smiled and amended her question, "Do you mean what should *you* do first?"

"Okay, jackass. What should I do first?"

"First promise you will never call me jackass again," he smiled, "and then go fix breakfast for the four of us."

"Are you crazy?" Abbe said.

"A team member, remember. They don't like you very much."

"I wish you would stop saying that," Abbe complained.

"They don't like you because they don't know you. Let them in, Abbe. Ask them questions. Don't know all of the answers. They are nice guys. They deserve to be treated with respect. Everyone does. Just go in and make some coffee, pop open some biscuit cans, and pour some juice. It will go a long way to a guy with a hangover, trust me I know."

Abbe smiled. "You may not have political experience in the government sense but you have just made the most meaningful speech that I have heard for weeks." She kissed him on the forehead. "How did you get so smart?" Then she asked, "Do they call me 'witch' or something?"

"Dragon Lady," he replied. Abbe covered her eyes with her hands. Nick smiled. "So…?"

"You get your shower. I'm going in to make breakfast." As she started to leave the room, she saw the napkin with the phone number sprawled across it. "Whose number is this?" she asked with a smile.

"Throw it out. She will never vote anyway."

"Nicholas Millar, you never cease to amaze me. Maybe we are a good team." Abbe walked out to put the coffee on.

———⊗⊗⊗———

Old habits die hard and Abbe didn't change overnight. But she did improve her image with the staff. The next few weeks were almost enjoyable for her. She actually got to go in for one vote. It was a non-issue and nearly unanimous but she actually went into the chamber and voted for the state of Pennsylvania and it was a thrill. She and Nick did nearly every museum and went to nearly every memorial. It was a daily history lesson. She did go back to Harrisburg frequently and sometimes Nick went and sometimes he stayed in Washington. One long weekend he went home to be with his family and Abbe went to Palm Beach to see her mother.

Laurie was the only one home when he arrived. "How I have missed my big brother," she cried as she hugged him.

"I've missed you too. What can you fix me to eat?"

"Well, some things never change," Laurie said and added, "fix it yourself."

"You, Laurie, are not your mother's daughter."

"Thank you."

"Where are Mom and Dad?" Nick asked.

"They had an appointment with Dad's cardiologist. He is not getting any better Nick. They say he is losing the elasticity in his heart. He is too old to be a candidate for a transplant and that is about the only solution. He is never 'down' though. At least not in front of me or Pippa. Even though Dad is older than Mom, and he was older when we were born, I will never think of Dad as old. I knew he was older than the other kid's dads, but Dad was always so healthy and active. Let's face it, he was young when he was father to the other four, but he was getting on when he married Mom and they had us. But, it breaks my heart to see him deteriorate like this."

Nick listened carefully and chewed on his bottom lip. About this time, Calpurnia, meandered in and sat at Nick's feet. He reached down and rubbed her ears and as a result she flopped down on the floor and put her head on his shoe. "Remember when we were little and we were never satisfied with how old we were?" Nick asked. "I couldn't even imagine being as old as Mike and Beau, they were grown, but I always wanted to be as old as Mandy. She is nearly twelve years older than I am. Can you imagine wanting to give up twelve years of your life to be someone else's age? She probably would prefer to be my age now."

"Shoot, I always wanted to be your age," Laurie said. "Having you one grade ahead of me, used to drive me crazy. Whatever you were doing, always seemed so much better than what I was doing. Well, except when you were grounded for doing it," she laughed. "But, kids do always want to grow up too fast I guess. Pippa wants to be a teenager. She and her friends pretend they are in high school and she is only in pre-school. Society promotes that too. All the party invitations and things for little girls have teenage stuff on them. She can't pretend without acting like she is using a cell phone and swinging her hips."

"It's really sick to complain about the next generation, you know. I think we made a pledge that we would never do that. Tell me about the boyfriend," Nick said.

"He's great. I can't wait for you to meet him. His name is Sahid, everyone calls him Sid. His parents were born in India but he was born here. He looks Indian but has a Brooklyn accent. That's where he is from. It is really funny. Cute, not funny," she amended. "I met his parents and they are so sweet. He is great with Pippa and she likes him. He is a really good doctor, Nick. Maybe I was supposed to be with a doctor all along. Dad was always so funny about thinking doctors and nurses shouldn't date. The old 'don't shit where you eat' theory, I think. Anyway, maybe we can all go to a club together this weekend. Got a date?"

"Do I have to have a date to go to a club with you?"

"No. I was just trying to subtlety ask about your love life."

"I plead the fifth," Nick said.

Kris and Emily came in the back door. "Nicky, great to see you," Emily said. "Have you eaten? Can I fix you something to eat?"

"Mom!" Laurie shouted.

"What?"

"Isn't he capable of fixing something himself?" Laurie asked.

"I don't really have an answer for that. He's been away and he's back. I missed him," Emily pouted.

"Oh, brother," Laurie said.

"Hi Dad," Nick said standing and walking over to Kris and giving a hug. "You doing okay?"

"I'm okay," he said in a resigned voice. "Better than I have a right to be," Kris added.

Emily later told the kids that Kris was given a stronger drug and was told to take it easy. He was to slow down a little, no lifting, and do plenty of resting. Later Kris was resting in his bedroom and Nick peeked in. "Come in, Nick. I am just resting, which means doing nothing. I could use the company. How are things going for you and Abbe in Washington?"

"Winding down. It has been a good lesson for us both, I think. Abbe is becoming a little more patient. Not a lot, mind you, but a little more. And I guess I am getting a little more focused. I know now I don't want to travel or move around. I am ready to settle in one place. I want to come back to Philadelphia and live here. Well not here, in this house forever." He laughed. "I will one day move out and get a place on my own. I still don't know what I want to do for sure, but I am sure I will find something."

"No one is rushing you, son. Your mother and I love having you here and you can stay here as long as you need to do so. But, we also know you need to get on with your life too, and be on your own when you are ready." He changed the subject slightly, "And so what about you and Abbe? I'm getting old enough to ask personal questions, I guess, Nick. You don't have to answer though."

"It's okay. We are winding down too. That has been a good lesson as well. I know there is someone out there for me, it just might not be Abbe. PLEASE don't tell Mom I said that. She will try to get involved. So will Laurie. Abbe and I haven't really talked about it either."

"Plenty of time, Nick. Your mom and I have had more time together than we ever thought possible. I have had two lives really. One before your mom and one after," Kris said. Kris smiled as he looked at his son, "Nicky, would you do me a favor? I know this is sort of random, but would you read to me?"

"Sure Dad. What do you want me to read?"

"Psalms, I think. You choose."

"You got it." Nick pick up the well-worn Bible from the night stand and read for a few minutes until Kris went to sleep. Nick started to make the sign of the cross on his forehead but stopped and instead leaned over and kissed him on the cheek.

"Hi Nick," Annie said cheerfully. "I feel like it has been ages since I have seen you. You look great. Have you seen the President yet?"

"Nope, but I have been tied up in traffic because of his motorcade a couple of times."

"Well, that's something," she said. "Where are we going?"

"I thought we would go to the Parisian Café. How does that sound?"

"Very French."

They walked to the car and Nick opened the door for her. As soon as he got in and started the car, Annie began to talk. "Guess what? I am learning to cook. I thought since I like to eat so much, I should learn to cook. I am working in the Millar House kitchen for dinners. I have been trying some new things and people seem to like them, well, some more than others. But the big news is that I have been accepted to go to the Culinary Institute. I will go to classes three days a week and work in their dining hall two days. They serve meals to the public. Maybe I could cook for you one day. They mostly do lunches and sometimes do catering. Isn't that great? I think it will be really fun. I will start next quarter. It isn't real college but it is something practical. I should be able to get a job in a restaurant when I finish. What do you think?"

"I think it is fantastic!" Nick said. "What a plan. It's great, Annie."

"I did look through the entire college catalog and I couldn't really find anything that seemed perfect and everything was going to take at least four years. I wanted to get Angel settled before that. There is a day care at the Culinary Institute. Thanks so much for sending me all of the menus. I have learned a lot from them too. It was sweet of you to do that. And Angel loves it that you send the children's menus too. She plays restaurant with her friends. Oh, and I almost forgot. I got a list of the books that all high school graduates should have read, and I am reading them. I just finished *To Kill a Mockingbird*. It is such a wonderful book. I finished it and the next day I started reading it again. So I read it twice before putting it back in the library. The library at the house is pretty good. They have most of the books and if I ask about one, they seem to get it some way. I finished *1984* but I didn't like it too much. But now I am reading *Little Women* and I love it. Have you read those books?" Annie asked.

"I have, and I didn't like *1984* very much either. *Little Women* is my sister's favorite book. *To Kill a Mockingbird* is probably mine. Well, one of my favorites. I have been reading biographies of presidents. It just seems the thing to do in Washington. I am not terribly busy, so I get to read quite a bit."

At the restaurant, they looked over the menu. Annie said, "I'll have the macadamia-crusted mahi-mahi and a green salad with vinaigrette on the side, please."

Nick said, "The lady makes such great choices, I will have the same." They smiled at each other. Nick picked up his iced tea glass and tipped it to Annie. "To you and your plans. Cheers."

"Cheers," she replied. "No one has ever toasted me before. You always teach me something."

"And I think I am the one who has learned the most from you," he said beaming. "You really are amazing. How are things going at Millar House? Are the people nice?" he asked.

"They are so nice, Nick," Annie answered. "Most of them are smart, well-educated, have good jobs. They just chose the wrong guy. Some were married a pretty long time. But, they said they didn't want to put their children through a divorce or they didn't think they could make it on their own, so they stayed. They are quickly getting it together. Having a nice income helps but it still takes time. One woman married right after college but her husband wouldn't let her work. After a while, he didn't even like for her to leave the house without him. She stayed until he hit her little boy. She could take it, but she didn't want her son to have to. So she took off as soon as he left for work one day. Everything was in his name, so she doesn't have any money or a job yet either. But she will. My hero is a girl who came a few days ago. She has just been married about a year and one day she said something her husband didn't like and he beat her up. She grabbed her car keys and was out of there. Once is enough she said. We all clapped when she said that."

"They are all nice to me," Annie went on. "No one is judgmental. We are all in the same boat, sort of. No one knows what I was doing," she said sheepishly. "My counselor does," she corrected, "but I don't talk about it in group. My counselor says no one needs to know anything except that I was abused. I guess I am 'worst case scenario' in a way."

"You are 'worst case scenario'?" Nick repeated. "What do you mean?" He was clearly puzzled.

"I am the worst thing that can happen under the circumstances," she answered clearly. "I'm okay with that. You helped me get away and I will never do it again. I am the worst case scenario!"

"Oh, Annie. You aren't the worst case scenario of anything. If anything, you get the prize for most resilient or independent, or just plain amazing! Maybe you should think of doing counseling yourself," Nick said smiling at her.

"Like those Weight Watcher people who lose weight and then get to be a leader? It would be cool to help other women like me, well, not like *me* but who have been battered like me. I can tell people that if I can do it, anyone can."

"Annie, you should be the poster child for gutsy women. You are the best case scenario. I'll call you in a few days from DC and you can give me a progress report on the changes in your life."

Chapter Seventeen

"**M**om," Nick said into his cell in a muffled voice.

"Nick? Are you okay? You sound kinda funny," Emily said.

"Well, I have just had some stitches in my mouth. I'm sending you a picture but promise not to scream." He waited for her reaction.

"Oh, my God, Nick," she gasped. "What in the hell happened to you?"

"I got mugged, or robbed or something. I don't know what you call it. Two guys came up and clobbered me. They just took the money out of my wallet, not the cards or anything. They just wanted cash. I would have given it to them if they had asked," he lamented.

"Nick, how many times have I told you to watch where you are going. You shouldn't be going into some of those areas you go in alone," Emily said with motherly dismay.

"Mom, I'm holding the phone out until you finish. I don't need for you to yell at me," Nick said without moving the phone from his ear.

"I am sorry, sweetheart. How many stitches and where? Your eye looks terrible. Does it hurt?" she asked earnestly.

"All the stitches are inside my mouth. Well, there may be one or two on my lip. I don't know how many. I have a shiner and a slight concussion, which is really just a headache. I'm on a bus going home from the hospital and everyone is looking at me. It is not pretty, I guess. But, I'm okay."

"You were totally by yourself?"

"Well no one else in their right mind would venture into that neighborhood," he said sarcastically.

"What does Abbe say?"

"She hasn't seen me yet. I don't think I'll call her. I will just let her yell at me in person."

"Why were you there?"

"I had just played a pick-up game of basketball with some teenagers and was heading back home. About a block away two older guys grabbed me. Damn, I just remembered, they took my basketball too."

"And what lesson have you learned, Nicholas?" his mother asked.

"Not to call you the next time I get mugged."

"And," she said.

"Stay out of bad areas," he said like an obedient son.

"Oh my God, Nick, what happened to you?" Abbe asked in disbelief. Leo, the press secretary, was with her.

By this time Nick was exhausted. At the hospital, they had given him a shot and a pain killer and he wanted to go to bed. "I was mugged," he explained simply. "I'm okay. I had some stitches put in my mouth at the hospital. I'm on drugs, so just let me go to bed."

"Just tell me what happened. Where were you?" she asked, lightly running her finger over the swollen part of his eye.

Nick winced, "I went to Borden Meadows to play basketball with some teenagers at the center there. When I was going home, some guys grabbed me and took the bills out of my wallet." He continued to walk toward the bedroom. "I just talked to my mom, so no need to yell at me. If you have any human compassion, you will let me go to bed." He got to the room and flopped on the bed.

Abbe and Leo followed him into the room. "Do you need anything, man?" Leo asked. Abbe sat on the bed and patted his back. Finally she and Leo left the room and closed the door.

"Nicest guy in the world," she said. "He would never make it in politics."

Leo said, "I am not sure he'll make it anywhere," and shook his head.

As it happened, Abbe had been invited to a dinner of Pennsylvania party people the next night. Nick was going with her. She had looked forward to it for weeks. Finally, she would have an audience. The next morning she let Nick sleep late. She did hear him get up once in the night to get a drink of water and take a pill. She got up and made sure he was okay. Now she was waiting for him to get up while she read bios on the people who were going to be at the dinner.

"Hi," Nick said as he wandered in to the living room. He had showered and was wearing a pair of jeans and a white tee shirt. His hair was still damp. His eye was nearly swollen shut by now and the shiner was a bright red and purple. His upper lip was swollen and he had marks on his cheek bone on the other side of his face and a long scratch across his chin. Just above the neck of his tee shirt, Abbe could see he was bruised. She wondered how much he had been hit in the body, or if his face got the majority of the hits.

"Can I get you something to eat?" she asked.

"Yeah, something soft," he said, and added, "and something to drink with a straw. Abbe," he began with a serious tone, "I know I look like hell, but I will go tonight. Maybe you can put makeup on my eye or something," he said.

Abbe smiled at him. "I think I would have to use a paint roller to cover your marks, kiddo. If you feel like going tonight, we'll go. If you don't, we won't. I will explain to them. They aren't having this dinner for me. I have just been invited to fill a chair."

"I want to go, Abbe." Nick knew how much it meant to her. "I just don't want to embarrass you."

"We'll see."

By seven that evening, Nick was feeling better. He stopped taking the pain killers at lunch time and was getting along okay and he insisted that they go to the dinner. He still looked like the walking wounded, but seeing an attractive young man in a tux with a shiner was a conversation starter. He stopped counting how many times he was asked, "What does the other guy look like?" His standard answer was, "A hell of a lot better than I do." People were sympathetic and Abbe was caring. One time she introduced Nick as her 'boyfriend'. Nick was surprised but tried not to show it.

A group called America's Glory performed for the audience and Nick recognized someone he knew in the group from his high school. The group sang mostly patriotic songs and the audience loved them. After the performance, Nick went up and talked to Lisa and brought her back to the table. He introduced her to Abbe. "Senator Metzger, this is Lisa Gibbons from my high school." Lisa was very pretty and a wonderful performer. She sang one of the show-stopping solos in the performance.

The two women exchanged pleasantries. Nick explained that he worked for Senator Metzger. Abbe was asked a question by someone else at the table and Nick and Lisa had a moment to reminisce. Nick told Lisa he had been to the high school reunion and who was there. Lisa had been traveling with the group for nearly a year. "I'm confused," Lisa suddenly said. "The last thing I heard about you was…"

Before she could say anything else, Nick explained, "I made a career change recently." He tried to smile but the stitches prevented much of one.

"Does she know?" Lisa asked.

Nick then put his hand over his mouth to prevent injury and stifle a laugh. "She knows," he answered. Later, when Nick had time to think about it, he wondered if his past would continue to creep up on him occasionally. Then he wondered about Annie. She seemed to have made a new life for herself quickly. Would she one day come upon someone who knew her before? Still, he thought, she looks nothing like she did the night he met her. Surely, no one would even recognize her.

Nick convinced Abbe to have a big going away party, since when she and Nick left, the staff would be out of jobs too. It was possible the newly-elected senator would keep some of them but he had no obligation to do so. The new senator, John Robertson, was well-known in Washington. He had been budget director for the president two terms ago. He won the election handily. He was an effervescent personality in front of the cameras but did not suffer fools easily. He knew and liked Abbe's father, but considered her a no-name wannabe. He had no time for her. Abbe finally got it. She was put in Washington to deflect attention from the election. However, the news was not all bad. Abbe was to be appointed Deputy Mayor of Harrisburg. It had been concluded that because she had been out of Philadelphia for so long, she couldn't claim residency. The party was starting to groom her for bigger and better things in Harrisburg, and make up for her heart-breaking, or at the very least frustrating few months as senator.

Abbe rented one of the small ballrooms in the Omni hotel. She hired a band and invited all of her staff and their significant others and also many staff members from other staffs. Nick had convinced Abbe that all of the real work gets done by staff members and they have a long memory. If she ever wants to come back to Washington, she should get on the good side of people who can help her get things running smoothly. Nick told her that both his mother and father were adamant that you should reward the people who really help you in life. Kris felt strongly that nurses were the key to a smooth-running hospital and Emily proclaimed that if you really wanted to get something done in court, you must get along with the bailiff, and court stenographer as well as the judge. They both agreed that time spent talking to guards, cafeteria personnel, and clerks paid high returns. Those to whom you report, may at the moment like the Christmas gift you give them, but those reporting to you will always remember you gave them a gift. So, Abbe had a party.

The band was awesome, they were told, the food exquisite, and a good time was had by all. It was nearly three am when the last reveler went home and Nick and Abbe started packing up the apartment the next morning at nine. The moving van came at ten and they were on the road by three that afternoon. It was a bittersweet moment. Abbe had asked Nick to come to Harrisburg and live but he wanted to go back to Philadelphia. He drove her to Harrisburg and stayed overnight and drove to Philadelphia the next day.

"Hey, Annie, how are you?" Nick asked into his cell on his way to Philadelphia.

"Okay," she answered.

"You sound down, Annie. What's going on?" he asked.

"Well, I am disappointed I guess. I got accepted to culinary school but it doesn't start until next semester. I applied for a Habitat House and there is a waiting list a mile long. You know I am not allowed to stay here forever!" she stated affirmatively. "I can't afford an apartment. I am just sort of at loose ends, I guess. I've been working as much as I can at a restaurant near here. It is pretty good money and I make good tips. Angel and I may be able to share an apartment with Tamika and Shaundra. That would work I guess."

Nick wasn't accustomed to hearing Annie as anything but upbeat. "It will be fine," he said. "It takes time. Everything will work out." His father always said that and he took comfort in the words that were such commonplace logic. "What if I stop by and take you to dinner?" he asked. Going to dinner was the last thing he really wanted to do. He had on jeans and a tee shirt and hadn't shaved. He would have to go home and shower and change. Once he was home, it would be hard to get away. He was tired. The party, the goodbye to the staff and then to Abbe, and the move back home were all talking a toll.

"No thanks. I appreciate the offer but we are having a speaker for dinner and it is mandatory. Hey, I did get my Pennsylvania driver's license yesterday though and I am number three on the list to get a car from here. Seems people donate cars for tax credit or something and I might get one. That way I won't have to take Angel on the bus to day care at the culinary school. Marty got one the other day. It was given by a family who inherited it from an elderly person when they died I guess. It is really ugly. It is big and gray and looks like a boat. But it runs, and Marty was crying she was so happy. I don't care what kind I get either." She paused and said, "There are some really nice people in this world, Nick. I didn't used to think so, but I do now."

It made Nick happy and sad at the same time when she said that. "And you know," Nick said, "some of those nice people, who do nice things, were helped out once by some nice person. So it just goes on and on."

"Well, I hope I can do something to help someone some day," Annie said wistfully. Suddenly she changed the subject. "Guess what?"

151

"What?"

"Since I have some time before I start school, I am taking another speech class. Not the kind of speech class where you give speeches," she explained. "The kind where you learn to speak right, 'speak properly' I mean." She giggled. "I loved the first class I took, so I thought I may as well do something while I am waiting. There is a student at the university who is doing some kind of thesis on proper speech and she is helping me. The first lesson was learning when to use 'I' and when to use 'me'. Like *I* will give the book to you, or you can give it to *me*. You know of course, it is the subject/object thing. People get confused when they are talking about two people. '*I* will give the book to you, or you can give it to John or *me*.' For some reason people want to say 'John or I'. I learned it once in school but I have forgotten a lot of grammar. I have just been lazy about my speech. I really know the correct way, but just haven't bothered to speak correctly."

"You and most of America," Nick said. "I am sure lots of us could use a refresher course. You are amazing Annie."

Chapter Eighteen

Moving back into his room at his parents' home was not the most ego-enhancing thing to ever happen to Nick. He had at least kept busy the last several months and now he had nothing to do again. Finally, he went down to Yumsters and talked to the owner about working as a waiter. He had loved it as a college student. And, as he pointed out to his family when he told them he had been hired, "I have always been good at taking orders."

Nick knew that the family wasn't all that excited about him working as a waiter after several degrees and many years of study. But he had to do something, and it was the only thing that sounded appealing to him. The lack of status did not bother him in the least. He liked Marge, the owner, and she always liked Nick. He only balked when she told him he had to wear black pants and a black shirt. Finally she relented and let him wear a white shirt and black tie. All the other waiters were happy to go without a tie, so none complained that he dressed differently. Nick was a great waiter. He was personable and the patrons enjoyed talking with him. He was reliable, always there, never late. In a pinch, Marge could count on Nick to fill in when someone didn't show. He had on more than one occasion, worked two shifts in one day and even filled in cooking a couple of times. Though he claimed he only stirred and plated food.

"I'll miss you," Emily said hugging Nick.

"Mom, I will be a few blocks away. You can practically see my apartment from here," he said.

"I know. I'll still miss you."

"I won't. More for me," Laurie said teasing.

"Like you will be here long!" Nick said. They all knew Laurie was about to become engaged to Sid. "Mom and Dad may someday have their nest back, emptied at last."

"Love you son," was Kris's only comment.

"See you guys. But not too soon I hope," Nick added.

Nick's apartment was small but had everything he needed. It was just a larger version of his room at home. In fact, it had most of the furniture from his room at home and a just few other things that Emily gave him. He liked it. It was sparse, but he didn't seem to notice. There was nothing on the walls and only a small rug at the door on the hardwood floors. His routine was simple too. Nick worked and coached a little CYO basketball and went to church, of course. On occasion, when he would tell Emily or Laurie that he was going to see Abbe for a weekend they would perk up. He didn't volunteer much other information. They were hopeful that either things would work out with Abbe or the girl of his dreams would show up one day at the restaurant or at the apartment building and suddenly Nick would be "in love". They also hoped an employer with a real job would show up at either place and offer him a wonderful career, but that didn't happen either. He went to see Abbe less and less often. After a couple of months, Nick seemed settled into a routine and didn't come around as often for dinner. He would come sometimes during the day when he wasn't working or when his dad was there alone. He would take Kris out or spend some time with him at the house. Nick seemed content, happy even, "just being a waiter".

"Hi Nick. It's Curt." The voice on Nick's cell sounded frightened. "I need your help, Nick. I'm in trouble. Will you help me?"

"Sure, Curt, I'll try. What do you need?" he asked earnestly.

"I'm in jail. Will you bail me out?"

"How do I do that?" Nick asked.

"You need to go to bail bondsman. Tell him who I am and that I have collateral. I can put the business up if I have to, or the house or whatever. Then have him get here as soon as possible. I don't want to spend the night here, Nick. It sucks here. It really does," Curt said.

"Do you want me to call your wife?" Nick asked.

"No, that's why I am having you contact the bail bondsman. If she finds out, she might keep me from getting the money together for bail. Just get a bail bondsman to come and get me the hell out of here."

"Should I be able to tell him what you have been charged with?" Nick asked.

"Assault."

Nick didn't know what to ask next or what action to take. This was all out of left field for him. Curt filled him in on where he was and begged him to get on with it. Nick looked in the phone book for a bail bondsman and tried to find one near his apartment. None of them were. Most were located near the jail. Finally, he just took a stab in the dark and called Bob's Bonds—You Ring, We Bring. Bob did indeed answer the phone and had Nick give him the information over the phone. In reality it seemed Curt could have done it himself but he seemed to want Nick to be the middle man. He wasn't sure why. The bondsman did suggest that Nick meet him at the jail.

Nick had been to jails before. But, it was always a non-personal, mission visit. He had conducted classes a few times or just come to listen to inmates, so they didn't feel abandoned by society. He had never known any of them well. He walked into the jail and was met by Bob, whose real name was Sammy Carruthers. He was short; came to about Nick's chest and "swarthy" was the word Nick could think of to describe Sammy. Although, he thought maybe "slimy" might be as good a description. He was about to think that he had chosen badly but he looked around and they all seemed swarthy and slimy. He was repulsed by the entire scene. And he was very puzzled about what Curt had done, or been charged with doing.

Nick sat out on a bench while the business of the bondsman was transacted. Sammy came out and told Nick it would be a few minutes until Curt would be released, had Nick sign a paper and he left. Nick was to take Curt home. Nick sat for three hours, waiting for something to happen. When he inquired, he was told it would happen when it happened. Finally, the door opened and Curt came out.

Curt looked terrible. Nick didn't think to bring anything for him. He didn't expect it to take this long. Curt told Nick he had been given a court date and it was in two weeks. He was told he was lucky. He could have stayed in jail waiting for two weeks but bail was set and paid.

"Nick, I need your help. My wife has no idea where I am. It's three am and I'm not home. If she hasn't called the police yet, she will. Will you call her? Tell her I am with you. Tell her we got drunk, went to your apartment and went to sleep. You just woke up and realized she probably didn't know where I was. Say I'm still sleeping and that you will send me home in the morning," Curt said. "I don't want to get into it with her tonight." Then he added, "You'll have to take me to get my car in the morning. I left it parked where they arrested me."

"What in the hell is this all about?" Nick asked.

"Just call my wife. Every minute you wait makes things worse. I'll tell you after you call her."

Nick called Curt's wife and said what he was told. Lillian was asleep and didn't realize what time it was. Curt, in reality, probably could have snuck in and not been caught. Nick didn't like lying to her. She seemed like a nice lady. She was concerned for Curt; offered to come and get him. She thanked Nick for thinking of her. Nick felt terrible. He acted in a devious way. He was never devious. He never out and out lied. Even as a teenager, he always told the truth and took his medicine. He was appalled with himself as well as Curt. He drove Curt to his apartment.

"Okay, Curt. Now tell me what is going on. What happened?" Nick demanded.

"I slapped around a hooker. She was trying to rip me off. She was threatening that she would call my wife if I didn't give her five hundred dollars. She had my wallet and so she knew my address. She wouldn't give it back to me, so I took it from her. Someone in another room called the police. The cops must have been next door, because they were there in an instant. I called my attorney and he said it would be 'he said/she said' if it went to court. He doesn't think it will. He said the ho's don't usually go to court."

Nick felt bile come up into his throat. His heart pounded in his temples. He sat down on the edge of the coffee table and put his head on his knees. Finally he looked up and asked, "How badly did you hurt her?"

"She's not hurt. I just slapped her around. She deserved it. She is a thief and a con."

Nick couldn't talk. He walked into the bathroom and splashed water on his face and grabbed one of the pillows and a blanket from the bedroom, walked back and threw them on the sofa. Finally, he said, "You can sleep here. I'll take you to get your car in the morning and I never want you to ask me for anything like this ever again."

Two weeks later Nick found himself in court room sixty-three. He sat in the back row, scrunched low in the seat, with a baseball cap pulled down as far on his forehead as possible. He wanted to be there to know what happen to Curt but he didn't want to see Curt or for Curt to see him. All the action was in the front of the court room. Curt and his attorney and someone, probably from the prosecutor's office Nick thought, were there. He didn't see any police officers or any women. The bailiff called Curt's name and he and the attorney went up to the bench. They talked for a few minutes but Nick couldn't hear the conversation and then the judge said more loudly, "Case dismissed". Nick jumped up and went for the door nearly running into a woman in sunglasses also wearing a baseball cap. "Excuse me, I'm sorry," he said as he jogged down the hall and then down the stairs and out the door. She ran the other way down the hall.

Nick went to see his dad from the court house. "Hi, Dad," he said as he entered the house.

"Nicky, what a nice surprise. What's up?" Kris asked.

"Not much," he answered with little enthusiasm and sat down at the table.

Kris looked at his son. Something was definitely up. Nick looked terrible. "Cuppa tea?" he said using the British question.

"Sure." It was a perfunctory answer. Nick didn't even get up to help. Ordinarily he would have sprung into action to make the tea for his dad. He sat with his hand around his chin. Finally he said, "I'm having sort of a moral dilemma."

Kris smiled at him. "You, Nick? When you have a moral dilemma, we are all in trouble."

"Maybe it isn't a moral dilemma. I know the moral issue. I just did the wrong thing and I feel so guilty," he confessed. "But, I felt like I was in a box and was forced into it." He paused, "But that's just an excuse."

Kris didn't know where to go with this, so he waited and listened.

Finally, Nick looked at his dad and said, "I helped someone who did something wrong and he got out of it. And I lied to someone. I just out and out lied. A boldfaced lie to get someone out of a jam." Then knowing it was terribly confusing, Nick told his dad the entire story of Curt's phone call, the bail money, and Nick's own complicity.

Kris brought Nick a cup of tea and sat down next to him and patted his leg. "Curt is a complicated young man," Kris said. "You got involved before you knew what was going on. You helped a friend. You didn't know what he had done. And maybe it was a mistake to call his wife and lie to her, but you didn't create the situation, Curt did. Sometimes we do things in the spur of the moment that we wish we could take back. But we can't. You can't call his wife now and tell her the truth. It could end their marriage. She may know the truth anyway. Or she may find out when Curt does something else stupid or mean. The chances are she knows Curt pretty well. It doesn't seem to me that you can do anything at this point. Maybe Curt learned his lesson," he said optimistically. But then said, "Though it doesn't really sound like it since there were no consequences. But you let Curt know that you thought it was wrong and not to ask you to ever do anything like it again. What else can you do?"

"I don't know. I keep going over and over it. His wife seems so nice, Dad. I feel sorry for her, and the other woman too," he added. "He hit someone. He hit a woman, Dad. I just ..." he trailed off.

"Friendship is a funny thing. I would have laid down my life for my friend, David, when he was alive. I miss him every day. And yet we didn't have the same moral standards for sure. Still, if he had asked me to do what Curt asked you…I probably would have done it. And felt crappy afterwards. I guess it **is** a moral dilemma: do you turn down your friend when he asks a favor, or do you do something you feel is wrong? There is no good answer. Curt just came back into your life and you wanted to help him. I will say this, Nick, not many people would spend even ten minutes being concerned about what you did. Your standards are high and sometimes even you may not be able to meet them."

"Thanks Dad. I always feel better talking to you. I think I'll go for a run. That usually helps too. Love you."

"Back at you, son."

After his run, Nick showered and was just coming out of his bedroom when the door bell rang. He was dressed but he was still drying his hair and the towel was around his neck. He ran his fingers through his hair as he answered the door. The woman standing there looked vaguely familiar but Nick couldn't place her at first. She had obviously been crying, her face was puffy and red. Then Nick saw the baseball cap she was wearing was the same as the woman in the courtroom. "Lillian," he said in whispered recognition.

Lillian stood seemingly unable to move, with her hand on her chest. Nick bit his bottom lip and finally reached to put a hand on her shoulder to help her in the door. She started to slap Nick, but she recoiled, holding her hand out as if to strike him but unable. Finally, she began to cry and let him help her in the door. He walked her to the sofa and she sat. At last she found her voice and said, "I wanted to slap you so bad!"

"I'm sorry you didn't. I deserve to be slapped by you. I'm sorry," he said not knowing how to go on. "Can I get you something? I don't have much but," he tried to think what he could offer her. "Would you like a cup of tea? My dad is English and he insists that everything is better with tea."

Surprisingly, Lillian nodded yes. Nick put on the electric kettle that his dad thought that every home must have, and came back into the room.

"I don't even know why I am here," Lillian began. "I guess because Curtis always made you sound like such a paragon of virtue that I was shocked. Curt is incorrigible but I thought you were different. Then when I saw you at the courthouse, I was really mad at you. I don't know where you fit into all of this," she said with exasperation. "I have been learning things about Curt nearly every day." She stopped and looked directly at Nick. "I didn't know that Curt ran around on me until after he was arrested. A letter from the prosecutor's office came and I opened it. That was when I first learned about the arrest. Then I hired a private investigator and after only half a day of investigation he told me of years of betrayal and worse yet, shady business dealings. It seems Curt gives low-ball appraisals to friends who own holding companies, and they buy up property for commercial development. They pay off Curt. Are you in on that?"

"Me? No way. I had lunch with Curt the day I met you and I saw him the day he called from jail. That's it. I hadn't seen him for years; not since high school. I don't know why he called me to bail him out. I felt terrible calling you. I am really sorry. If I had it to do over again, I would have refused to do it. I'm really sorry," he said again. "Furthermore, I hate what Curt has done. At least what little I know. What he was charged with…sickens me."

"Me too! Now I have to drag my kids through a divorce and it will probably be sticky. Curt's family owned the company originally but I have worked there for ten years building it up. Curt isn't very good at business. He'll try to keep it. I would love to take the girls and go back home to my hometown in Vermont, but if I leave, I think he may get everything. Then I wouldn't be able to support them. I don't know," Lillian was so tired she was weary to even talk. Nick brought her a cup of tea and some Fig Newtons, the only thing Nick could think to serve her. She hadn't eaten all day and actually ate them. Her blonde hair was curling from lack of attention and showed an indentation from the baseball cap. She ran her fingers through it and fluffed it up.

"Do you have a good attorney?" Nick asked.

"No, I only know real estate attorneys."

"Well, maybe there is a way I can help." Nick got his mother on the line and asked her for a name of an attorney for Lillian. "One that looks out for the distaff side of things, Mom."

He put Lillian on the line with Emily and she wrote down the recommendations that Emily gave her. Afterward, Lillian seemed to want to talk. "I don't know why I married Curt. I felt sorry for him I guess. He told me he had a bad first marriage and wanted to make up for it. I guess I thought I could change him. He was bitter toward his family. He never wanted to be around them but I have a big family and he would always be willing to visit mine. He liked your family too and talked about them. I guess that was what was missing in his life."

Nick picked up the conversation as she trailed off. "I think you are right. Curt and I didn't have that much in common. We played sports together but he wasn't into student government or academics and I was. He did like my family though, now that I think about it. He always wanted to date my sister, Laurie, but I wouldn't let him. He was pretty condescending to girls, I thought. We rarely doubled. We messed around in class when we had one together. Curt never knew when to stop though. I was willing to act up until the bell rang but then I turned it off. Curt kept it up until he got into trouble and then couldn't understand why I wasn't in trouble too. He thought I got special treatment. I just knew when to stop. My parents were fairly strict; reasonable, but I would be in big trouble if I 'dissed' a teacher. Curt talked back to them regularly. But we got along pretty well. Sports was our common bond. He spent a lot of time at my house. His dad was maybe an alcoholic, I'm not sure. His mom always seemed tired and never wanted us around his house. My house was always perpetual motion, especially when everyone was home. Curt liked that."

"Thanks, Nick. I truly don't know why I came here. It was only that I couldn't believe you were involved in Curt's messes and yet you called me for him. At first I thought maybe, you know, you just got out the priesthood and didn't know any girls or something. Maybe you were with Curt that night. Curt said you weren't. Then, I was so angry when I saw you in court because you were supporting your buddy.

Now that I think of it, you were not there for Curt, you just wanted to know whether he would get off, just like me."

"I am so sorry I was involved at all. Actually, I wanted to make sure he did show. The bondsman had me sign as 'indemnitor'. If Curt didn't show up in court, I would have been stuck for the bail money. I hate to admit it but I didn't even read it. I just signed the paper. I'm thinking I am pretty naïve for my age. I feel pretty foolish. I still think I would feel better if you would haul off and hit me," he said smiling.

"Not likely. I'm a wimp," Lillian said smiling herself for the first time.

"So am I," Nick said. "If I can do anything, please, let me know. I owe you one."

"I think your mother has been a big help. I feel better now that she has given me a name of someone to contact. I don't look forward to all of this but I'll make it."

"You know where I live," Nick said. He added, "And I work at Yumsters. Stop in and I'll buy you a meal. Are your girls okay?" he asked.

"They are at their friend's house and going to stay overnight. I didn't want them to see me so frazzled. I don't know where Curt is, or care. I yelled at him until I wore us both out. He left. I just don't know how I got myself in this mess. I have always been so against divorce and now I can't wait to begin the proceedings."

"Is all of your family in Vermont?" Nick asked.

"Pretty much."

"Do you have friends here?"

"Yes, some. Mostly mothers of the girls' friends. But no one I can really confide in. They are all happy little homemakers. I mean, they are really nice but I don't think I could tell them about this, now anyway. I guess after a while everyone will know. I just feel like I need a support group of some kind."

"Would you like to talk to my sister? She just went through something similar. Well, not really similar. Her husband had a long-term relationship with a woman and Laurie didn't know anything about it until the woman got pregnant. She's getting a divorce. I'll give you her phone number and if you feel like talking to someone sympathetic, you can call her. I'm a pretty good listener too," he added sincerely.

Lillian stared off in to space. "I am really sorry to take up your time. You must have someplace to go."

"I don't actually. Would you like a glass of wine? Maybe something else to eat? I can fix us a sandwich."

"You know," Lillian said cautiously, "that sounds pretty good. Don't go to any trouble."

"Want to come into the kitchen with me?" Nick asked.

"Sure. How long have you lived here?" she asked while walking into the kitchen and looking around.

"Not long. I was in Washington DC for a while and then back at my parents. My apartment is a little stark, isn't it?" he said smiling. "I'm not too into decorating. I am used to pretty plain surroundings."

"It doesn't look bad. You are fairly neat for a guy. It is just," she searched for the right word, "simple."

Nick laughed, "I like that. I am simple."

"Not you, just your apartment," she laughed.

"No really," Nick said, "I am simple."

They had a glass of wine and then a sandwich and Lillian told Nick about her family and growing up in Vermont. Nick had been skiing there as a child and he told her about being in Stowe and how much he liked it. Lillian told about some of her ski trips. Curt didn't ski and she hadn't been since they have been married. They had another glass of wine. Lillian slipped off her shoes and pulled her feet up under her on the sofa when they went back into the living room.

"You look tired," Nick said. "Would you like for me to drive you home?"

"You are very polite. I do think the wine has had an effect. Let me think about it."

"Lillian, would you like to stay here tonight? You can have the bedroom and I will sleep out here. Probably neither one of us should be driving and you look really tired," Nick said. "I can find something for you to sleep in and I have an extra toothbrush. I just went to Dr. Ryan yesterday and he gave me one you can have."

"You go to Ted Ryan? He is the best. I go there and the girls do too. He is so good with them."

Nick said, "My sister's little girl goes there too. She was afraid of dentists but she loves Dr. Ryan. I just went to him for the first time this week. I like him!"

"Well, we have a lot in common. We both despise Curt and like Dr. Ryan."

"And maybe some other things too," Nick added.

Nick pulled out a pillow and blanket so he could sleep on the sofa. He didn't say anything about the fact that the last person to sleep on the sofa was Curt.

In the morning, Nick heard Lillian in the shower and he went into the kitchen and put on coffee. They each had a piece of toast and Lillian left unceremoniously, thanking Nick for letting her stay.

"Any time. I am here if you need me," he said.

Two weeks later Lillian stopped in at Yumsters. Nick was pleasantly surprised to see her. After seating her and asking what she would like to eat, he put in her order and asked for a few minutes to talk with her. The manager on shift was happy to let him, Nick so rarely asked for time off. "How are things going?" he asked Lillian vaguely.

"Curt has been arrested again. This time for fraud. It is about the deals I told you he was making. I swear, I didn't tell anyone but you. I don't know how they found out."

"I'm sorry," Nick said. He really didn't have any words of wisdom for this sort of thing. It was all out of his league. They talked generally but Lillian said she had to get back to the children and asked if she could just take her meal home. Nick had it boxed, added some things for her girls and brought it back to her. Lillian agreed to keep Nick posted on what was happening to Curt.

Chapter Nineteen

"Nicky, I never see you. What are you doing that keeps you so busy?" Laurie asked as he came in the house.

"Not a lot. I have been putting in a bunch of hours at the restaurant," he answered. Calpurnia slowly walked up to him and Nick squatted down to scratch her behind the ears.

"Mom and Dad are out to lunch. They will be sorry to miss you. Have you seen Dad?" Laurie asked.

"I try to come over every other day or so. He looks frail. He always says he feels fine. I took him out to lunch Monday."

"He does seem frail. But he never complains. Mom doesn't say much. She seems to think if she doesn't acknowledge it, it doesn't happen. I know she is worried though."

Nick said, "Yes, I asked her to go out one day and she wouldn't leave Dad, even though he told her to go. So how is everything with you?" he asked.

"You mean my love life?" Laurie said laughing. "Great. I am so lucky to have found someone so truly wonderful. Love is a good thing. You should try it."

"Maybe I will," Nick said.

"You almost sound like you mean it," Laurie said.

"It could happen," Nick said smiling enough to make Laurie suspicious. "I have to go. I just came to bring these things for Dad," he handed Laurie some books and magazines.

"Wait," she called to him as he turned toward the door. "What's up with you? Have you met someone?"

"I have met lots of someones," Nick said teasing.

"You know what I mean," Laurie said not giving up. "Are you back with Abbe? Are you and Abbe still 'a thing'?"

"A thing?"

"But you are seeing someone, aren't you? Abbe or someone else?" she further probed.

Nick shrugged refusing to answer.

"You are! Tell me," she begged. "Someone you work with?" she guessed.

"Laurie, give it up. Worry about your own love life and not mine." He leaned over and kissed her on the nose. "I have to go to work. I live to work!" he shouted as he went out the door.

Laurie watched out the window as Nick walked to his car. His phone had obviously rung for he put it up to his ear and he smiled. Something is up with him, Laurie said to herself.

On Saturday night Nick was at the door of Yumsters seating people when he heard a familiar voice. "I don't care where my table is, but I want a sexy waiter."

"Abbe! How are you? You look great."

"And so do you. I have missed you, Nick. When do you get off?"

"In about an hour," he answered.

"Can you meet me at the Omni? I have a taxi waiting to take me. I just got in from the airport. Emily said you were here."

"Sure."

Nick had the desk call Abbe when he arrived and she asked to have him sent up. She was standing at the door when he came off the elevator. She was in a pair of slacks with a silk shirt worn on the outside as if she had pulled it out from the waist band. She was barefoot and her hair was pulled back and tied with a ribbon. She threw her arms around Nick when he came inside. "I have missed you, Nicky!" she said. Nick didn't think she had ever called him "Nicky" before. She continued to keep her arms around him and kissed him, a deep passionate kiss. "Shall we talk first, or go to bed first and talk after?"

Nick smiled, "Let's talk. We have a lot to catch up on."

Abbe went over to the fridge and pulled out a bottle of Pinot Grigio she knew Nick liked. She handed it to him with an opener and went to get glasses. When she sat down on the sofa she summoned Nick to sit next to her with a look. He opened the bottle and poured the wine. When Nick sat down, Abbe crossed her legs and her foot crossed over his foot. "Cheers," he said. She repeated it. As soon as Nick took a sip of wine, she kissed him lightly again.

"Tell me what has been happening with you," Nick asked.

"Everything has been coming up roses, Nick," she said. "As you know, I have been working as Deputy Mayor in Harrisburg and they are going to run me as Attorney General and it seems like a shoo-in." She was grinning ear to ear. "My worthy opponent just got into a little domestic trouble. Seems he had a wife and a lover. Never a good combination. His wife says she has forgiven him, but he won't get many votes from women. I really seem poised to win."

"That's great Abbe."

"I'm on my way, Nicky. Finally! It is happening. I've been thinking," she said tentatively. "Since you aren't involved in a solid career right now, why don't you come to Harrisburg. I'll find something for you there and we can be together again. We're good together Nick. I'll prove it to you in a few minutes," she said seductively.

"Abbe," Nick began, "I am not a politician. I can't help you. We had a great run. I can't thank you enough for taking me to Washington with you. It was great for me. I needed it. I needed you. I'm grateful. But I have a life here now. It may not seem like much of a life to some but it is what I want. I like what I am doing. I am just now beginning to set out plans for my life here. I'm a late bloomer," he said.

"Well how about we have some pillow talk for old time sake?" she asked.

"I can't believe I am saying this but, I need to go. I can't say it isn't temping. But, it isn't fair for us to start something back up that we can't finish. Thanks Abbe. Good luck on your run for Attorney General. I'll be waiting to hear." He kissed her lightly and stood and walked to the door and waved as he left.

Abbe poured herself another glass of wine. She filled the glass to the brim. "To me," she said. Then she added, "To Nick, nicest guy in the world. You would never make it in my world, anyway."

On the way home in the car, Nick punched in a number. "Sorry, I know it is late. I just wanted to know how your day went."

Nick reached for his cell before he had opened his eyes. He rolled over and propped himself up with a pillow. "Hi, Mom," Nick said as soon as he saw her name come up on his phone.

"Hi, Nicky," Emily said softly.

"Anything wrong?" he asked concerned by the tone of her voice.

"We just took Calpurnia to the vet and he had to put her down. I hated to do it without telling you but she was in pain. You know she hasn't been well for so long. It's just that we should have told you to go with us."

"It's okay, Mom. I'm sorry you had to do that. I should have taken her for you. I'm sorry." Nick struggled to find the words to say to his mother. "I have been at loose ends lately. I'm sorry I haven't stopped in more. How is Dad doing?"

"About the same, I guess," she answered.

"Would you like another dog?" Nick asked. "Do you think a dog would be good for Dad. You know, company when he is resting?"

"Nick Millar, if you bring another dog into this house I will kill you. If you want a dog, you get a dog and take it with you. Do not get a dog and leave it with us!"

Nick grimaced, "Sorry Mom. I will not get you a dog."

"Good. Now what is going on with you?"

"Not much. I am working most evenings. I am still coaching basketball at the CYO. The kids are pretty young though. I would really rather work with teenagers. But by the time they are teens they either play at school or don't play at all. I went in to Holden one day and found some guys and played."

"Nick. You are going to get yourself killed just walking into neighborhoods armed with only a basketball. I thought we had an agreement that you were going to stay out of bad areas."

"We did?"

"You're hopeless," Emily said in disgust. Then she said cautiously, "One of the neighbors said she thought she saw you at the movies the other night—with a girl. Is that right?"

"Could have been," Nick answered without the details Emily was searching for. "Want to go to a movie this afternoon? I don't go in tonight until late."

"I can't go to a movie. I have to go to the grocery and run some other errands." Then she had a tinge of guilt and said, "Sorry, honey. Are you okay? You sound down."

"I'm fine, just have things on my mind. Tomorrow I am off after lunch. I'll stop in and see you and Dad if you are there. Don't stay home on my account though."

"Okay. I will be out for a while but your dad will be here."

"I need to talk to Dad anyway. Tell him I'll bring dessert."

I will, Nick. Love you!"

"Love you, Mom."

"Hi, Nick," Lillian said as he opened the door for her.

"How did it go?" he asked.

"He got six years for fraud," she said sadly. "I thought that would make me happy but it doesn't."

"You are a good person, Lillian. When does he go in?" Nick asked as he motioned for Lillian to come in and sit down on the sofa.

"I think they took him. I don't know anything about this stuff. Someone from his attorney's office told me they didn't think he would serve much time, if any. They made a deal. That's why he was sentenced so quickly. The prisons are crowded, he said, and they might let him out right away on parole since he isn't dangerous. I didn't talk to him. I just heard the judge say six years; then I left. What am I supposed to tell the girls?" Lillian asked but wasn't looking for an answer.

"I don't know. Will they hear from someone else? I always think it is better to tell someone myself instead of having someone else tell them," Nick answered. "Would you like me to go with you?" he offered.

"No. The girls are in Vermont for the week with my parents. What I would really like is to go to dinner with you. That's terrible of me isn't it? You are the only person I am comfortable with right now. I don't know what other people know or don't know. Are you busy?"

"Let me make a phone call. I'll be right back," Nick left and went in his bedroom and came out only a few minutes later. "Let's go out," he said. "Where would you like to go?"

"I don't care. Someplace big and noisy," she answered. "Are you sure this is okay? I feel I am taking advantage of your kindness."

"It is perfectly fine. How about City Tavern?"

"Great."

"Let me go change quickly. Even I won't go to City Tavern in a tee shirt. Give me a second," and Nick left the room. Soon he was back wearing a white knit shirt and blazer with chinos. He grabbed his car keys and they were out the door.

City Tavern was busy but they could easily fit in two for dinner. They were seated immediately. When the waiter came to the table for drink orders, Nick looked to Lillian. She ordered a glass of Riesling and he a light beer. "I may not be able to drive home," she said. "My car is at your place. Do you think I could stay again?"

"Sure," Nick answered. "Every time your husband is sentenced to prison, you can stay over at my house," he said with a smile.

"The first time, he avoided being sentenced," she said.

"Well, in those cases too," he said.

Before they had even had their appetizer, Lillian's phone vibrated. She picked up. She listened, said only a few words and hung up. She looked up at Nick. "He got out. Overcrowding. He will just have to report to a parole office they think. Or maybe wear an ankle bracelet. Well, it makes it easier on the girls I guess. I may not have to tell them anything. I think he will stay away from us anyway. I think," she said again less positive. She took another drink of her wine.

Chapter Twenty

Nick put his hand firmly on Annie's shoulder, almost at her neck, as he led her to the car. It was the most intimate he had ever been. He opened the door and closed it behind her. "So this play we are going to is a dinner theater?" she asked after he was behind the wheel. They were both dressed up; she in a ruby red dress with a matching sweater and heels and he in a blazer.

Nick explained, "You are assigned tables and there is a buffet. You eat your meal first and then the play starts. You stay at your table and watch the play. I think they might serve dessert during intermission. I don't remember," he said. "You'll like it. It's a musical, *My Fair Lady.* We talked about it once, remember?"

"I remember. It is about an uneducated, poorly-speaking woman that some guy tries to make over."

Nick looked at Annie and frowned. "It doesn't sound very good when you explain it like that. I thought you liked the movie."

"I sort of liked it, but it bothered me that this guy didn't really care anything about that girl. He just wanted to change her. It just occurred to me, is that what you want to do? Am I your project? Do you just want to help me learn to speak properly and get an education and then you will move on to another girl?"

Nick was shocked. "Annie, how can you say that? I care about you. I...." He was at a loss for words.

"Well," she began, "How would I know what you are doing. Maybe it is what priests do when they are no longer priests. We have been to dinner several times, lots of times, several movies, dancing at clubs, sometimes we take Angel places. We have been doing things, going places together for a pretty long time, in a way. Why? Why have you been doing all these things?"

Nick pulled into a parking lot and stopped the car, clearly frustrated. "I like to be with you," he answered simply. "I enjoy going places with you. I know I do introduce you to some new things but mostly that's because this is my home town. And I have maybe had some advantages and have experienced some things you haven't but I don't mean to make you feel uncomfortable. I'm sorry if it seems like that. I thought you liked to do those things." He bit his lip and waited for her to respond.

"Were you in love with the girl you went to Washington with?" Annie asked.

"No!" Nick quickly answered. "I liked her. She gave me a job and something to do when I needed to get away. I definitely wasn't in love with her."

"Is this a date?" she asked bluntly.

Nick paused and looked at her. "A date?" he repeated softly.

"You know, a guy asks a girl out. They go somewhere together. They hold hands sometimes. He takes her home and kisses her goodnight. I think that, is a date!" Annie looked at Nick, "Sometimes you do hold my hand. Sometimes you even kiss me on my forehead or cheek. Or nose! Once you kissed me on the nose! But I think on a date, a guy kisses the girl more passionately on the mouth than you ever do. I was just wondering, are we dating? Or are we palling around? Or, is this lab work? You know, are you testing me; seeing how I am doing by taking me out in public?"

Nick signed loudly. "Oh, Annie. I'm crushed that you can even think that. I'm crazy about you. I don't want to be with anyone but you. I don't think of us as pals and I certainly don't consider going out with you as lab work." Nick got very serious and looked directly at Annie and said, "I think I am in love with you, Annie. I know I am. But, I admit I'm scared. I'm afraid I will make a mistake and go too fast and lose you. I know you didn't really want a relationship right now. You wanted to get on your feet. And I guess because I am older than you and ready to settle down, I was trying to be cautious so I wouldn't scare you off."

"That's really funny. Liza Doolittle dumps the perfect, hunky guy. Like that would ever happen! Just tell me, don't you ever want to really kiss me? Don't you want to have sex with me?" She quickly added, "I know the first time we were going to have sex was weird, but don't you want to have sex with me now? I kinda owe you, if nothing else."

"Stop!" Nick shouted. "Don't ever say that. You don't owe me a damn thing, Annie. And I wouldn't have sex with you as payment for anything. That has been the whole point. I wanted us to have a new relationship that had nothing to do with how we met. You are a different person. I'm a different person. I'm crazy about you. One of the reasons I went to Washington was to get away from you. I didn't want to mess things up for you. You needed to get things straightened out and so did I. Yes, I damn well want to have sex with you. I have wanted to have sex with you ever since we met. But, I want you to want me. How can I make you understand that? I want you to want me," he repeated. He tried to calm down a bit. "Annie, sex is just sex. I want to make love to you; make love with you." Nick stared off for a minute and then turned and looked at Annie, "I'm not really in the mood for a play. I'll take you back to your apartment." He was silent for a moment and then he put his hand firmly on the back of her head and pulled her to him and kissed her passionately. Then he held her at arm's length, "Unless you want to go back to my apartment instead," he said looking at her.

Annie smiled and kissed him on the nose, "I thought you would never ask."

The door bell rang six times in rapid succession. Nick was reading a book and put it down to answer the door. Emily, Laurie, and Beau, were all standing there with Khiem Li and Kris in the background.

"Hey, what's up?" Nick asked somewhat surprised they were all there together.

"It's an intervention!" some of them shouted.

Nick looked at his dad as they were walking in and Kris said, "I'm only here for the beer."

Khiem Li also parted herself from the group and said, "I am not a part of this either."

Laurie, Emily, and Beau sat down on the sofa and chairs surrounding Nick. Khiem Li, physically separated herself from the party by pulling up a bar stool and sitting several feet away. When Kris came back in from the kitchen he handed out the beer and sat on a bar stool next to Khiem Li.

Laurie began, "The rules for an intervention are thus," she said trying to sound official. "We talk, you listen. You are not allowed to interrupt us. Got it?"

"No! What in the hell are you talking about? I have my drugs and alcohol under control," he joked. "I…" he started to say but Laurie took the floor again.

"Shut up!" Then she giggled. When they were children, they were not allowed to say "shut up" in the house. "We talk, you listen, remember?" she asked. Nick put his hands in the air in a captured prisoner sort of way.

She looked Nick up and down. "You are dressed up. You actually have on a shirt. And it is tucked in, and you are wearing a belt," she said rather amazed to see Nick not wearing a tee shirt and jeans. And he smells great, she said to herself; what up with him?

Laurie began again in a serious tone, "We are here to tell you that we have been patient, but no more. You have to get a real job! Working as a waiter just postpones looking for something and makes your resume look ridiculous. Shut up!" she said again as Nick started to say something. He took a long drink of beer from the bottle and stretched his long legs out in front of him. "You just can't be a waiter forever, Nick," Laurie said. "It is a part-time job for a college student or someone who is just waiting to do something else; like until they start school or something. It isn't a life-time occupation. At least it shouldn't be for someone with hundreds of degrees, like you." Nick didn't respond but Laurie was puzzled by the slight smile on his face. What is up with him, she asked herself. He's got something going on. He is moving out of town or …something. Maybe he does have a girlfriend. He only comes around to see Dad. He never comes for dinner or anything. He can't work that much, she thought. Oh my gosh! He hasn't joined another church, Episcopalian or something, so he could be a pastor, has he?? That would be just like him! Or would it? No, he would never do that. Laurie was truly puzzled.

Beau took over, "Look, man, you have got to get a job; a real job, bro. You've got to work forty hours a week in a place where you are around people! You can't stay holed up here." Beau paused and looked around the sparse room. "Where is your television, man? Don't you have a TV? Don't you even watch football?" Emily indicated by pointing that there was a small television behind Beau. He continued, "You have been out, you know, from the priest thing, for over a year or two. You should be sitting at the grownups' table now. Get a job. Work in an insurance office or something. You don't have to love it, man. You just have to work a forty-hour week, going in each day at the same time and getting off at the same time every day, like everyone else," Beau said.

"None of you do that," Nick said, meaning as professors, Beau and Khiem Li set their own hours around their classes and certainly did not work a forty hour week. Laurie was working a four-day week and Emily and Kris were retired.

Beau said, "Shut up!" Kris laughed and Khiem Li shook her head in disagreement with the group. Beau had said his piece so walked into the kitchen for something to eat. He shouted back in, "There is nothing to eat in here. Nothing!"

"I work in a restaurant," Nick answered back.

Obviously Beau was looking through the cabinets and he listed things off: "Cereal, kids' cereal I might add, graham crackers, soda crackers, peanut butter, and Fig Newtons, well at least that's something." He went on, "A can of peaches, lots of applesauce." He moved to the refrigerator. "In here he has milk, yogurt, string cheese; not much else. This is pathetic."

"I repeat, I work in a restaurant," Nick said slightly irritated.

Emily took over the intervention. "Honey, we want you to be happy." Nick started to say he was happy but she glared at him and he didn't say anything. "We are all worried about you." Then she looked at Kris and Khiem Li and amended it to, "Some of us are worried about you. We want you to have a ...fulfilled life. I have to agree with

Beau and Laurie. I think now you just need to get something full-time where you can meet people—not people who are telling you what they want for dinner. And you need a plan for your life. One job may lead to another. You are a well-educated person, Nick. And you are cute," she said as only a mother could say. "You need a wife and kids. You would be such a wonderful father, and husband," she added. "You are not getting any younger, Nick. You need to get married." Her tone got serious. "Abbe said you are the one that broke it off. I understand she may not be the one but, you'll never meet anyone working in Yumsters, Nick."

Before she could say anything else, there was a tiny knock at the door. Nick said under his breath, "Just in the nick of time." Khiem Li was closest to the door so she got up and opened it. There stood Annie and Angel. Annie was obviously surprised to see everyone there. She was taken aback and unsure of what to do.

"Hi," Annie said sheepishly. She stepped in the door but didn't move farther. She was dressed in slacks and long blouse that was belted. She had on a little makeup. It was a more sophisticated look than usual. She looked very attractive. "I'm sorry, I didn't know you all were here," she said self-consciously. Khiem Li closed the door and gave her a hug to make her feel accepted. Khiem Li took Annie's hand and led her into the room. Annie felt maybe she was interrupting something and was trying to decide what to do.

Emily said, "Annie, your braces are off! Your teeth look beautiful. We haven't seen you for so long. We heard you are in school and have an apartment." Annie smiled, somewhat embarrassed. They all welcomed her warmly and Angel ran to Nick and he picked her up as Annie walked over to him. Angel put her arms around his neck and gave him a toddler hug and then continued to lay her head on his chest, a little shy. The family was somewhat surprised that she was so comfortable with Nick. Still, Pippa loved being with Nick so it seemed reasonable that Angel did too.

"Are you all quite finished? May I talk now?" Nick asked.

"Sure," one of them said.

Nick turned to Annie and said, "I was just about to tell them about my new job but they wouldn't let me." Annie smiled at him. "Well," he began, "I happen to like the restaurant business and I am going to work with Marge for the next three months and she is going to train me in managing Yumsters." A quiet cheer went up and Nick said, "Shut up," more softly than the others had. He went on, "The reason she is training me is because she wants to sell the place and retire." He let that soak in and Emily started to say she was sorry Marge was leaving but Nick put his finger to his mouth to quiet her. "And I'm buying it." That took longer to soak in. "I have my trust fund money, I saw a lawyer and a banker, it is not a stretch, it is a good buy, and I like it," he strung together in one sentence. "So, there!" he said with a smile. One by one they each gave their congratulations saying they thought it a good plan. If Nick liked the restaurant business, this was wonderful, they thought. The perfect solution. Everyone was talking at once giving their thoughts and opinions.

They were all pleased for Nick. Beau and Laurie started to give suggestions on changes they thought he should make to the restaurant but Nick put his hand up to silence them once more. "I think now, Angel has something she wants to tell you," he looked at her and she grinned.

Angel looked up from Nick's chest and turned to face the group. "Mommy and I are going to marry Nick," she said with glee.

Nick put his arm around Annie's shoulder and waited for a reaction. They were all stunned; thrilled but stunned. No one said anything for a moment.

Emily was the first to move. She went to Annie and hugged her and then Nick. Suddenly Emily turned to Kris. He was standing back looking very happy. "You knew!" she said to him. He smiled. "You rat, you knew and didn't tell me." Kris walked over to Emily and put his arms around her. "I can't believe you knew and didn't tell me. You let us come over here and act like idiots."

"I did tell you I didn't think it was a very good idea," Kris said in his defense.

Emily turned to Khiem Li, "Did you know too?" she asked.

"No," Khiem Li answered. "I just didn't think coming over was a very good idea," she said smiling.

"Where, when?" Emily asked Nick and Annie.

"Soon," Nick answered. "In the Millar House chapel. Just family. And Tamika and Shaundra and whoever Annie wants from Millar House," he added. And then he said, "Well, I am not so sure about some of you guys. You may be busy anyway, 'intervening' in someone's life," he added with a smirk.

"Why did you let us go on like that, making fools of ourselves?" Laurie asked.

"It was fun," Nick replied, "and you are really good at it."

Emily looked at Nick and said, "There is no diamond on this woman's hand! I wouldn't expect you to be romantic, Nick, but I wouldn't expect you to be cheap either."

Everyone laughed. Annie spoke up, "Nick wanted to get me a diamond but I always thought it looked so great for couples to have matching gold bands; just simple bands. It was me! That was what I wanted," Annie said, taking culpability.

"Okay then, I think that is sort of classy too. Classic gold bands," Emily said thinking it over. Perfect for them, she thought. Perfect. The perfect rings for the understated couple.

"We already have them," Annie added. "But, Nick is romantic," she said in a forceful but small voice.

"This is great, son," Kris said. "I am happy for you both; all three," he amended. "I'll go get some more beer," he said and headed for the kitchen.

Nick said, "Dad, there are two magnums of champagne in the fridge drawer. Annie and Nick looked at each other and smiled. "We were actually going to tell you this weekend, but since you barged in here…," Nick trailed off.

"I'll help you with the champagne, Dad," Beau said and walked to the kitchen with Kris.

Annie looked at Nick and said, "I've never had champagne."

Emily insisted on taking Annie shopping for a trousseau. Annie tried to talk her out of it to no avail. Laurie went with them and the three spent the day having Annie try on clothes in every boutique and department store in Philadelphia and the suburbs. While it was true that Annie had very few clothes, and even fewer that she had actually purchased, instead of them having been given to her, she didn't want Emily to spend money on her. Emily convinced her that she did the same for all her girls and she insisted she do it for Annie. Besides, she said, one of them had to have some clothes and it didn't seem like it was going to be Nick. Even after all of the purchases of everything from lingerie to shoes, Emily was taking notes and planning to supplement further. Annie looked good in everything; so she was such fun to shop for, Emily thought.

Annie and Angel would move into Nick's apartment after they were married. Emily took that as a reason to do some decorating to the apartment but it was so small that not much could be done. Annie and Angel were living with Tamika and Shaundra in another apartment not much bigger. Annie had very few things to bring with her.

Nick moved his things from the tiny second bedroom he had been using as an office, and they moved Angel's bed and toys in there. Nick and Annie did let Emily decorate Angel's room, but she couldn't do much more than coordinate a valance and a bedspread in a princess theme and find some ways to decorate what little wall space there was with Disney prints. Emily finally decided to let the apartment be with these few changes, and then maybe someday, when they have a house she could be more "helpful." At least this is how she was trying to justify her participation to Kris.

Nick was sitting at the back of the chapel with his cell up to his ear when Kris, Emily, Laurie and Pippa came in. He was listening but not talking. He put his hand up to his forehead and then massaged his temples. He looked up at his dad. "Everything okay?" Kris asked. Nick made a face of disgust and taped his cell against his temple.

Pippa began dancing with Laurie and twirling and giggling so loudly that Angel heard her from the bedroom she and Annie were using to dress, and asked to come out of the room. Annie finally relented and Angel ran out of the room to play with Pippa. Angel and Pippa were in identical dresses; another one of Emily's ideas. The girls looked like darling flower girls, even though there were no formal bridal attendants. Just Kris, Emily, Laurie, Tamika, Shaundra and two other friends of Annie's were coming to the wedding but hadn't come into the chapel yet.

"What's wrong, Nick?" his mother asked tenderly. "Where is Annie?"

Nick motioned toward the hall. He turned off his phone and looked at his dad again and then put his elbows on his knees and rested his head in his hands. "Cold feet?" Emily asked. Nick didn't move or answer.

Kris looked from Nick to Emily. It took all of his energy to walk up the sidewalk to Millar House. Emily tried to get him to sit down. "I'll go talk to her," he said. Nick didn't move.

Kris walked slowly to the room Annie was using to dress, and tapped lightly on the door, saying, "Annie, it's Kris. May I talk to you a minute?"

"Okay," she answered softly but didn't come to the door. Kris turned the knob and opened the door to find Annie sitting on the edge of the bed in the pale-blue sheath dress she had chosen with Emily for the ceremony. Her size five shoes were on the floor in front of her. She was holding a piece of tissue that had shredded in her hand. A ribbon for Angel's hair lay curled on the bed. Kris sat next to her and pulled her to him. She rested her head on his chest and he patted the back of her head, smoothed her hair and then kissed her on the head. Finally, she looked up and into his eyes. She tried to smile.

"Annie," Kris said, "if you don't want to marry Nick, you don't have to. No one is going to make you. If you aren't in love with Nick, certainly his mother and I don't want you to marry him. You shouldn't marry him. It wouldn't be fair to Nick either. If that is the case; if you are not in love with Nick, I will go tell him for you. Nick will get over it. He is an adult. If this isn't right, it shouldn't happen."

Kris stopped talking and rubbed Annie's shoulder as he now had his arm around her. They sat for a moment and Kris began again.

"But, if you do love him, is there something stopping you from going in there to him, because he is confused and worried and maybe hurt? Can you tell me? Or, if you want, I will go get Nick and have him come back here and you can tell him." Kris cupped her chin in his hand. She looked so fragile and young. "No matter what it is, it will be okay Annie."

Finally Annie said, "Nick is the most wonderful person in the entire world. Any woman would be crazy not to marry Nick. But," she stammered, "I think maybe he shouldn't marry *me*. I have a child. He should have his own children. It is a package deal if he marries me. Do you know about me?" she asked directly.

"I know Nick loves you," Kris answered. "I know Nick could marry any of a number of women and he wants to marry you."

"But do you know about me?" she repeated. "Do you know how we met?" Annie knew how close Kris and his son were and honestly wondered if Nick had told him.

"No. But I don't need to know. That is all between you and Nick. No one else needs to know anything that is private between the two of you. And, Nick has a big family. And we are pretty invasive. So it is a package deal for you too." Kris paused and looked at Annie intently and asked, "Are you in love with my son?"

A tear ran down Annie's cheek and she wiped it away with her shredded tissue. She took a big breath. "I don't know how love feels," she stated simply. She looked at the floor. Kris waited for her to go on. He continued to pat her without either talking. Finally she looked up. "How would I know what love feels like?" she asked rhetorically. Then she said, "My stomach turns over every time I hear his voice on the phone or see him walk into a room."

Kris smiled and nodded his head in agreement, "My stomach still flips when I see Emily or hear her voice."

Annie said softly, "When we aren't together, I look at the clock and try to imagine what he is doing and then I count up how long it will be until we will be together again." Annie finally smiled, "When we are together, just reading or watching a movie, I never want the moment to end. But when he does leave, I can almost feel the warmth of his body still sitting next to me and I remember what he smells like."

She finally jumped out of her trance and amended, "I can smell his soap and shampoo. Do you know what I mean?" she said embarrassed.

"I do," Kris answered. "I really do, Annie."

"But, maybe I pushed Nick into this. I don't know. This is like a fairy tale. It doesn't seem real. My life has never been like this. My life is never anything like this." She paused and looked up at Kris, "I am not like you and Nick. I'm not good like Nick. Nick is so wonderful. He's so smart and well educated. He deserves a smart well-educated woman. I'm just not good enough for him. I really don't think I am," she said softly.

"But he does!" Kris said. "Annie, don't put yourself down. You are smart! And you are getting an education! I think Nick is incredibly proud of you. And we all see what a wonderful mother you are, how hard working, and tenacious; not to mention cute as a button and funny as hell." He smiled. "I think Nick thinks he is incredibly lucky to have found you." Annie took a big breath. "The point is, Nick has no doubts and is ready to make a lifetime commitment to you. The question is, are you ready to make a lifetime commitment to him? It is a big deal, and it is up to you, Annie. It's your choice. You are in charge of your life. No one is going to make you do anything you don't want to do. No one. Not any more, Annie. You are a strong person. You get to decide. Only you know what is best for you and Angel. Don't worry about Nick. Nick can take care of himself."

Annie and Kris walked into the chapel with Annie holding on to his arm. There was no music, no flower girl throwing rose petals. Just Kris walking Annie to meet up with his son. Nick stood up and turned to face her. Nick was sure his heart was going to beat out of his chest. Kris took her hand and placed it in Nick's. They walked together to the altar and the family and friends followed. Pippa and Angel stood between Emily and Laurie wide-eyed as they watched Nick and Annie say their vows.

There was a small reception at Kris and Emily's house that evening. It was mostly family and a few family friends. Mandy and Alison came but Mike and his wife were unable. Beau, Keim Li and some of their family was there. John and Janey came, and Marge was there as a guest and some other friends from Yumsters, as well as Annie's friends from Millar House and a few neighbors. There was food in the dining room as well as outdoors and most of the party ended up being on the patio and in the garden. They did not have much time for a honeymoon because Annie was about to start her last quarter in culinary school and Nick was soon to take over the restaurant. There were so many places that Nick wanted to take Annie he had trouble deciding. Finally, he chose a few days in New York City.

Chapter Twenty-One

Nick and Annie stayed at the Plaza in New York for their honeymoon. It was Emily and Kris's wedding gift. They went to a musical. They took the Staten Island Ferry to see the Statue of Liberty. Nick called it the poor man's tour. They shopped and ate in a different restaurant each meal. For lunch one day they had corned beef at the Carnegie Deli. Annie loved it. She even loved the rude waiters. One night, there was a beautiful buffet in one of the Plaza ballrooms and they dressed and went down. Annie was overwhelmed with the array of food. They looked at the trays of various appetizers and then the crab legs, lobster rolls, boiled shrimp, and oysters at the seafood table and proceeded on to the salad bar, carving station and huge dessert table and wondered where to begin. "I want to start with something light," Annie said. "I want to take a long time to eat and don't want to fill up quickly. You choose," she said. "Just give me a taste of something I have never had to begin.

Annie sat down and Nick walked around the room looking at the wonderful variety of food. Keeping her request for something light, he made his selection and took it back with two forks to the table. Annie closed her eyes and Nick carefully put a small forkful in her mouth. She continued to have her eyes closed while she savored its goodness. Finally, she said, "It is wonderful. What is it?"

"Soufflé," he answered.

"How do you spell it?" she asked. "I want to write it down." Nick smiled.

"A soufflé," Annie said dreamily. "I've never had soufflé. I thought about putting it on my list of things to try some day. I just never thought I would actually get to."

When Nick and Annie arrived back from their honeymoon, Nick called his mother as soon as they got into the apartment. "Hey, it's Nick. How is everything going?" he asked.

"Nicky, now don't go crazy on me, but your dad is in the hospital. We are all with him and I think you and Annie should come. Angel is at Beau's house with one of the kids. Pippa is there with her."

"Is Mike there?" Nick knew that was the test of how serious the problem was.

"Yes, and Mandy and Alison."

"When did this happen, Mother." His frustration was beginning to show.

"He has been here for three days, but he told me not to call you, Nick. Kris was adamant that no one was to call you. He is getting weaker and weaker, but I think he is waiting for you Nicky." Emily couldn't talk anymore. She handed the phone to Beau.

"Sorry, bro. We couldn't call. He wouldn't let us. Come on now though. I know he wants to see you. He has had some time with each of us. Mom just went in to tell him you are on your way."

Nick grabbed a bottle of water and he and Annie jumped in the car and drove to the hospital. Indeed, everyone was there. Nick couldn't remember the last time that was true. All six Millar children were in the same room. Nick was told to go in as soon as he got there. He took Annie's hand and took her in with him. They both hugged Emily and Annie kissed Kris on the cheek. He squeezed her hand. Then Emily took her back out with her, leaving Nick alone with his father.

"I didn't want to interrupt your honeymoon," Kris said with some effort. Nick tried to stop him from talking at all but he had things to say. "I have talked everyone else," he said. "I have been waiting for you." Kris took his hand and put it on the side of Nick's face affectionately. "I'm okay with this, you know. And I know you should be okay with it too. The two of us have a greater understanding of it. It will be hard on your mother. I know you and the rest of the family will help her. Especially you Nick," he added. Kris closed his eyes for a minute before going on. Then he began again.

"I have been so blessed, Nick. I have had wonderful friends over the years and incredible children. I fathered four sons, Mike, Beau, Geoff, and you. Each of you is as different as day is to night. But, you have similarities too. I am sorry you didn't know Geoff. He was gentle, like you Nick. I have been thinking about him a lot lately. I have had lots of time to think about each of you and how incredibly proud I am to be your father. The most amazing thing about the six of you with me now, is how well you all get along and always have. Mike and Beau had a different mother, Alison and Mandy had a different father, and you and Laurie are the product of Emily and me. But, you each have so much love and respect for one another and for me and Emily. It is overwhelming." Nick tried to interject that it was due to Kris but Kris continued on. "I have had some time with each of you. I am fortunate that I have had the time to tell each of my children how I feel about them."

Nick bit his lower lip and didn't take his eyes off his father. "I love you," he whispered.

"You have always been incredibly special, Nick. I know it sounds trite or patronizing, but I really mean it. Honestly, son, you have a gift. You have the heart of a servant; a disciple; a kind and loving soul. I had a dream about you the other night and you were washing feet. There was a long line of shabbily dressed people and you blessed each one and washed their feet. I got in line and you washed mine too. You never looked up at me. I wanted to tell you that it was me and you didn't have to wash my feet but you just nodded your head and continue to wash them." Kris paused before going on.

"I know it was difficult for you to return home after leaving the priesthood. As in everything else you have done, you have re-entered our lives with so much grace and love. We can barely remember not having you here with us, you are such an integral part of our lives now. When I see the things you do as a layman, I have no doubt that you are where you have been called to be. I am so proud of you. And I am incredibly happy that you and Annie are together. You deserve to be happy. So does Annie. Annie is a phenomenal young woman. You literally 'found' her and changed her life. But, I can see that she 'found' you too when you were lost. You are meant for each other, I am sure of it." Kris seemed to rest for a minute before continuing. He closed his eyes and then opened them and looked directly at Nick. "Now I want to ask you to do something."

"Anything," Nick was able to utter.

"I want you to give me Last Rites." Nick started to protest but Kris stopped him. "I know you can. I asked a priest. He left things for you," and he nodded toward the table.

"You are the one who taught me the difference between 'can' and 'may', Dad," Nick said with difficulty. "'May' means you have permission. And yes, I may perform The Anointing of the Sick under some circumstances. But 'can' means you are able. I don't think I am able, Dad." The words caught in his throat.

"Yes, you are. You'll be fine."

And so he did. The words swirled in his head. Penance, Absolution, Eucharist, Viaticum. He spoke. He heard himself say the words he had said before. Never did he think he would say them again, especially for his father. It seemed unreal. He chanted the words but his thoughts were elsewhere. The communion is the provision for the journey. For the journey. My God, my father is about to die. How can I do this? How can I?

When he concluded, Kris asked him to get Emily and come back with her. Again Nick did as he was told. Emily came in and sat on the edge of the bed and Nick stood behind her. "I love you," Kris said to his beloved wife.

"And I am mad at you," Emily said flirtatiously. "You are always making me do something I don't want to do. When we first met, you made me run a mini marathon. Do you remember? You said it would be fun, but it wasn't. It was miserable. I couldn't walk for two days. Then you made me have these rotten children. I had already had two kids and I had to start over with another two. And now," she stopped to wipe away a tear, "you are going to leave me here and make me go

187

on without you. And you are going to say I will be fine. But I won't. I won't."

Kris smiled, patted her hand and said, "Yes, you will. You'll be fine. I promise."

The evening after the funeral mass, the family had a reception for close friends and family. Nick walked up to the podium and began, "Welcome. On behalf of the Millar family, I welcome you. I am Nick, the youngest and favorite son." Michael and Beau booed him. Nick laughed and continued. "Actually, I was chosen to speak to you today because I was out of town when they had the vote." Now Mike and Beau applauded. "We are here today to celebrate Dad's life. We have promised it would be a joyous occasion, not somber or sad. Dad was the first to say he had a wonderful life, not without obstacles and heartbreak, but he said the good far outshone the bad. We are to celebrate.

First let me introduce those of us who were privileged to call him Dad and then when we all mingle in a while, you will know who we are. Michael is the eldest and he is with his wife Alice. Mike and Alice waved. Their two daughters were unable to come today and are in California. Beau is next and his wife is Kheim Li. They waved. They have six children and they are all with us today. And two grandchildren Chloe and Chelsea are here. Maybe Beau is the most like Dad after all." The audience laughed. Nick went on with the introductions. "Alison is next and her husband is Brent and her sons Kris and Mike. Then it is Mandy and her husband David." All showed they were present. "Mandy and David have four girls: Ella, Beth, Sonja, and Trudy. Sonja has a son, Troy, and Beth has a daughter Nichole. It is a good thing I have notes," Nick confessed. "I'm next, and my wife of two weeks is Annie," he smiled unabashedly. "With Annie is her daughter, Angela; soon to be my daughter." Annie smiled shyly and Angel nestled close to her mother but didn't take her eyes off Nick. "And last but certainly never least, Laurie, our little sister and the baby of the family. She is with her fiancée Sahid and her daughter Pippa." The audience looked appreciatively at the family.

"As you might have imagined, we do not all get together that frequently. If nothing else, this has been an opportunity for the siblings to be with one another and talk about Dad and our respective childhoods. Earlier we were discussing how tough Dad was. We all agreed; he really was a strict disciplinarian. We were each telling about times we had been in trouble. My story is that one day I borrowed Dad's car when I had just started driving. That afternoon I had to come home and tell him that I had parked in a no parking zone and the car had been booted! When I saw that big ugly yellow boot clamped to Dad's car when I got to it, I was scared to death. I knew he was going to freak out—and he did. He sat me down and lectured me for what seemed like hours, with words like *irresponsible* and *undependable,* coming up more than once. The word *stupid,* which was a word we were not even allowed to use in our house, may even have been uttered. He was furious. I was devastated and that wasn't even the punishment. I was grounded for two weeks, not allowed to drive. Once Dad said something it was a waste of effort to try to get him to change it. It was written in stone. And I knew that he would not relent just because the homecoming dance was that weekend. I would have to find someone to drive me and my date." Nick paused, "Now that I think about it, I think my date drove. And never dated me again, I believe." Nick smiled.

"Anyway, Dad gave me hell. When he was finished, I started to go to my room to decompress and try to get back some tiny piece of dignity after being verbally demoralized. When I started to leave, he shouted out, 'Where are you going?' I mumbled something inarticulate, and he said, 'Let's go play some hoops.' That was Dad. He beat you up, figuratively, and then it was over. He forgave you.

We went outside and played hoops and a while later he asked me if I thought having the boot on the tire, hurt the tire in any way. I said I didn't know. He then told me a few months previously, he had overstayed a parking meter and they had booted the same tire. I was in shock. He had torn me apart and he had done the same thing. So I said, 'And you weren't even grounded.' He laughed and said that in a way he was. That he didn't play golf for a month! Again that was Dad. He rigorously believed in discipline, even self-discipline, and maybe we are all the better for it. So, the glasses are charged. Let's drink the first toast to Dad and the lessons he taught each of us. The toast is, 'To Kris.'" Each person in the room raised their glass and said, "To Kris."

Nick then began again. "The next toast will be to my mother because in the last thirty-five years or so, you can't think of my dad without including my mother. My mother has made it very clear that she absolutely wants no pity. She wants no one to say 'poor Emily'. She told me a story that her mother-in-law, my father's stepmother, Laura, told her. Laura was one of those people who could remember where she was the moment she found out that John F. Kennedy had been killed. Laura was a big Kennedy supporter and was devastated by his death. But, when someone said something about 'poor Jacqueline' she lit into them. 'Do not feel sorry for Jacqueline Kennedy,' she said. 'Be sad, she has lost her husband, but remember—she was married to the most wonderful man in the world, if even for a short time and had his children. So do not feel sorry for her.' Mom says that is exactly her situation and please do not feel sorry for her either." Nick smiled warmly at his mother. "The toast is to Emily."

"To Emily," the guests said in unison. The family milled around in the crowd and met and talked to each guest, and listened to stories they each told of Kris. Many remembered Mike and Beau as children and the loving live-in, Grace, who lived with them for several years and helped Kris with the boys when they were small. Grace passed away several years ago as had David, Kris's old college roommate who began his career at University the same day as Kris. Many remembered Geoff, Kris's son killed at eighteen. No one mentioned his ex-wife, the mother of his sons. Carol was not a part of the boys' lives from early on. Kris had the responsibility of parenting the children on his own. Many people remembered when Kris and Emily married and Emily's two girls who were teenagers, and lived with them in the house. They laughed at how Kris had to change gears from raising boys to living in an all female household. And most everyone there remembered when Nick and Laurie were born and how happy Kris and Emily were with this new family they had created together. Kris's life indeed was a long and happy one.

Later, the family was all at Emily and Kris's house. Most had changed into more comfortable clothing. Beau and Mike called to Nick, from the kitchen that they were going out to play touch football. Nick was wearing only a tee shirt and it was getting colder outside, so he ran upstairs to find something to wear over his tee. In his parents' room he saw a University of Pennsylvania Hospital sweatshirt on a table. He pulled it on and ran back down stairs.

Emily, Laurie, Annie and Khiem Li were all in the kitchen beginning to put together some leftovers for snacks. Emily turned white when she saw Nick enter the room. She walked to him. "Take that off," she screamed. "Take it off. It isn't yours!" she hurled at Nick. She grabbed the front of the sweatshirt with both hands and crumpled it in her fist. She pulled on it as she again demanded, "Take it off!"

Nick was in shock. He stared at his mother as he pulled the sweatshirt over his head and started to undo the arms which had turned inside out. Before he could, Emily snatched it and pulled it to her with her arms wrapped around it. They all looked at her in disbelief. "I'm sorry, Mom. I'm sorry," Nick said with great sympathy and confusion. No one else said anything.

Finally, Annie walked up to Emily and faced her and put her arms around her, Emily still hugging the sweatshirt. "It's okay," she whispered as if to a child. "It's okay."

Emily put her head on Annie's shoulder. "It is all that's left," she said. They all looked at her confused.

But, Annie patted her and said, "It smells like Kris doesn't it?"

Emily shook her head. "I am so afraid the smell will go away. I slept with it last night. It is all that's left," she said again sadly. Then she began to sob for several minutes. No one spoke but let her release the pain. In a while, she started to regain her composure. "I didn't want to do this," she complained. "I wanted to stay strong. I promised myself I wouldn't do this."

Nick went to her and put his arms around both Annie and Emily. "Mom, you need to do this. This is the right thing to do."

"I can hardly look at you," Emily said to her son as she became more composed. "You have his eyes. You have those incredible eyes; and his long legs. And your hands are just like his. Your fingers are so long." Finally, she said, "It's stupid. I'm sorry. I think I am going insane."

Nick pulled back and smiled at his mother. "You aren't going insane. You are starting to grieve." He gave her a mischievous look. "I'll get brown contacts. And stoop. And wear gloves," he said smiling at her. "Hey, Mike, after the game leave Mom your sweatshirt. It will smell like you. I have one in the dirty clothes hamper you can have too, Mom."

"You have his wicked sense of humor too!" Emily said as she righted herself and blew her nose. I guess the sweatshirt isn't all that's left of him." Then she added with obvious sarcasm, "It's just the best part." She patted Nick's face. "Don't you dare get brown contacts!"

Chapter Twenty-Two

Three months after Nick and Annie's wedding, Laurie married Dr. Sahid Ahimil and the family welcomed him warmly. "You did good," Nick told his sister in the vernacular. "How did we get so lucky?"

"Thanks for standing up with me, Nick. I miss Dad, but I love it that you were here for me."

"Always!" Nick proclaimed.

Laurie and Pippa moved into Sahid's condo until the house they were building could be completed. Emily insisted that Laurie move out and that she would be fine on her own. Nick stopped in to see Emily nearly every day on his way to the restaurant or on the way home. Emily did some travel. She and her sister went to Hawaii for two weeks and she traveled to see Alison and Mandy and their families more frequently than she had before. She stayed busy with Millar House, played bridge, and kept up with old friends. Not that she didn't miss her husband and grieve; she did. But, per his instruction, she got on with life.

Annie finished up her culinary certificate and Nick and Annie became co-owners of Yumsters. There was a very small apartment above the restaurant that had been used mainly for storage. Nick had it cleaned out and redecorated into a place where Angel could be nearby with one of them or a sitter from the university if they had to be working. It turned out to be a darling little girl's apartment. Nick called it 'The Playhouse'. Either Nick or Annie could run up and see Angel or have a meal with her; Annie worked on the menus there. There were lots of toys, a little table and chairs, books and crayons, a play kitchen, and a little bed in the playhouse. The back yard was fenced and Angel played out there in good weather. The staff loved to play with Angel and she was friendly and sweet to everyone, but Nick was her absolute favorite.

The transition of ownership was easily established. The customers knew Nick and there was no noticeable difference in patronage the first few months. Nick did work with his wait staff on his philosophy of how to be a good waiter. "First," he told them, "you should tell the customer that as their waiter, you will walk around to their table frequently. But, you will try not to be a bother by constantly coming up to them, possibly interrupting conversation, asking if they need anything. Should they need something, they need only to glance in your direction and you will approach them. Furthermore," he instructed, "you need to explain to the customer that any waiter can get something that they may want if their personal waiter is not immediately available to them. The entire staff is at the disposal of the customer."

"Secondly," Nick said, "the menu is to be explained as flexible. Accompaniments to meals are merely suggestions and can be switched for any on the menu, as are salad dressings. If they are unsure of which dressing they might like; the waiter should bring more than one. Each diner should feel they are creating their own meal if they wish. Wine will be served in half portions as well as full glasses. Some people don't feel they should have a second glass of wine," he explained, "but a half glass might finish off a meal nicely." Another policy that Nick felt strongly about was not clearing the table until everyone had finished eating. Nick was a slow eater himself, and he disliked it when dishes were whisked away while he was still eating his meal. He did not want that to happen to his diners unless it was requested.

"Lastly, the old adage that 'the customer is always right' is right," he told them. "If the diner says something is not good, accept their opinion and get them something else. Furthermore," Nick told his staff, "do not to let anyone go away unhappy. If there seems to be any concern that you don't feel comfortable answering, get me and I will handle it." He added that if anyone did not feel comfortable acquiescing to the whims of the customer, then perhaps they should work at another restaurant. They had very little turnover of staff.

Annie got pregnant in the spring. She had a good pregnancy, rarely complained. She enrolled in two college classes. She decided to pursue a degree, though she claimed she would be eighty before she finished. She loved working at Yumsters. Everyone loved Annie. As her pregnancy progressed, people stopped in just to see if she had delivered yet. She looked enormous. She was such a tiny person, that Nick said she looked as if she had swallowed a watermelon. Her water broke just as they were closing one night and Nick drove her to the hospital. Angel was picked up by Laurie.

Labor was long and difficult. After nine hours there had been little progress. Eleven hours and labor had nearly stopped. The decision was made to do a C Section. Nick walked with Annie on the way to delivery but stopped outside to let the family know what was going on.

"I hate this," Nick told his mother. "No more children. I can't stand to see her in such pain." He wished his dad were there to explain things and be with him through it all. "Annie is great, I'm the one who is no good at this," he complained.

"Nick, she'll be fine. Now it will go quickly. They will give her medication and she won't be in pain," his mother explained. "I thought you had been trained to spend time in hospitals, Nicky. I thought you spent time with people in their greatest need," she teased.

"I hate it," he said again. "And I was never trained to see my wife go through this."

The next time he talked with her he was totally euphoric. "It's a boy," he said with pride. "He's seven pounds, ten ounces. But Mom, he is nearly twenty-two inches long! He's nearly as tall as she is," he exaggerated. "Annie's fine but exhausted. They are going to take her in and let her sleep. She is already pretty out of it."

"What is his name?" Emily asked. Neither Annie nor Nick wanted to know the gender before the birth, but Nick was adamant that Annie should choose the names. Kris told Nick he always thought the mother should name the babies because they did all of the work. That sounded right to Nick. Annie took it one step further, however, and wouldn't tell Nick the names she had decided on. They did talk about names and agreed that they liked some more than others. Annie didn't want to name the baby after Nick or Kris. She didn't think it was fair for one child to have the name of a parent or someone special and not another. She didn't want Angel to have any hard feelings about the new baby.

"I don't know," Nick answered. "Annie didn't tell me. She wanted to surprise me. We will have to wait until she wakes up," he said.

"You should tell Angel about the baby. I'll put her on," Emily said.

Nick waited until he heard Emily put the phone up to Angel's ear. "Angel you have a baby brother," Nick said.

"A Matthew," Angel said clearly. "I have a baby Matthew."

"Matthew?" Nick asked. "How do you know that, Angel?"

"Mommy told me. It was our secret from you, Daddy. He is going to be Matthew like in the Anne book."

Emily took the phone back. "Matthew? Do you think that's right, Nick."

"Yes, it makes sense. He's Matthew like in *Anne of Green Gables*. I told Annie she was like Anne, funny and talkative and she told me I was like Matthew Cuthbert, the old guy who was so nice to Anne. It's kind of a joke, but it makes sense. That way she could name him after me. Only Annie!" he exclaimed with true admiration.

When Annie woke, she confirmed the name Matthew. She chose David for a middle name because she liked the story of David slaying the giant. She wanted her son to know he could do anything, no matter his size.

"Are you getting any sleep?" Emily asked as soon as Nick answered the phone.

"Yes," was his one word answer.

"You are? How is that possible? Nicky, don't tell me you don't help out with the middle of the night feedings."

"Mom," Nick said defeated, "I don't wake up. Annie jumps up when he starts to open his mouth to cry. She is afraid he will wake

Angel. I tell her to wake me but she doesn't. She says it will take too long to get me to wake up. Now, are you happy? I feel like a heel." Then he added, "And don't tell me how Dad got up in the night every night. He was a doctor, he never slept or something. I do try to help out during the day," he said apologetically.

"Where are you now?" Emily asked.

"I'm at the restaurant but Tamika is going over to be with Annie this afternoon and she is taking Shaundra to occupy Angel. She said she would try to get Annie to nap, but she won't. She would rather sit and talk with Tamika. That's restful, I guess." Then Nick thought about it and said, "Annie will probably be baking cookies or something for the kids instead of resting."

"She will be fine. Annie's a jewel, Nick. You know we all love her don't you?"

"How could you not, Mom. She is amazing."

"She is amazing, Nick. I have never seen anyone make such a turnaround as Annie. She was homeless. She had been abused. She had very little education. Now you would think she had graduated from Bryn Mawr. I am so happy that you two found each other, Nick."

"God is good, Mom. Gotta go. Talk to you later."

Sometime later, Emily called Annie. "Annie, Nick says he sleeps in while you take care of the baby, is that right?" she teased.

Annie laughed, "According to Nick, he doesn't do anything at the restaurant either. He just doesn't want anyone to know how good he is at cooking or taking care of the baby. He's great, Emily. He does everything there and at home. He is fantastic with Angel. She adores him. He was up all night with her the other day when she was sick. She calls him when she wants something, not me. But, I have food so Matthew calls me!" she said jokingly. "There could not be a better father than Nick. I know Kris was wonderful but Nick ranks right up there. And remember he has not had the experience that Kris had. Nick is learning on the fly. He's amazing."

"It must be love, he said the same thing about you," Emily told her.

Emily invited Nick, Annie and the kids to dinner one Sunday evening. It was the kind of meal Nick remembered as a child: chicken and noodles, vegetables, and trifle she had learned to make because his dad liked it. Matthew, of course, slept through the meal and nursed later. Emily loved to cook for the family. Emily had on black jeans and a silver blouse belted at the waist. Even now in her advancing years, she was petite and perfectly groomed. Nick sensed that his mother wanted to tell them something and she finally was able to get it out. "I want to move into a senior condo," she explained. "I don't like rattling around in this house by myself. So here's the deal. I move out and you guys move in. That way we keep the house in the family. Got it?" she asked as if there should be no questions.

"Well," Nick said trying to take it all in. "That would be wonderful, but there are others who maybe would like to live in this house. It is their birthright as much as mine," he said. "I can't take this house," he said with finality. Then he added, "What about primogeniture?" Emily and Annie looked at him blankly. "Historically, the oldest son inherits everything, not the youngest," he explained.

"It has already been agreed. Everyone wants you to have it. Your dad wants you to have it. He told me."

"Recently?" Nick asked flippantly.

Emily looked at Annie. "How do you keep from whacking him sometimes? Before he died, Kris told me he thought you should have this house. He talked to all the kids. Everyone is living in a house they love. They all got started a little before you did. This is your house, Nick. Everyone wants you to have it."

Nick made phone calls to all the family to check things out and make sure there would be no hard feelings in this transaction. But no one objected. Actually, everyone was in favor of it because it would keep the house in the family. So, in a few months, Annie and Nick and the two children moved into Nick's childhood home. They asked Emily to live with them but she wouldn't hear of it. She had already signed a lease for a condo. The location of the house was perfect for them; so near the restaurant and the school. And Nick loved this house. Nick didn't want to move into the master suite that had been his parents, on the main floor. Besides, they reasoned, they wanted to be on the same floor as the children, so they moved into one of the bedrooms upstairs and made the downstairs bedroom a playroom. They spent the next few weeks redecorating, not because they didn't love it as it was, but because Emily insisted that they redecorate. She helped Annie choose things, making sure they were Annie's choice and not hers. Annie has good taste, Emily thought. She likes things of quality and fairly conservative styles and colors. The two women spent many afternoons together making plans and finding just the right lamp, rug, clock, or whatever to finish off a room. The grand piano was to stay. Only Nick played and Emily wanted to hear him occasionally. Nick and Annie hoped that their children would one day want to play also.

Chapter Twenty-Three

T he door bell rang just as Annie was coming home from the grocery, entering through the kitchen. She went through the house and got to the front door as the bell rang for the second time. Upon opening the door, she saw an attractive woman standing with a cake on a plate in her hands. "Hi," she said. "I'm Stacie Martin. I live over on Blanchard and just wanted to welcome you to the neighborhood. I've known Nicky forever," she said with a flirtatious look. "When I heard he got married and moved back into the house, I couldn't wait to meet you."

"Please come in. I'm Annie," Annie said as she motioned for Stacie to enter. "This is so nice of you. Please come into the kitchen and have a cup of coffee or tea with me," she said sweetly. Stacie followed still carrying the cake. Annie motioned for Stacie to sit at the table. She sat and put the cake on the table. "Tea or coffee?" Annie asked.

"Coffee," Stacie answered. "I'm not pregnant, so I celebrate by having caffeine," she said laughing. "I have four children," she explained. "And my husband is a devout Catholic, like Nick." Then she thought about what she said. "Well, not like Nick. He wasn't a priest. I just mean. You know what I mean." She laughed. "I talk a lot. But I'll stop. Tell me about you, Annie. I am so thrilled Nick fell in love and got married. And I am so, so, glad you guys moved in here. Now I'll stop. Tell me about you."

Annie liked Stacie already. "Well," Annie said, "I haven't had lunch and would love to have a piece of this Angel Food cake. Will you join me?" Stacie nodded eagerly. "I have some strawberries in the refrigerator. What would you think of me making a little sauce to go with it; sound good?"

Annie threw together some strawberries, a berry jam, dried cranberries, and a little orange juice in a small sauce pan and in a few minutes the women were having a slice of cake with a warm sauce artistically poured over it. Stacie was impressed. "I have never tasted anything so wonderful. Maybe you could write that down and I could serve that to my mother-in-law on Sunday."

"Sure," Annie said. "And if you could give me your recipe for Angel Food cake, we will be even."

Stacie laughed. "Trader Joe's! You take it out of the package and put it on a plate. I'm sorry, I'm no cook. I'm friendly though, you have to admit. Obviously, Nick knew what he was doing marrying you and buying a restaurant. Everyone is talking about Yumsters and how great it is. We haven't been since you guys took over. I intend to go now though." She barely paused before continuing, "The four of us will have to get together soon. My husband is Greg. He's an actuary. Do you know what they say about actuaries?" she asked. She went on, "Actuaries are accountants but without the personality." She laughed. "Greg is sweet though. Nice guy. He isn't from here either. He is from Ohio. Anyway, let's put something on the calendar. Maybe weekend after next. I will need some fresh company after my mother-in-law leaves."

"Let me make the sauce for you," Annie said. "I'll make it on Saturday and you can pick it up and warm it up on Sunday."

Just then Nick came in the back door carrying the sleeping Mathew in a pumpkin seat and Angel balanced on his hip. "Stacie, great to see you," he said and gave her a hug. He walked back and put his hand on Annie's shoulder and she took Angel in her arms. "I'm glad you've met Annie."

"I'm the lucky one. I may have found my own personal caterer. Annie, I just thought, the first Wednesday of the month I get together with two other women I know you will like. Will you meet with us? We go out for lunch. We used to play tennis once a week but it didn't work out very well with just the three of us and even at that, one or two of us was always pregnant and couldn't play. Do you play tennis?" she added in one breath while making over the children.

"I would love to meet your friends," Annie answered. "I don't play tennis but would like to learn. Maybe I could take some lessons and then play," she looked at Nick as she answered.

When Stacie left, Annie seemed to have second thoughts about meeting Stacie's friends. "I don't know, Nick, maybe it isn't a good idea to get together with neighbors."

"It is a wonderful idea, Annie. You've met your match in Stacie. Stacie is great. I have known her since kindergarten, I think. You can trust Stacie. You'll like her friends. I'm not sure who she is talking about but trust Stacie."

"I have never played tennis but I think I will like it," she said more to herself.

Angel went to kindergarten where Nick went to school. Though now Angel was to be called Angela, her "big girl" name. For the most part she was called Angela, but at home she was more often than not Angel. She was a beautiful and pleasant little girl and loved school. Annie took everything about school seriously. She read every memo that came home in Angela's little backpack. She volunteered at every opportunity. She went over every drawing and paper that her daughter brought home.

Annie loved living in this house. It was a home beyond her wildest dreams. Stacie became her best friend and she also liked the other two women that Stacie introduced her to. She got to know other neighbors, participated in school activities, went to homeowner meetings, and because so many people knew her from the restaurant, was soon a pillar of the neighborhood. But even with all of her other responsibilities and interests, she continued to work on her Bachelor of Arts Degree in Counseling. She never wasted a moment of time. During any lull at the restaurant she worked on her studies. She attended morning classes while Angel was at school. She also made time to volunteer at Millar House and take food to missions and food pantries.

Annie and Nick ran the restaurant together. Annie created new dishes and the menu changed frequently which pleased regular patrons. They did, however, keep some favorites on the menu; one of which was soufflé. Annie named it Honeymoon Soufflé but never explained it. Annie cooked along with another cook they hired from one of the downtown hotels, and one or two sous chefs, frequently someone they hired from Millar House. Nick worked on the books, the physical building, and kept all the employees happy. The employees were happy. He hired mostly college students as wait staff and scheduled the number of hours each wanted to work according to their semester of studies. He made job duties flexible and each took turns as maître d', and cashier as well as waiter if they wished. Nick was always available to customers and no one ever left unhappy. Though rare, if there was a complaint, he tried to ratify it quickly. If that was not to be, there was never a charge for the meal. Nick was willing to do anything needed from waiting tables to cleaning the bathrooms. The bathroom was one of the first things they changed in the facility. Originally, there was only one, designated as a family bathroom. Annie told Nick that women did not generally like to use a bathroom that men used. He, of course, was an exception, she diplomatically explained, but men were disgusting. So they had two bathrooms put in and the women's was luxurious. The men's room was more functional, though it also had a changing table. Annie was adamant about that. Each morning when flowers or other adornments were put on the tables, so also was the women's bathroom furnished; hair spray was put out, hand lotion, potpourri, and the fixtures were state of the art. Many people commented on the luxury of the Yumsters' ladies' loo.

Business was very good. The children grew and blossomed. It was the family Annie dreamed of having and that Nick had experienced. The children were "close" just as Nick and Laurie had been. Both Nick and Annie tried to be home in the evenings as much as possible. Nick would come home if only to tuck the children in and read a story, if he couldn't get away any more than that. Annie had more regular hours. She saw to it that everything was ready to go so she could be home by the time the children got home from school. The restaurant was closed Sundays and Mondays. They made the most of this time with the children. At the end of every evening, restaurant leftovers were taken to shelters. Someone, often Nick, would close the restaurant and drive to a mission. It was as routine as turning the "Closed" sign. Everyone in the Philadelphia social services community knew Nick and Annie. Whenever they had an opportunity, Nick and Annie would serve at one of the missions. The entire family volunteered at Millar House.

Nick resisted the temptation to enlarge the restaurant. He liked the intimate atmosphere and apparently so did the clientele. They took some reservations, but always kept a few tables available for drop-ins. Thursday, Friday and Saturday evenings there was usually a line of customers and a wait of sometimes an hour. Patrons would leave their names and come back. No one complained. Nick did not want to duplicate the restaurant either. It was a one-of-a-kind and they wanted it to remain so. However, so many people asked Yumsters to cater parties for them that they were becoming overwhelmed. Annie loved to work on special menus and new dishes and so they eventually opened a catering company. They hired Beau's daughter, Brit, to run it. She had a degree in business and loved working in the restaurant as a college student. Nick said he wanted to name the business and surprised Annie when she saw the first catering truck with "Annie Yums" on the side.

The catering company was just as successful as the restaurant. It catered weddings as well as smaller celebrations in St. John's, but also in the surrounding areas as well. Annie worked on the menus from home after the children were in bed. They hired the staff to cater functions from both the Culinary Institute and Millar House, or women who had moved on but had once lived in Millar House, like Tamika. She was a full time employee.

Nick called the house from the car. "Hi, how is everything going?"

"Good," Annie answered. "Matthew is irritating Angel, and Angel is complaining and irritating me. Normal. Everything is normal," she said smiling. "Where are you?"

"I am home. I am sitting in the car in the drive. Will you get the kids and have them sit on the stairs with their eyes shut and then I'll come in. I have a surprise."

"I love surprises. At least I think I do. I am kind of scared though. Is it a good surprise or, oh never mind," Annie said. "I'll go get the kids. Give me thirty seconds."

Nick gave her two minutes and walked in the door. The kids were sitting on the steps but both had taken their hands from over their eyes and squealed in delight when they saw the two puppies in Nick's arms. Nick put the yellow lab in Angel's arms and the black lab in Matthew's. Both puppies began to lick their little faces and as the children squirmed, the puppies jumped down and began running around the room. Annie was laughing so hard she was crying. Nick sprawled on the floor and the puppies began to pounce on him, licking him in the face between jumps. Finally he got hold of the yellow one and took it in his arms as he sat up. Annie sat down next to him and grabbed the black one.

"Mommy gets to name them," Nick said.

"I want to name them," Angela announced.

"Sorry," Nick said. "It's Mommy's job. She names all babies."

Annie could barely hold on to the puppy. She tried to determine the sex but it squirmed so much she had to ask.

"Both girls," Nick answered.

"No fair," said Matthew but he was ignored and soon sat with his mother and petted the dog.

"Well, I think we should name them Jo and Meg. Jo will be the black one because she was the black sheep of the family."

"Great names for our 'little women'," Nick said. He went out to the car to get the crates and supplies he bought to go with the puppies. When he returned, both kids were standing on the steps pointing to the puddles in the hall. Annie was coming in with paper towels and cleaner. "Oops," he said.

"It happens," said Annie. Then she said mostly to herself, "I have never had a dog before," and grinned.

Chapter Twenty-Four

"Nicky, have you seen the babies?" Laurie asked. She was propped up in bed but looked very fit and healthy. She had on a pink cotton robe over her gown. Her hair was pulled back behind her ears, her makeup perfectly applied.

"I just saw them. Sleeping," he said as he kissed her. "Twins," he said. "Are you crazy? And girls. You now have three girls. I can't even imagine."

"Oh, the beauty of fertility drugs. I just have to be sure I don't get pregnant again. It is the gift that keeps on giving, you know."

"You could have six, like Beau."

"Not going to happen. Thanks for taking care of Pippa."

"Our pleasure. When I get home, I'll send Annie over with Pippa to see the babies. Maybe tomorrow if it is okay with you, I'll bring our two. Though you should get all the rest you can now," he said thoughtfully. "Maybe you don't want visitors."

"Of course I do. They need to see their cousins. Mom just left. She is going to stay with me for a few days when I go home. Although, I think it interferes with her schedule. She is the busiest person I know."

"I know. She is busy. I have to plan weeks ahead to have lunch with her. But that's a good thing. Where is Sid?"

"He's roaming the halls, telling all his friends about the babies. He will be great with them. He has more patience with Pippa than I do."

"That is the true feminine mystique. How can women and daughters be so close and fight so much?"

Laurie laughed. "Men just don't get that, do they?"

Nick was seated on the floor with his back against the chair in which Annie was seated cross legged. She was studying; he was reading. Annie nudged him to look at Matthew as he was making his way down the hall coming toward them in his pajamas. "Hey, big guy, what's going on?" Nick said softly to him.

Matt plopped down in his dad's lap and said solemnly, "I'm sad about school." Nick saw the dark lashes around his son's blue eyes were damp. He loved kindergarten, so Nick was surprised he was sad about first grade.

"Tell me about it," Nick said. "What is making you feel sad?"

"I'm afraid I don't know enough words," he explained.

Nick tried to interpret the child's statement. "You know lots of words. What makes you think you don't know enough?" he asked.

"We are going to read this year," Matt explained. "What if I don't know all the words?"

"Well, Matt," Nick explained, "that is the beauty of first grade. You aren't supposed to know all the words. The teacher is going to teach them to you. But it will take her all year. She will just teach you a few at a time. I think you already know some of the first ones she will teach you," he said. "But, Matthew, you don't just learn to read in first grade. You do other things too. And you get to go out to play at recess. Remember Miss Marshall told you there will be recess every day? And you get to eat lunch in the cafeteria. Remember that? And be with your friends Jared and Nathan. It's all fun, Matthew. So no worrying in first grade! I tell you what," Nick said. "Let's not worry until…," he thought it over, "until your second year in high school. When you are in your sophomore year, I will help you and worry with you. Okay? Until then, you can just have fun."

Matthew was getting sleepy from being in Nick's arms. "Okay, Daddy. But when I am a scotomore in high school you won't forget; you'll worry with me?"

"I will." Nick got down on all fours. "How about a ride on ole' Horace the Horse? Kiss Mommy and get on."

Matthew kissed his mother and mounted Nick's back and road back to his bedroom. Nick sat in the rocker in his room and rocked Matthew and read three stories he chose from very young story books. "Don't grow up too fast on me, buddy," Nick whispered to the sleeping child as he put him in bed. Jo was already curled up on the foot of the bed waiting for Matthew.

Just as Nick was leaving Matt's room, Angela's light came on. He stopped at the door. "Hi, babe. You can't sleep either? First day jitters for fifth graders too?" he asked.

"I'm just afraid I will have Mrs. Meanster and not Miss Nelson. No one likes Mrs. Meanster and everybody likes Miss Nelson. What if I get her? A whole year!" she exclaimed.

"That's not her name!" Nick said with outrage. "What is it?" he said with a smile.

"Mrs. Kingster," Angela said glumly, "but everyone calls her Mrs. Meanster." Nick sat down on the side of the bed moving Meg slightly as he did. She raised one eye, and rolled over on her side.

"I am sure you are right but I would be careful calling a teacher a name like that because you might slip and she would hear you. It would probably make her angry but it might make her feel bad too. I don't think you would want to make her angry or hurt her. Besides, Angela, in my experience, sometimes the teacher you fear the most ends up being your favorite. Remember last year when the boys in your class would act up all the time and you couldn't hear stories and do fun things because they were so badly behaved?" Angela nodded. "Well, a teacher who is more strict won't let that happen. She will keep the boys quiet so you can do the things you like to do. So having a teacher like Mrs. King-ster," he emphasized the proper pronunciation of her name, "might just be a good thing. So tomorrow is what we call a win-win situation. Either you have Miss Nelson and you are glad, or you have Mrs. Kingster and you can be glad. Either way—great school year. After all, this is fifth grade! You can handle anything any fifth-grade teacher has to hand out. I predict this to be the best year ever," and he kissed her on the nose. "And, this year is…the year of the father-daughter dance!" Nick said in an announcement voice putting his hand out as if holding a mike. He then put his arms in the air and made them sway. "We are going to get down and boogie!"

"You're going to embarrass me, aren't you?"

"That's my plan."

"Daddy, how did you and Mom get together?" Nick's heart stopped. That was the question they never answered.

"What do you mean?" he said to stall.

"How do you meet the right person?" Angela asked. "All the boys in my class are jerks. How will I ever find a nice guy?"

"When you don't look," Nick answered. "Truly, Angela, it happens when you least expect it. And guys are jerks right through high school usually. You shouldn't start to think about finding the right one until after college. Anything else?" he asked.

"What's Mom doing?" Angela asked.

"She's studying. Do you need her? She will be in here in a flash if you do."

"No, I'm okay. I just wondered what she was doing. When will she get to stop studying all the time?" Angela said wrinkling her eyebrows.

"Well, this is the last class before she finishes her degree. Next semester, she will be a college graduate. But, knowing your mother, I don't think she will ever stop studying. She is always trying to learn more. I am incredibly proud of her. Aren't you?" Angela nodded.

"Where did you get that?" Nick asked looking at the framed photograph of himself when he was ordained, that was on Angela's night stand.

"Gran Em gave it to me. It's okay isn't it, for me to have it?"

"Sure."

"You look really different now. You were really young then but you look sad. Were you sad?"

"No. I was really happy but they told us not to smile for the official picture. I don't know why. They sent the pictures to our parents. I didn't even see mine until I came home for a visit one time. Mom used to have it on the piano."

"I'm glad she gave it to me. I don't have any pictures of mommy when she was young. When I was at Gran Em's last week, she let me look through all of her pictures of you when you were a little kid. I think she is going to give us the books but she still likes to look at them sometimes."

"Yeah, I'm sorry we don't have any pictures of your mom when she was younger too. But we will make up for it by taking lots of pictures now, okay? And your mom is still young, by the way!" Nick looked at the book on Angela's night stand. "What are you reading?" he asked.

"*The Secret Garden*. It's really good," she answered.

"May I read some to you? You aren't too old to have me read to you, are you? Please, please, say no," he teased. Nick read for nearly fifteen minutes before Angela fell asleep.

When Nick got back to Annie, she asked, "Everything go okay?"

Nick smiled and said, "First day of school jitters for both."

"Are you sure you don't want more kids?" she asked laughing.

"No," Nick answered quickly. "I am pretty happy with the ones I have. Besides I think ole' Horace the Horse is about to go out to pasture." He lay down on the floor on his stomach and Annie came down and rubbed his back and shoulders.

"This is what I get for marrying an old guy," she said laughing. Nick turned over and pulled her down on top of him.

In time, Matthew had the same love for school as Angela. They both did well academically and loved participating in school activities. As he progressed through the grades, Matt became interested in sports just as Nick had. He excelled in basketball which was no surprise to anyone. But he was also interested in drama and music. He played trumpet at school but in addition took piano lessons for a while. Angela also took piano lessons but Annie finally tired of trying to persuade her to practice, let her discontinue her lessons, and Annie took Angela's lesson time. After a while all the piano lessons stopped. No one had Nick's talent, and they were always glad to have him play and they would happily listen.

Angela was a teacher's dream. She was more outgoing than Matthew and would tackle any project. She loved academics but was also an all-round girl. She had lots of friends and loved listening to popular music and texting. Both children were encouraged to have their friends to the house and Nick and Annie made their friends comfortable in their home.

The restaurant and the catering company both flourished. After a while, Nick had to give in and expand the restaurant and also added a patio in what was once the back yard. They were no longer closed on Mondays. Now it wasn't just a local restaurant but people came from all over the area. It received incredible reviews in Spotlight Philadelphia Magazine.

Nick didn't get home until late one night and the kids were already asleep. Yumsters had been crowded from the moment it opened that day, and they barely had time to change from the lunch to the dinner menu. Everyone was working flat out. Nick seated customers, waited on tables, and even plated meals to get things to customers in a reasonable time period. It was a hectic day but everything went smoothly. He sent Annie home at five. The children were old enough to stay alone for an hour or two now. Angela had taken Safe Sitter training at the Y and had been babysitting for neighbors occasionally. She was always willing to stay with Matthew when they needed her to do so. She had been taught that it was a family responsibility, not a job, and she was not paid to sit with Matthew. However, neither child wanted for anything. Nick and Annie played the tight-fisted parent role but in reality their children were as indulged as any of the others in the neighborhood.

Annie was up in bed when Nick got home. He went up and sat on the bed to talk with her. She was in flannel pants and one of Nick's tee shirts, propped up watching television which she turned off when he entered the room. Nick relayed the facts of the rest of the evening after she left and he noted she was not as interested in the conversation as usual. "Everything okay?" he asked tentatively.

Annie handed Nick a letter she had received. It was addressed to Ann Marie Bertonelli Millar. It was from a private investigator in Oklahoma City who was hired by Annie's mother to find her. It was her mother's dying wish to see Annie. They didn't know how the investigator had found her but Nick explained that it was not that difficult to find anyone today.

Nick waited for Annie to say something. He knew her silence indicated she was upset that her mother had found her. Nick took her hand, "It's okay, baby. No one is going to hurt you. Your mother is dying and it is perfectly normal for a dying person to want to tidy up the loose ends of their life."

"So, you think I should go see her?" she asked, perplexed.

"I think a dying person's wishes should be met if possible. Don't you?" he asked back.

"I have a wonderful life now. I don't want to go back," she stammered. "I wanted to forget everything about my past, even my mother. She was never a real mother, Nick. She never took care of me. I don't even know her. I really don't. I was so young when I left. I have nothing to say to her."

"Well, maybe she has something to say to you, Ann. How old was she when you were born?" Nick asked.

"I don't know, really young, barely a teenager, I think."

"And how old were you when you left?"

"Not much older than that, I guess."

"Well haven't you learned some things since then? Maybe she has too. She might want forgiveness, Annie. Not many people are vengeful on their deathbed."

"I can't do it. I can't." Nick cuddled with her but said nothing. Annie vacillated, "I don't want to be away more than one day. Will you go with me?" she asked pleadingly.

"Of course, I will," he answered. "I'll do anything for you."

"I hate for you to see where I came from."

"I am incredibly proud of what you have done with your life," he answered.

Reluctantly, Annie flew to Oklahoma City on a Tuesday night, and as promised, Nick was with her. The children stayed with Beau and Kheim Li. They chose to go during the week when it would be lighter at the restaurant and the children had the routine of school to occupy them. They stayed in a hotel in Hastings, Oklahoma, near the nursing home where Annie's mother had been in hospice care for several weeks. Nick tried to keep Annie upbeat by taking her to dinner at a bistro recommended by the desk. And while she loved the meal and took copious notes, she was glum as soon as they were back at the hotel. When he tried to console her, she started to cry.

"You have no way of knowing how I feel," she told him through sobs.

"I know I don't," he said. "And I will never know, unless you tell me."

"I feel like shit," she said. "I feel like I have never been away and I am right back where I started my miserable life in the first place."

"And where do I fit in?" he asked.

"I don't know. You are too good to be here."

"Annie, you left here. You live in St. John's now and you belong there. You are here only to grant your mother's dying wish. Because you are a wonderful, giving person, Annie," he added.

Annie slept fitfully and kept as close to Nick as physically possible while he slept. In the morning they showered and dressed without much conversation. When Nick asked if she wanted to go to breakfast, she said no. She didn't feel like eating.

When they walked into the nursing home, Nick was flooded with memories of when he had been assigned to visit the dying when he was first a priest. He remembered the difference between the first time he made his call there and the last, when he had some experience in dealing with death and dying. Not that it was ever easy. Annie was pale. Nick could see the dread in her face. He stopped at a bench just inside the door of the facility and sat her down. "Annie, I'm not making you do this am I?" he asked painfully.

Annie shook her head.

"Are you okay?" he then asked.

"I can do it," she said with determination and tried to smile.

"I love you," Nick said. "We'll do it together. I am right beside you."

After being told the room number they walked somberly to the room holding hands. Nick tapped on the door and on being told to come in he took long strides across the room, threw out his hand and announced, "Mrs. Bertonelli, I'm Nick Millar." He gave her an infectious smile and then asked, "So do you know who this beautiful young lady is?"

The woman in the bed was barely eighty pounds. Her body had shriveled around her and she looked twenty maybe thirty years older than her biological age. She was totally devoid of color and her hair was thin and limp around her face. She smiled though when Nick approached. She had an IV in her arm, but she shook hands with Nick and then she folded her hands on her lap. Finally she looked at her daughter and said, "You're Ann Marie. I didn't think you would come."

"Hi Mama," Annie said in a voice nearly as weak as her mother's.

"I prayed you would come, Ann Marie. But I didn't think you would," she added, continuing to stare.

Annie was at a loss for words, so Nick took over. "Annie got your letter, Mrs. Bertonelli, and here we are. We came in last night. We live in Philadelphia, I don't know if you knew that."

Mrs. Bertonelli responded by saying, "I didn't know where you were, Ann Marie, but I wanted to see you one more time." She began to tear as she said, "I wanted to say I'm sorry to you. My preacher told me to tell you. He said you would want to hear it as much as I wanted to say it. He said you may not want to forgive me, but that's okay," she said weakly.

"Oh Mama, I do forgive you," Annie said looking at Nick. He smiled at her. There was a long uncomfortable pause. To help them along, Nick suggested that Annie show her mother pictures of the children. Annie carefully took out the pictures from her purse and showed her the school photographs from this school year that Nick suggested she bring.

"A boy and a girl," Mrs. Bertonelli said. She held on to Angela's photo. "She is beautiful, like you Ann Marie. She looks like an Angel."

Annie faltered hearing her mother say that. While she tried to compose herself, Nick said, "Her name is Angela and we call her Angel." He went on, "Our son's name is Matt; Matthew," he elaborated.

"Ann Marie, I don't know how you can ever forgive me for the things I did to you. You don't have to forgive me, but I do have to tell you how sorry I am for what I did. I can't remember everything. I was either drunk or stoned most of the time. I have been clean and sober for eight years now."

"That's great, Mama," Annie said sweetly.

Mrs. Bertonelli looked at Annie and said, "I know I did lots of horrible things, but the one I regret the most was the time when I left you alone for all those days I was in jail. You were so little. About six or seven, I think. You were hiding in the closet when the police came to get me. When I got my coat, I told you not to leave the apartment until I got back. I was gone three days and when I came back, you were there, alone in the apartment. There was hardly anything for you to eat. I know you were so scared. I should have let them take you. Maybe they would have found you a good home. Instead, you stayed with me several more years while I ..." she couldn't go on.

"It's okay, Mama. I was okay. I made it, didn't I?" Annie said. Nick grimaced thinking of the things Annie had endured as a child.

"You took care of me, most of the time, Ann Marie, when I should have been taking care of you. And then when you needed me most, I let you down. When you said you were pregnant, I called you a tramp. And then you went away. Who can blame you? You were just a baby yourself." She began to cry softly.

Nick sat with his hand over his mouth while Mrs. Bertonelli was talking but then got up and crossed the room to put his arm around Annie and he nervously massaged her shoulders. He wondered if he should step outside to give the two of them some time. Maybe Annie didn't want him to hear everything. But she grabbed his hand to indicate she wanted him there and he sat down next to her.

Annie shook her head. "Mama," she said, "I forgive you. I forgive everything." She looked at Nick. "I have a wonderful life; a wonderful family. My husband has forgiven me for all of the things I have done. I have to forgive you. Nick tells me that we do what we think we have to do to survive. Sometimes we do things we aren't proud of. But then we grow and learn and we may not have to do them anymore." Annie started to sputter at that point. She was trying so hard not to cry that she was holding her breath. When she did finally breathe, it was a gasp. Nick reached into his pocket and fingered his rosary. He then transferred it from his pocket to his left hand that was holding Annie's. He placed it between their hands and Annie clutched it until it made marks in her hand.

"Ann Marie, you have given me such a generous gift. That's what my preacher said it would be; a generous gift. I am happy. I am truly happy for the first time in my life. I see that my only child is well and has a wonderful family of her own. I know I didn't do anything to make your life good but I am so happy that it is. Did you graduate from high school?" she asked suddenly.

"I did, Mama, and I went on and got certification from a culinary institute and then after Nick and I were married, I got a degree from the University of Pennsylvania." She beamed at her mother.

"You went to college," her mother said with admiration. "I am so proud of you."

"Thank you, Mama," Annie said.

An aide came in to check on her patient and Nick and Annie stood. "I should go, Mama. We have a flight going back tonight. I don't like to leave the children very long. I have never been away from them before," she explained.

"You are a good mother, Ann Marie." Then she paused and looked at Annie. "Derek was here. He says he needs to see you. He has something he has to tell you. He left his phone number and address." She lifted her hand to reach the table next to her bed and handed the card to Annie. "I didn't ask him anything and he didn't tell me what he wanted, Ann Marie. But he acted like it was important."

Annie was white. Nick was concerned she would faint. He put his hand on her cheek and she touched his hand and said she was okay.

Nick went over and shook hands with Mrs. Bertonelli one more time. "It has been a pleasure," he said and meant it. "Would you like for me to say a prayer, Mrs. Bertonelli?"

"I would like that."

Nick carefully took her hand and Annie went over to the other side of the bed and took her mother's other hand. It was small and fragile, even in Annie's petite one. They each bowed their head as Nick prayed. "Dear Father of mercy and God of comfort, we ask that you look graciously on Mrs. Bertonelli and have mercy on this thy servant, giving her unfeigned repentance for all the errors of her past life and steadfast faith in Jesus Christ. For if we say that we have no sin, we deceive ourselves, and the truth is not in us. But if we confess our sins, he is faithful and just to forgive our sins, and to cleanse us from all unrighteousness. We ask for God's gracious mercy upon Mrs. Bertonelli, thy loving servant, and that the Lord bless her and lift up his countenance upon her, and give her peace, both now and forevermore. Amen."

"He has," Mrs. Bertonelli said. "Now he has."

"You did what you thought you had to do, Mama. I'm okay. I have a wonderful life. It's okay, Mama. I forgive you." Annie waved to her mother as she backed out the door. Nick took her hand and they walked out the door, down the hall and out of the building without a word.

Once they were in the car, before Nick could ask, even though he wasn't sure he would have, Annie said, "Derek is Angel's father. Her birth father. You are her father in every sense of the word." She paused and looked at Nick. "Would it be crazy for me to see him?" she asked. "I mean, for us to see him. I wouldn't go without you. What if he wants to see Angel? I have never told her anything. I was always afraid she would ask about him, but she hasn't really. I don't ever intend to come back here again. If I am going to see him, it would have to be today. I don't want him showing up on our doorstep. If I have to see him, I would rather it be here."

"Let's do it," Nick said. "Do you know how to get there?" They drove the short distance in silence. They pulled into the drive and Annie put her hand on Nick's leg.

"Nick, I love you more than I thought humanly possible. I don't want to be here because I have any feeling for Derek, but I need to know what he is thinking so he doesn't do anything to hurt Angela."

Derek answered the door. He was about Annie's age, small framed, close-cropped hair and wire-framed glasses. He obviously recognized Annie or else Mrs. Bertonelli had called him, Nick didn't know which. Again, Nick sprang into action to get things going. "I'm Nick Millar, Annie's husband. You must be Derek." Nick held out his hand and Derek shook it. Derek looked at Annie and she him. A woman came up behind Derek and asked them to come into the living room. They all sat down awkwardly.

Derek began, "Ann Marie, I didn't know how to get a hold of you so I visited your mother. I would like to have a relationship with our daughter and for my boys to know her." He said it bluntly, without any preparation. It hit Annie right between the eyes. Annie thought for sure she was going to faint. She put her head between her knees and tried to breathe. Nick put his hand across her shoulder and massaged her neck. She finally sat up. At first she was angry. Why now does he want to know Angel? Where was he when she needed food and clothes? she asked herself. But, she was tired. It was emotionally draining to visit her mother and now to see Derek. She didn't say anything.

Derek stopped to let Annie process the information but now went on, "I don't want anything else from you, Ann Marie. I have a good life." He nodded toward his wife. "Lacey and I have been married for twelve years. We have two boys." Derek stopped and stood up and walked around the sofa and sat back down again. "I know I treated you terribly. I left you to take care of Angel on your own. That was terrible; a really horrible thing to do to someone." He seemed repulsed by his own negligent actions. He continued, "All these years. I let you take care of Angel without any help. I didn't contribute one penny to help you. I am so sorry. My parents feel badly too for how they treated you. They now realize they have a granddaughter that they have never met." He went on, "Ann Marie, I truly am sorry. That's all I wanted to say. I talked to your mother and she said the same thing. She said she was a terrible mother and I know I was a terrible person not to take care of you or our child." He waited for Annie to say something, obviously very unsure what it would be she would say.

"So, what do we do now?" Annie asked.

Derek shrugged. "It is up to you. I promise I will not bother you. If Angel wants to see me or talk to me, I would really like that. I would like for her to know the boys and for them to know her. But," he added, "it has to be okay with you too."

Nick finally spoke, "Annie and I have talked very little about the possibility of Angel meeting you. I, personally, think she should have at least the option to meet you. However, right now she is in the throes of high school and any little upset is a major crisis for a teenager and I don't know if this is the appropriate time, right now in the middle of the school year I mean, to meet with her, but I don't speak for Annie. Whatever Annie wants is what will be done. We might even need some professional help on this one. We want to make sure it is handled right."

"I need to think about it," Annie said. "I will let Angel know in due course about you. Someday she should know you and your family. Someday. Like Nick says, maybe it should be when she is eighteen and out of high school. Or at least when she is on summer vacation and not in school. I don't know. Maybe we should talk to someone," she said in a daze.

"That's fine," Derek answered. "I can wait until you think the timing is right."

Annie stood up, appearing to be ready to leave. She quickly sat back down looking ill.

Lacey said, "Derek, let's give them a minute. This has been such a shock and Ann Marie just saw her mother today too. This was unfair. I'm sorry. It shouldn't have been done like this. We just didn't know how to get in touch with you except through your mother." Lacey and Derek walked out and sat on the porch so Annie could get herself together.

"It is a shock, Annie. I'm sorry it came at you like this. I love you, sweetheart," Nick whispered. "Together we can handle anything." He changed his tone. "This is a good thing, Ann," Nick said affirmatively. "Angela's father wants to have a relationship with her. We can handle that; someday, anyway. We have to do it, for Angela. She deserves to know her father."

Nick and Annie went back to the hotel and called home. Annie needed to hear Angela's voice but when she did, tears came and she couldn't talk. "Mom's had an emotional day," Nick explained. Nick also called the restaurant and checked to see that it was running smoothly. Annie made several pleas to Nick that she wanted to explain everything to him but Nick insisted that they go eat dinner first. They hadn't eaten all day. There was a small Italian restaurant near the airport and they showered, dressed and drove there.

The restaurant was not crowded. It was early for dinner and there were only four occupied tables. The wait staff was friendly and Nick and Annie talked with them about entrée suggestions. Nick ordered a bottle of Merlot. When the wine came, he poured it and clinked glasses with Annie. "To you, Annie. May you be granted peace at long last," he said.

Nick suggested they just eat their meal and for Annie not to worry about explaining everything to him now. Annie, however, wanted to talk. She began her story, "Nick, I was just a teenager when Derek and I first met. We went to school together. We had been in the same class but I dropped out. It is a small town. Everyone knows everyone's business and Derek's parents knew about my mother and didn't want me anywhere near their son. You know about forbidden fruit. I think the more his mother protested, the more attention Derek paid to me. When I got pregnant she went ballistic. She shamed me into going to her aunt's farm for the duration of my pregnancy out in the boonies. Derek was up for a soccer scholarship and she didn't want me screwing it up. Derek didn't know where I was. I had nowhere else to go, no money, and no health insurance so I didn't have much choice. My mother kicked me out of the house, just like she said. I lived with Derek's aunt and uncle and helped them out with their kids. We didn't have cell phones then, so I tried to call him when his aunt and uncle were away but his mother always answered and threatened me. When I went into labor, his aunt took me to the hospital and someone came and gave me some papers to sign to give up the baby. I wouldn't sign them. Derek's mother came after the birth and gave me a check for five thousand dollars to give up the baby and go away. Annie wiped away a tear. "At first they wouldn't even let me hold the baby. What I remember the most is when my milk came in. I was so sore and miserable. No one explained anything to me. I was so alone. Finally, I talked to one of the young nurses and told her my story. I told her that I wanted my baby. She got in touch with a social worker and the next day they took me and the baby to a foster home. They checked on my mother and knew I couldn't go there. But, evidently they couldn't make me put the baby up for adoption. I don't know. I didn't know half of what was going on. But they did keep Derek's mother away from me. I don't think she knew where I was. I stayed there for a few weeks or a couple of months, I guess, but they weren't very nice. Especially the husband. I was afraid he was going to rape me, so I took off."

"I knew Derek was going to Ohio State, so I cashed my check and took a bus to Columbus. I guess his mother forgot I still had the check and she didn't stop payment on it. Around the university there were lots of rooms and little efficiencies to rent so I found a place right away and took a job in a diner and found a good sitter for Angel; a student who lived above the diner. I didn't know how to find Derek, so I put an ad in the student newspaper. I just used initials and said I was in town and looking for him and said where I was working. Several boys came around who read the ad but not Derek," she said with a disgusted look. "Finally, over a year later, he showed up where I was working. He had flunked out of school but hadn't told his parents. He moved in with me. He never got a job. He hardly left the little apartment. He was just another mouth for me to feed. He was depressed about school and knew he had to face his parents sometime. He stayed about three or four months, then he left. I assumed he went home but I never heard from him again. I wasn't going to chase after him this time."

"Unfortunately, I was getting pretty depressed myself, but I loved Angel. She was the first thing that ever belonged to me. She loved me! The lady who owned the house where I lived was really nice and helped me out. After a while, I worked at the diner and took Angel to a nearby cooperative day care. I worked five days at the diner and one day at the cooperative helping with the kids. I was doing okay. But then the lady who owned the house had to sell it and I was going to have to find something else, and all the others were too expensive. I didn't know what I was going to do."

"I had become friends with one of the campus policemen who came to the diner. He was married at the time and we were just friends. But then he told me he got a divorce and started flirting with me. He was really nice to me. He brought me flowers one day. He was good to Angel too. He was always bringing her something. He came to the diner nearly every day. He would just sit and watch me.

My boss didn't care because he didn't interfere with my customers. He took me to the movies once or twice. He bought me little things. He really seemed nice."

"He said he had a chance to go to Philadelphia to be a cop. He asked me to come with him. He said we would get married and I could have a complete new start." Annie looked at Nick and made a face of disgust. "I was just stupid and didn't know what to do. He was always good to Angel. I wouldn't have gone if he hadn't been. For a while he was good to me too. I just didn't realize how controlling he was. He started telling me what to wear, how to fix my hair, and made all the decisions and I mean every decision. I was so worn out taking care of everything by myself, it didn't seem so bad in the beginning. But, when we got to Philadelphia, he didn't mention marriage again and he didn't get the police job. I never knew why. So he took a night watchman job for a while and hated it. He slapped me once when I said something he didn't like. Then he cried and asked me to forgive him." Annie made a scornful face. "I felt sorry for him. I thought he was just depressed because he didn't get the police job and thought being a night watchman was beneath him. Then they said he stole something from an office and he got fired. He couldn't get another job and he started to get mean.

Everything I did was wrong. He ridiculed me; accused me of all kinds of things. I couldn't think of a way to get out of the situation. I thought I would go back to Columbus but I didn't even have enough for the bus ride. He never let me have a penny. Finally, we got evicted from our apartment and had nowhere to go. He actually found an unoccupied apartment and we lived like squatters. I guess we were squatters," she said remorsefully. "Things got really bad. I wanted to get a job but he wouldn't let me. He kept saying guys were looking at me. He got paranoid about it. He never wanted me to go out of the house without him. We had nothing to eat, very little anyway. He did go with me to get food and diapers for Angel at a government sponsored place. That was practically the only place I got to go."

"Suddenly, he came home one day and moved us into another furnished apartment. He brought in groceries and got us some clothes and toys for Angel. Then, he told me he 'borrowed' the money from some guy who hired him to get girls to work the streets. He had to pay the money back or the guy would have him killed. He threw some trashy clothes at me and told me to get out there and bring him what I earned. He said I was a tramp anyway having a child out of wedlock and always flirting with guys. I never even saw any guys; I certainly didn't flirt with any. I refused to go out and he beat me up. When I healed, he told me to do it again. I refused and he beat me again. Finally, I told him I would go out if I could have someone watch Angel. I didn't trust him with her. I found someone and went out. I didn't know what else to do. I thought maybe I could keep a little of the money and take off one day. He watched me like a hawk. I tried to get away once but he found me. I wanted to get a real job but he wouldn't let me. I would have worked anywhere, done anything. I felt like I was caught in a trap. I hadn't been out there very long when you came along. I don't know what would have happened to us if you hadn't come there that night." Annie laid her head against Nick. "It's disgusting, isn't it? I'm disgusting." Tears ran down her face. Nick fought back his.

"It is disgusting," he finally said softly. "It is disgusting what one individual will do to another. You, however, are not disgusting. You are wonderful. You did what you had to do to take care of Angel. Is Derek disgusting?" he suddenly asked.

"No, not really, I guess," Annie said softly. "He was just young and confused or scared or something, I guess. I don't know. I don't harbor any ill will against Derek. His parents had quite a hold on him, I guess. I don't know," she said again. "He seems to have his act together now."

"How can you let Derek off the hook and be so hard on yourself?" Nick asked rhetorically. "Derek left and you stayed. You took care of Angel. Derek never helped you with his child. Now, this other jerk. He really is disgusting, Annie. He hit you and forced you to do something you didn't want to do. He is the bad guy in this situation."

Nick thought for a minute. "Annie, do you know that prostitution is legal in some countries. Actually, in some states; well just Nevada I think. But it is legal in most of Europe, and Canada, and in Australia, and New Zealand I think. Even here it is considered a victimless crime. I'm not saying it is a good thing; or a bad thing for that matter. I'm just saying it isn't …," Nick faltered trying to explain. Suddenly he changed his tone and said, "Did you know that it is mentioned in the Bible? More than once, Jesus talks about prostitutes. Once he told someone that tax collectors and prostitutes would enter the kingdom before they would, because they hadn't believed in him. Jesus had a soft spot for them as he did for others who were oppressed or scorned. He didn't want them judged by pious Christians."

Nick changed his tone slightly, "When you ask for forgiveness from a priest, he says 'Go in peace and sin no more.' That's it. If you have asked for forgiveness, you are forgiven. So let's let it go. Stop punishing yourself for something you had little control over. Let's get on with things that are under our control. Angel was fathered by Derek. That is a fact. It really isn't much different than if you had been married once before. My mother had children from her first marriage. So did my dad. Derek is Angela's father and she should have contact with him if she wants, don't you think?

"I think so but I am so scared. What if she hates me?" Annie asked.

"She loves you. We'll get some help and find out how and when to tell her about her father. She wants to know, even if she hasn't asked. She is probably afraid to ask, thinking it is something really bad. Since we haven't told her anything, she might think her father is in prison, or an addict, or who knows what. Derek seems like a straight up guy. I think Angela has a right to know him," Nick said.

Two weeks later Annie heard from Mrs. Bertonelli's minister that she had passed away. She wanted Annie notified but not until after she had been cremated and her remains scattered. She wanted there to be no service other than a prayer by her minister. She had only a small amount of money she had saved from her job the last few years as a maid in a hotel. After the cremation expenses were paid, the small remainder went to her church. Annie was happy about that and she and Nick sent a donation to the church in memory of her mother as well.

Chapter Twenty-Five

"**N**ick," he answered.

"Hi, Nick."

"Is this Congressman Metzger?" Nick asked smiling as he spoke into his phone.

Abbe laughed. "How are you Nick? I haven't talked to you in ages."

"Great, we are all great. How are you Abbe? I am so happy for you. You finally made it. You must be thrilled," he said.

"I am over the moon. Thanks for the flowers. I can't believe I really get to go this time as an honest-to-goodness congresswoman."

"A duly-elected congresswoman. Congratulations, Abbe. I am incredibly proud of you. This time you will knock Washington on its ear."

"That's why I called Nick. I want you to come with me. I really mean it, Nick. We were good together. There is no one I trust more than you."

"You must be joking," Nick said.

"No, I am serious. I want you to be my chief of staff again. You can keep your restaurant. You can go back and forth. I need you Nick. You keep me on an even keel. I trust you more than anyone on earth. I know that you will tell me the straight scoop. Please, please, please."

"Abbe, you are going to Washington because in the years since we were there, you learned what you needed to know. I don't know a damn thing more than I did the day we left. You need someone who knows the ins and outs of congress. Not me. Besides, I made my life here. I don't just have my business here, I have a wife and two kids. I'm not going anywhere. Thanks Abbe, I'm flattered. But, no thanks."

"I was afraid you would say that. But, will you and your family come to Washington to see me?"

"You bet. And when you need to get away, we will always have a room for you."

"Man, Nick. Why did I ever let you get away?"

"It was fun Abbe. But it wasn't meant to last. It was a temporary gig, for both of us."

"Okay, but I am going to stop in sometime and meet Annie. She must be something special."

"She is."

The restaurant had closed for the night without incident. Customers left in an orderly manner before closing time so all the staff had time to manage their cleanup duties and get out early and Nick was the last to leave. Someone from Shared Feast came to pick up the leftovers and Nick was just taking out the last of the trash when a shadow moved in on his right. He jumped. "I'm sorry, man, I didn't mean to scare you," a voice said. A young African-American man walked up to Nick. "A woman down the street told me to come here and see if you could help me out," he explained. "My wife and I have had one problem on top of another," he said sadly. "We are from Montgomery. We were driving to upstate New York to live with a cousin for a while and look for work but our car broke down. It's down the street a few blocks." Nick was looking at the young man trying to decide how to help. "To tell you the truth, I think it is just out of gas." The man didn't seem like a panhandler, and Nick had seen many. He didn't quite know what to make of him. He was well-groomed, dressed in what may have been designer jeans and a tan sport shirt. Before Nick could invite him in or find something for him to eat, a policeman ran up.

"Put your hands against the building and back your feet up. You know the drill," he said in a condescending manner. "Sorry, Mr. Millar. One of the neighbors called and said this guy was prying around the houses. We'll get him out of here."

"Wait," Nick said. Nick knew the police officers in the neighborhood. The tiny little police force in St. John's had only a few employees. There was little crime in St. John's. Nick often wondered what kept them busy. Nick hoped he would get the name right, "Willie," he said, "I don't think there is a problem here. This young man was just asking me for some help. Someone told him to come here," Nick tried to explain.

"Well," Willie answered, "there is a problem because he is a vagrant. And we don't tolerate vagrants here in St. John's," he said with authority. "Several people saw him walking behind the houses. Who knows what he was going to do." With that he placed handcuffs on the man and led him to the car where he evidently read him his rights as they walked.

Nick was still puzzled and tried to think what to do. He put the trash in the bin and started to walk to the police car but Willie took off before he could say anything more. Damn, he thought. Now what should I do? He thought maybe he would stop in at the station on his way home and see if he could do anything. He went back into the restaurant to finish up. He put all the receipts together and closed out the cash register putting the money in the bag for the bank. He went back into the kitchen to make sure there was no food left out of any kind, and then pushed the button on the dishwasher as his last act. He thought he heard a noise in the back. He walked to the back door and heard a gentle knock. He opened it to see a young black woman with a child in her arms. "Can you tell me where they took my husband?" she asked. "He wasn't going to hurt anyone," she said. Tears began to make their way down her face and she wiped them away. "The last four days have been a nightmare," she choked out. The child, under two years old, Nick thought, began to cry also when she saw her mother cry. Like the young man, the woman was well dressed, and well groomed.

Finally, Nick composed his thoughts and said, "Come in." Nick started to take the woman and her child into the dining room but thought about the little girl and decided the best place to take them to talk might be the playhouse. They still had toys up there and a crib. The child could play and the mother could explain to him what exactly the situation was. He unlocked the door and led them into the playhouse. He put some toys on the small wooden child's table and the little girl stopped crying and pulled from her mother to get down to play with them. "Let me run down and get something for us to eat," he said diplomatically. "Then you can tell me what is going on."

"You aren't going to call the police, are you?" she asked frightened.

"No," Nick said sadly, and he ran down the stairs to get food. He grabbed some apple sauce for the little girl, a spoon and a soft roll. He then poured milk into a carafe and put some glasses on a tray with the other things. He looked in the fridge for something quick and that didn't needed reheating. He opted for some sliced roast beef, cheese, grapes, and threw a couple more rolls on the tray and took the stairs two at a time. He put the tray on the table in front of the loveseat.

"Help yourself," he said. "Tell me what you can and let's see if we can't get this straightened out."

The woman pulled the child back up onto her lap and fed her the applesauce. Then she handed her pieces of the roll. She reminded Nick of Annie when Angel was small when he first met her and she would pull off little pieces of things for her not wanting her to choke. He could tell she was a loving mother.

"We are from Montgomery," she began. "My name is Nan and my husband is Thomas. This," she pointed to the little girl, "is Jessie." She took a bite of a sandwich she made from the roll and meat, chewed and swallowed, to give herself time to collect her thoughts. "We were on our way to upstate New York. Let me start at the beginning," she said. She had another bite and began again. "Thomas lost his job at Hyundai. He was an engineer. They let go of nearly half of their engineers. He graduated from Georgia Tech," she said with pride. "I was in graduate school. I am a teacher but couldn't find a job so I went back to specialize in Reading Resource thinking maybe that would be a better field. I am not so sure it is now," she added. "Thomas couldn't find another job in Montgomery. He tried everything. He got a severance but it didn't last long. So he took any job; fast food, delivering papers, anything to bring in money. He worked night and day. I wanted to quit school but he didn't want me to. We decided to sell the house. We have quite a bit of equity and thought we could buy a smaller one or rent until we got better jobs. The housing market was terrible and we couldn't sell it. A realtor convinced us that we should rent it and then sell it when the market is better and we rented it for the mortgage payment. In the meantime, we were going to go to New York and live with my cousin and try to find work. We used up most of our savings. We didn't have a lot because we had my tuition and Thomas had school loans we had been paying and we had made double housing payments the last several years thinking that was a good strategy. Obviously it wasn't. So we started out with only a few thousand dollars with us. We have always tried to get along without using a lot of credit cards and we only have one and it was nearly maxed out."

"We got to Lexington and Jessie got really sick. We, of course, have no medical insurance. We couldn't afford COBRA coverage. I got her into a doctor and he put her in the hospital overnight for observation. We had to pay for the hospital, doctor, tests, and prescriptions. It took everything we had. And we had to stay in a hotel one night. We started pulling things out of the trunk we had brought with us to pawn. I had never been in a pawn shop in my life. Neither had Thomas. I called my cousin to ask her to wire us some money and she told me she and her husband split and she moved back with her mother. No room for us. Every day I thought it couldn't get any worse and it did. Well," she reconsidered, "Jessie got well. That is the blessing. They never could figure out what was wrong with her but she is okay now. We slept in the car last night at some rest stop. We got here and the car ran out of gas and we are flat broke. Thomas asked a woman in the neighborhood if she could tell us about a shelter or church or somewhere we could go for help and she said your restaurant was down the street. She told him to go behind the houses and go to your back door. Another bad idea! I guess she didn't think it would be good for a black man to walk down the street and go into the front door of your restaurant." With that Nan stopped talking and finished her sandwich. Jessie was content to play with the dolls she found in the doll bed.

Nick listened intently. Finally he said, "Nan, you and Jessie stay here. Stay in this apartment and don't come out until I get back. I am going to the police department and see if I can talk some sense into Barney Fife," he said sarcastically. "Use anything you need here. There are towels, maybe some clothes. I don't really know what is here but use whatever you need. I don't plan to be gone long. Do you have a cell?" he asked.

"Not charged," she answered. "I want you to know," she began, "we aren't like this." She began again, "I mean, we have college educations, we did everything right. I don't know what happened." She began to cry again.

"I know," Nick said. "I am going to help you. I will. I promise. My wife will help too. She will want to help." Nick thought that over. "I had better call her. She'll worry." He took out his phone and called Annie telling her he would be late. Some stuff came up. Nothing to worry about but don't wait up. Nick took off leaving Nan and Jessie in the little apartment.

An hour and a half later, Nick unlocked the door and came into the playhouse with Thomas. Nan ran to him. Nick explained that he refused to press charges and furthermore insisted they let Thomas go. He told them he would be responsible for Thomas and he would go with him the next morning when they could check his home ownership, which was the only thing Nick could think of that might impress the cop and make him realize Thomas wasn't a vagrant but a property owner. "Now," Nick said, "how about you guys getting some sleep. The loveseat pulls out into a bed, though it is small. It will be cozy," he remarked. "But there is the crib and I know there are sheets somewhere." Nick had stopped by Thomas's car and they filled it with gas from the can Nick had taken with him. He had Thomas pull into the parking area behind the restaurant and helped him bring in suitcases so they had clothes. "We have a washer and dryer," he explained, "if you need it tomorrow. Just don't leave this room tonight. Here is my cell. Call me if there is a problem." He left them the home phone number. "No one should come in tomorrow until about nine. And come to think of it, it will probably be me, and my wife."

Thomas asked, "What will your wife think of all of this?"

"She will be glad to help and will give the cops a piece of her mind. Compared to me, she is a pit bull. She will tolerate anything but intolerance. Annie will help you in any way she can."

"My God," exclaimed Nan, "is this nightmare over?" Then she checked herself, "I mean, can we really go to sleep tonight in a clean bed and try to start over in the morning?"

Nick said, "At the very least, you can stay here a few days. Do either of you cook?" he asked with a smile.

"Nan bakes!" Thomas said boastfully.

"Okay, then," Nick said. "You are hired for a week. Then we will see what happens." He smiled. "I have to get home. My wife will start to wonder what happened to me. See you in the morning. Stay in here," he advised. "When we get here in the morning, we will get you something to eat. Do you have everything you need? Need anything before I leave? "Then he added, "Oh crap, I forgot, Thomas you didn't get to eat."

"I'm okay, man, you've done enough."

"I'll be right back. No, come with me and tell me what you want. There is a fridge upstairs you can put things in." Thomas ran down with Nick and they put together some food and he had Thomas take it upstairs and Nick then locked the door.

Thomas and Nan fit in beautifully at Yumsters. They lived in the playhouse for about three months. Nick and Annie offered to have them move into their house for a while but they wouldn't hear of it. They liked the playhouse. It gave Thomas and Nan a chance to get their lives in order. Thomas helped out in the restaurant in any way he could. He cleaned, painted, waited tables, made repairs and when he couldn't find anything to do at the restaurant, he worked at Nick and Annie's house; it always needed some attention.

Nan was indeed a good baker and she baked all of the regular menu items and came up with some of her own. She and Annie developed a warm relationship just as Nick and Thomas did. In the spring, Thomas and Nan's house in Montgomery sold and that enabled them to buy a small house nearby. Thomas got a job as a mechanical engineer at Watson Engineering in Bristol. Nan, however, still did not have a teaching job but loved working in Yumsters. She could leave Jessie with a sitter in the playhouse, just as Annie and Nick had done with their children, and would run up and see her any time she had a break. Nick and Annie spent lots of time with Jessie too. Annie would let her help with a special dessert, and Nick would carry her on his shoulders while he straighten and set up tables. Sometimes Angela would watch her for them at the house. More often than not, they all had Sunday dinner at Nick and Annie's house. Annie and Nan prepared Easter dinner together at the house and they hosted Emily, and Beau and Khiem Li's family, and Emily's daughters and their families. Nan and Thomas were a part of the extended Millar family very quickly. Thomas played football with Matthew and Nan showed Angela ways to braid her hair. They all loved Jessie.

Nan took all the day-old baked goods to one of the missions each day. She sometimes stayed and served a meal there. She was becoming as well-known at the shelters as the Millars. She trained young women from Millar House to be bakers. Nan stopped talking about going back to school or teaching. She loved working at Yumsters.

Chapter Twenty-Six

Nick had been waiting for thirty-five minutes in the school parking lot for the bus to arrive. He knew he was early. Angela had texted him about every ten minutes telling him where they were. But, it was the first time Angela had been away for this long and he was anxious to see her. Annie pulled up next to him. "Where are they?"

"Just down the road. Be here in ten minutes." Other cars started arriving to pick up their children. Soon they saw the big lumbering bus creeping down the narrow street and could hear the kids shouting. One by one the children piled off, each met by happy parents and siblings anxious to hear about their trip. Angela was near the back but finally came down the steps. Annie ran to her.

"Mom, Dad, we had such an awesome time. Representative Metzger got us tickets to everything. We got to go to the House of Representatives, we saw her office, and we got a special tour of the White House. It was like we were special visitors. And Dad, she told everyone how you used to work with her and how the two of you were a special team in Washington. She let me sit in her chair in the House of Representatives. It was incredible. She treated me like I was royalty because she likes you so much. She told me you are one of the smartest people she knows."

"Well, she exaggerates incredibly," Nick said laughing. "Remember, she is a politician."

"Nick, I've been thinking," Annie said.

"Ouch, I bet this is going to cost me," Nick replied.

"Just listen, okay? I have a business proposition."

"Hey, I like being propositioned."

"Please be serious," Annie pleaded.

"I'm sorry. I will. Go for it. Wait, let's go into the library and sit at the desk." Nick and Annie had a partners' desk they bought a few years ago. They loved sitting across from one another even if they were working on different things. It was a beautiful piece of furniture and there were two red leather Queen Anne chairs flanking the desk. Nick and Annie each sat down at their respective side.

Annie folded her hands on top of the desk. Nick looked at her intently, obviously curious.

"When is our slowest time of day at Yumsters?" she asked.

"Mid-afternoon," Nick answered. "It slows down about two and picks up again about four-thirty or five," he suggested.

Annie began again, "And you know even though we have to get ready for the dinner crowd, we don't have a lot for the wait staff to do then. They don't like to work split shifts, so we pay them for the full shift even though they don't do much. Right?" she asked.

"Right."

"Well," she said slowly. "What if we would do something to bring in people just during that time?"

"Like what?" Nick asked perplexed.

"Afternoon tea," was her complete answer.

"Like English afternoon tea?" he asked.

"Exactly. Your dad told me about it a couple of times. It really isn't much work. We could have a set menu and a set price. We would still serve the regular menu also like we always do, but I am betting most people will want tea when they hear about it. We would serve a plate of delicious baked goods; scones, of course and other tea cakes. Nan says she can bake them. We could do hot cross buns at Easter. And we would also have a plate of tea sandwiches: smoked salmon, cucumber, and a couple of others. They take no time to prepare. It is really pretty easy. We would serve them on tiered pedestals. We would serve hot water in a tea pot with a tea cozy over it and a bowl of tea bags. Or, no, we would serve two steeped teas," she said thinking it over. "One regular tea and one herbal, no caffeine. That's it. And we would charge per person. No real substitutes. If you want afternoon tea, you get a plate of cakes and a plate of sandwiches, and tea!" she said with finality. Then she added, "I guess we could serve any drink they want. We have them anyway." She paused and looked for a reaction from Nick. "Well?"

"It's brilliant. We could advertise in Philadelphia tourist brochures. You, my dear, are a genius. There is just one thing," he said pausing.

"What?"

"You and I have never really had afternoon tea. We really should experience it once first, don't you think?" he asked.

"Where do they have it?" she asked innocently.

"England," he answered. "Let's go to London on the kid's next break. We'll take them out of school for a few extra days. It will be an educational experience. I just don't think you should serve afternoon tea if you haven't had afternoon tea!"

"Oh, Nick. I have never been out of the United States before! I have a passport though. I got it when I was in Millar House." Nick just smiled.

The timing was perfect because Nan and Thomas could take care of everything at the restaurant while Nick and Annie and the kids were in England. They were only there a week but did everything they wanted to do. They did all the touristy things: The Tower of London, Changing of the Guard, Westminster Abbey, Madame Tussaud's, the new observation wheel, the London Eye, shopping Oxford Street and they had tea at the Ritz. They ordered three-tiered tea trays for the sandwiches from Harrods, tea pots, and tea cozies from various places and had them sent home. It was a wonderful trip and the family enjoyed every minute.

Serving afternoon tea from two until five was a big hit. Annie was right, it was little work and good profit. Some ladies came once a week with friends. Other people stopped in on their way to or from Philadelphia attractions. It was extremely popular.

———— ∞∞∞ ————

"Dad," Matthew said to Nick.

"Yes, Matt,"

"Do you think I'm gay?" he asked his dad.

"Not really. Do you?" Nick asked wondering where this came from.

"I don't know. I don't think so but some guys called me that."

"What guys?" Nick asked.

"Guys from the year ahead of me."

"Just what exactly did they say, Matthew?"

"They said 'Hey Millar, you're gay!'" Matt quoted.

"What do you think they meant by gay?" Nick asked his cherub-faced son.

"I know what it means, Dad! It means you like guys more than girls. But," he explained, "I don't like girls. They really annoy me, Dad. Does that mean I am gay?" Matt asked with a concerned look on his face.

"I don't think most guys like girls at your age Matt. It doesn't mean you are gay. It means you are still interested in Lego, and Star Wars and other things and you just aren't ready to like girls. About when you go into your teens, you start to think more about girls." Nick took a moment to lecture to Matt, "Too many kids, and adults too, use the term gay to mean something negative. It really is a term to describe a group of people who just want to live their lives like everyone else, being treated fairly and not being ridiculed. They deserve the same respect as everyone else." Nick thought he may have gone over Matt's head with that speech but it seemed important to tell him how he felt personally. "Matt, do these boys say anything else that bothers you?" he asked.

"They said all priests are gay. I don't think they know that you were a priest. They said it about Father Naylor when he came to give a talk."

"Wow, that's a pretty broad statement." Nick sighed loudly and tried to think of how to explain to his son in a simple way. "I think maybe that these boys have just learned a new word 'gay' and they are trying to use it as much as possible. Sometimes guys do that. These guys are trying to get attention with their new vocabulary word. There are several ways to handle people like this. One is to just ignore them if you can."

Matt interrupted. "Michael Harper tried to ignore them and they followed him down the hall calling him fag until he cried."

"That's sad, Matt. Well, what if you just acted like it doesn't matter to you. When they say, 'Hey Millar, you're gay', what do you think would happen if you said, 'How's it going?' Or if you said, 'What's happening man,' as if what they are saying makes no sense so you don't acknowledge it. But the trick to this, Matt, is to look them right in the eye. They are trying to embarrass you; make you feel bad. If you look them in the eye and say, 'How is it going?' it didn't work. Does that make any sense at all?"

"I guess so. I'll just look them in the eye and say, 'Whatever!' That's what Angel says to me when she doesn't want to argue with me."

"Matt, that is brilliant. That is the perfect non-confrontational answer. How many kids do these boys say this to?"

"Nearly everyone in my class."

Have they ever hit or hurt anyone, Matt? Do they bully kids or just say silly things?"

"No, they aren't bullies; they are both really little guys for their age."

Nick smiled at his son. "Just look them in the eye, Matt."

It was Career Day at Matt's school and Nick was asked to talk about running a restaurant to the seventh grade. The teachers decided that parents should not talk to their own child's class, so Matt had other parents coming into his sixth grade. It didn't take long for Nick to realize which boys in seventh grade were fixated on the word "gay". Today's word, however, was "sex".

Nick had just started to tell the class about Yumsters when one of the boys raised his hand and asked, "Were you a priest? My mom said you were a priest once."

"That's right," Nick said, to the teacher's amazement. "I was, but now I run a restaurant, and I would like to tell you some of the good things about it and some of the pitfalls." He tried to race ahead.

The same boy interrupted saying, "But, when you were a priest, did you sign a paper saying you wouldn't have sex?"

Another boy jumped in, "So, did you go without sex, or did you break the rule?"

Nick looked to the teacher who made no effort to stop the boys or try to get things back on track. Finally, Nick said, "Listen, you guys, you seem to have a lot of questions about sex. I think maybe you should ask your health teacher and maybe he can talk to you about sex. But, I am here to talk about restaurants and he began to discussing the hours that the restaurant was open and how he tried to be home with his family as much as possible. He talked as fast as he could and tried not to have pauses that the boys could fill in. He went on describing the menu, the duties of the waiters, and what time the bakers come in, and finished without a question period. He ended, leaving a container of cookies for the class. As he left the room, he passed another father ready to come in and talk about being a corporate attorney. Nick nodded to him and said, "Good luck—tough room." On the way home, he stopped and bought Matt a very large Lego set he been wanting and that Nick had a week ago said was too expensive.

Chapter Twenty-Seven

Nick was sitting on the sofa reading the paper when he heard a car drive up in front of their house and he saw it jump the curb as it parked. Angela had been pacing and was looking out the window now. "Have him come in, Angela. You are not to leave until I meet him," Nick said sternly.

"Dad, we're late." She grabbed her hoodie and purse.

"I want to meet him!" Nick said again.

"Oh, all right!" Angela said, furious that she had to go get her date and bring him in.

By the time she got to the car, the boy was getting out. He tried to kiss her but she rebuffed him knowing Nick was watching. Once inside, the boy sheepishly said, "Hi, Mr. Millar," and held out his hand. Nick shook his hand and asked him to sit down. Angela rolled her eyes.

"How are things going, Chad. It is Chad isn't it?" Nick asked. Chad's face was pink and his eyes glazed.

Chad nearly laughed. "That's me."

"Well, Chad," Nick said, "have you been drinking?"

"Oh, not much. I had a beer or two. We were celebrating. We won district last night," he said with pride.

"District! Wow, that's great," Nick said with feigned enthusiasm. "What kind of keys do you have for your car?" Nick asked.

Chad was trying to figure out what Nick meant and took out his car keys and looked at them in his palm. Nick took them from his hand. "Angela isn't going out with you tonight, Chad. Her mother and I have rules about drinking and driving." Angela was about to cry but wanted to see Chad's reaction. "Tell you what, Chad. I will be your designated driver. I will drive you home in your car. You look tired, man. How about you go home and get some sleep." He turned to Angela and said, "Follow me, sweetheart, and bring me back home." Nick tossed her the keys to his car. She didn't say anything.

Chad was compliant. He walked with them to the cars and told Nick where he lived. He didn't seem to notice that Angela wasn't with them. Nick talked to Chad on the way to his house but there was little conversation on Chad's part. He nodded off a couple of times. Nick pulled to the curb in front of Chad's house and turned off the engine. Chad made no effort to get out of the car, so Nick went around and opened the door for him. They walked up the front steps and Nick rang the bell. Again, Chad made no effort to do or say anything. He stood facing the door to his home. Chad's mother, Mrs. Anderson, came to the door. "What's going on?" she asked suspiciously. By this time Angela had joined them.

Nick explained without judgment. "I'm Nick Millar. Chad came over to our house to pick up our daughter, Angela, tonight. Unfortunately, Chad has been drinking and Angela's mother and I don't allow Angela to go out with someone who has been drinking. I drove Chad home." He put out his hand for her to take Chad's car keys. Chad walked on into the house but the rest of them stayed at the door.

Mrs. Anderson was upset, but not with Chad, with Nick. "Who are you to judge my son as drunk. He was perfectly capable of driving home. Teenage boys these days have a beer once in a while, so get used to it! Are you so sure that your precious daughter doesn't drink?"

Nick had had enough of being nice. "Mrs. Anderson, your son is drunk and he certainly had more than one beer. He couldn't park the car in front of my house." Before they could say any more, they all heard retching as Chad lost it all in the hall. Nick looked directly at Mrs. Anderson. "It seems Chad must have caught the flu on the way home. Hope he is feeling better tomorrow." He and Angela walked back to the car and Nick drove them home.

At first Angela didn't say anything. Finally, she said meekly, "He is one of the most popular boys in my class. I was so excited to go out with him." She leaned against her dad and continued, "We could have been like those kids we read about in the paper who are killed when they hit a tree, couldn't we?"

"Angela, I want you to date the popular boys, if that's what you want. But I want you to have enough self-worth to stay home when it isn't safe to be with them. You can blame it on us. When I was a kid and pressed to do something, I knew I shouldn't, I would say 'I can't, my parents would kill me.' Come to think of it, I think they would have."

"I don't want Chad to be killed hitting a tree either, even by himself. That's why I drove him home. I don't know why his mother was protecting him, or thought she was. Maybe she was just embarrassed. I am not saying Chad is a bad kid. Teenagers do have a beer now and then. I did when I was a teenager. But if he can't make the judgment call about whether or not he is capable to drive, someone has to make it for him. I will pick you up anytime, anywhere, baby, if you need a ride for any reason. Call me. Call your mom. Don't risk your life to be with someone just because they are popular."

"I'm glad we married you, Dad," she said sweetly. She use to say that when she was little but she hadn't said it for a long time. It gave him pause for thought about getting on with letting her meet her father.

When they got home, Matt and Annie had just returned from the grocery. Angela came into the house yelling, "Mom, Dad is trying to ruin my life," but the tone of her voice showed she wasn't really upset. She ran upstairs.

Annie replied, "We all try, dear." She kissed Nick and asked, "Where have you two been?" Nick explained the situation but didn't mention his concern about Angela needing to hear about her birth father because Matt was in the room.

Nick sat down at the table looking somewhat weary. "Matt," he said. "What would you think about military school?"

"Huh?" Matt replied.

"I'm thinking it might be a good thing if you went to a military school for high school. When I was at Notre Dame, I knew kids from Howe and Culver military academies near there. What do you think, Annie? Shall we send Matt to military school?"

"What did I do?" Matt asked.

"Nothing son, but maybe we can keep your record clean if you go to a military academy. Sound fun?"

"Well, no! Mom, what's up with Dad?"

Annie answered, "He's insane honey, but don't let it bother you."

"Annie, what do you have against military academies?"

"Well now that you mention it, it may be that they prepare young boys to fight in wars," Annie said. "And besides," she went on, "I thought you were a pacifist?"

"You make a good point. Well, if military academies are out, would you home school both of them?"

"Nick, you are insane," Annie said as she poured him a glass of iced tea and sat it in front of him.

"Not even if we made the playhouse into a little school?" he asked. Annie ignored him.

Angela came bounding down the stairs and into the kitchen. "Home schooled? I don't think so. I'm going out with Corey," she said cheerfully.

"Corey?" Nick said. "A half an hour ago you had a date with Chad. When did you make plans with Corey?"

"I texted him from the car on the way home," she stated matter-of-factly. "You were driving, not me. I never text when I drive. Besides, it's not a real date. It's Corey. Corey is my bf. He is there for me when my father screws up my life."

"Angela, about that," Nick said.

"I'm just kidding, Dad. You did the right thing. Corey and I are going to a movie. Okay?"

"Okay." Angela started for the door. "Just one more thing, Angel," Nick said following her.

"I know, 'Don't do anything illegal, immoral, or stupid'," she said quoting what her dad so frequently said and his father before him.

"Actually, that isn't what I was going to say but now that you mention it, don't do anything illegal, immoral, or stupid. How would you feel about being a nun?" he said quickly. Angela rolled her eyes. She looked at her mother and Annie shrugged her shoulders. "Did you see that Oprah show a few years ago with the young nuns? They seemed really happy. The ones I knew were happy I think. They wear sensible shoes; no foot problems," he was muttering now. Nick got up and walked Angela to the door. "What I really was going to say is," he paused trying to find the right words. "I love you." Angela looked at him to hear the rest. Nothing more was said. Finally, he said again, "I just love you." Angela kissed him on the cheek.

"I will think about being home schooled," she said with a wink. Then she added, "But absolutely not about being a nun. Hey, maybe I would like a military academy. Being with mostly guys...not too bad, Dad. I'll think about it."

Nick sat down on the sofa, his elbows on his knees, and head in his hands. Annie came in and put her arm around him. When he looked up, she planted a kiss on him that continued as she flattened him on the sofa. She continued the kiss as she was on top of him, then stopped suddenly, kissed him lightly on the forehead and got up and walked away.

"Hey, that's not nice. You can't just start something and walk away leaving me like this," he complained.

Annie turned and smiled at her frustrated husband. "I just wanted you to remember what it was like to be a teenager," she said sweetly.

Nick pulled a pillow from the sofa over his face and said to himself, I remember.

"Nick, guess what?" Annie said with glee.

"I give up."

The Schmidts are going to sell the ice cream shop next door. You know, we thought they would. I know you don't want to expand any more. But I have been thinking...."

"Oh God, help me," Nick said in jest.

"Just listen, Nick."

"I am listening."

"I know it isn't very big. It is narrow and straight back. But, I think we could make it into a bakery and Nan could run it for us," she said with finality.

"A bakery?" Nick said trying to catch up.

"Yes, we could do all of our baking there. Our kitchen is crowded now. But if we did all of the baking next door, the kitchen could be used for everything else. And," she went on, "we could sell some of the scones and tea cakes we serve at tea, in the bakery. It could just be a sweets bakery. We would bake the rolls and bread for the restaurant, but only sell the sweets in the bakery. Bread is too time-consuming. We will just bake what bread we need, like we do now. But sweets don't take very long and we could sell them in the shop. Nan could run it. What do you think?"

"I think you must never sleep. Do you ever rest? Do you ever stop coming up with brilliant ideas?" Nick beamed with pride. "I'll go talk with Morgan. We have the option and they have to offer it to us first. What do you want to name it? Have you thought of that too?"

"I was thinking 'Yummies'. Too dumb?" she asked.

Nick thought it over. "Yumsters the restaurant, Annie-Yums the catering company, and Yummies the bakery. No, it is perfect, of course. You are scary."

"I think we should bake éclairs," Annie said. "I've never had an éclair and they sound so elegant."

"Well then, we will have éclairs," Nick stated affirmatively. "But," he said sadly, "we don't have time to go to Paris to taste them first. I will try to find you one somewhere around here."

Chapter Twenty-Eight

"**D**ad," Angela said smiling, "you aren't going to embarrass me tonight are you?"

"Of course I am," Nick said smiling back. "It is my duty as a father to embarrass you."

"What are you worried about Angel?" Annie asked. "I'm the one who is going to embarrass you. I look ridiculous in your cheerleading outfit. Your dad is a fantastic basketball player. You know he's better than anyone on the parents' team and probably better than most of the boys on the school team."

Nick was smiling at them both. "Of course, I can only last one quarter. By half time you will have to call 911. And you look unbelievable in the cheerleading outfit," he said addressing Annie. "How many mothers can even fit into their daughter's outfit?" This was the first year that Nick and Annie had participated in the parents versus the varsity basketball team. It was a tradition that went back before Nick's time as a student. His father and mother participated for two years when Nick played varsity basketball. It is not a very serious game. By the end of the evening, the parents usually are getting beaten badly and start cheating and fouling any chance they get. It is a fundraiser for the athletic program.

"Tipper Archer and Melody Allan said their mothers had to buy new cheerleading skirts and borrowed letter sweaters from some boys. Believe me, they can't fit into their daughters' outfits," Angela said with pride. "You do look great, Mom."

"Mrs. Archer, can't even fit into this room," Matt said sarcastically.

"Matt! That's enough," Annie chastised. Nick grabbed Matt and gave him a noogie, rubbing his knuckles in his hair.

"Let's have dinner. I have to go to school early. We haven't practiced very much," Nick lamented.

"Your team doesn't stand a chance, Dad, no matter how much you practice," Angela said. "Our guys are tough. You old guys are going to be…" She put her hand up to her forehead making an "L", "Losers!"

Nick now grabbed Angela and acted as if he were going to give her a noogie but instead made an irritating noise in her ear.

Nick's team had only eight players. They tried in vain to get other dads to play but they only came up with eight. That meant they could not foul out and couldn't substitute much. Brent Walker, who sometimes played with Nick, agreed to coach them since he had a torn ligament and couldn't play. There was no shortage of cheerleaders for the parents' team. Twelve women volunteered. Annie tried to get out of it when she learned they had so many but three of her friends were on the team and wouldn't let her. "It is all four of us, or none of us," her friend Nadia said. "You can be head cheerleader," Stacie said. "You are the only one who can get the crowd to look at us," she said to flatter Annie. "And you are so tiny, we can easily lift you up or put you on top of a pyramid."

Annie looked worried. "Our insurance plan isn't that good. Let's don't do any lifting."

It was a good crowd. The gym was filled to near capacity. Jonathan and Nan came for moral support. Both Nick and Annie were glad to see them there. Nan was making a wonderful success of the bakery and Jonathan was happy in his new job. Angela took Jessie over to the student cheer section and gave her pom-poms and said she could help them cheer. Beau and Khiem Li sat on the bottom row of the bleachers. Beau, however, heckled Nick more than supported; in a friendly, brotherly way. All of Angela's friends were there teasing their mothers who were cheering and fathers who were playing. Nick noticed that Chad was starting but didn't say anything to him.

The first quarter was fairly routine. The two sides seemed almost evenly matched. Nick did shine for the dad's team and the varsity team was not prepared for him to be so good. He made four baskets and both of his foul shots. The score was sixteen to fourteen in favor of the varsity. The second quarter the varsity stepped it up. By the half, they increased their lead to thirty to twenty-one. They accomplished this mostly by tying Nick up so he couldn't get the ball. The dads were spent by half time. The two cheer squads competed for attention during the half and it was a shouting match for the entire break.

In the third quarter, Nick played really well. He faked, bumped, and out foxed Chad several times. Chad tried to take the ball from Nick as he started down court but Nick bumped him out of the way and Chad faked a fall to the ground trying to get a foul on Nick. Nick went to the basket and dunked it. He ran back down court and reached down and helped Chad up from the floor. Chad said nothing. Nick patted him on the shoulder. Annie had teased Nick earlier in the day, asking if he was going to slap everyone on the butt all evening like most players she had seen on television. Nick said it had been part of priest training to be very careful where you touch people, especially children. The dads continued to be able to get the ball to Nick and they ran the score up to thirty-eight, thirty-seven in their favor by the end of the third quarter.

The fourth quarter the dads crashed. It was just as Nick feared, they just plain wore out. The fit teenagers were running circles around them. They were exhausted. They began to clown around. They called time out and tried to get the women cheerleaders to go in for them. They sat when the other team had a foul shot. Nick would run a few feet and hurl the ball at the basket so he wouldn't have to run farther. They lost fifty-eight to forty-four. All of the cheerleaders came onto the floor and many supporters too. It was a good night and everyone had a good time, despite the fact a lot of middle-aged men were going to have trouble getting out of bed the next day. As the players were all going to the dressing rooms, Nick stopped Chad. "Great job, Chad. You are a good ball handler."

"Thanks," he muttered embarrassedly. He started to walk away but he stopped and turned back. "You are pretty good too..." he looked for the words.

Nick laughed, "For an old guy?"

Chad made a face of regret. He continued to stand and Nick waited to see if there was something more. Chad said, "I'm not drinking. I stopped," he turned and walked away.

Nick ran up to him. "That's great, Chad. No wonder you play so well. You are really healthy. I'm proud of you. Are your parents here?" he asked.

Chad shook his head, obviously wishing they were. "My mom never comes."

Nick thought, why do parents screw things up so badly sometimes? He put his arm around the boy's shoulders and walked him to the locker room. "If you ever need a job, come around to the restaurant," he said. Chad looked up at him and almost smiled.

Chapter Twenty-Nine

"**N**an, let's close up. You need to get home. I'm sorry I'm late. I'll stay and close. You go on home," Nick said as he came into the bakery. It had been a phenomenal success. Nan loved working there and she had a talent for baking. The bakery closed at seven. Nick usually ran over to make sure everything was okay before Nan went home, then went back to the restaurant until closing there. "Nan?" No answer. He knew she hadn't gone home because her car was still there and all the lights were on in the bakery. She must have late customers he thought, looking at his watch and seeing it was nearly seven twenty. "Nan?"

Nick walked into the main part of the bakery and saw a man leaning up against the glass case. The man had his back to Nick and he couldn't see his face. "How's it going?" Nick said in a friendly voice. The man moved slightly and as he did, Nick saw Nan crumpled on the floor. He pushed the man out of the way and bent over Nan. He saw blood puddling around her body as he raised her head from the floor. He looked up at the man to try to make some sense out of what was happening. Nick tried to think of what to do. He put his hand to Nan's neck to check for a pulse and heard a sharp noise. He fell over Nan's body.

"Nick. Can you hear me, Nick?" Annie was standing beside the hospital bed holding his hand, trying to wake him. All of the medical information had been explained to her. He had seven hours of surgery to make repairs to the skull and where the bullet grazed the brain. They didn't know the extent of the damage but were very optimistic. There would be a lot of swelling for a while they told her, so they couldn't tell right away. There would probably be some lack of mobility on one side but it might be temporary. He might have verbal problems initially. The doctors were generally optimistic but always ended with "time will tell" or "we will have to wait and see".

A nurse, Laurie, and Emily were all in the room with Annie. Annie was stern. "Nick. You are okay, Nick. Wake up. Squeeze my hand." He made no effort to move. The others decided to go for coffee and Annie was left with the nurse.

"Give it time, Mrs. Millar. He has had a lot of anesthesia. Be prepared he may not seem to recognize you at first. That's normal. We have to be patient." The nurse nodded toward the call button. "Call if he opens his eyes or moves in any way." She smiled at Annie. "He is going to be okay. It may take a while, but he'll make a good recovery. He's a healthy young man. He was lucky. There wasn't as much damage as there could have been," she said positively. "With therapy he will probably walk and talk again. Just give him time to come out it." She patted Annie on the back as she left the room.

Lucky, she thought. Lucky to come into the bakery in the middle of a robbery. Lucky to find Nan dead. Lucky to be shot in the head. And probably! That word stuck in her craw also. He will probably walk and talk again! It seemed like this was the longest night of her life. But he was alive! They were lucky, she admitted it. It seemed like she had been waiting forever for him to wake up. She moved back and sat in a chair watching his chest move ever so slightly. She leaned her head back against the back of the chair and closed her eyes for just a second she thought. "Ahh," she heard the voice whisper. She looked to Nick. His eyes were still closed. She waited. "Ahh," he repeated. This time she saw his mouth move ever so slightly. *Ann*. He's trying to say *Ann*, she said to herself.

Annie carefully took Nick's hand, trying to avoid the tubes and taped areas. "I'm here, Nick. I'm here," she said through tears. "I need you, Nick," she said under her breath. "I can't go on without you." He was making an effort to open his eyes, they fluttered but he couldn't keep them open. "I'm here, Nick," she said again, gaining some of her inner strength to encourage him. "Can you squeeze my hand?" She slipped her hand under his to see if he could. His fingers moved ever so little. She stared at the barely perceivable movement.

He whispered again, "Annnn." This time when she looked up, he was awake; his eyes were open. "Annn," he said once more. His head was bandaged so that he was propped to look right at her. She couldn't tell if he could see her or not. She didn't want to move to press the call button. She didn't want to do anything that might make him close his eyes again. She gently rubbed his hand. He looped one finger around hers and held on to it. She kissed his hand then put her cheek against his. His cheek was warm. A tear fell from her onto his cheek and she gently wiped it away. She sat on the bed holding his hand for nearly ten minutes with neither saying anything. Occasionally, Nick would close his eyes but then immediately open them willing them to stay open. He stared at Annie but made no effort to speak. Finally, she pressed the call button.

Annie stayed with Nick in his room that night. Once she woke hearing him paw at his chest. She went to him and he woke pointing to his neck. Finally, she realized he was missing his crucifix. When she took his hand, he touched her wedding ring and she looked at his hand and saw his ring was missing also. She spoke to a nurse and they came up with the crucifix, his rosary that he always carried in his pocket, his wedding ring and his wallet. They didn't want him to wear the ring because of swelling but said he could have the crucifix back around his neck. Annie took the wedding ring and strung it on the chain before she put it on him. She put the rosary in his hand and he went back to sleep.

Nick began to make some progress in the next few days. First it was just staying awake. Then it was being aware there were people around. Finally, he was trying to communicate with the doctors and nurses. He met with both physical and speech therapists. They were optimistic. Doctors said it would take some time for both his leg and arm on one side to gain strength. He was told he may never run down the basketball court, as before, but Nick knew he couldn't play like that forever. He could probably still play one-one-one with Matt and shoot hoops eventually. That was what he hoped for. It was possible that he might have a slight limp, but Nick was not concerned. He began to talk a bit, in choppy incomplete sentences but he had no trouble with cognitive understanding. He was indeed lucky.

One morning he woke to see a small shadow in the doorway. "Hi, Dad," a little voice whispered. Nick looked as if he was going to try to have a go at saying the name but he didn't. Instead he held out his hand. Angela walked slowly to him. "Hi, Dad," she said again with the same timidity. He squeezed her hand.

Nick saw that she had been crying. He looked directly at her. "I'm okay," he said with effort. Angela searched his face for a flicker of a smile but there was none. She would have to be content with his statement, and she did feel better that she had heard him speak. At home, there had been lots of people in and out but no one really talked to her. Her mom was so frazzled, everyone was trying to help her and no one said much to the children. Matt and Angela had been huddled together ever since it happened. Annie told them she didn't want them to go to the hospital until Nick was a little stronger. She wanted to protect them from seeing him struggling to walk and talk. Angela couldn't wait any longer; she felt a compulsion to go, but Matt didn't want to come with her. He was afraid; both afraid of being late to school and afraid of seeing his dad. Angela promised to text him as soon as she left the hospital.

"I was so scared, Daddy," she said reverting back to her younger name for Nick. "I had to see you. I have been so scared," she repeated. "I took Matt to school. He said to tell you he loves you," she said sweetly.

Nick pulled his hand from hers and put it on her face. He looked directly into her eyes and said clearly, "I'm okay." He wiped away a tear from her cheek. Angela noticed he used only his one hand, his other had not moved from his side. Before she could think of a way to learn any more about his condition, Annie appeared at the door.

Angela blurted out, "I'm sorry, Mom, I had to come," and began to sob. Annie rushed in and took Angela in her arms.

"It's okay, Angela," Annie said cradling Angela's head against her chest. "I shouldn't have tried to keep you away. I just didn't want to frighten you. I probably frightened you more by keeping you away. I'm sorry. Dad's fine. I'm glad you got to see him. We are all going to be fine. Dad's doing great and will be home soon. You and Matt can both come back with me tonight if you want. Okay?" Angela shook her head. "I'll write you a note to get into school late."

Flowers continued to arrive for Nick. Annie finally had to ask that they keep the cards but pass the flowers on to nursing homes. A huge basket of spring flowers came from Abbe. It took up the entire table. That one, everyone made sure made it to the room. Congressman Abbe Metzger was a name everyone recognized in Pennsylvania. The card was signed simply "Love you Nick, Abbe"

Nick still had no memory of the incident. He didn't ask. The day he was to leave the hospital to go home, the decision was made to tell him about it. Annie had spoken to a psychologist who was a friend of Nick's father and he had agreed to meet with them before Nick was released. After the psychologist, the surgeon would explain the wound to Nick and the surgical procedure that took place. The medical staff all agreed that it was important for Nick to first understand what had happened to him. Nick was dressed and propped on the bed in his room, Annie at his side, when two men came in and introduced themselves. The older of the two came up and thrust his hand at Nick saying, "I'm Brad Seigers. I knew your father well. He was a great man. I have retired but my son, Jon, has taken over my practice." He indicated by gesture that the young man with him was his son. Jon Seigers then came up to Nick and shook hands with him and continued the conversation. Brad sat down against the wall as his son took over.

"Nick," Dr. Seigers said, "what do you remember about the night all this happened?"

Nick thought for a minute, trying to find the easiest word to explain that he could verbalize. "Zip," he finally said shaking his head.

"Do you know what happened to you, Nick?" the doctor asked.

"Stroke?" Nick asked. Annie put her hand to her mouth. My God, she said to herself, he has no idea. The poor guy thought he had a stroke! Nick also thought it might have been a brain tumor but he wasn't ready to hear about it until now, so he didn't ask. Either seem possible to him.

"I'm afraid not, Nick. I can understand why you thought it was a stroke but in fact you were shot. Do you remember being shot?"

"No." Nick was stunned.

"You were shot, Nick. You were shot in the head where you have the bandage. Have you any idea where you were when this happened; when you were shot, I mean?" Dr. Seigers probed.

Nick frowned. He obviously had not thought about it. He finally answered as a question, "Yum sss?"

"Is that the restaurant you own?" Dr. Seigers asked. Nick nodded. "Actually, it took place at the bakery. It is next door to your restaurant isn't it?" Again Nick nodded. He let that sink in. "So, Nick, you understand that the shooting took place at the bakery?"

"Yes," Nick answered.

Dr. Seigers went on slowly almost sounding as if he were in court. "Now as I understand it, the bakery is next door to your restaurant, but there is no door connecting the two. Is that right?" Nick looked confused and looked at Annie.

Annie repeated the question to Nick, and Nick nodded affirmatively. Dr. Seigers continued, "Evidently, Nick, you entered through the back door. Do you know what happened next?" Nick bit his lip and shook his head that he did not know. "Do you know that someone else was in the bakery when you came in?" he asked.

Nick again looked to Annie and then back to the doctor. "The gun mun?" Nick questioned forming the words the best he could.

This time the doctor nodded in agreement. "Yes, but someone else was in the bakery too. Do you remember?"

Nick continued to chew the inside of his mouth and shook his head no. He closed his eyes for a moment and then opened them and looked at Annie. "Nan?" he asked sorrowfully. Annie now nodded in agreement. Nick put his hand over his mouth. "Shot?" Again Annie nodded her head. "Hurt?" he asked in a pathetic voice, afraid of the answer. Annie looked to Dr. Seigers.

"Nick, your friend Nan, was shot and killed. She was on the floor when you came in. They think she was dead by the time you arrived.

Do you remember anything now?" Nick took his hand from his mouth and covered his eyes then put it back on his mouth again. Finally, taking Annie's hand in his. Nick shook his head.

"Are you doing okay?" Dr. Seigers asked. "Do you need some time? Or do you want me to go on?" he asked Nick.

"Okay," Nick answered very softly.

Dr. Seigers continued on. "The gunman was still in the bakery when you came in. Do you remember seeing him?"

"No," Nick quickly answered.

"Nick, do you know a man named Curt Norris?" Dr. Seigers asked. Nick turned white and swallowed audibly. Annie reached up and stroked his face. She was afraid he was going to pass out. The nurse, who had been standing back, walked up and offered him a drink of water, holding the straw for him. He took a small sip. "The police tell us that Curt Norris has confessed to killing your friend, Nan, and also shooting you. He actually called 911 from his car and sat until they arrived and arrested him." Dr. Seigers waited for some response from Nick. He got none. Nick was kneading Annie's hand, lacing his fingers in and out of hers nervously.

Finally, Nick said, "Why?"

"I can't answer that for you, I am sorry. I don't know his motive. The police may know but they have not made that known to the public," Jon Seigers said. "Mr. Norris didn't have money from the bakery on him when arrested, but we assume he was going to rob the bakery."

"Oh God. Why....Nan? I...give...," Nick said, trying hard to be understood.

"You would have given Curt money?" Annie said. "Is that what you want to say?" He nodded. "We know you would have, sweetheart. Probably Curt knows that too. I don't know why he killed Nan. Or, shot you," she added. "None of it makes any sense to any of us, Nick. We just don't know why Curt did it."

A tear ran down Nick's cheek. "Jon thun," he wailed. "Jess," he tried to say but had trouble pronouncing both names. Annie began to sob and leaned into Nick's shoulder.

Annie held on to Nick's neck, wrapping her arm around him, whispering in his ear. "I am so sorry, Nick. We are all so sorry. We loved Nan. We all feel so bad for Jonathan and Jessie."

Nick pointed to himself but couldn't speak. "I…" he started to say. "Fault," he finally stammered.

"No," both Dr. Seigers and Annie said at the same time. Dr. Seigers took over. "The reason I am here is to help you process this information and know the facts. Nothing is your fault. Mr. Norris pulled the trigger two times. He aimed it at two people. One lived and one died. You lived, she died. She happened to be there. You happened to come into the building after he shot her."

"Me," Nick shouted. "Want me?" he asked.

"We don't know what was in the heart or mind of Mr. Norris. We only know he did a very bad thing. We know that you just showed up. You did nothing wrong. Your friend, Nan, was in the wrong place at the wrong time. She did nothing wrong either. You are both, innocent victims."

Nick continued to shake his head. "My 'ployee," he said with difficulty.

"It doesn't matter that she worked for you. It doesn't matter that you knew Mr. Norris. You have done nothing wrong. Tell me what you are thinking, Nick!" Dr. Seigers demanded.

Nick shrugged his shoulders. "Came for me?"

"We don't know if he came for you. It appears he came for money. It doesn't matter. His motivation has nothing to do with you. Nan worked for you because she wanted to do so. You didn't hold her captive. She was working that night because she had agreed to do so. You are not responsible in any way for what happened that night. Only Mr. Norris is responsible. You know that, don't you Nick? I bet you have counseled people yourself in similar ways. You have told them that we are only responsible for our own actions, not those of others." Dr. Seigers changed is tone slightly. "Nick," he paused so Nick would look at him. "This has been a shock for you. You needed to hear what happened because you may start to remember some of it. You may never remember it. The human brain has peculiar devices.

Sometimes it tries to protect us from pain. I want to know that you are processing this information in a healthy way. Talk to me."

"So sad," Nick said mournfully.

"Yes, it is that," Jon Seigers said.

"Jon thun, Jess," Nick said.

Annie put her hands on either side of Nick's face. "Nick, it is sad. It is so sad. Nan was like one of the family. We loved Jonathan and Jessie too. It's horrible. It is just plain horrible."

"Fune ral?" he tried to ask in a phonetic way but couldn't get it all out.

"Yes," Annie answered. "They had the funeral on Tuesday at the Baptist church. It was wonderful. There was beautiful music and lots of tears. Everyone gathered around to help Jonathan and Jessie. Nan's mother and sister came. They took Jessie back with them. Jonathan wants to see you but was waiting until you were ready." Nick continued to shake his head in disbelief.

"Nick, I know you want to go home. Are you able to go home? If you need help, I am here. If you want to stay here a day or two I can arrange that. Do you want to stay?" Dr. Seigers asked.

Nick shook his head. "Home...kids," he said. He looked at Annie. "Ann," he said.

"Okay, Nick, but I am here. I think we need to spend some time talking about this. Will you come to see me next week?" Dr. Seigers said.

Nick shook his head but without really listening. He was still thinking about Nan being killed; about Jonathan and Jessie without Nan; about Curt killing Nan and shooting him; about Lillian and Curt and their children. "God!" he said as he leaned back against the pillows. He was so exhausted. Annie lay down next to him, turned on her side and slid under his arm. The Doctors Seigers left the room.

Chapter Thirty

At home, Nick was sad and moody and even impatient with the children. He asked to see Jonathan but he had taken some time off and was out of town. It was a painstakingly difficult task to go down stairs in the beginning, so Nick stayed mostly in the bedroom upstairs. He only went out to go to therapy at the hospital. Annie stayed home as much as she could when he first came home and then Emily came and stayed with Nick so that Annie could take care of the restaurant and getting things at the bakery straightened out. She had to get rid of the inventory, so she took it to Millar House and other shelters. She and Nick agreed not to open the bakery for a while. Emily was so grateful that Nick was not more seriously hurt, she didn't push him to do anything. She went into an indulgent-mother mode and cooked anything she thought he might eat and ran around trying to find ways to entertain him.

The next week, Beau stayed with Nick once or twice but one day Nick asked him to go home. Beau couldn't stand the silence that Nick seemed to require and wanted the television on or a computer game going. Nick didn't seem to tolerate the noise well. It was the same for Angela and Matt. They would go in to see Nick but he had little to say to them. If they started to play around and get silly, Nick would send them out. Angela went downstairs one day in tears. "Mom, will Dad ever be all right again?" Annie was beginning to wonder too.

Laurie came to visit one day. Nick was dressed and sitting in a chair in the bedroom. "Hey, loafer. What's going on?" Laurie asked.

Nick shook his head, indicating nothing was going on and that was okay with him.

"I hear from the grapevine that you are giving everyone a hard time," Laurie said. Nick looked shocked and shook his head. He rolled his chair over to his computer and got into MSWord.

"I am giving who a hard time?" he typed in.

"The kids and Annie, I guess. Don't you talk at all? I didn't know you typed everything out. You were talking some the other day," Laurie said.

"This is just faster," Nick typed as a reply.

"Annie and the kids said you are grouchy. Is that right Nick? That is so unlike you. You are usually so intolerably positive," Laurie said smiling.

Nick thought for a minute. Then he typed, "This is hell."

"Are you in pain?" Laurie asked sincerely and honestly.

"Not physical pain but," then he stopped typing. He looked at Laurie to see if he could trust her; to see if she could understand what he was going through. After all, she was his sister. He typed again, "I feel really bad about Nan and Thomas. And Jessie," he added. Then he went on as if to cover his honest expression of feeling with something more obvious. "I still have headaches and the medicine upsets my stomach and makes me throw up so I try not to take it. Ann and the kids think I should just get on with things and stop complaining," he ended.

"Nicky, Annie and the kids were scared shitless. They are so grateful you are going to be okay. I hate to see you having problems with them. They love you. They want to help you. They really do," Laurie stated affirmatively.

"I know," he typed.

"How can I help?" Laurie asked. She would do anything for her brother. Nick shrugged his shoulders.

"I'll talk to your doctor and see if he can change the medication to something you can tolerate better. Okay bro?" Nick nodded. Laurie kissed him on the cheek and went down to talk to Annie.

"How did he seem?" Annie asked.

"Okay, I guess. He is pretty broken up over Nan's death. I guess that's normal, don't you?" she said feeling she had to defend Nick.

"Did he talk to you?" Annie asked.

"Yes." She casually added, "Well, he typed mostly."

"He typed!" Annie shouted. "And you let him get away with that? Laurie, you are as bad as your mother. He is supposed to talk. He can talk, you know." Annie sat down at the table and put her head on her arms.

Laurie looked at Annie. "My God," she said, "I have turned into my mother. I don't know why I let him get away with that. I'm sorry Annie. I'll come back tomorrow and have a go at him. I guess I am just so thankful he is alive…" she trailed off. "I'm sorry, Annie. I'll be better next time. I am a nurse. I should know better."

Later in the afternoon, Nick heard the back door slam even upstairs, where he was sitting in a chair. He then heard Annie's footsteps on the stairs. She walked up to him still wearing her jacket. She took it off and threw it on the bed. "We had a little caregiver conference today, Nick. I met with all your therapists. Guess what? They want to discontinue. They tell me you don't even try to get better. Your speech therapist says she thinks you can make almost all of the sounds, but you won't try. I think you like to be silent, don't you Nick? You know how to keep from talking. You are good at it. Does it remind you of when you were a priest? Do you like shutting all of us out? I am disgusted with you. Poor Nick Millar. Let's all feel sorry for Nick. Nick, with the perfect grades, perfect teeth, from the perfect family. Not so perfect anymore. Boo hoo! Other people have had really bad things they have had to deal with and they get on with their life. Not Nick. Everything has to be perfect for Nick. It has been easy so far, so if it gets hard, you just quit." Annie was furious and lashing out at Nick with everything she had.

Nick stood up and put his hand in his pocket and bit his lip listening to Annie. "When you put your weak hand in your pocket like that, I just want to slap you. Take it out of you damn pocket and use it. I never see you try one thing with that hand. Your physical therapist and occupational therapist say the same thing. It's too hard for you, isn't it Nick. Everything is supposed to be easy. I've had it."

Nick still hadn't said anything. They stood looking eye to eye without either flinching.

Finally Annie said, "I want a divorce. You aren't the man I married. You are a quitter. You can have the house and sit here all day and feel sorry for yourself. Maybe Mommy will come and help you. I will take the businesses and continue to make something of my life and the children's." She turned and walked out of the room and downstairs.

Later both kids came home from school but Annie asked them not to go up and see Nick right away. She was hoping he would come down to see them. He didn't. Annie went upstairs one time to get something and heard noises from their bedroom. Nick was talking, chanting, maybe singing. It was slurred but audible. She tried to listen from the hall but couldn't understand. She went back down stairs.

Angela and Matt were having a snack and talking when suddenly the three of them heard a noise from upstairs. It first sounded like a knock but then became apparent it was pounding on the floor above them. The three of them ran up the stairs. Annie took a breath and opened the door. Nick was lying on the floor face down. She stopped the children from going in. From the door she asked, "What's wrong?"

Nick turned is head to face her and said, "Get me up!"

"Why?" Annie asked. Matt started to push past Annie to help his dad but Annie held him back.

"Help up!" Nick demanded.

"Why?" Annie asked again.

"Fell," he said with some effort. By now he was glaring at her. His four-pronged cane was across the room.

"And?" Annie said.

"Need help," he said through clinched teeth.

"What? I can't hear you. Say it louder," she instructed.

"I need help!" he said loudly.

"Say it louder, Annie said.

"I need help." He said it softer this time instead, totally defeated.

"Finally," Annie said as she and the kids pulled Nick to his feet and helped him sit on the bed. "What were you doing in here, rocking and bopping?" Annie asked.

"Having funeral," Nick said.

"Oh Nick, I'm sorry you couldn't go to the funeral. She sat down on the bed next to Nick and leaned her head against him. "I was hard on you today, I admit," Annie said. "I will give you all the help you need, if you will help yourself too. Is it a deal?" She kissed him on the cheek. Nick tried to smile. It was a little lopsided but could be perceived as a smile. The first one since the shooting. "Let's go downstairs," she suggested. "Now here's the deal. You are supposed to use both railings and alternate your feet. Got it?" Nick nodded as he walked to the stairs. "And," she added, "you are to talk in complete sentences. I don't care how long it takes you."

"Okay," Nick answered.

"Okay what?" she asked.

"Okay, I will walk, ddddown sstairs holding...on," he managed to get out with some difficulty.

Annie recognized she had him where she wanted him and went on. "And, the next time I see you with your hand in your pocket, you had better be going for your car keys."

They slowly made it to the bottom of the stairs and Nick turned to Annie. "I'm sorry."

Annie looked at him and grinned. "You are sorry what?"

"I am sorry you are sooo mmmean," he grinned back.

"You are not. I'm the best thing that ever happened to you," she said smugly.

"I know," he said defeated.

"Nick," Annie said suddenly, "I'm an idiot!" Nick turned to see what she was talking about. "This isn't about you feeling sorry for yourself for being hurt. This is about you feeling bad because you can't *fix* things. You are used to taking care of things; helping people get their act together, making them feel better. You couldn't *fix* Curt and you sure as hell, couldn't *fix* Nan. You know what that makes you Nicky?" Nick shook his head. "Mortal. You are just like the rest of us. I know you have done some wonderful things. You helped me so much. You have helped lots of people. But, you aren't God. Some things are out of your hands. Even if you had remained a priest, Nick, Nan would still be dead and Curt would still be in jail." She put her hands on her hips and looked directly at Nick and said, "You are going to have to get over yourself."

Nick nodded as if she had struck a chord. He suddenly felt released, in some way. He couldn't have done anything, he thought to himself. He really could not have prevented it. She's right. I am not God. He pulled Annie to him and put his head on her shoulder. He whispered in her ear, "You have perfect teeth too."

Annie laughed. "It was the first thing I could think of. I am not used to yelling at you. I'm not good at it."

"Actually…you are," he said as he kissed her.

After dinner they were all in the kitchen. Matt was doing homework at the kitchen table and Angela was texting a friend while sitting opposite him. Annie was at the sink and Nick was carefully carrying dishes from the table to the sink, visibly limping but walking on his own nevertheless. The house phone rang. Angela started to jump up but Annie motioned for Nick to get it. He was standing nearby.

He picked up the receiver and said, "Hell o," carefully exhaling as he had been instructed in speech therapy.

"Matthew?"

"Nick."

"Oh Nicky, I am so glad to hear your voice. How are you?" his mother asked.

"Okay," he said without expression. Emily went on to ask what he had been doing, how his therapy was going and routine questions to be expected of one's mother. He answered as best he could; usually with just the word, "okay". Finally, surmising that he was getting tired of talking to her she decided to ask to talk to Annie and find out how it was really going.

"How is Annie?" she asked.

"Annie's mean," he said clearly.

Emily laughed. "She finally kicked you in the butt, didn't she Nicky?"

"Yeah. Mean, also smart. Deadly com-bi-na-tion." Nick handed the phone to Annie saying, "It's for you."

263

Jonathan finally did come to see Nick. It was hard on both of them. Jonathan told Nick he had asked for a transfer and his company agreed to move him to San Antonio. No one could blame him for wanting to relocate. He moved to Texas as quickly as he could. His company agreed to sell the house for him. Jonathan promised to keep in touch.

Nick took on his recovery with a vengeance. He never missed a therapy session. He went as often as they would have him. At home, he walked up and down the stairs over and over. He began to walk the dogs using a weight on his leg. He would walk while Annie and Angel ran. He arm wrestled with Matt to strengthen his arm. He swam at the Y. He shot baskets for hours on the drive using his weak arm. He played the piano. Slowly progress was made; many months of painful effort. Finally, he could speak plainly, a little slower perhaps than before but not noticeably so. His smile was just a tiny bit lopsided which Annie swore was sexy. And, he walked with a barely perceivable limp, which Annie also said was sexy. But, at last he was healthy and fit and they were grateful for that.

Chapter Thirty-One

"Are we all assembled for the family vacation forum?" Nick asked.

"Dad," Angela said quite irritated, "there are only four of us. We are here. Get on with it."

"Okay then," he continued. "Since all are present and accounted for, we will not have to call roll."

"Dad!" Angela and Matt shouted in unison. Annie rolled her eyes.

"Your mother and I have given it much consideration and we have decided on a destination for our family vacation. We are going to," he paused for effect, "Camden, New Jersey! Yeah! Let's show a little appreciation here. Home of Campbell's Soup. I believe they have the largest soup tureen ever made displayed there." Nick was playing to an unappreciative audience. Stone silence.

"Okay then, our second choice was Death Valley but I will go on to the third: Disneyland, Los Angeles," he said without feeling.

"Oh, Daddy, really? Disneyland?" Angela flipped out her phone to text her friend.

Matt, too, was thrilled. "Disney in LA, wow, Dad. That's great."

"No tureen," Nick said in a sad voice. The children failed to see any of Nick's humor.

"Wait until I tell, Jason. He won't believe it." Matthew also left the room.

Nick looked at Annie, "If you want to make them happy it has to have a coaster."

"I know," she said consoling him. "But they love you for it. We will try to find some educationally-worthwhile activity while we are there."

"In LA?" he asked.

"Now I never took you for a prejudiced person, Nick Millar. Los Angeles has lots to offer and we will visit Mike and the family in San Francisco. We will have a wonderful time. Besides, they are growing up so fast. Soon we will be vacationing by ourselves."

"Why do they have to grow up?" Nick asked sadly.

"Because you are getting old and can't handle them much longer," she said smiling.

"I don't know if I can handle them growing up either."

"We will do it together. And when they are grown, we will have time to go all the places you want to go, though not Camden or Death Valley. We can cruise!" she said decidedly.

"It just goes so fast," Nick complained. "Angela is in high school, Matt in middle school."

"More time for you and me," Annie said as she flattened herself against him and laid her head on his chest.

"This is starting to sound better," he said smiling and kissing her.

"Nick, I've been thinking," Annie began.

Nick covered his eyes.

"I am serious," she said.

"Let's hear it."

"I want to sell the bakery and the catering company. I think we should just concentrate on the restaurant and even scale back what you and I contribute at the restaurant. Maybe this has all been a warning for us. Angela will be in college before long, Matt in high school. Let's stop working so hard. Let's have regular hours, hire more management staff for nights and weekends and start to take it easy." She waited to see Nick's reaction.

"I couldn't agree more. I have been thinking the same thing. If it is okay with you, I was thinking about talking to Lillian about it. When she was here the other day, she seemed lonely. Her girls are away in college now and she is alone. I think she might like to manage either nights or weekends. She has great business and people skills."

Lillian had contacted Nick a few months after the shooting, not knowing if he would see her. Annie and Nick welcomed her with open arms. She was now a member of the extended family.

"Perfect," Annie said.

"This way we can get more involved at school. I never want to miss another activity because I'm working," Nick said sadly.

"And we can join that gourmet group in the neighborhood," Annie said enthusiastically.

"I could play some golf," Nick added.

"*We* could play some golf. I want to learn, Nick. Can I play too?" she asked.

"Of course. When the kids are away in college, we can take golfing vacations. It will be a great thing to do together."

"And, I have been thinking that I might like to do a cook book," Annie said. She looked to see Nick's reaction.

He laughed. "Why do I think we are going to be just as busy as we were before?" he asked.

"But, we will be doing things we like, and we choose," Annie said.

Nick smiled. "I can't see you ever sitting still Annie. I will just have to try to keep up."

Chapter Thirty-Two

"I guess I should have known it was you," Curt said as soon as he sat down opposite Nick and picked up the phone. Curt had lost weight. He was pale. His hair was buzz cut making his receding hairline more apparent. He was wearing a lime-green prison jumpsuit. "I was sort of expecting you."

"That's funny," Nick said solemnly. "I wasn't sure I was coming until today." Nick was looking good. He had been spending lots of time outdoors and was tan and fit.

"Oh, I knew you would come. Count on Nick Millar to do the right thing," he said with sarcasm. "Why *are* you here?" Curt asked and really wanted to know the answer.

Nick paused. "I guess because I wanted to know why. Why did you shoot Nan? Why did you shoot me? It has been killing me, man. Why Curt? You surely knew I would have given you money if you needed it. Didn't you know that?" He waited for an answer. The timing of the conversation was spasmodic because of the phone system.

Now Curt paused. "I knew you would give me some money. But, what I wasn't sure about was how you felt about my wife. Correction— my ex-wife. Lillian was just like everybody else. 'Nick the saint. Nick the good guy. Nick the savior.' It gets a little tiring after a while. I had heard it all my life and now my ex-wife was under your spell. I thought maybe you two had a thing going on." Curt stopped to let Nick respond.

Nick took a breath exhaled loudly. "I have my own wife, Curt. I adore my wife. I have no desire to...." He stopped. "This is stupid,

Curt. You killed my friend because you thought I was having an affair with your ex-wife? That's pretty paranoid even for you."

"You get everything, Nick. You always have." Then Curt changed his tone, "I didn't really think you two had an affair. You are too perfect for that. But, she liked you. She compared me to you."

"And so you killed our friend?"

"No, I wasn't going to kill anybody," Curt said in a sad voice. "I went there to take your money because I needed money and I knew you had some. But she wouldn't give it to me. She took it out of the cash register like I asked her, but then she changed her mind. I guess she was standing up for you too. 'Don't take good Nicky's money'," Curt said imitating a woman's voice. Nick winced. "I don't know what she was thinking, actually. She just said, 'No!' She held on to the money and then started to put it back in the cash register. She picked up her cell and I shot her."

Curt began to talk in very slow sentences. "I don't even know how to shoot someone. I had never used the gun before; any gun," he amended. "I just pointed it at her I guess, and shot. I don't remember. I just know she grabbed her chest and went down. Before I could think, you came in. You pushed right by me holding the gun. It was like you didn't even see me. But I shot you too." Curt stared off into space looking ill.

Nick couldn't believe what he was hearing. He still had no memory of the event. "Why did you call the police?" Nick asked.

"I knew I would be caught. I don't get away with things. I figured I may as well call the cops myself. I saw by the look on your face that she was dead. In one instant she was dead and my life was over too. I thought you might be dead too, but when they put you on the stretcher I could see you were still alive. I didn't want to kill you, Nick. I didn't want to kill her either." He paused, "There was something about the gun."

Curt's face turned ashen. He was quiet and his eyes began to well, he blinked back tears. "It was like the damn gun had a life of its own. I felt like it did the shooting, that I didn't." Now the tears ran down his cheeks and onto the prison jumpsuit. Curt went on, "The gun was there in my hand. Only, I didn't feel it. I don't remember pulling the trigger." Curt was nearly in a trance relating the information. "I shouldn't have brought the gun," he said in almost a whisper. "I shouldn't have brought the stupid gun!"

Nick was speechless. He sat with the handset up to his ear, the other hand over his mouth. Curt wanted to talk. "I'm going to be in prison now, for the rest of my life." He was speaking in nearly a whisper. "The stupid gun. The ironic thing is that I have owned the gun for years. It was licensed. I had it for protection. Realtors meet with people they don't always know. Lots of realtors have guns," he trailed off.

Finally, Nick tried to speak. His speech problems were only noticeable now when he was stressed and it took him some time to put the words out. "I'm sorry….you brought the….g gun too." Nick sat back in his chair and tried to compose himself. Finally, he said, "Nan is in heaven, but you, Curt, are in h….hell." The words were barely audible. He almost said something else, but stopped for a minute to gain control. Neither man said anything for a good two minutes. Curt started to leave. But Nick said, "Do you," he paused, "want me," he paused again, "to come back?" Nick exhaled audibly.

"You would come back?" Curt said looking incredulously at Nick. "You would actually come back to see the person who shot you and killed your friend?"

Nick swallowed hard. "I think so," he said into the mouthpiece.

Nick was to pick up Matt at school after basketball practice. He got there a little early and went into the gym to watch the practice. He saw Matt's nemesis, the boy who gave Nick trouble on career day, sitting on the bench in street clothes. Matthew actually said he was having no trouble with the boy now. He left Matt alone. On impulse, Nick walked up and sat next to him. "What's goin' on?" he asked. The boy shrugged. "Is the team any good?" Another shrug. He continued his questioning, "Why aren't you playing?"

"Missed grades," the boy answered.

"Ouch," Nick said. "Any subject in particular or all in general?"

"Math. I hate it," the boy responded.

"You get any help at home?" Nick asked. Something about some old bruises on the boy's arms and a fading cut on his face made Nick uneasy.

"No my mom doesn't know how to do it and neither does her obnoxious boyfriend," he answered.

Nick thought to himself that the boy's answer just said a lot. "Your name is Dean, right?" Dean nodded. "Where do you live?" Nick asked.

"On Broadly," he answered.

"Do you know where the restaurant, Yumsters, is?" Nick asked the boy.

"Yeah, my mom and her boyfriend go there sometimes."

"Stop by there after school and I'll get you some help with math," Nick told him.

"Really, are you a math whiz?"

"No, but I can do most of it. Anything I can't do, I am sure someone there can. The wait staff is mostly college guys. They all know math. Will you give it a try?"

"I might."

"Come in the back door," Nick said.

The next day after school, Dean was there with his math book. Nick saw him come in and came out of the kitchen to meet him. "Let's have a snack first. That's what we always do at our house before we start homework," Nick told him. "What do you like? We have caramelized bread pudding, Crème Brule, chocolate espresso mousse, kiwi tort," Nick listed with a smirk.

"Don't you guys have anything normal?" Dean asked sincerely.

Nick laughed. He pointed to a table. "Sit there and I will bring you the specialty of the house." Nick came back with a plate of chocolate chip cookies and a large dish of vanilla ice cream over which he had put chocolate sauce, whipped cream and a cherry. He brought with him two spoons. Dean began to eat the ice cream eagerly. Nick took his spoon and dipped into it.

"Hey," Dean said, "you're eating my ice cream!"

Nick smiled at the boy and said with a grin, "Actually, you are eating my ice cream." The two sat and ate for a while and then Nick

271

tried to start up a conversation. "Tell me about your family," he said. "Siblings?" Dean looked confused. "Brothers and sisters?" Nick amended.

"No, just me and my mom and dumb butt."

"Your dog? Cute name," Nick said to keep things light.

"No." By now Dean was smiling. He continued eating the ice cream. Nick had put his spoon down after a couple of bites. "Dumb butt is my mother's boyfriend."

"Oh, I take it you don't like him. Do you see your dad?" Nick took a chance and asked.

"No. Don't even know him. He is probably in prison or something. My mom won't tell me. She just says to forget about him."

"Do you forget about him?"

"No, I wish I knew who he was. Well, he probably is a bum."

"I don't know," Nick said. "Maybe he is president of Nike, or the inventor of Marine Hero, or designs roller coasters. He could be anything, couldn't he?"

"It doesn't matter what he is, he doesn't want me."

"Well, you don't know that either. Sometimes adults screw things up for their kids even if they don't mean to do it. Maybe you will meet up with him one day." Nick could only think of Derek wanting to meet Angela and feeling neglectful that they keep postponing it.

Dean and Matt started to hang out a bit together. He obviously liked coming to the house when he wasn't being tutored at the restaurant. The boys would shoot hoops or play electronic games. Annie would invite him to stay for dinner sometimes and either she or Nick would run him home. It all reminded Nick of Curt, and how he would spend time at their house. One day the two boys came into the house and Dean went immediately up to Nick and handed him a manila envelope. He was anxious for Nick to open it.

"B plus in Math," Nick shouted. He slapped Dean's hand. "Wow, you did it! What a comeback. You must feel so good about this."

"Yeah. The best thing is, I actually understand it now. It isn't that hard. I think I can get an A next semester." He was beaming.

Nick read the name on the report card, "Dean Michael Thomlin, I am very impressed."

"I know, it's a stupid name. I hate the name 'Dean', he said.

"It is not stupid. Dean means exactly the opposite. It is an intelligent name. It means a person of importance. Someone in charge; a preeminent member of a group. It's a great name."

"Do all names have meanings?" Dean asked. By now he thought Nick had the answer to all questions.

"Most do, lot's are from the Bible and are Greek or Hebrew. Some are Roman names and have meanings." Annie was listening and hoisted herself up to sit on the counter.

"What does Matthew mean?" Matt asked.

"A kind man," Nick quickly answered looking at Annie who was laughing at him.

"What does Angela mean?" Matt then asked.

"You should know that, Matt. It means angel."

"What does Nick mean?" Dean asked him.

Quickly Nick answered, "An irritating chip in the skin." The boys were starting to catch on that Nick was making it up but continued.

Dean then pointed to Annie and said, "What does your mother's name mean?"

Annie put her hands on her hips and glared at him. "I am not his mother!" she said indignantly. Nick came over and stood next to her laughing.

"I mean your wife," Dean said embarrassed. "What does her name mean?"

"Her name is Annie. It means orphan with bad hair and a dog." The boys laughed.

Dean said, "The dog's name is Sandy. That is my mother's boyfriend's name. Well, it is his nickname," he said smiling. "What does Sandy mean?"

Nick said very factually, "It actually means ugly dog." The boys cracked up. Glancing at his watch, Nick asked, "Do you need a ride home?"

"No thanks, I rode my bike. See you later....'Chip'," Dean said giggling.

Angela came in the kitchen just as Dean was leaving. "Your dad is crazy," Dean said to her when he went out the door.

"Tell me something I don't already know," she said sarcastically. Nick turned to face Annie and picked her up off the counter where she was sitting. She put her arms around his neck and wrapped her legs around his waist. "Gross!" Angela said when she saw them. Nick then kissed Annie. "Eeew! Get a room!"

Nick said to her, "I choose this room. Shall we use the table or the floor?" Annie shook her head laughing.

Angela walked out of the kitchen saying, "Dad, you are so infantile."

"Good vocabulary word, Angel. Know any others?" Nick said back.

"Juvenile," Angela retorted.

"How about sophomoric? Aren't you sophomoric this year, Angel," he asked.

"I am a sophomore. You are sophomoric. And immature, I might add," Angela said as she left the room and went back upstairs.

"Why do I always feel like the designated grownup in this outfit?" Annie asked rhetorically.

Chapter Thirty-Three

Both Angel and Matt were good students and well behaved for the most part. Angel sometimes got crossways with Annie. However, Nick reflected back when he was a teenager and remembered that Laurie and his mother sometimes got into it. When he thought back far enough, Emily and her older two daughters argued on occasion too. Mothers and daughters, he thought. He was glad he didn't have that problem with Matt. Still, the jury was still out since Angel was older than Matt.

Nick was so like his father before him and when the girls did get into it, he would try to be peacemaker. When Annie's temper would flare and she would get right into Angela's face, he would grab the back of her shirt and pull her back to him, just as he had seen his father do to his mother.

Angel was a pretty little girl literally. She was barely five feet tall, like her mother, and of small build. She had darker hair than Annie but the same turned up nose and confident manner. Her skin was flawless and she wore very little make up. Her hair was blunt cut about shoulder length and had a few strands of highlighter. At home she usually wore her hair in a simple pony tail. As a teenager, she had lots of dates but not one particular boyfriend. She and her friends often went out in groups. She seemed to have her head on straight, as her parents saw it, and came in at curfew and didn't obsess about boys. She was goal oriented and wanted to get into an Ivy League school and study law. As a sophomore, she was active in student government, played soccer in the spring and volleyball in the fall, she was a Homecoming Princess, and volunteered at Millar House playing with the children and organizing runs and competitions for them. She, on occasion, helped out at the restaurant. As a family, they got along very well and she had called Nick 'Dad' since she was small. He adopted her at age five. She and Matt actually got along well and spent lots of time together when their parents had to be at the restaurant. Angel was protective of Matt and would never let him stay alone, even if she had planned to go out. She would change plans and either invite a friend to come over to watch a movie with them or she would stay home with Matt alone. That's why it was such a shock when she did not make curfew one Saturday night. Her girlfriends were having a birthday party for her. Her birthday was in a few days.

Angel was to be home at eleven. Annie and Nick had been watching a movie, though both had fallen asleep at some point; they both woke for the ending. They switched to the evening news after that. Matt was in bed. At eleven-ten Annie called Angel's cell. No answer. She and Nick agreed not to panic until after eleven-thirty. Annie couldn't decide if she was angry or worried. It was just so unusual for Angela to be late and not call. Neither of them could remember exactly who she had gone out with. It was one of her girlfriends. It may have been the one who was having the party. But they were unsure which one was having it and which one picked up Angel in her car. They both vowed they would not let either child leave the house again without knowing specifically who they were with. It was just that Angela had never been a problem in this regard and they had been a little lax in asking questions.

At eleven forty-five, just as Annie was looking up phone numbers of friends, Angela came in the door. With a smug look on her face she asked, "What are you guys doing up?"

Annie was livid. "Where have you been? Why were you late?" she asked. Nick stood next to Annie as she faced Angela.

"I was out. I came home when I felt like it," Angela answered.

Nick and Annie were in shock. Angela started up the stairs but stopped and turned saying to her mother, "Why do you care what I do?"

"Come back here," Annie ordered.

Angela stomped down the stairs and faced the two of them. "What?" she shouted.

"Come on you guys, Matt's asleep," Nick said. "Angela, what happened? We were worried about you. You never do this. You are always considerate and let us know when you are going to be late. What's going on, sweetheart?" Nick asked.

"Nothing! I'm home. Home sweet home with my loving parents. We are the all-American family, aren't we?" Angela said.

"Have you been drinking?" Annie asked, thinking that may be the cause of the strange behavior.

"No. Wouldn't that be naughty! I'm not naughty. I'm a good little girl—just like my mommy."

Annie and Nick were totally perplexed by this strange behavior. Finally, Nick said, "Let's go to bed and sleep on it. We will talk about this tomorrow." Annie started to say something but held her tongue. Angela stomped up the stairs.

Nick and Annie sat back down in the family room and talked for a few minutes trying to figure out what just happened. Nick got a glass of water to take up with him and Annie began turning out the lights and when they came back into the foyer to go upstairs they heard footsteps coming down. Angel was walking down stairs in just her panties, bra, and high heels. She stepped on each stair, pushed out her hip and posed before going down to the next. "Is this how you do it, Mom? Is this how you dressed as a ho?" she asked. Nick and Annie walked over to the staircase in shock.

"What are you doing, Angel?" Annie asked.

"Do not, call me Angel," Angela shouted at her mother. "How dare you call me that! How dare you talk to me after a lifetime of lies!!" she hurled at Annie. "'Angel, those jeans are too tight. Angel, that skirt is too short.' My God, Mother, were you afraid I was going to turn out like you? A hooker, like you, Mom?"

Nick could take it no more and walked over to Angela and slapped her across the face. He was as shocked as Angel. As soon as his hand swiped her face he was pulling her to him. "I'm sorry. I'm sorry," he pleaded. Nick, the pacifist, the peacemaker, had struck his daughter. In his entire life, he had never struck an individual. Angela flinched but didn't cry. It was not a painful slap and she was too angry to feel it anyway.

Angela pushed him away from her and said, "And you Dad. But you aren't my real dad. You adopted me. How did you get into this mess? Did you two think that with his goodness and your badness it would all even out, Mother?" she asked. "My real dad is probably in a prison some place," she said almost to herself. "My dad is probably a serial killer and my mother is a ho."

"Angela, stop," Nick pleaded. "What are you talking about?"

"Everyone knows. I was the last to know, but now even I know. Mom was a hooker. Melody put it on TeenSpace. Her dad treated you one time when your john beat you up. You remember that Mom? Or did it happen so many times you can't remember? Anyway, it is all over TeenSpace. Everyone knows now. Angela's mother is a hooker! And who is Angela's father? It could be anyone, couldn't it Mom?"

Nick and Annie were standing with their hands over their mouths in shock. Angela was standing in front of them staring in defiance. No one knew what to do next. Nick reached for Angel but she pushed him away. Tears were beginning to streak down her face leaving black marks from the mascara she layered on for effect. Her eyes were ringed with black. Nick handed her his handkerchief and she wiped her nose. She was shaking and Annie took off her cardigan and tried to put it on her shoulders but Angela threw it on the floor. Nick was desperate to think of something. Finally, he said that they should go into the library. It is a smaller, cozier room he thought. They needed to be together in closer proximity than in the foyer. He took Angel's arm and gently led her into the room, looking at Annie to follow.

When the three of them got into the room, he sat Angel down on the loveseat there and brought the throw from the back of it around her. He sat next to her on the edge of the loveseat and reached for Annie's hand and pulled her down to sit on the table in front of it.

"It's true, isn't it?" Angela said softly without looking up.

"That's a ridiculous question," Nick shouted. "You are letting someone make an outrageous assertion and using what they say as presumption of guilt, then asking her to defend herself."

"I have no idea what that means, Dad. I speak English," Angela said defiantly.

"I am saying you are swinging at a bad pitch. Anyone can say anything on the internet and it doesn't mean it is true. The truth is that your mom had a hard life. She had an abusive boyfriend." Nick tried to get things calmed down. "Angela, your mother had none of the advantages that you and Matthew and I had. She made sure you had the things she didn't have. She made something from nothing. She started out with nothing and made a good life for all of us. I am in awe of your mother. I am incredibly proud of her. I am so proud of her," he repeated. "I had an easy life. Everything was easy for me. I had two loving parents, and money, and position in the community. I went to the best schools. I had everything handed to me. But your mother didn't have anything handed to her. She had to earn everything for herself." As soon as the words were out of his mouth, he regretted them.

Angela interrupted, "And she earned it by selling herself. She earned it by being a prostitute!"

Annie sat on the edge of the table with her head on her knees and didn't look up.

"How can you accuse your mother of something you have read on the internet? You know she was abused. More than once she was abused. She was abused by her mother and then her boyfriend. Yet, she kept you healthy, and fed, and clean. And then, she got an education and training and made a career for herself. She made a life for herself, and you. She has worked hard to make sure you and Matt have what you need, and me," he added. "I was…aimless. Even though I had all the advantages, it was your mother who made my life worthwhile. She got me back on track and gave me direction and incentive. She knew how to run the business. She does all the real work. I just take orders. I have always just been the one to do what I am told. She is the brains behind it." He paused. Annie still did not say anything.

"Do you have any idea, how humiliating it was to be in a room with four so-called friends and have them show me Melody's TeenSpace message? They were all laughing at me." Angela said as she began to cry again.

"I'm sorry," Annie whispered. "Oh, God, I'm so sorry."

"That was a terrible thing for someone to put out there, Angela," Nick said, trying to be pragmatic. "No one should put out stuff like that." He tried to think of something to say.

"The terrible thing is that everyone thinks it is true!" Angela said.

"Look," Nick said trying to be logical, "the only truth is that it was cruel. No one is looking for the truth on the internet. Anyone can say anything and your friends know that!" he said emphatically. "We'll try to get to the bottom of this." The three of them sat silent for several minutes.

Finally, Angela said she wanted to go up to her room. Nick thought it fruitless to keep her there with them. They were each suffering. They would have to work it out tomorrow. "Go to bed, sweetheart. I am sorry someone put that vile message on the net. We are a family. We will work this out. We love you, Angela. Your mother and I love you. We love you as much right now, as we ever have. And we will always love you. And I will always love your mother." He ended, feeling like he was babbling but not knowing what else to say. Annie said nothing.

Angela left the room and Nick tried to pull Annie off the table to sit on the loveseat next to him. She refused. He got up and sat next to her on the table. He tried to take her hand but she continued to hold her hands on her knees. He settled for putting his hand on top of hers. His large hand was on top of her tiny ones. She was so small and wounded so badly. He ached for her. He put his arm around her and whispered, "It will be okay. It will all work out." And then he realized that was what his father always said. It was always so promising and profound when he said it and Nick always believed him. But now it sounded it trite and cliché. Finally, struggling to make her feel better he said, "We are in this together. I love you. When you hurt, I hurt. We will get through this. It will go away. It will. No one believes it anyway. No one. We look everyone straight in the eye." Finally he put his head against hers and said, "I love you, Annie. I love you."

Chapter Thirty-Four

Nick pulled into the garage the next morning and noticed that Annie's car was gone. He wished she had gone with him to mass. Angela and Matt were sleeping when he left and he decided not to wake them. Angela finally succumbed after hours of sobbing. Annie did not sleep at all. She and Nick had talked until neither could talk any more. She finally went downstairs to the kitchen table while Nick stayed in the office at the computer. When he left for six o'clock mass, she was still there but going up to shower. When Nick came into the house he saw the note on the kitchen table. Just a few words, but a stab in the heart.

"Nick, I was afraid this would happen. I am so sorry.
None of you deserve this.
I love you. Goodbye."

Nick stuffed the note in his pocket.

Nick rang the door bell and patiently waited for an answer. He looked at his watch. He had waited until 9 a.m. before driving over. Mrs. Allan answered the door in her robe. "Yes?" she asked confused.

"I want to talk to Dr. Allan," Nick said clearly.

"I'm sorry. He doesn't talk to people at home. You will have to call his office and make an appointment," she said clearly irritated.

Then she recognized Nick. "Aren't you Mr. Millar, Angela's father?" she asked.

He ignored her question. "I think Dr. Allan should talk to me. I picked this up on the internet, and while I think there are a lot of errors on the internet, I believe there is some validity in this piece." He read from a piece of paper he was holding, "Releasing information to non-medical people, about confidential medical issues, or to third parties without the permission of the patient, is a breach of patient-doctor confidence and is illegal. It is punishable by law and can result in heavy fines and other disciplinary measures. If there is damage to the family life, reputation, or job of the patient, the physician involved will be forced to pay compensation." He stopped reading and said, "Dr. Allan released information that is harmful my family."

Dr. Allan stepped from behind Mrs. Allan and came to the door. "What is going on here? Are you threatening me? Should I be calling the police?"

"If you wish. I am telling you, that you are hurting my family. I want it stopped, now. It is too late to take it back, but at least, stop it. My daughter, my wife, my son, and I have all been damaged by this atrocity. Stop it! At the very least, you owe my daughter and my wife an apology. You will never know the harm you have done." Nick took a deep breath, "That's ironic," he said. "My father was a doctor too. The Hippocratic Oath was posted in his conference room. I have read it many times, sitting, waiting for him. I know people quote it as saying, 'First do no harm.' It isn't exactly worded like that really, but it means the same thing. You, Dr. Allan, have done great harm."

"I have no idea what you are talking about," Dr. Allan said in an irritated voice and he started to shut the door.

Nick caught the door and held it open. "Go read your daughter's TeenSpace entry. I will sit here on the step while you read it." Nick let go of the door and turned, stepped down two steps and sat on the top step putting his head on his knees.

In only a few minutes, Dr. Allan was back at the door. "Come in Mr. Millar," he said.

Nick walked dazed through the Allan's home and sat in the chair pointed out to him by Dr. Allan in the elegantly decorated office. He sat across from Dr. Allan who was sitting in front of the desk looking at the computer. Melody's TeenSpace entry was in front of him. Dr. Allan too, seemed dazed. He looked up at Nick and asked, "What do you want me to do?"

It took Nick a minute to articulate his answer. "I want it taken off. I want an apology to my wife and my daughter." He added, "As soon as possible."

"Helen," Dr. Allan shouted into the hall. "Go wake up Melody and get her down here."

Nick rose from the chair and started out the room. "Don't you want to stay to...talk to her?" Dr. Allan asked.

Nick shook his head. "I have to go home. I have a mess to clean up at my house," he said simply. Melody was coming down the stairs as he was leaving. He did not turn to see her but went out the door without closing it behind him.

Once at home, Nick looked at TeenSpace. Melody's entry had been removed. An hour later, there was a new posting. *"My father, Dr. Timothy Allan and I, Melody, both apologize to Angela, her mother and the entire Millar family for the vicious things I said in my last entry. We know Mrs. Millar to be a wonderful mother and a caring and productive citizen. She has given of her time and resources to the school and the community. We know of all the causes she and her family take on to make the world a better place. We are deeply sorry for the cruel things I said. We beg forgiveness, although we know what I have done is in truth unforgiveable, and pray that those who read the entry will embrace and respect the Millar family as they so deserve to be embraced and respected."*

Matt came into the room. He just woke up but he could sense something was wrong. He went to Nick and put his arms around him. "Hi, Dad," he said sweetly. "What's going on with Angela?" He climbed onto Nick's lap, his long legs dangling.

Nick explained it as simply and as briefly as he could. "Someone put something nasty on TeenSpace about Angela and Mom. It has been taken off but everyone is still hurt over it. Mom went out for a while."

"When will she be back?" Matt asked.

"I don't know."

"What did it say?" Matt asked sincerely.

Nick stammered. "It was ugly, Matt," he said. Then he reconsidered and thought about Matt hearing what it said from someone else. Who knows what Angela is going to say when she comes down, he thought. "Matt, it was about your mom. You know she had a really hard life for a while. You know that don't you, son?" he stalled.

"I know she had Angel and she wasn't married. Is that what you mean, Dad?" he asked innocently.

"Yes, and your mom had nothing, Matt. She had no money, no one to help her out. No one! She had to take care of Angel and herself, by herself. And she did it. Someone put on TeenSpace that your mom did some things that are not considered 'nice' in neighborhoods like ours," Nick said. "Now, she..."

Matt interrupted, "What Dad? What did they say Mom did?"

Again Nick was torn with giving too much information and not giving enough. He did not want someone else to tell his son what was said about his mother. "They said she worked as a prostitute," he finally said bluntly. Then he asked the boy, "Do you know what that means?"

"That she got money for sex," he answered. "Did she?"

"I don't think that is a fair question to ask. It is like the question 'Do you still beat your wife?' You know, Matt, this is why we tell you to be careful about what you put on the internet and on social networks. Anyone can say anything, whether it is true or not. And people get hurt." He waited for Matt's response.

"I heard Angel crying and it was Melody Allan who put it on TeenSpace, wasn't it?"

"Yes, but she has taken it off and has apologized."

"So, do we have to forgive her?" Matt asked.

Nick smiled, "Yes, but maybe not right away."

Matt put his arms around Nick's neck. "Mom is a great mom. Melody is a jerk and so is her whole family. I bet Melody's mom would have to pay *them* to have sex with her!"

Nick laughed out loud. "You may be right, Matt, but we aren't going to talk about anyone's personal life on TeenSpace or anywhere else, are we?"

Matt shook his head and continued to rest against Nick. A few minutes later the door bell rang with impatience. Matt jumped up and ran upstairs to change out of his pajamas. Nick considered not answering but heard Stacie's voice saying, "Somebody, let me in." He got up and opened the door. Stacie practically fell in the door. "Is Annie here?" she asked breathlessly.

"No."

"Did you guys read the TeenSpace entry?"

"Yes."

"Shit," Stacie said. "Where is Annie?"

"I don't know."

"Shit," she said again. "She left? You really don't know where she is?"

"I don't know where she is. She left this note." Nick took the note from his pocket and showed it to Stacie. He wouldn't have shown it to anyone else but he thought maybe Stacie might know where Annie would go.

"The kids told me about it a few minutes ago," Stacie said. "I knew Annie would be upset but I didn't think she would leave. When do you think she'll come home? You do think she'll come home don't you?"

"I don't know."

"I wish she had come to me when this happened. I can't stand that Melody anyway. She's a pig. Nick," Stacie said slowly, "Annie and I are really good friends. She has told me about," she hesitated. "Annie has told me about her crappy life. Annie is the best person I have ever met. It kills me to think someone would do something to hurt her."

"Stacie, have you ever told anyone else about the things Annie told you?" Nick asked.

"Never. I swear, on a stack of bibles. I haven't even told Greg. Annie is my best friend. I would never betray her confidence. Honest, never. Margo called just before I left. She just heard about it and thought it was crazy. No one is going to believe one word of it, Nick. No one! If I hear from Annie, I'll let you know. Call me when she comes home?"

"Sure." Nick took a breath. "Stacie, are you sure you don't have any idea where she might be?"

"No. Do you?"

Nick shook his head. "I would go look for her but I don't have a clue. I don't want to leave the kids here and just drive around aimlessly. That doesn't sound very productive. So, I guess I will just wait." He looked at Stacie, "You are sure you don't have any idea where she might have gone?"

"I don't Nick. Honest, I would tell you if I did. I know you are worried. I am too. I will help any way I can. Call me if you hear from her and I will call if I hear, okay?"

"Sure," he answered unconvinced that either of them would hear anything.

Nick went upstairs to their bedroom. He opened the door to Annie's closet and stood looking in. He had no idea what to look for. He was hoping something would tell him where she had gone. Everything was neatly hung in place. He marveled how organized she was. Everything was by category: pants on pants' hangers, blouses above them on the higher rail, skirts together, dresses, suits, and casual and workout clothes all hung systematically. It wasn't a large wardrobe. Neither of them cared too much about clothes; not nearly as much as Angela, or even Laurie or his mother, he thought. Her shoes were all in plastic boxes and labeled except for the ones she wore regularly. Again, he recognized for the first time, how little Annie had of her own. She was always quick to get the things the children needed or wanted but rarely did she bring things into the house that were just for her. He wondered if he should have encouraged her more; pampered her more. She worked so hard. She always worked so hard. He opened a couple of drawers to the dresser. Again, nothing looked out of order, but fastidiously folded and carefully placed; underwear, socks, a few scarves. He flipped open the jewelry box on the dresser and looked at the few things there. He remembered the jewelry that Abbe owned and how sparse this collection was by comparison. He saw the pearl earrings he bought her one birthday, her thirtieth, he thought. The diamond studs were there. He bought those for her on their tenth anniversary. She helped pick them out, insisting they not be very large. She felt that she was too small to carry off much jewelry. The little cross he had given her when she lived in Millar House was not in the box. She never took it off.

How can I have no idea where she has gone, he asked himself? Surely, if she just grabbed her purse and keys and took off, she'll come back. She's got to come back. Still, he felt like a heel not looking for her. And, for the first time since they were married, Nick felt inadequate. What kind of a husband am I, he thought? I have never convinced her she is a worthy person. What a failure I am.

When Angela came downstairs it was nearly noon. Nick wasn't going to make her come down until she was ready. Her face was puffy and red. She had on no makeup and her hair was pulled back in a straggly pony tail and she was wearing gray sweat pants and a white sweatshirt. "I heard Mom leave. She didn't come back, did she?" Angela said.

Nick shook his head.

"It's all my fault. I believed that garbage. She isn't ever coming back is she?"

"I don't know, sweetheart. I have to believe she will," he answered.

"Should we call the police?" she asked.

"She left of her own accord. They can't do anything," Nick told her.

"Aren't you going to look for her?" she asked.

"I would if I thought I knew where to look, Angela. I don't. Maybe she just needs some time alone." He knew it sounded as if he wasn't trying to find her but he didn't know what to do next. He thought about calling Laurie or Khiem Li but he knew they would call him or bring her home or something if they knew anything. He was hoping not to have to tell anyone about this. He was hoping Annie would just walk in the door and the four of them would be together again.

Nick didn't move. He waited for Angela to say something. "I'm hungry," she said softly.

"I bet you are," Nick said. "Matt and I just had toasted cheese sandwiches. What sounds good to you?"

"Nothing really. I'll have some ..." she considered alternatives. "I'll make a peanut butter sandwich, I guess," she said. Nick followed her into the kitchen but sat at the table not offering to help. The kids had been making sandwiches for themselves since old enough to hold a table knife.

God, it has been a long day, Nick thought. Sometimes Sundays are so short, being the only day they have completely "off". The restaurant is closed on Sundays. Usually neither Nick nor Annie work on Saturday either, but the restaurant is open and there is a responsibility to check in and make sure everything is working smoothly. And if it isn't, Nick usually runs in. But on Sunday, unless there is a natural disaster, like a power outage or flooded basement, they are home free. Usually the time goes so quickly. They try to spend as much family time as possible. Sometimes they do special things with Angela and Matt and sometimes they get together with Laurie, her husband, and her three children. Once in a while when the children have other plans, Nick and Annie go for a drive into country or go to antique shops. But today, is just one long frickin' day, he thought, doing absolutely nothing. Matt went to his friend Sean's house next door. He was coming home at four.

Angela slowly ate her sandwich and drank a glass of milk. When she finished, she took her dishes over to the sink, rinsed them and put them in the dish washer. Then she quietly walked over to Nick and sat on his lap. He wasn't expecting this and had to quickly uncross his legs to accommodate her. She put her head on his shoulder and asked, "Do you hate me?"

"Of course not," he stated flatly. "I love you."

"What if," she began but faltered, and began again, "what if Mom doesn't come home?" She paused and asked, "Will you keep me?"

"Angela, how can you ask me that? Of course, I will 'keep' you. You are my daughter. I would lay down my life for you," Nick said to reassure her. "Mom will come home. She just needs some time."

"But I am not like Matt. I'm not, you know…half you!" she shouted through tears. "You adopted me. I am not your natural child," she sobbed. "If she doesn't come home…"

"There is nothing more natural to me than you, Angela. You are my daughter. Matt is my son. There is no difference to me. I could not love you more than I do." Then Nick felt panic kick him in the stomach. What if Annie didn't come home. Could Derek get custody? This is crazy, Nick thought. I can't even think like that. I'm being stupid, he thought. I am her father. The only father she has ever known. I am her legal father. Still Nick felt uncomfortable just from Angela's question.

Angela said, "I shouldn't have said all those terrible things to Mom. I shouldn't have believed those things. I know Mom had a hard life. I know we were in a shelter because she was abused. I guess that was when Dr. Allan treated her, when she was being abused." Angela looked thoughtful, "It is hard to believe that Mom would let someone hit her. She is so strong. I know she is little but I can't believe she took it. That just isn't like Mom."

"It was a long time ago, Angela. She didn't think she had a choice; she didn't think she could do anything to stop it, and she didn't have any place to go."

Suddenly Angela changed the subject. "I don't want to go to school tomorrow. I'm not going. Maybe I should change schools."

"Okay," Nick said agreeably. "You don't have to go to school tomorrow. We will talk about changing schools later."

The two of them moved into the library and sat. Angela picked up her iPod and Nick tried to read a book. He stared at the page, would turn to another and realize he had not read at all. Occasionally, he thought maybe he had nodded off. Time moved interminably slowly. He tried to read a news magazine but never got past the pictures. Finally he put in his ear buds but didn't turn on the iPod. He felt like an imposter. He had never pretended to listen to music before but he couldn't just stare into space. He wracked his brain trying to think where Annie may have gone. He tried to think of who to call; what to do. Should he have her credit cards traced or something? It seemed such an unreal situation, he couldn't think of anything rational to do. He sent a text to Stacie, *"Anything?"* he asked. She came back with the reply, *"Nothing"*. Finally, Matt came home and joined them. Matt was usually an up-beat child and he helped raise the mood a bit. He enthusiastically told what game he and Sean played and detailed scoring and maneuvers, neither of which did Angela or Nick really listen to or understand. "I'm hungry," Matt declared.

"I am too," Angela said and Nick wondered how they could go from one meal to another without any activity between. Matt had been out but he and Angela had spent the entire day in the house; highly unusual for either of them. He thought about getting Angela to go out for a run with him but didn't want to see any of the neighbors.

Suddenly Nick jumped up and said, "Let's go out."

"To dinner?" Matt asked.

"No, out," Nick answered. He looked at Angela's feet and saw she was wearing flip flops. "Put on some sneakers," he told her. She looked puzzled but went up stairs to put them on. Matt was wearing jeans and sneakers as was Nick. "Go to the bathroom," Nick ordered Matt. Matt also looked confused but left the room to do as he was asked. Nick pulled out a grocery bag and emptied the fruit bowl in it, then pulled down the loaf of bread and made some peanut butter sandwiches, put them in plastic bags and threw them in with the fruit. He made a couple of very quick phone calls and then ran upstairs to use the bathroom also. When they reassembled at the door, Nick ushered them out to the car without explanation.

"Where are we going?" Matt asked as he got into the back seat.

"For a drive," Nick answered and started driving toward town. They drove for a while and Nick started looking for streets. Angela once turned on the radio but Nick pushed the button to turn it off. He slowed and tuned on to a side street. The sun was starting to set.

"This doesn't look very nice," Angela said looking around. "Are there restaurants here?"

"No," Nick answered and slowed down more.

"I'm hungry, Dad," Matt said.

"Good," Nick replied without further comment and turned onto another street just as rundown as the first. Then he pulled slowly to the curb just as a woman was walking by. He put the passenger side window down and she walked over to the car.

"Nick, how are you honey," she said smiling. "We don't usually see you guys on Sundays. Oh, are these your kids?" She looked at Angela in the front seat. "She looks just like Annie." Angela didn't know what to say. The woman had wild hair and was wearing black baggy pants with an equally baggy flimsy top. Her complexion was rough and dark. She had what appeared to be a sleeping bag slung over her arm and a shopping cart was parked behind her.

"Hi, Dolly. You doing okay?" Nick asked. "Where is Betts? She is usually with you."

"She's in the hospital. Broken pelvis. Her old man threw her down some cellar stairs," she said calmly. "I'm doing okay."

"Which hospital?" Nick asked. "I might be able to stop in tomorrow and see her."

"Doctor's" she said factually.

"St. Catherine's has an opening," Nick said. "Interested?"

"No. Sorry Nick. Thanks anyway. I got to keep going." Nick opened the bag and threw her an apple. She caught it and walked away.

"Who was that?" Matt asked as they drove away.

"Dolly," Nick answered without further comment.

"Where does she live?" Matt asked.

"Here," Nick answered without anything more.

Angela was frightened, "Do you think Mom is out here?" she asked tearfully.

"No! We come by here on the way home from Millar House sometimes to see if anyone needs a ride to a shelter or something to eat. Dolly has been here forever. She doesn't want any help. Can't help someone if they don't want help," he added. He drove on down the street but didn't stop any place else. Then he turned on another street and pulled to the curb and parked. "Okay, guys, let's get out."

"Here? Why are we getting out here?" Angela asked her eyes wide. Nick got out and walked around and opened the door for Angela to get out. "Where are we going?" she asked starting to panic. "It's horrible here."

Matt and Angela had to walk fast to keep up with Nick's long strides. "That man just peed on that bush," Angela said revolted. The man turned and saw them as they approached. He reeked of stale sweat and urine. Nick reached in his bag and pulled out a sandwich.

"Hand this to him, Matthew," Nick instructed. Matt did as he was told. The man made a gesture like a tip of the hat. "They are serving at Barrington Mission," Nick told him.

"Okay, Governor," the man replied.

"He was peeing on a bush," Angela said again more to herself this time.

Up the street there were three more men and a woman. Nick opened his bag and tossed them each an apple or orange. They waved. "They are serving at Barrington," he told them. Another man seemed to appear from the shadows. He frightened Angela. Even Matt jumped when the man walked up to them. "Here's a sandwich," Nick said as the man approached. The man nodded as he took it from Nick and faded back into the dusky night. They crossed the street and started back toward the car giving out fruit and sandwiches until the bag was nearly empty. Just before they got to the car, Nick walked away from the children to what looked like a pile of trash and bedding. Nick bent over and touched it. "You okay?" he asked the man curled inside. The children didn't hear his answer but saw Nick put the last sandwich in a hand. Nick patted the bundle. He knew it was futile to tell the man where he could get a bed. "Get in," Nick said to the kids when they got to the car.

"Where are we going now?" Matt asked as he got into the back seat.

"Barrington," Nick answered.

Both children were totally confused and thought maybe the events of the day had made Nick whack out. "Dad," Angela said, "are you going to make us eat at the mission?"

"Nope, you are going to feed the hungry. You guys say you are hungry but you don't know the meaning of the word." They drove a few more blocks and Nick pulled into a small parking area next to a shelter. There was a line going down the street from the open door. There were a few men in line, but most were women with children. Some were entire families. Nick got the kids out of the car and told them to follow him. With long strides, he walked around to a side door and knocked on it. The kids ran to keep up. Someone shouted something and he replied, "Nick." The door opened. They walked into a gymnasium-type room that had tables set up in long rows. About twenty people had already been served and were sitting at tables. Nick walked over to the serving line and was greeted by a large black man who touched knuckles with him. "Got some volunteers for you Amos," Nick said.

Amos looked at Matthew and smiled, showing several gold teeth and a warm attitude. "Young man, how about we put you on mashed potatoes," he said looking at Matt.

"Yes, sir," Matt answered.

Mashed potatoes was the last item to be served before the person went to the table. Amos showed Matt how to use the ice cream scoop device used for putting potatoes on the tray. Before he started, however, Nick knelt down and put his hands on either side of Matt's face. "Matthew," he said. "Look the person in the eye. Say something to them. Say 'there you go' or 'enjoy' or 'have a good evening' or whatever you feel like saying. But look at them Matt. Give them their dignity. They are no different than you, only hungrier." He patted him on the shoulder and watched him put the first serving on the tray and saw Matt was following his instructions.

Nick turned to Angela. "See that girl over there?" he indicated a young girl who looked to be in her teens sitting against the wall. "Go over and see if she is okay. Ask her if she has eaten, if she wants you to get her something, or if she wants to talk to you. Can you do that Angela? If she gets hostile, just say 'sorry' and walk away. I'll be right here." Nick knew that sometimes people come in but don't want to socialize. She nodded and walked over to the girl. Nick walked behind the servers and asked one if she wanted a break and he took her place next to Matt and served green beans. Occasionally, Nick would glance over to Angela and the girl. Angela was sitting next to her now and they were talking. After a while the girl left and Angela asked what she could do next. Nick pointed to a trash can and told her to walk around and collect trash from the tables. She did as he asked. When she came back with the can full he told her where to put it. Then he asked the person next to him, serving greens of some kind, if Angela could fill in for her. Matt was in the groove now and actually enjoying serving. Angela heard Matt's comments and began to talk to people also.

"Dad," she whispered, "that girl I talked to is pregnant. She's my age, Dad, and she's pregnant. She said her stepfather 'knocked her up' and her mother doesn't believe her. She said she didn't have any place to go tonight and I told her St. Catherine's had an opening. That's right isn't it Dad? Didn't you say St. Catherine's?"

"That's right, sweetheart. You did the right thing. There are people there who can help her. There didn't used to be much help around, but now there is if you look for it," Nick told her.

"I can't imagine not having you and Mom there to help me, no matter what. Dad, you think Mom will come home don't you?" Angela started to tear again.

"I think she will," he added simply and served up more green beans. God, I hope so, he said to himself. They worked for nearly two hours and then the crowd thinned and finally someone from the staff closed the door. The kitchen staff came out and started to take things back into the kitchen to be washed. Nick, Matt and Angela carried some things in and finally Mrs. Ellery, a staff member in charge of volunteers, was telling people they could leave. She came up to Nick and thanked him for bringing extra help. The kids knew Nick and Annie helped out at shelters once in a while but they never thought about it really. The experience had an effect on them both.

"Dad, that was cool," Matt said as they were walking to the car. "I like it that we actually did something to help someone. At school and church we usually just collect stuff like canned food before ballgames and stuff. But this is really, like, you can see the people you help."

Angela agreed. "I can't believe how many little kids there were. That's so sad. I thought homeless people were just alcoholics and druggies. I didn't realize there were families and kids and everything. Dad, it was so scary out there where we were walking around. It would be so horrible to be homeless. Millar House is so nice, I guess I never thought about people living on the street."

"Millar House is small, Angela. It can't hold all the people who need help. And besides, it specializes in women who have been abused and their children. Some of the men who are out on the street are alcoholics and addicts, but others are broken and sick and are off their meds. Some are veterans who got messed up in one of the wars. Each person has his own story. Some just had bad luck. We are all God's children. Equal in his sight." Then Nick went off into what Angela called 'Priest Mode' and began quoting scripture:

"I was hungry and you gave me food, I was thirsty and you gave me something to drink." He drifted off, "Truly I tell you, just as you did it to one of the least of these, who are members of my family, you did it to me."

"Dad, do you miss being a priest?" Angela asked.

Nick answered carefully, "I loved being a priest but I love being a father to you and Matt, and being a husband to your mother even more."

Angela said, "I knew I could count on you for a schmaltzy answer." She smiled and even though he couldn't see her in the dark of the car, he knew she was smiling.

Nick stopped and got a pizza on the way home. He couldn't stand the thought of going back into the empty house. Annie, Annie, he said to himself, please be there, but he somehow didn't think she would be. As they neared their house, he diverted a street and drove by Yumsters. There was a light on upstairs in the playhouse. His heart jumped. Neither of the kids said anything so must have not noticed or thought that was unusual; he drove on home. Once inside the house, Angela ran to the phone and checked for messages but there were none. They opened some sodas and served up the pizza. After he had a piece, Nick told the kids he thought he would go over and check on the restaurant. He wouldn't be away more than thirty minutes he told them and as he went out the door said, "Lock the door and don't open it while I'm out." He tried to appear casual but once out the door he ran to the car and took off quickly.

Nick bounded up the stairs at Yumsters and flung open the door to the upstairs apartment. Annie was sitting in the rocker with her legs up under her. She was wearing jeans and a sweatshirt, her hair was pulled back in a ponytail, she had no makeup on, and her face was shiny and pink from having tears wiped away so often. When Nick looked at her he thought she looked fifteen. "Hi," he said sheepishly.

"Hi," Annie said without emotion.

Nick came over to her and knelt down in front of her. He put his head on her lap and said, "I love you."

"I love you too but maybe love isn't enough. You are all better off without me. My past is always going to haunt me. I don't want to be an embarrassment to my family," Annie said.

"They took it off, you know, and apologized, Ann," Nick said to her.

"I know. I checked. But some people will always wonder."

"About what?" Nick asked.

"About my sex life. What I did is so ugly. I don't even care so much what other people think but I do care about the kids."

"It is so over for the kids. They think it was all made up. They just want you home. Angela feels really bad that she accused you."

"But, Nick, you and I know it is true," Annie said looking at him.

"Annie, we have all made mistakes in the past, and I'm not sure that we need to apologize for them to anyone, even the kids. It was a long time ago. And besides, there are sorority girls who have had more sexual experiences than you, just on their spring break. This is all going to blow over. No one who reads it, thinks it is true. Everyone thinks Melody made it all up. No one believes you are anything but the wonderful mother and ideal citizen that you are. If you run away, you look guilty. Face the bastards, Annie. Look them right in the eye. They will never believe a thing the Allans say again. I doubt the Allans ever come out of their house again." Nick smiled, "They will probably move!" he said gaining momentum. "Melody will change schools. They are the ones who look bad, not you. Truly Ann, Dr. Allan broke the law. It was against the law for him to tell anything about anyone he treated. And it was ethically and morally wrong. I don't know how his daughter heard it, but it doesn't matter. Trust me, she isn't going to ever mention it again and neither is anyone else. Annie, seriously," he slowed his tone, and said sweetly, "Annie, you are a wonderful giving and forgiving person. Don't be ashamed of how you survived. It is no one's business. Let it go. It is time. We need to get on with things. You need to forgive Ann Marie. She was a child. Forgive her Annie. You have forgiven everyone else. Forgive Ann Marie."

"I don't know," Annie said in exhaustion. "Maybe I should stay away for a while any way."

"Annie, I can't do it without you," Nick said.

"Yes, you can."

"No," Nick said. "If you go, I go. The kids will have to fend for themselves. Mom can take them. No, Beau and Kheim Li. Or," he said taking time as if formulating a solution, "we could sell them."

Nick kept a straight face but a slow smile came across Annie's. A tear rang down her cheek and she wiped it away. She looked at Nick and said, "No one would buy them!" Then she broke down in sobs. Nick picked her up from the rocker and held her in his arms like a small child and he sat in the rocker.

"We'll have to give them away," he said with a smile. Finally, she calmed and laid her head against him. "Have you been here all day?" Nick asked. He added, "Because if you have, I am the dumbest person in the world."

"No," Annie answered. "I drove to the shore first but there were happy families everywhere. I had only been away a couple of hours and I missed you all so much." Nick wiped another tear from her cheek.

"Oh, I have more bad news," Nick said when he thought of it. "I told the kids they don't have to go to school tomorrow."

"You what?"

"See, I can't take care of these kids. We definitely have to sell them. Or," he said contemplating," we could all go to Hershey Park tomorrow?"

"Okay, I guess. I have never been to Hershey Park," Annie said as he carried her down the stairs and out to the car.

Chapter Thirty-Five

"Cheese fondue! Love it!" Nick exclaimed. They were walking into the library. A small table had been set for the two of them and a candle was flickering in a crystal bowl with rose petals artfully scattered around the container. Annie removed the candle putting it on a side table and placing the fondue pot in its place. "What's the occasion?" Nick asked, a little afraid he had forgotten something. He poured them each a glass of wine from the carafe Annie had placed there.

Annie arranged the accompaniments and sat across from Nick. "Well, both kids are out with friends tonight and I thought we could have a special little dinner alone—without discussing basketball, phone apps, rap music, or boys!" she said smiling. She raised her glass and tipped it to Nick. "To us," she said smiling. "We so rarely have time just us, I thought we should do something special for dinner."

"And something special after dinner?" Nick asked with a smile.

"Seriously, Nick, I have been thinking how great our lives are. When I met you, I thought you were the most wonderful person I had ever encountered. And after all these years, I still think you are. I was worried about you marrying me. I was afraid you would change your mind after a little while and think you had made the wrong decision to marry me and adopt Angel. I was afraid I was a project of yours and you would be finished after a while and want out. But you didn't. And, we made a life for ourselves, Nick, the two of us. We did! We had Mathew and became a family. We made this house; this neighborhood, ours. We made friends. We grew the restaurant. We made meaningful contributions to society. We have raised two great kids. Really. We are so lucky. We have had a couple of bumps in the road, but all in all we have been so fortunate. Blessed!" Annie was beaming.

"I love you Annie. You were never a project. I have always loved you and I will always love you. And we are blessed. We do have two great kids. I am happier than I have a right to be or ever thought I would be, but Annie, there is something still missing from Angel's life. At the risk of you getting mad at me and no longer wanting to do something special after dinner, I have to say...."

"Stop!" Annie had a resolute look on her face. "You really know how to ruin a mood. I know what you are going to say. I don't want to talk about this. Someday, Nick, we can tell her about her father. Someday, Nick. Not now. Not when everything is so good. Please Nick, let it go." Annie buried her face in her hands. Nick reached across the table for her hand but she pushed him away.

"Annie, we have to tell Angela about her father. We should have done it a long time ago. She needs to meet him and his family. Like it or not, they are her family too. It is the right thing to do." Nick moved his chair over closer to Annie. "Tell me what you are afraid of. Why don't you want to do this? I know you know we should."

Annie began to cry. Nick pulled out his handkerchief and handed it to her. "What do you think will happen if we tell Angela about her father, and how he wants to meet her; know her; have her meet her half brothers and his wife. Let's talk about it."

"She could stop loving me. She could hate me for..., I don't know. I don't want her to hate me."

"She loves you."

"But will she still love me, if she meets him?"

"Annie, did you stop loving her when you met me or when you gave birth to Matthew? Love expands. There aren't boundaries. She loves you and me. She can love you and me, and Derek. Some day she is going to meet someone and fall in love with him. Will she stop loving you then?"

Annie was not to be consoled easily. She looked at Nick, "But what if she wants to live with him? What if she wants to go to college in Oklahoma to be near him and the boys?"

Nick answered back, "What if she doesn't? What if she just wants to know him and his family; her family? What if she just wants to know what her father looks like, what his voice sounds like, what he likes to do; if they have similar interest and talents? What if she just wants him to see her play soccer or come to her graduation? What if she just wants to make sure he isn't a serial killer or drug dealer?"

Nick stood up and pulled Annie up to him and walked her over to the loveseat. When they sat, he held her close. Finally, he said, "Annie, we can't control every single thing in Angela's life. We can't *what if* everything. What if she gets leukemia like the Stewarts' daughter? What if she is crippled in a car accident like her friend, Barry? What if she falls in love and gets pregnant her senior year? What if she goes to college in San Francisco and never wants to come home again? It is highly unlikely any of those things are going to happen, and we shouldn't take time to worry about them. By the same token, we should know that if something would happen….we can handle it."

Annie stayed close to Nick's chest and said softly, "I raised her. I took care of her. He left. Maybe he doesn't deserve to know her."

"Now I can understand that sort of feeling, Annie. I really do sympathize with you. But 'deserve' is one of those funny words. Derek maybe doesn't deserve Angela's love. But do we deserve this wonderful life you just said we have. You said we have been blessed. Don't we have some sort of obligation to allow someone else to be blessed as well? Maybe the word we are really talking about is *grace*. Grace is the most beautiful word in the English language. Grace is giving someone something they **don't** deserve and not asking for anything in return. You are the epitome of grace, Annie. You give so much to so many. So, how about it? Do you want to tell her or shall I?" Nick smiled.

A smirk came over Annie's face. She said looking up at Nick, "I guess this is what you get when you marry a priest." She then put on a look of determination. "I'll tell her. Matthew is at a friend's house. Now is as good a time as any. I'll tell her when she comes home. I'll tell her when she gets ready for bed. I can do this. But, you can forget about anything "special" for you tonight. You made this happen; so deal with it!"

Nick smiled, "I've taken my share of cold showers. I can handle it. But when you feel great because you have made so many people happy; I'll be here to celebrate with you."

"What's up," Angela asked as her parents walked into her room. She was in her pajamas but was sitting cross legged leaning against a chair pillow, with her cell phone on her lap. Annie crawled up on the bed and snuggled next to Angel. Nick sat at the foot of the bed with his back against the footboard. "You guys are freaking me out. What's going on?" she asked.

Nick smiled. "Obviously we don't come in here enough, Annie. You don't think we just came in here to discuss the weather?" he asked Angela as he pinched her toe.

"Duh. Not together. You two never come in here together. What did I do?" she said joking.

"We just want to talk. Actually, we have some good news; well, hopefully good," Annie began. She took her daughter's hand. "I don't know exactly where to begin so I am just going to jump in. Angel, you have never really asked me anything about your biological father. We never talked about it and I guess we should have. I don't really know how you are going to feel about this, but Dad and I talked to him recently." Angela looked shocked. "He would like to see you, talk to you, if it is all right with you."

"He's here? He lives in Philadelphia?" Angela asked.

"No sweetheart. He lives in Oklahoma. But, we could meet somewhere and get together with him and his family sometime if you want." Nick explained.

"You talked to him? When?" Annie explained about meeting up with Derek and Lacey when she and Nick were visiting her mother. "So, he's married and has kids?" Annie answered that he was married to a nice lady and had two younger boys. "So, are they my step brothers?"

Nick shook his head and said, "Actually, Angel, they are your half brothers. Step children are not blood related. These little boys are your half brothers because you have the same father."

Angela immediately looked panicked. "Matt and I have the same mother. Does that mean he is just my half brother too?"

Nick scraped he teeth over his lower lip. "Well, technically maybe. But, I adopted you, so you and Matt were raised as brother and sister. Legally, you are brother and sister." He stopped and tried to think how to go on but Angela gasped.

"Legally? Who is my father, legally? I mean, does your biological father take over if he finds you?" She started to panic. "Do I have to go away? Do I have to live with him in Oklahoma?"

"No, no, no!" Nick said. "We are your family; mom, Matt and I are your family. You live with us. Derek would just like to meet you. He would like for you, your mom, and Matt and me to maybe meet them somewhere for a weekend or something, just so you can meet him and his family. That's all. We just think you are old enough to make that decision now. You can decide if you want to meet him. You don't have to. It is up to you. Mom and I have talked about it and we have agreed to do what you want. And you can take all the time you want to decide."

"You said Derek. His name is Derek?"

"Yes."

"Is he okay? I mean he isn't a rapist or anything? He didn't rape you Mommy?" she turned to Annie.

Annie was somber. "He didn't rape me. The pregnancy was because two teenagers were careless and didn't think about the consequences of unprotected sex. I was a willing participant. I didn't have much guidance as a child, Angela. I knew better but I …." she trailed off.

"Well, why didn't you get married? Why didn't you stay together. Were you in love? How long were you together?" she asked. Obviously she had thought about it occasionally.

Annie explained simply and without judgment about being sent away by Derek's mother and trying to find Derek at Ohio State. She went on to say that Derek left and they never contacted one another again. "Maybe for a day or two I thought we were in love, but we weren't. We were too young to know about love. I love your dad. Nick!" she clarified. "He is the only person I have ever truly loved but back then I was a teenage girl who wanted someone to pay attention to me because my mother didn't and I didn't have a father. I shouldn't have gotten pregnant but Angel my life would have been so empty if I hadn't. I love you so much. And I loved you from the first moment I saw you. Before that. I loved you from the moment I knew I was pregnant. I will never be sorry I got pregnant."

"I can't believe it," Angela said in an amazed tone. "I never thought I would ever see my father. I thought he must have raped you since you didn't want to talk about him. I want to see him. I mean, I want to see what he looks like. Do you have pictures of him?" she asked her mother. Annie shook her head.

"I had a wallet-size senior picture once, but I tore it up when Derek went away. I probably shouldn't have but I was upset. All this is still a little hard for me but I want what is best for you, Angela, and I admit a child should probably know her biological father if he is willing. I didn't want you to meet him at first. I just wanted everything to stay as it was; just the four of us. But, Nick convinced me that you might think something was missing from your life if you didn't know anything about your father. So, I am trying to be open about this whole thing."

"Are you mad at him, Mom? Derek, I mean. I don't know what to call him. I can't call him my dad. Dad is my dad. I mean, Nick is my dad. Anyway, are you mad at him, Mom?" Angela took her mom's hand in a very adult way. "Nothing can take away my love for you, Mom. I know you did everything you could to take care of me when no one else did. Are you still mad at him for going away and leaving us?"

Annie sighed. "I guess I am. I should be grateful because it let me meet Nick and marry him. I feel sure Derek and I would never have made it. We were much too young. And even though I was able to pull myself together and grow up quickly when I got pregnant and when you were born, Derek didn't grow up so quickly. He was still like a teenager and wasn't ready to take on any responsibilities. He didn't have a clue how to be a husband or a father. We couldn't make it. It just wasn't possible. But I guess I am still a little put out that he didn't even try to help me in any way. I really needed help, both financial and emotional but Derek didn't help. He didn't have a job and he couldn't cope. So he left without even thinking about what I needed and I guess went back to his parents."

"But Nick was a grown-up when I met him. With Nick I was able to have a family. Many years later, Derek matured evidently, and was able to have a family with his wife, Lacey, who seems very nice, by the way. Now you know why dad and I preach about making responsible decisions. One wrong decision can change your life forever. And you can't depend on someone else to make it right." Annie smiled. "Enough preaching. Derek seems like a nice guy now. I am sure he is a responsible dad to his boys. He wants to do the right thing now by getting to know you. At least he thinks it is the right thing. And dad thinks it is the right thing. I guess, I don't know. It's hard for me. I just haven't been very prepared for all this."

Angela hugged her mom. "I am not very prepared either, Mommy. But I think I want to see him. Maybe just once."

Chapter Thirty-Six

The resort where the two families agreed to meet was located in the mountains overlooking Asheville, North Carolina. It was a beautiful stately old building and had been the summer home to writers and artists in the 1920s. It was located on sprawling grounds and combined modern facilities with a look from the past. Both families knew Asheville, but neither had stayed at the resort so both were agreeable for this to be their getaway spot to meet and get to know one another. There was a golf course, though the husbands promised not to play this trip, and there was a beautiful spa craved into the landscape that the women had hopes of using. There were also swimming pools, restaurants, and shops on the estate.

The two families were told to meet in Conference Room B in the hotel. The child psychologist, Grant Morgan, had been recommended by Nick's doctor at University Hospital, and was to meet with them and help get things rolling. Nick cautiously opened the door and smiled when he saw Derek and Lacey and two little boys already inside. Grant was immediately at the door. Nick thrust out his hand, "Nick Millar," he said as introduction. He then turned to Annie and his children and introduced them to Dr. Morgan who preferred to be called Grant, and they each shook his hand. By then, Nick was across the room shaking hands with Derek and Lacey and kneeling to shake hands with the two boys.

Grant looked at Nick and said to himself, I wonder if I am even needed here. Nick circled back around and put an arm around Angela and introduced her to the family and then Matt. It was awkward at best but the little boys helped Angela by showing her the Matchbox cars they had brought with them. She looked at Derek as she shook his hand but then looked away. She smiled uneasily at Lacey. Matt was good with the boys since he could relate to their toys. As they were chatting, Nick firmly put his arm around Annie's waist and pulled her to him. He then took her chin in his hands and touched his index finger to her nose to let her know, all was well. Angela backed away from Derek nervously stepping on Nick's foot. Nick quickly put his hands on her shoulders and held her in place to keep her from tripping and then brought her next to Annie. Matt was still making conversation with Simon and Patrick, the Hutchinson's two boys, and Derek was talking to him also but looking at Angela and Annie. It was uncomfortable but the formalities had been disposed of and the first step made.

Grant slapped his hands together and said, "This is great!" with just a little more enthusiasm than was necessary. Grant was thirty-five and looked twenty-five and was just a little too Californian for comfort. He had enthusiasm that the two cautious families found somewhat annoying. Still, they didn't know how to proceed on their own. Grant instructed, "Everyone find a seat, nodding to the chairs and sofas around the room. Each family found four seats together and sat in a row. Grant laughed. "Do you see how you sat?" he asked. He came around to the circle of seats and handed each person a nametag. "Now," he said, "sit in alphabetical order. You may need to help the younger boys," he instructed. Finally Angela, Annie, Derek, Lacey, Matt, Nick, Patrick, and Simon were seated. "Later we will change seats and sit in age order," he quipped with no one knowing if he was serious. "Let's begin," he said in a voice booming a little too much for the size of the room. He seemed to notice and began more softly. "Starting with Nick, I want you each to say one statement about how you feel about being here; just one." He looked to Nick. Nick smiled and said, "I am glad to be here and get on with this." He started to say more but Grant put his index finger in the air to indicate just one thought from each participant.

Patrick was next in order since they started with Nick and Grant prodded him to help him by saying, "What would you like to do at the hotel today?" Patrick answered, "Go swimming!" He did the same for Simon who answered he also would like to swim.

It was to Angela now. She sat frozen. Grant asked, "How do you feel about being here?"

A few seconds passed and she answered cautiously, "I'm nervous."

"That's very honest," replied Grant. "Ann," Grant asked, "what would you like me to call you?"

Annie shrugged. "Ann's okay. Nick and my friends call me Annie." It came off sounding a bit defensive. Realizing it, she said, "Anything's fine. Anything." Annie looked pale and very serious. She had lost a few pounds in the last few weeks and she looked waifish. She seemed to have purposely dressed down, with very little make up and her hair in a pony tail. She wore a simple white shirt and black pants. It was in contrast to Angela who had brought three outfits for the day because she couldn't decide at home what to bring. She tried on all three and went back to the first and was nearly late getting ready.

Seeing Annie's reticent posture, Grant asked softly, "How do you feel about being here, Annie."

"Resigned," was her one word answer. Grant searched her face for some expression of anger and saw none but felt there was some underlying her answer. He would get back to it later.

Derek was somber also and didn't take his eyes off Ann Marie. He bit his lip as Grant then asked him, "Derek, how do you feel?"

Derek paused as if hearing the question for the first time and trying to think of an appropriate answer. "I feel grateful," he finally stated.

"Lacey?"

Lacey answered quickly, much like Nick. "I am glad this is finally happening."

"Matt," Grant said. "How do you feel?"

Matt looked down at his feet and said, "I'm confused and don't know how I am supposed to feel." He looked troubled.

"Actually, Matt, there are no right or wrong ways to feel. I think confused is a good answer though." To the group he said, they could all move to more comfortable seating around the room now. They could sit wherever they liked. He gave them a few minutes to move.

When they were dismissed by Grant, Nick quickly got up and moved to one of the sofas against the wall, Angela sat next to him. Annie sat in a chair she pulled up on the other side of Angela. Lacey moved a chair also and sat next to one of the boys. The others filled in. Once everyone was seated Grant moved two metal chairs to the center of the room facing each other. "Now let's have Ann and Derek up here in the hot seat," Grant said smiling. Derek stood immediately but Annie stayed seated, looking down at her hands. Nick reached over Angela and patted Annie's hand. Derek was now seated facing the empty chair.

"Annie, it's okay," Nick said to her. She gave him a sideward's glance. Nick said nothing but nodded his head to indicate she should go sit. Grant watched. Annie rolled her eyes at Nick and gave him a look of exasperation and got up, walked to the chair and sat. She didn't look at Derek but to the side of him. Everyone in the room could tell she was upset; angry. Angela slid her hands under her thighs and stared at her mother sitting across from her biological father and bit her lip. Nick was rubbing his face with his right hand. Derek was biting the inside of his mouth and Lacey was staring at Derek. It was a room exploding with small actions.

Finally, Grant turned to the boys and said, "Hey guys, how about the three of you take a break and go into the other room and play some Lego. How does that sound?" Matt jumped up obviously thrilled to be released but the two little boys were unsure what to do. Lacey turned and explained to them they could go with Matthew and play in the next room where there were some fun things to do. The boys left the room willingly. "If you need anything," Grant explained, "Tracey is going in there with you and will get you anything you need." Grant's assistant followed the boys into the next room.

Grant now turned his attention to Annie who still had not looked up. "Ann," Grant said. "I feel your anger. I think we all do. Let's have it. Tell us why you are so upset." Annie sat up a little straighter in her seat. Her feet just barely touched the floor. She looked first at Grant and then at Derek. "Say it Ann. Start with I am upset because…." She looked backed to Grant with abject hostility. "I am upset because….," Grant began again.

Annie gritted her teeth and began slowly and deliberately, "I am upset because this crap is tearing my family apart!"

"What is happening?" Grant asked quickly.

Annie took a deep breath and said very slowly and deliberately, "Matthew thinks he is losing his sister. Angela was his sister!" she nearly shouted. "They have been extremely close. They enjoy being together. She has always watched out for him. They felt like they were brother and sister. Now," she paused to wipe away a tear, "he is her half brother. And one of three half brothers. Now she has two darling little half brothers who will take her attention. They will have gained a sister but Matthew has lost one." She put her hands over her face and willed herself to not cry. "We were a family. Now we are just torn apart."

Ann continued talking in a soft voice, almost as if to herself, "Nick is the only father Angela has ever known. He was there for her when she needed someone. He carried her on his shoulders. He read to her when she couldn't sleep. He stayed up with her when she was sick. He helped her with her homework. He made sure she didn't get in with the wrong kids. He taught her to drive. And, Nick has never treated her any differently than Matt. He has two children, no difference; both his kids. And now is he supposed to just relinquish that role. Let Derek take over and walk her down the aisle when she gets married. Now he is just Angel's step dad? Derek is her 'real' dad?" she put her fingers in the air making quote marks. "Well he sure the hell didn't want to be her 'real' dad in Columbus." She paused, "Derek seems like a 'real' dad to his boys. I assume from day one he has done all of the things a dad is supposed to do for his boys. He has two great little guys. And now he wants Angel." The room was silent. Lacey was sobbing noiselessly and Nick patted her arm.

Angela got up from her chair and sat on Nick's lap, her head against his chest. He rubbed her back, saying gently, "It's okay, sweetheart. This is okay. It will all be okay."

Finally, Grant said, "How do you feel about that Derek. How do you feel about what Ann said about you?"

Derek had gone pale. He took several deep breaths. Finally, he said, "She's right. Everything she said about me is true. I was not a father to Angel. I was horrible to Ann Marie. I left her to do it all without any help from me." He looked directly at Annie. "I'm sorry. God, I'm sorry. I know it seems like an easy thing to say, but I truly am sorry. I never wanted to hurt anyone by doing this; by getting to know Angela. I certainly don't want to hurt Matt or Nick. I'm sorry." He stopped talking. He began again. "Nick is in every sense Angel's father. He deserves that title. I would never want to take that away from him, even if I could, and I can't. It is easy to see how much Angela adores Nick." Angela was resting her head against Nick and had his handkerchief in her hand. "And Matt is the young man I want my boys to be; he would be a wonderful role model for my boys. I'm sorry Ann Marie if I have hurt you again. I never wanted to do that."

Derek rubbed his hand across his mouth several times before beginning again. "I have tried to be a good father to my two boys. I know that seems unfair. I try to be a good husband to Lacey too, even though….," he didn't finish his thought. "Ann, I recognized several years ago what a louse I had been to you and Angel." He paused to explain himself, "It took me quite a while to get on my feet once I was back home. I worked and took night classes at State. It took me seven years to get my degree. All that time I didn't have two nickels to rub together. When I screwed up at Ohio State, my parents refused to help me with college expenses. I met Lacey at school. She was working on her Masters that summer while she was on break from teaching. I got a job with Donnovans when I got my degree and we got married. She had saved a little from teaching but I had nothing. I was thirty and starting out like I was twenty-two. I told Lacey about you and Angel before we were married. We agreed that one day we would try to find Angel and help out if she needed anything. After the boys were both born, we decided we should try and find her. I only knew you had been in Columbus. We went back and talked to people at the diner, the apartment, and the day care. No one was there who still knew you. I looked in the obvious places and the phone book but couldn't come up with anything. Last year I saw Carol Linden, from high school and she told me she was a nurse at the hospital and that your mother had been put in hospice. I went to see her and she told me she was looking for you too. She said if the private detective found you and you came to see her, she would give you my address and number."

Derek paused obviously trying to think how to go on. "I have felt guilty for so long, I didn't know exactly what I should do to help you when I found you. When you and Nick came to our house, it was obvious that you are doing well now. I was so relieved to know your life was good. But, I thought maybe Angel might want to know who her father is….her biological father. Maybe she had wondered about it. I wanted my boys to know her. I thought it would be good for the kids to know each other. I didn't think about Matt. I just didn't think. I wouldn't want my boys to come between Angela and Matt. But, I don't think it has to be like that. I'm serious when I say I would love for Matt to be a role model for my boys. And, I have never met anyone quite like Nick. Nick is the most…." Derek bit his lip trying to think of a word to describe Nick, "non-judgmental person I have ever met. And the best father! I can tell. If I could be half the father he is, to my boys, it would be great. I'm not asking for Angel to move in with us and live away from the family she loves. I just would like us all to know one another. Couldn't we all get together once in a while, just so we could see you all; get to know each other? Does that make any sense?"

Annie had calmed herself and was listening to Derek. He had made a good case and she had no rebuttal. She stared thoughtfully into space for a moment and then finally looked at Derek. "You're right. We can get along. I can be civil. I didn't want to upset Angela. I have just been dreading this moment for so long." She paused and wiped her eyes and blew her nose. "I'm sorry. I don't mean to suggest that I think you are a bad person. Like Nick says, you are just like everyone else—getting better as you go along. I have no right to judge. I have made my share of mistakes. But, I beg you….beg you, please don't hurt Matt or Nick or Angela. They didn't do anything to deserve any pain we could cause them. We are the ones who screwed up." She smiled at her phraseology. "And Lacey and your boys….they are innocent too. Obviously, you are willing to try to include Angela's family in your circle. If you can do that, so can I."

Grant clapped his hands enthusiastically and said, "Let's get on with it. Let's get to know each other. Call the boys in here and we will begin to build some bridges." The boys came back into the room and Grant instructed everyone to sit in a big circle again. He helped move the chairs to accommodate. Wanting to get things moving while Annie was still open to discussion he began. "When I call on you, you can ask any question you want of any one person in the room. I encourage you to include different people each time you have the floor. I think you will find you have something in common with everyone here. Let's start with Nick. I think Nick will be comfortable with this exercise. Nick. What would you like to ask someone?"

Nick obviously took the exercise very seriously and calmly said, "Lacey. What grade do you teach and why did you choose that grade?"

Lacey smiled and answered, "I teach sixth grade. I love sixth because they are young enough to participate in classroom activities without embarrassment but old enough to engage in interesting discussions."

"Great," Grant said. "Lacey, you ask one."

Lacey spoke, "Angela, what sports do you participate in?"

Angela answered that she played soccer and volleyball this year. She was asked by Grant to ask a question. "Simon, what is the best book you have ever read?"

Simon answered quickly "Harry Potter! Did you read it?" he asked. Angela smiled and answered she did and Matt pointed to himself to suggest that he had read it and liked it too.

"Your turn, Simon," Grant instructed.

"Matt, what is the best Lego you ever built?" he asked proudly.

Matt thought for a moment and answered, "The White House, from the Architectural Series." He knew he should ask the next question so he went on to do so. "Derek, what kind of car do you have?"

Derek answered, "We have two cars. Lacey usually drives the van and I drive a Toyota crossover." He saw Matt make a face so asked, "Disappointed it isn't a sports car?" Matt nodded. Derek said with a smile, "So am I." They all laughed and it took the tension from the room. Now it was Derek's turn. "Nick, you guys mentioned when you were at the house that you bought a restaurant when you were married. What did you study? Hospitality or business or food science?"

Nick smiled, and flashed a quick look to Annie. She too was smiling. "I was a priest," he said simply. "I was a Roman Catholic priest for a number of years. But," he quickly added, "I was not a priest when I met Annie." Derek gave a look of disbelief. He motioned with his hand to go on. Nick continued, "I went to Notre Dame undergrad and went into the priesthood when I graduated and was a priest until I was in my early thirties. I no longer felt called and left. I had worked in a restaurant in college and liked it and went back to that. Quite honestly, I was not very qualified or motivated to do much else. I like it because I get to be around lots of people, Annie and I get to work together a lot, and there is never a dull moment," he said while smiling.

Annie spoke up. "I know it isn't my turn, but Nick does more than just run a restaurant. Nick uses every opportunity to contribute. He hires guys that need stability and a role model in their lives. He treats his customers as if they are the only person who matter in the world. He works with shelters and pantries and ministers to the homeless. It is a mission as much as a job for Nick."

"Hey, I think it is my turn now," Nick said to get the attention off himself. "Patrick, who is your favorite NFL player?"

"Peyton Manning!" he shouted out, happy to be included in the game. "My turn?" he asked. Grant nodded. "Angela, do you remember my dad, from when you were little?" he asked with confusion.

She answered, "No, Patrick, I don't remember him. I was really little when he went away. But I sort of remember when my mom and dad got married. That was cool. And I remember when Matt was born. He was really little and loud!" she said laughing. Then Angela stopped suddenly realizing she was to ask a question and her face darkened and her eyes filled with tears. Bravely she asked, "Derek, why didn't you want me?" Annie lowered her head.

Derek answered immediately, "Angela, it had nothing to do with you. It really didn't have anything to do with your mother either. It was just me. I didn't feel capable of being anything to anyone." Derek got very somber. "I remember just before I left, I was watching your mother fix your dinner and feed you. And then she bathed you and dressed you for bed. She read a story to you. It was about a fish; *Rainbow Fish*," he remembered. "And I thought about how good she was with you. And I wondered how she knew what to do and I didn't feel like I knew how to do anything. I was just taking up space; living off the small amount of money your mother was making. I felt so ashamed. I was just plain depressed. I thought you would both be better off without me. I left the next day when she went to work and you were in daycare. I can't stress enough, Angela, it had nothing to do with you. It had nothing to do with your mother. It was me. I was incapable at the time. I didn't think I could add anything of value to your life, so I left." Derek was obviously finished with what he wanted to say so he looked to Grant. Grant nodded to indicate he should now ask his question.

Derek looked Angela in the eye and asked, "How do you feel about me? Did you ever think you wanted to meet me or did you never want to?"

Angela began softly, "I always wondered about you. Mom never mentioned you, so I didn't either. And I had my dad. My dad is awesome. All my friends want to have my mom and dad. They are great. I guess I thought that maybe Mom had been raped or something and so she didn't want to talk about my biological dad. I know my mom had a really bad time on her own, and so I guess I thought you must not be very nice to let her take care of everything herself."

Angela thought for a minute. "I never tell anyone that Nick adopted me. Mom and Dad never mention it either. But, I always thought maybe everyone knows Nick isn't my dad because he is so tall and I'm so short. Matt looks like Dad. That made me wonder about my dad—my bio dad. I did wonder what you looked like. Do you think I look like you?" Angela started to cry. "Matt looks like Daddy, but I don't." Nick winced and reached for Annie's hand.

It was Derek's turn to wipe away a tear with his handkerchief. Then he said, "Angela, I think you are too beautiful to look like me. You look just like your mother. You look just like she did at your age." He took a breath and began again, "I'm not tall like Nick. Your mom and I didn't have any tall genes between us. But, I think you and I have some other things in common. I went to college on a soccer scholarship. Maybe you get some of your ability from me. I like to read and I love movies, not just macho shoot 'um ups, but movies some people think of as 'chick flicks'." Derek smiled. "I like music. I like the old Eric Clapton and Springsteen and stuff from the past but I like Green Day and Maroon Five too." Angela smiled. "Maybe we can talk about music later," Derek said, hoping he had made headway with Angela.

Angela was excited that Derek was interested in what she liked but she didn't want to be disloyal to her parents. "Nick likes music too. He knows everything about music, old and new," she blurted out. "And Matt too. Matt likes some rappers that are really pretty good."

"Well, maybe we can all talk about music together," Derek said sweetly.

Seeing things were going well, Grant decided he no longer had to mediate or lead the discussion. "Who in this room likes to go swimming?" he asked. Everyone raised their hand. Grant had talked with each couple separately and they agreed to go swimming in the hotel pool if the timing seemed right. "Well, let's break this off and you guys can change and meet back at the pool. I will be here in the hotel all night tonight and until noon tomorrow, so if there is something any of you want to discuss with me, I will be at your disposal. Anything we should discuss before we go?" No one spoke up so he dismissed the group. They all went back to their rooms and changed for the pool.

Swimming was a perfect activity for the families. Nick and Matt played with Simon and Patrick in the pool, and Annie and Lacey spent some time talking, sitting on the side. Derek swam laps with Angela for a while. Then they all played a simple version of water volleyball. Everyone went back to the rooms to rest until dinner. They had dinner on the veranda of the hotel. It was a very congenial evening.

The next morning Lacey and Nick were the only ones who wanted to go for a run and they went out early together. Later, Annie, Lacey, and Angela did some shopping. Nick, Derek and the three boys went to a mini golf course. That evening they had dinner together again at a pizza place that had karaoke. It was not crowded and they all participated in several different arrangements. Both Lacey and Annie shed a tear when Derek and Angela sang a duet of *Uptown Girl*. Nick kept the evening light by playing with the boys and teasing the girls. The two families had a good evening. The next morning at breakfast they looked at calendars and planned the next time they would get together.

Chapter Thirty-Seven

"**H**urry up you guys. Go change clothes," Angela demanded. Nick and Annie had just come in from the car. Nick had taken Ann to lunch at an inn in the Amish country and surprised her with a gift, a beautiful diamond ring to replace the gold band she had insisted she wanted when they were married. She put the diamond ring on her right hand, however, saying she couldn't possibly replace the band; it meant too much. She thought the diamond ring the most beautiful thing she had ever seen. Nick was pleased. They ran upstairs to change clothes.

In St. John's, Halloween is the biggest holiday of the year. All of the merchants, including Yumsters, have their windows decorated by children artists in early October. There are contest winners. Bus tours come to see the art work. There is a Halloween parade the Saturday before Halloween with floats. Nearly every high school in the area participates. On Halloween night, everyone in the neighborhood dresses in costume. Just before dark, the small children make their way around the neighborhood and candy is passed out. Prizes are given in each age bracket for costumes. Then everyone gathers in one of the cul-de-sacs in the neighborhood for food and drink. Adults pull out all the stops and have every imaginable drink concoction and snack.

Nick has been going to St. John's Halloween Night since a child, and his children have never missed it. Nick never liked to dress up, as an adult anyway, but this year was an exception. Nick wore black pants, and black shirt with a clerical collar. And Annie; she wore a very short red dress, black fishnet stockings and stilettos. They won first prize. All their friends came around to congratulate them. There was much discussion about how Annie was too wholesome, too sweet, to be convincing in her costume. Stacie and her husband, Greg, thought their outfits a riot. Greg asked if the couple met in a confessional. Everyone laughed.

Angela walked toward her parents with her friend, Corey. Corey said, "Your parents are so cool. Everyone is talking about how outrageous they look. My mom said your mom can't look anything but pure, even dressed like that. I love their costumes. And yours, of course, and your brother's." Angela was dressed like a nun, and Matthew had on a pin-striped suit, hat, and red tie depicting a pimp.

"You are looking good, Angela. I think you will like being a nun," Nick said.

"Yeah right, Dad. I do like the sensible shoes though," she said as she pulled her long skirt up a bit and showed her purple sneakers. "Oh, here they are," she announced excitedly as she looked up. "Corey, this is Simon and Patrick, my little brothers," she said as she introduced him to the two young boys who ran to her. She gave them each a hug. "It is so great to see you guys. You've grown since I saw you last month," she said sounding like an adult. "And this is my father, Derek, and his wife, Lacey." They each gave Angela a one-armed hug and shook hands with Corey. "Come on guys," she said as she took each boy's hand and they left to go collect candy. Suddenly she stopped and ran back to her parents. Angela hugged Annie and said, "Thanks, Mom. You're the best!" Then she went to Nick and hugged him and said into his ear, "Derek is my father, but you will always be my dad! Love you guys!" and she went off to Trick or Treat with the boys, shouting, "Hey, Matt, come with us."

About the Author

Sandy Kendall's previous book, The Boy from the O, was a finalist in fiction for Best Books of Indiana 2011. An author of several children's books, Sandy graduated from Indiana University and taught English and Reading Resource in middle schools. She and her husband, Dan, now live in Indianapolis.